REAPER'S STAND

JOANNA WYLDE

BERKLEY BOOKS, NEW YORK

THE BERKLEY PUBLISHING GROUP
Published by the Penguin Group
Penguin Group (USA) LLC
375 Hudson Street, New York, New York 10014

USA • Canada • UK • Ireland • Australia • New Zealand • India • South Africa • China

penguin.com

A Penguin Random House Company

This book is an original publication of The Berkley Publishing Group.

Library of Congress Cataloging-in-Publication Data

Wylde, Joanna.
Reaper's stand/Joanna Wylde.
pages cm—(Reapers motorcycle club; 3)
ISBN 978-0-425-27236-7 (paperback)
1. Widowers—Fiction.   2. Motorcyclists—Fiction.   3. Motorcycle clubs—Fiction.   I. Title.
PS3623.Y544R47   2014   2014020000
813'.6—dc23

PUBLISHING HISTORY
Berkley trade paperback edition / October 2014

PRINTED IN THE UNITED STATES OF AMERICA

10 9 8 7 6 5 4 3 2 1

Interior text design by Kristin del Rosario.

PRAISE FOR THE *NEW YORK TIMES* BESTSELLING REAPERS MOTORCYCLE CLUB SERIES

REAPER'S LEGACY

"Raw emotion and riveting characters, I fell in love from page one!"
—Katy Evans, *New York Times* bestselling author

"Wylde's second Reapers Motorcycle Club contemporary (after *Reaper's Property*) mixes a super-hot bad guy, a struggling young single mother, and sex that blisters the imagination, resulting in a thrill ride as raw as it is well written."
—*Publishers Weekly*

"Drama, angst, laughter, and some intense sexual high jinks reign supreme as our hero and heroine fight to keep their hearts safe from the attraction that batters them both."
—*RT Book Reviews*

"Joanna Wylde has a great voice in this genre . . . This is such a well-done motorcycle club book."
—*USA Today*

"[*Reaper's Legacy*] hooked me so hard that I could not put it down. Ms. Wylde's world-building skills are exceptional. She will completely take you into the biker world where the motorcycle club has [its] own values, rules, laws, and ways of doing things."
—*A Bookish Escape*

"[Joanna Wylde] knows how to balance great characters; a realistic, gritty storyline; [and] hot-as-hell men and women . . . with the perfect amount of romance and tenderness."
—*Ana's Attic*

"A really good bad-boy biker book! Exactly what I've been looking to read."
—*Maryse's Book Blog*

Berkley titles by Joanna Wylde

REAPER'S LEGACY
DEVIL'S GAME
REAPER'S STAND

ACKNOWLEDGMENTS

This is my fourth book in the Reapers Motorcycle Club series, and as time passes it becomes harder to write my acknowledgments. The list of people who have supported me grows longer and I'm afraid I'll forget someone. You have no idea how much I appreciate all of you.

Thanks to everyone at Berkley who has made this possible, especially Cindy Hwang. I have an incredible team behind me and I appreciate all their efforts. It's worth noting that I've been repeatedly blessed by the Cover Gods—the Berkley art team has been amazing, and I hear almost daily from readers praising their efforts.

I also want to thank my agent, Amy Tannenbaum, Betty, my MC friends, my beta readers, my writing posse, all the bloggers who have supported me and everyone on my Junkies page. Special thanks to Chas and Jessica, because it doesn't matter whether or not a book is good if nobody ever finds out about it. Kylie, Hang, Lori, and Cara—you know exactly how much you've helped me, and don't think I take it for granted. Thank you for all the time you've given me.

Finally, thanks to my family, whose endless patience and willingness to step up makes my writing possible. I love you very much.

AUTHOR'S NOTE

Throughout this series, I've tried to offer readers insight into MC culture and how I do my research. I'm very fortunate to have the continuing support of real women affiliated with clubs, and like each of my books, this one has been reviewed for accuracy. *Reaper's Stand* was the first in which my club friends didn't find major errors regarding club life, so maybe I'm finally figuring it out.

I've tried to make each book in the Reapers Motorcycle Club series different, rather than following a set formula. This has challenged me as a writer, but I've enjoyed exploring a variety of character types along the way. I think you'll find that *Reaper's Stand* has a different feel than the books that came before it. For example, *Devil's Game* was a coming-of-age novel. *Reaper's Stand* is the opposite—it's a book about mature characters who are already fully formed as individuals. Every time I try something new, I worry that readers won't be willing to make the leap. So far you haven't given up on me. I hope you enjoy *Reaper's Stand*.

PROLOGUE

COEUR D'ALENE, IDAHO
PRESENT DAY
LONDON

Should I look him in the eye when I killed him or just shoot him in the back?

Tough call.

I crouched in the kitchen, digging through my purse as if searching for keys. I knew right where the gun was, of course, but pulling it straight out just seemed so . . . obscene. The smell of dinner on the stove filled my nose. Chicken chili, with whole-grain corn bread in the oven for a side because it's healthier.

It'd been baking for ten minutes already, which meant I had about twelve more minutes to end his life before the bread burned.

Reese sat out in the dining room, reading one of his motorcycle magazines and drinking his favorite beer while he waited for food. I'd been sure to buy a half rack earlier, and I'd met him at the door with a cold one open and ready to go. He was on his second now. I wasn't under any illusions—two beers wouldn't be enough to slow him down if he came after me, or ease his pain if my aim was off.

Still, a man deserves a beer before dying, right?

My fingers brushed the cold metal of the gun. I pulled out my phone instead and looked at Jessica's picture, studying her pretty, smiling face on graduation day. So full of hope and promise. She'd raised her right arm to wave at the camera. Her pinkie curled forward, offering a glimpse of the sparkling tips on her new acrylics. She'd wanted them for graduation so badly. They hadn't been in the budget, but I couldn't tell her no.

You have to understand—none of us ever expected Jessica to graduate.

Hell, she shouldn't even be alive. My bitch of a cousin had done drugs all through both pregnancies, yet somehow Jessie pulled through. Not unscathed. She had the usual developmental quirks . . . poor impulse control, bad judgment. Quick to anger. They came from fetal drug effects—the gift that keeps on giving for a child's whole life. But at least she *had* a life. Her little sister died in the NICU two days after her birth. Never got a chance.

Fuck you, Amber. Fuck you very much for doing that to your kids.

I glanced up at the oven timer and realized I'd wasted nearly three minutes thinking about Jess. I supposed I could kill him *after* pulling out the bread, but putting it off would just make things harder.

Or maybe I should feed him first?

No. He'd had his beer, but if I had to sit across from Reese over a meal I'd never make it. I couldn't look into those blue eyes and laugh. I'd never been a good liar. This past month had been heaven and hell rolled into one big bad joke.

Right. Time for the punch line.

I pulled out the small pistol and stuck it into the pocket of the loose sweater I'd picked so carefully for just this moment. I also took out my keys, my ID, and my cash, stuffing them into my jeans. Just in case. I didn't really expect to survive the night, but it never hurts to hope. The van was even gassed up and ready to go, on the off chance that I managed to get away.

Of course, I had no idea where I'd drive. *Burn that bridge when you get to it* . . .

Things started going wrong as soon as I walked into the dining room. Reese wasn't sitting at the head of the table, where I'd left him. Damn. I could've shot him in the back without warning if he'd just stayed put. Now he sat facing me, leaning casually in his chair, beer in hand. The magazine lay open before him and he looked up, offering me that mocking smile of his. God, I loved that smile, despite the fact that it could be cruel as all fuck.

"Something you want to talk about?" he asked, cocking his head.

"No," I murmured, wondering what he'd say if I shared my thoughts. *Gee, Reese, I'm so sorry I'm about to kill you, but if it makes you feel any better I hate myself for doing it—not a hundred percent sure I won't shoot myself next.*

I wouldn't, though. Not yet. Not until I saw Jessica for myself, made sure they'd kept their promises and she was safe and sound. After that?

Well. We'd just have to see.

He sighed, eyes flicking to my pocket, where my hand shifted nervously on the gun.

Paranoia hit yet again.

He knew. He knew all about it, I could see it in his face. Fuck. I'd failed her . . . *Don't be ridiculous. How could he possibly know?*

"Babe, you look like you could use a day off," he said finally. "Have you considered hitting the spa? Maybe get a massage?"

"That costs too much," I said automatically, biting back a hysterical laugh. Because money mattered now, right?

"I wasn't suggesting that you pay for it," he said, frowning at me.

"I don't want your money—"

"Yeah, I know, you're totally independent and you like it that way. Blah, blah. Just let me do something for you, for once. Fuck's sake."

Shit. Why did he have to be so nice?

I felt my eyes start to water and I looked away, forcing myself to detach again and focus. I needed to kill him, and I couldn't give him any warning. But he was facing me and all the way across the room, which was a bigger problem than it sounds. Pistols aren't exactly known for accuracy, and it's not like I had much in the way of experience.

I needed to get closer.

If I came up behind him, rubbed his shoulders . . . That would be close enough. God, I was a shitty human being.

"The food won't be ready for another ten minutes," I said. "You look sort of tense. Want a neck rub?"

He raised a brow as I circled the table.

"I think you should stay back," he said slowly. I paused.

"What do you mean?"

"Well, I'd hate to make it too easy for you, sweetheart."

My chest tightened. I offered a weak smile, because like I said— I'm a shit liar.

"I don't understand."

"I'm assuming you're planning to shoot me in the back of the head," he said quietly, and that's when I realized he wasn't relaxed at all. He might be leaning back casually, but every one of those solid muscles roping his body had drawn tight, poised to attack. "That's a bad idea. You shoot that close, you'll be all covered in blood spatter. Means you'll have to risk tracking more evidence out of the house or taking time to clean up. Either way, complicates things."

Well. At least it was all finally out in the open. Almost a relief. I pulled out the gun and held it up, using my left hand to brace my right as I carefully sighted on him. I expected him to explode up at me, to fight back. Instead he just sat, waiting.

"Go ahead, do it," he said, a sad smile toying with the corners of his mouth. "Show me what you're made of."

"I'm so sorry," I whispered. "You'll never know how much I wish this weren't happening."

"Then *don't* do it. Whatever it is, we can work through it. I'll help you."

"You can't."

He sighed, then looked past me and jerked his chin.

"It's over, babe," I heard a man say from behind. Huh. I guess it was. Fortunately, I had just enough time to pull the trigger before he hit me.

CHAPTER ONE

My back was killing me.

It was nearly two in the morning, and I'd just finished up the late-night cleaning shift at the pawn shop. I'd been letting myself get soft the past couple of months. Too much time spent managing the business, not enough time scouring bathrooms, because I'd forgotten just how much work scrubbing a toilet really is.

Well, scrubbing toilets, floors, dusting, vacuuming. London's Cleaning Service did it all, and while we might not be the cheapest crew in town, we were the best. I knew this because I turned down more accounts than I took these days. Thanks to my hard-earned reputation, finding new clients was easy. Workers? Not so much. Most people aren't fans of spending their nights wiping up after others, and even with my higher-than-average starting pay, people flaked on me.

Tonight, for example.

I'd gotten a call from Anna—one of my crew leads—to say she had two no-shows. Because the life of a cleaning lady is nonstop glamour, that meant I got to spend my Friday evening scraping dried pee off the floor in a men's bathroom.

Charmed existence, I know.

At least my aching back and I could crawl into bed soon.

I pulled up to the house and noticed a blue Honda Civic parked in front. Mellie's car—my young cousin's best friend. She must be spending the night with Jessie, I realized. I bit back the surge of annoyance. On the one hand, I really preferred it when Jess cleared stuff like this with me ahead of time.

On the other, there were worse things than having the girl home on a Friday. Most of them were worse, actually. God, I loved her so much, but Jessica was impossible. I reminded myself yet again that it wasn't entirely her fault—the counselors told me over and over that I needed to help her learn to cope with her limitations, because it's not like she'd grow out of them.

Decision making wasn't Jessica's strong suit.

According to the experts, that part of her brain just hadn't developed quite right, thanks to her mother's ongoing chemical romance. I wasn't sure how I felt about that. I knew she wasn't like other kids. But you know what? We all have to learn to get along in this world. Nobody's born with a clean slate, and she wasn't a little girl anymore.

I unlocked the front door to find Mellie sitting on the couch. Her knees were drawn up, her eyes were huge, and she clutched a can of Diet Coke like a shield.

My parent radar crackled to life.

"What did she do now?"

"We were at a party," Mel whispered. "It was around ten o'clock. She ran into some girls who graduated a couple years ago—Terry Fratelli and her friends—and they invited us out to the Armory for a party with the Reapers motorcycle club."

I swayed, grabbing the back of my old, green wing-backed chair to catch myself.

"Fuck."

Mellie's eyes got even wider. I didn't cuss. She *knew* I didn't cuss. Ever.

"What's the rest of it?"

The girl looked away, biting her lip.

"I'm so sorry for leaving her," she said, guilt written all over her face. "But there was no way I'd go out there and she didn't listen to me. She actually got kind of . . ."

Her voice trailed off and I filled in the gaps. Jessica liked to make fun of Mel when she wouldn't follow along like a well-trained puppy. Classic Jess. Such an idiot child—I wasn't quite sure how she managed to keep a friend like Melanie around, given the shit she pulled.

"Anyway, she promised me she'd text, and I told her I wouldn't say anything as long as she stayed in touch. But she stopped texting me around midnight and I could tell she was really drunk. Her messages weren't even making sense. I'm really scared for her, London."

This last was said with a sniffle, and I realized the poor girl was terrified. I came over and sat down next to her, giving her a hug. Mel spent so much time over here that she felt like my own sometimes.

"She's gonna be so pissed I told you."

"You did the right thing, baby," I said, running a hand across her hair. "She's being a selfish brat, putting you into this position."

"Well, on the bright side she'll forgive me," Mel muttered. She sniffed and pulled back, looking up at me with a wavering smile. "She always does."

I smiled back, but my thoughts were grim. Mel was too nice. Sometimes I wished she'd ditch Jessie and find a new best friend. Then I felt guilty, because even with her issues, Jess was my heart.

"I need to go find her," I said. "Do you want to stay here or head home?"

"I was thinking I could sleep here tonight?" she asked. I nodded, already knowing the rest of the story. Friday nights at Mel's house weren't pretty, especially on paydays. Her dad liked to celebrate the end of the week a little too much.

"Sounds good."

I tried calling Bolt Harrison from my van so Mellie wouldn't hear me. He managed Pawns, the same store I'd been cleaning that night. It happened to be owned by the Reapers MC. Bolt was their vice president.

I'd had the cleaning contract there for about six months now. They were becoming one of my most valuable accounts and had dropped hints about offering a second contract for The Line, their strip club. We'd already come in a few times when they needed extra help, and I had high hopes it would grow into something bigger. I originally ran the Pawns crew myself, but two months ago I'd turned it over to Jason, an older guy who'd been with me for almost five years. He was reliable, worked hard, and did a great job managing the people under him.

The MC paid well, and they paid in cash, which was convenient. In return, we kept our mouths shut about anything we might see, which honestly wasn't as much as you'd think. I thought there might be some prostitution happening in the back rooms out at The Line, but I'd never seen any sign of women being forced.

Not my job to tell consenting adults what to do with their bodies.

Even so, I made sure that none of the younger girls ever came out with me. Just because I didn't call the cops doesn't mean I wanted my people getting sucked into anything.

Anyway, I figured Bolt was the first place to start if I wanted to extract Jess from whatever trouble she'd gotten herself into this time. I liked Bolt and felt relatively comfortable around him—and he was my only choice, really. My other contact was Reese Hayes, the club's president. That man scared the heck out of me and I'm not ashamed to admit it. Something about him . . . The way his eyes followed me. Like he wanted to eat me, and not in a nice flowers and candlelit dinner kind of way. A hint of gray at his temples said he was probably just a little older than me, but his body was built like a man in his twenties. I don't know what bothered me more, his inherent scariness or the fact that his scariness sort of secretly turned me on. (Pathetic, I know.)

There was no way on earth I'd talk to him if I didn't have to.

"Yeah?" Bolt answered. I heard music in the background, loud music.

"Hi, Mr. Harrison."

"Is there any point in telling you to call me Bolt?"

I would've smiled if I hadn't been so stressed—we'd been dancing this same dance since I'd started. None of the club members understood why I insisted on being so formal, but I had my reasons. Just because the MC paid well wasn't any reason to cozy up to them. I liked my boundaries.

"Not really," I said, my voice betraying my worry.

"What's going on?" he asked, picking up on my tone. That was Bolt—he saw and heard everything, whether you wanted him to or not.

"I have a personal problem I'm hoping you can help me with."

Silence.

I'd probably startled him. I'd never come asking for help before. In fact, I rarely saw him these days. The first few months he'd watched us like hawks, but lately we'd started to blend into the background. Nobody pays attention to the cleaners, something I've always found fascinating. You wouldn't believe the things I've seen or the secrets I hold.

Of course, that might be why I found Reese so unsettling—six months into the job and I still hadn't disappeared yet.

"You probably don't know this, but I'm my cousin's guardian," I said, pushing forward. "One of her friends just told me that she went

to a party out at your clubhouse tonight. I'm worried about her—
she's a great kid, but not the best at making good decisions. Is there
any chance you can help me track her down?"

More silence, and I cringed. I'd insulted him, I realized. Implied
things about the parties at his clubhouse that we all knew were true
but nobody liked to talk about or admit. That they weren't safe for
young women. That the club couldn't be trusted.

"Is she an adult?"

"She's eighteen, but she just graduated two weeks ago and she's
young for her age."

Bolt snorted.

"Hate to tell you this, sweetheart, but she's old enough to make
her own decisions about where to party."

Now it was my turn to fall silent. I could say plenty—that she
might be old enough to party, but she wasn't old enough to drink
legally. That they could find themselves in a heap of trouble for providing her with booze. Of course, for all I knew the cops were out
there partying with them . . . But I kept my mouth shut, because I'd
learned a long time ago that if you give someone enough silence,
eventually they'll fill it.

"Okay," he said finally. "I get where you're coming from. I'm not
out there tonight, but Pic is."

Darn. "Pic" was short for "Picnic," and that was Reese's nick-
name. I had no idea why they called him that and I sure as heck
hadn't asked. He was the least picnicky person I'd ever met in my
life.

"Go out to the Armory and ask for him. Tell him I sent you, tell
him it's a personal favor. Maybe he'll track her down for you, maybe
not. Like I said, the girl's an adult. You know how to get there?"

"Of course."

He laughed. Everyone in Coeur d'Alene knew where the Armory was.

"Thank you, Mr. Harrison," I said quickly, hanging up before he could change his mind. Then I turned the keys in the ignition and my van roared to life, along with the check engine light that had been haunting me for the last week. I chose to ignore it, because even if I had someone look at it for me, I couldn't afford to fix the stupid thing.

If it could still drive places, it wasn't really broken. At least, that was the theory.

I shifted into reverse and backed out of the driveway. Oh, Jessie was going to hate this. Auntie London riding to the rescue in a minivan with the cleaning service logo on the side.

Ha. Not like it was the first time.

The Reapers clubhouse was about ten miles northeast of Coeur d'Alene, back on a private road twisting through the heavily forested hills. I'd never been there, although they'd invited me to a couple of parties when I first started cleaning Pawns.

I'd politely refused, preferring to maintain my wall of privacy. I'd cut back on socializing after my ex-husband, Joe, left. Not that I blamed him for ending it—he'd been clear from the start that he didn't want kids in the house. When Amber OD'd and nearly died six years ago it came down to him or Jessie, because I couldn't stand the situation any longer. The choice had been clear and the divorce had been amicable enough.

Still, I'd needed to lick my wounds for a while. Between building my business and raising my cousin, I hadn't even tried dating until I met Nate a few months back. On nights like this, I wondered if those years alone had been worth it. It wasn't that Jess was bad. It's just that she never quite figured out the whole cause-and-effect thing, and probably never would.

By the time I pulled up to the Armory it was nearly three in the morning. I don't know what I'd expected from the Reapers club-house. I knew it was an old National Guard building, but somehow that hadn't translated into "fort" in my head. But that's essentially what this was. Big, solid building, at least three stories tall. Narrow windows, parapets on the roof. There was a gate through a side wall leading to what looked like a courtyard behind the building.

Directly in front of the building was a line of bikes, watched over by a couple of younger men wearing the signature leather vests I'd seen around town over the years. Off to the right was a gravel parking lot with a good number of cars in it. I pulled into the end of the line and turned off the ignition.

It occurred to me that I'd be crashing a party right after cleaning for six hours. Great. I probably looked like an escapee from an insane asylum. I flipped down my mirror—sure enough, my blonde hair was ratty and my makeup had long since disappeared. Oh well . . . Wouldn't be the first time chasing down Jess had dragged me out when I needed a shower and bed.

Although she'd never dragged me anywhere quite as intimidating at this place.

I got out of the car and started toward the main door. One of the men walked across the gravel to meet me. I looked him over, feeling old. He had to be twenty at the most, and the scraggly beard he wore with obvious pride had hardly filled in. He wasn't muscular like his friend manning the door, but all wiry and pointing bones.

"You here for the party?" he asked, studying me skeptically. I couldn't blame him—my ratty jeans might not stand out too much, but my tank top had seen better days and the bandanna holding back my hair was stained with sweat. I probably had dirt streaks on my face, too. The light in the car had been so poor they wouldn't have shown up.

Oh, and did I mention the feeling-old part? At thirty-eight, I was pretty sure I could've been this kid's mom.

I decided I didn't like him.

"No, I'm here to speak with Mr. Hayes," I said politely. "Mr. Harrison suggested I come here to see him."

He looked at me blankly.

"I got no idea who you're talkin' about," he said finally. The oversized infant masquerading as an adult turned and hollered at his friend. "BB, you got any idea who 'Mr. Hayes' is?"

BB lumbered over toward us like a bear, dark hair hanging down his back in a braid. He seemed to be older than this one, but not much. I sighed. Good lord, they were just babies. Dangerous babies, I reminded myself, eyeing the chains hanging from their pants and the bulky rings decorating their hands.

Those were essentially brass knuckles.

"That's Picnic, dumbfuck," BB said, looking at me critically. "Why you callin' him Mr. Hayes? You got papers to serve? He's not here."

I shook my head. I wished it were something that simple.

"I call him that because I work for him," I said, keeping my voice matter-of-fact and composed. "I own London's Cleaning Service—several of your businesses are our accounts. Mr. Harrison sent me out here to find Mr. Hayes."

"Bolt sent her," BB told the little one. He nodded at me. "I'll walk you in. See if we can find him."

"Thank you."

I took a deep breath and steeled myself to follow. I'd heard so many stories about this place that I wasn't sure what to expect. If you believed the rumors, the Armory was a combination whorehouse/underground fighting pit, with piles of stolen goods packing every room to the ceiling. Fifty percent pirate cave, fifty percent drug den, one hundred percent dangerous.

BB opened the door and I followed him in, getting my first good look at the clubhouse.

Well.

The rumors were certainly wrong about the stolen goods. I'd like to think if they furnished the place with stuff they'd taken, they would've picked out things that were a little nicer than what I saw before me.

The room was large, and from the central location of the door it seemed to span the entire front half of the building. On the far right was a bar. Ancient couches and cast-off chairs lined the walls, and several battered, mismatched tables filled the center. To the left was a pool table, darts, and a jukebox that was either forty years old or a damned good replica. The place wasn't dirty . . . just very well worn.

It's funny, but looking around, my very first thought was that I was overdressed—and by overdressed, I meant there was literally too much fabric covering my body.

Wayyy too much.

The women ranged from full-on naked to dressed casually in tight jeans and low-cut tank tops. I stuck out like a . . . well, like a cleaning lady at a biker party. Half the guys had women on their laps, partially clothed and otherwise, and off in the corner I was pretty sure was a couple having full-on sex.

I snuck another quick look out of the corner of my eye.

Make that *definitely* having sex. Disgusting . . . yet strangely mesmerizing . . . I had to force myself to look away, hoping to hell I wasn't blushing like a little girl.

You're thirty-eight and you know where babies come from, I reminded myself firmly. *Just because you're not getting any doesn't mean they shouldn't.*

People started to notice me—big guys covered in tattoos, wearing leather vests with the Reaper colors on them. Their gazes ranged from curious to outright suspicious. Shit. This was a mistake. So Bolt sent me out there. That didn't mean it was safe, or a good idea. Bolt wasn't my friend. Sure, he probably valued me as a worker, but the club valued their strippers, too. Certainly didn't stop them from firing their asses right and left when their personal drama got out of hand.

Snap out of it.

I took another deep breath and smiled brightly at BB. He'd been watching me expectantly, almost like he thought I'd run away or something. I'm no wimp, though. I might choose not to cuss, but I know what the words mean.

I looked up to see a tall man with shoulder-length, wavy hair and so much scruff on his face he'd entered beard territory. He wore another of those vests. The name on his was "Gage," and below it was a smaller patch that said "Sgt at Arms." I'd never seen him at the shop, but that wasn't saying much—we came in after hours for a reason.

"Says she's here to see Pic," BB said. "Bolt sent her."

"That right?" he asked, eyes speculative. He swept them down my figure and I forced myself to smile at him.

"I'm looking for my cousin's daughter," I said. "She came out here for the party with some friends, apparently. Mr. Harrison suggested that Mr. Hayes might be able to help me."

The man smirked.

"Did he? Imagine that."

I wasn't sure how to interpret his words, so I chose to take them at face value, forcing myself to wait for him to continue.

"Back outside, BB," the man said. "I've got her from here. You're the cleaner, aren't you?"

I glanced down at my filthy clothing.

"How could you tell?" I asked, my tone dry. He laughed, and I felt some of my tension break.

"I'm Gage," he said. "Let's see if we can find Pic."

"I hate to bother him," I said quickly. "I mean, if he's busy right now. I see you're one of the club officers. Maybe you can help me?"

He raised a brow.

"Bolt sent you to talk to Picnic, right?"

I nodded, wondering if I'd made a mistake. *Well played, London. Alienate the one guy who stepped up to help you.*

"Then you should talk to Picnic."

I offered another smile, wondering if he could see how close my face was to cracking from the effort. He turned and I followed him across the room, avoiding catching anyone's eyes. Some seemed interested in me, but most were too busy drinking, talking, and doing more intimate things to pay attention to one grubby woman. In the center of the back wall was an open hallway leading farther into the building. He passed through it and I followed, growing even more nervous. Walking into the building had been bad enough, but somehow this felt worse. Like I'd hit the point of no return.

Certainly the point of no witnesses.

A door opened up ahead and two girls stumbled out, giggling. Jessica? No, but I recognized one.

"Kimberly Jordan, does your mother know where you are right now?" I asked, my voice cracking like a whip.

Everyone in the hallway froze, including Gage.

Kim stared at me, her eyes wide.

"N-no," she said. She peered around me, as if wondering if her mother might jump out at her next. Good. Maybe that would make her think.

"You wanna talk to the prez or not?" Gage asked, his voice cool. "Pick your battles, babe. You want this one or your cousin's kid?"

I swallowed, realizing that the Parental Voice of Authority might not be so welcome here. Oops.

"I'm here for Jessica," I told him. He smiled at me, his teeth bright and shiny in the dim light.

"Great, so let's leave them alone, all right? Girls, get out of here."

They brushed past us quickly, whispering with thrilled and excited eyes.

"Do you always have underage girls out here drinking?" I asked him, unable to just let it go completely.

"We're not serving anyone underage," he said flatly. I raised a brow, wordlessly calling him on his bullshit. He grinned. "You wanna look me in the eye and tell me you never had a drink until after you were twenty-one?"

I sighed. Of course I had. Not only that, I'd had lots of them and I hadn't turned into an alcoholic or gotten pregnant or anything horrible.

Nancy Reagan had been wrong—at least in my case. Amber probably should've just said no.

"Can we just get on with it?"

Gage shook his head, not even bothering to hide his amusement, then stepped forward and knocked on the unmarked door to our left.

"Pic? You busy?"

REESE

I sat on my office couch, wondering why the hell I didn't give a shit that a beautiful girl was currently sucking my cock. Sure, I enjoy a good blow job as much as the next guy. But tonight I wasn't engaged, just couldn't bring myself to care. This was unfortunate, because the babe kneeling between my legs had a mouth like a Hoover and a very loose sense of morals. She was the new headliner over at The Line— the boys had brought her out tonight just for me.

Birthday present.

Forty-three fucking years old.

Her fingers dropped low, running under my balls with a light touch as her tongue swirled around my dickhead. I reached over and grabbed my beer, taking a long, slow pull. The cold liquid slid down my throat and I decided I didn't give a fuck if she finished or not.

I want you happy, baby, but you can do better . . . Heather seemed to whisper in my ear.

I'd been hearing her voice since the day she died. Christ, I missed that woman, and I wished to hell those little whispers were more than my own sick subconscious. But I knew they weren't, because if Heather's spirit was really beside me offering advice, I wouldn't have fucked up so bad with my daughters.

I glanced across the room to the black metal filing cabinet. A picture sat on top of it, in a tarnished silver frame. My old lady. The shot was from one of the last family parties we'd had—right after she recovered from the mastectomy, but before that final round of chemo. Her arms wrapped tight around our two beautiful girls, all three of them laughing at something just out of the frame.

Hoover chose that moment to suck me in deep down into her throat and I closed my eyes. Damn, Bolt had told me she sucked cock like a pro, but he hadn't given her full credit. The woman had a *gift*. Every inch squeezed tight and I wasn't small. I groaned, letting my head fall back.

Why did it still feel like I was cheating on Heather?

Hoover popped back up, giggling at me annoyingly. I opened my mouth to tell her to shut up, but she sucked me back in before I had the chance. *Shit*, that was good. My boredom disappeared, leaving the clarity I only got during sex or a good fight. My body felt incredible, but my mind floated, blessedly detached. No guilt over Heather, no worry about the club, not even thoughts of my girls could touch me here.

I was like a machine, powerful and free.

My phone buzzed next to me on the couch and I glanced down to see a text.

> BOLT: Enjoying your party? I sent you another present. Try not to break it.

I glanced down at the brown-haired head bobbing in my lap and decided that my life might not be perfect, but damned if my friends didn't take care of me. If there was a God in heaven, I was about to meet this bitch's twin sister.

A loud knock came from the door.

"Pic? You busy?" Gage called. "You got company. Bolt sent her."

Reaching down, I caught the stripper's hair and gripped it, slowing her down.

"Send her in."

The door opened and a short, curvy blonde dressed in a dirty T-shirt and ragged jeans stumbled into the room, her eyes going wide as she took in the scene. Generous tits filled out the design on the front of her shirt, which read "London's Cleaning Service."

Fuck. *FUCK*.

That *cocksucking bastard*. Bolt was gonna pay for this, because London Armstrong was the last woman who should be in this building. This bitch and her gorgeous rack had been making my life a living hell for the past six months, because she was the last thing I needed in my life and I'd never wanted to fuck anyone more.

Not even Heather.

And that was a problem.

It didn't matter how nice London's tits would look squeezing my dick until I came all over that pretty face of hers. She was too nice, too clean, and way the fuck too grown up. Ms. Armstrong was a regular citizen walking the straight and narrow, and she had no place in my world. She'd run off screaming in the darkness if I cut loose with her . . .

To make things worse, I sort of liked her as a person, too.

Hoover made a sudden choking noise, and I realized I'd trapped her head, cutting off her air. I let her go and she jerked back, looking up at me in confusion as she panted, mouth red and wet. I patted her head, reassuring her.

Like a dog. *Christ*.

What the hell was Bolt thinking, sending London here? I sucked in a deep breath, because the woman—who was staring at me across my office as if I was an ax murderer—looked like she was about to turn and run for the hills.

I wanted to chase her when she did it . . . run her down, rip off her jeans, and shove deep inside while she screamed at me. Yeah, nothin' wrong with *that* scenario.

Fuck it.

Six months I'd jerked off picturing her boobs, but I'd done the right thing and left her alone. Not my fault she walked into my damned office and not my responsibility to save her now that she'd come here. Clarity washed through me again and I decided there was only one way to end this.

I offered her a predatory smile and raised a hand, waving her toward the couch.

Happy birthday to me.

CHAPTER TWO

LONDON

I'd never considered myself a prude.

I was wrong. I was *definitely* a prude, because I had nowhere in my head to put what I saw when I walked through that door. I don't know why it was so shocking. It wasn't like I hadn't seen people going at it publicly in the other room, and of course a private office like this would be perfect for a quick blow job . . . But when Reese Hayes yelled that he was busy, I'd expected him to be busy with some sort of nefarious, biker gang–related activity.

You know, laundering money or something.

Then he smiled at me, the kind of smile a shark gives a castaway right before it rips her leg off. He raised his hand, beckoning me toward the couch.

I stared at him (*oh my God he's got a woman's head in his lap!*) feeling something like panic, and opened my mouth to say I could come back later. Then it hit me—no, I couldn't come back later. I needed to find Jess and I needed to find her right now before she started wreaking havoc. And as much as I wanted to judge the club members for leading her astray, I knew darned well she could find trouble all on her own. If anything, taking her out of here would be an act of mercy.

They had no idea what kind of destruction she was capable of.

You can do this.

"Hello, Mr. Hayes," I said briskly, deciding a businesslike tone was the best way to set myself apart from his other . . . *friend.* Nope. I was a woman with a purpose and I didn't have time for fooling around.

Still, it took everything I had not to look at his lap, see if I could catch a glimpse of his endowments. This would be so much easier if I hadn't spent at least two or three sessions with my vibrator picturing a scenario just like this one, but with me playing the staring role. *Pull it together, Armstrong.*

"I'm London Armstrong and I run the cleaning service that works for your club."

I stepped into the office but didn't go so far as to walk over and offer my hand for him to shake.

There's only so much a woman can handle at once.

Hayes gave me the same look he always gave me. Calculating. Hungry with just a hint of speculation as his eyes swept down my body. He lingered a bit on my breasts, but didn't make a show of it. Nope. He was all business, except for the uncomfortable fact that a woman was actively giving him a blow job. I swallowed, feeling my cheeks flush.

His eyes flickered back up to mine.

"What can I do for you?" he asked, his voice low and gravelly. Sexy. I shivered, because I could think of all kinds of things I'd like him to do for me. Maybe even *to* me, although I hated to admit it. It'd been a long six years, and I hadn't slept with Nate yet . . . We'd been dating for nearly two months, but between our schedules we didn't get to see each other all that often. Hell of a dry spell.

I forced myself to consider Hayes's question seriously, despite the squelching, squishy noises coming from his lap. How did that woman keep sucking on him like that, oblivious to what was going on? It was *very* distracting.

"You needed something, sweetheart?" Hayes asked again, taking a swig of his beer. "If you're here to join in, fine, but otherwise come sit down and tell me what you want."

Join in?

My cheeks radiated heat and I knew I was lost. I'd done so well staying matter-of-fact up to this point, but there are limits. *Just get it over with! Then you can go home and have a very large glass of wine.*

I'd need a bucket to hold all the wine I'd be drinking tonight, I decided.

"I'm looking for my cousin's daughter. She lives with me."

"Have a seat," he told me again. Gage gave a laughing snort behind me, shutting the door on us. I glanced down at the couch, an old plaid monstrosity that had to be twenty years old. With my luck, I'd catch a disease from it.

"I can stand."

"Sit. Down."

His voice snapped, and I felt myself tremble. Reese Hayes was a scary man. He'd been playing nice so far, but I was all too aware of the rumors surrounding him. Nate was a sheriff's deputy, and he was full of stories about the Reapers, particularly their president. I'd blown him off, because the MC were good clients and I figured he was just prejudiced against them. No criminal gang could just exist in the middle of the community so openly, could it? Looking at Hayes now, I realized those stories might have been true after all.

His eyes were like cold chips of blue ice, and the hint of gray at his temples and in the scruff covering his chin gave him an air of authority that I wanted to obey almost instinctively. His arms were thick, banded with heavy muscles, and his thighs . . . I glanced away quickly, because those thick thighs of his framed the half-naked woman sucking his penis perfectly. Like I'd walked into a particularly high-definition porn shoot.

I wanted to die.

Under the best of circumstances this man made me uncomfortable, and I'd done my best to avoid him. So far I'd done a pretty good job, too—wasn't like he hung around Pawns in the evenings when my crew came in. Well, sometimes he did, but he stayed back in the office.

Maybe *that* was where he did his money laundering?

Feeling just a smidge hysterical, I wondered exactly how one would go about washing money. I flashed briefly on a vision of Hayes working an old-fashioned, crank-handled washing machine while a group of aproned bikers carefully hung hundred-dollar bills on clotheslines in a sunny meadow.

"Babe?"

I blinked, trying to remember why the hell I'd thought this could be a good idea.

"Yes?"

"Are you gonna sit down or not?" he asked.

"I'm really uncomfortable with"—I gestured toward the woman—"this."

"That's not exactly my problem," he said, dropping a hand to rest on her head. "But if it's an issue, you can take her place."

"No," I said quickly.

"Then sit the fuck down and tell me why you're here."

His voice tightened, and I realized he was running out of patience. Fair enough—he obviously had other things on his . . . ahem . . . mind. I carefully perched on the edge of the couch, facing the door. This was actually better, I realized. I didn't have to look at him now. Although I could feel the woman's movements through the furniture frame and that was very creepy.

"My cousin's daughter is somewhere at this party," I said quickly. "Her name is Jessica, and she has very poor judgment. I'd really like to get her out of here and home before she does something completely stupid."

Like set the building on fire.

"You got shit timing."

I didn't respond, because what the hell would I say? So far as I knew, Hallmark didn't make a "Sorry I Interrupted Your Oral Sex" card.

Maybe I should write their corporate office to suggest it?

Hayes grunted, and the movement of the couch stopped.

"Go find Gage," he muttered to the woman, who pulled free with a smacking noise I really, really didn't need to hear. A second later she stood and wiped her mouth, glaring at me. I shrugged, offering a faintly apologetic smile. The couch trembled again as Hayes shifted, and for one horrible minute I thought he was actually going to grab me and push me down into her place. Then I heard the sound of a zipper.

"It's safe."

I turned to look at him. He'd swiveled to face me, propping one booted ankle over his knee and stretching his arm out along the backrest. It was way too close for comfort. If I leaned over I'd be able to touch him. There was nothing on his face to indicate I'd just ruined his happy ending. No emotion at all.

Nada. *Yikes!*

"Tell me about her," he said. "Why is this a problem?"

Now there was a loaded question . . .

"It's a problem because she's young and stupid," I said, feeling fatalistic. "She's self-destructive and does idiotic things, and if I let her run loose out here, something bad will happen, trust me."

He cocked his head.

"And that's our fault?" he asked. "You afraid we're gonna corrupt her?"

I snorted, biting back an edgy laugh and shaking my head. God, if only . . .

"No," I replied. "Okay, yes. Probably. But the danger goes both ways. Jessica is—"

I paused, unsure how much family business I wanted to share with him. As little as possible, I decided.

"Jessie has a lot of issues. She makes bad decisions and drags other people into them. For example, she got her best friend arrested for shoplifting, even though the poor kid had no idea what was going on. I know you have no reason to do this, but would you please consider helping me find her so I can take her home?"

He watched me, eyes trailing over my face. I wished he'd show some sort of emotion. Anything. I couldn't tell what he was thinking, and that freaked me out.

"How old is she?" he asked thoughtfully.

"Eighteen. Just graduated from high school. But believe me, she's not an adult."

He raised a brow.

"She doesn't have to do what you say," he said. "Lotta kids that age live on their own already."

"She has to do what I say if she's going to be in my home," I replied carefully. "And she's definitely not taking any steps to support herself just yet, so I'm guessing my place is it for now. I'd just as soon not be responsible for a newborn, too, but knowing my luck, she's actively getting pregnant even as we speak. Nobody needs that."

He shook his head slowly, some unfathomable emotion in his eyes.

"You can't control this," he told me. "I have daughters. Did you know that?"

"I don't know you at all," I said, which wasn't entirely true. I could still remember the first time I saw him, because he was beautiful and if I weren't a mature, sensible woman I'd have said I had a crush on him. I definitely felt a strong physical pull—at least, when I wasn't terrified of him.

That wasn't okay.

I had a boyfriend. Nate. He was nice and he liked me and I liked him and he made me feel safe. I had a good life. I took care of Jessica and ran my business. I took care of her friends sometimes, too, and inconvenient crushes on bikers—ones I worked for, no less—weren't on the table.

But as fabulous as Nate was, I hadn't been able to keep myself from watching Reese Hayes these past months, and there was more than enough gossip about him floating around town to feed my fascination once I started listening. Hayes had two grown daughters, he'd been president of the Reapers for the past decade, and his wife, Heather, had died from breast cancer six years back. Right after I'd won custody of Jessica, actually.

I knew about Heather Hayes's death because I'd attended her funeral.

She'd gone to high school with Amber, and while we hadn't really known each other back in the day, I'd wanted to pay my respects. I'd never seen a man look more devastated than Reese Hayes had that cold, dark March afternoon at the cemetery. We'd gotten late snow, and his girls had been crying hysterically the whole time.

He didn't cry, though. Nope. Reese Hayes had looked like a man who'd lost his soul. Since then he'd gotten a reputation around town as a total slut, a reputation that seemed to be well deserved, based on what I'd seen here.

Not your place to judge, I reminded myself.

When I started my cleaning business, I learned early that everyone has secrets to hide and it wasn't my job to uncover them. Get in, do the job, get out, go home. Easy and simple.

"If you knew me, you'd know I feel sympathetic toward you," he said. "Like I said, I have daughters. But I've learned the hard way that you can't control them. I'm a hard man and not even I can control them. You don't stand a chance with this kid. Why don't you just go home?"

Enough. I stood quickly.

"I'm not leaving without her. Will you help me, or do I need to start searching by myself?"

He didn't move and his expression didn't change, but the air in the room cooled.

"Sit your ass down," he said, his brilliant blue eyes flashing. The absolute authority and will in his tone was indisputable, reminding me that this was a very dangerous man.

I sat.

Hayes rose to his feet, coming to stand in front of me. Then he leaned down and rested his hands on the back of the couch on either side of my head. His gaze pinned me, and my adrenaline surged.

What the hell was he planning to do?

"You do realize where you are?" he asked softly, which was way scarier than it would've been if he'd yelled at me. Quiet menace, carrying visions of bodies buried in shallow graves . . .

"You're in my club. Outside this room are twenty men who will do anything to back me up. *Anything.* And outside this building are forests and mountains that reach all the way to Montana. Only witnesses out there are deer and maybe a moose or two. You sure you wanna piss me off? I just pulled my dick out of a willing woman's mouth for you, so it's not like I'm in a good mood to start with."

I couldn't breathe. My heart beat so fast that I thought it might explode out of my chest, and I knew for a fact that pissing him off was definitely the last thing I wanted to do.

"Now ask me nicely to help you," he said, the words slow and deliberate. I nodded, taking a minute to steel myself.

"Mr. Hayes, will you please help me find my cousin Jessica?"

"No."

Sudden moisture filled my eyes, and I felt myself quivering. I blinked quickly and forced back the tears through sheer will. I'd be damned if I'd give him any more satisfaction. Silence fell between us, his face six inches from mine, palpable tension hanging in the air. In the distance I heard music and noise from the party, all too aware that I was utterly at his mercy.

"Can I go?" I asked quietly.

"No."

At least he was direct. I licked my lips nervously and his eyes followed the movement. I couldn't look at him anymore, so I lowered my gaze.

That was a mistake.

"Lower" was his body, and one glance was enough to tell me that just because he'd sent his girlfriend away didn't mean he'd lost interest in sex. Nope. Nice big bulge in those jeans.

Yikes.

My eyes skittered away, stopping at the big knife strapped to his leg. A hunting knife. Inside at a party. Nothing scary about that at all, right?

"Convince me to help you," he said softly, his voice growing smooth, almost silky.

"How?" I whispered.

He chuckled.

"How do you think?"

I closed my eyes, trying to think. Sex. He was talking about sex. Okay. It wasn't like I didn't know about sex . . . Was I willing to sleep with a man to find Jessica? Give up on my relationship with Nate?

My gut twisted, because I'd already given up so much for her.

"It's a very bad idea to mix work and personal business," I told him. "I've got two crews working for you right now. I think getting involved would be a big mistake. Not only that, I'm seeing someone already."

Hayes gave a low chuckle.

"I don't want to get involved and I don't give a shit about your boyfriend. But I wouldn't mind fucking your tits—that'd motivate me to help. Your call."

I gasped.

It wasn't exactly a secret that I had a decent-sized chest, but I'd never had someone be so . . . crude . . . about it. I didn't know what to say. My eyes flew around the room, desperate to look at anything but his face hanging over me. Then I spotted a picture up on the file cabinet. A beautiful woman stood next to two teenage girls. Heather Hayes and her daughters. Those girls were grown up and moved out now, one of them in the past year.

Now Hayes lived alone. Inspiration struck.

"Who cleans your house?"

He blinked at me.

"What the fuck?"

"Who cleans your house?" I asked again, my thoughts coming together quickly. "If you help me find Jessica, I'll come out to your place and have my crew do a full cleaning, no charge. You can sleep with anyone, but how many of those women can you trust to clean your house?"

He rocked back on his heels, cocking his head at me. A strange light came into his eyes.

"Didn't see that one coming," he said, his mouth quirking at one corner. "But any of those girls out there will clean for me."

"I'll bet they expect something in return, don't they?" I asked, sensing I had him. "I'll bet they want to be your girlfriend or whatever it's called . . ."

"Old lady."

"I'll bet they want to be your old lady," I continued, getting into it. I leaned forward, willing him to agree with me. "And I bet they get annoying after a while. My crew comes in, we clean, we leave. No stress, no fuss, and no strings attached. How's that for something of value?"

"Not your crew, just you."

I frowned at him. He sat back on his heels, seeming relaxed enough, but I still felt the coiled tension in the air.

"All right," I said, figuring I should stop while I was ahead. I held my hand out and he took it, wrapping his strong fingers around mine. They were warm and solid. I'd bet his arms would be, too.

He didn't say he wanted to hold you, I reminded myself firmly. *He said he wanted to "fuck your tits," and that's a place we don't need to go.*

Obviously I should start sleeping with Nate sooner rather than later, before my hormones destroyed me entirely.

Don't question. Just find Jessica.

"So what does she look like?" he asked. I dug into my pocket and pulled out my phone, flipping quickly to her graduation picture.

Good lord, my little cousin was stunning.

Jessica was tall, with long legs toned from running. Her hair was a rich, chestnut-brown and her eyes were bright with thick lashes. She looked like an all-American princess.

He gave a low whistle.

"Pretty girl," he said slowly, and I glanced quickly at his face, hoping desperately I wouldn't see lust in his eyes. He took the phone and abruptly turned and walked out of the office, leaving me to scamper after him like a puppy. I followed him back into the main lounge area where I'd first come in. I spotted Gage leaning against the wall, eyes seeing everything as he surveyed the party. Reese walked over to him and handed him the phone.

"So we lookin' for her?" Gage asked.

"Yup," he said. "She's goin' home with London, just as soon as we find her. And she's out for good after that, got me?"

"Sure," Gage said casually. "But she's upstairs right now with Banks and Painter. Probably already on her back."

I shivered, closing my eyes. *Please, please, please be using condoms . . .*

"This way," Hayes said, and I followed him through the partiers and across the room. The crowd parted for him like a wave, making it all too clear who was the boss.

At the far end of the room, past the bar, was a staircase leading upstairs. Hayes started climbing and I followed. On the second level we passed through a large game room holding a pool table, old couches, a giant TV, and several generations of video game consoles. There were people here, too, although not as many. Just the occasional couple on a couch.

Eyes forward. Not your place to judge.

Hayes led me up one more level, into a narrow hallway lined on each side by narrow wooden doors.

"Armory used to have barracks space up here," he said. "I don't think it was ever really used, but that's how they built them back then. Now they're our guest rooms. She's probably in the one at the far end, because it's the only one open."

He strolled down the hallway casually, as if we weren't in a race to stop my cousin from getting pregnant. I forced myself to follow with measured footsteps, coming to a halt next to him in front of the last door. I heard moaning inside, and I closed my eyes, wishing I were at home in bed, where I belonged.

"You sure you want to do this?" Hayes asked, and something softened in his hard eyes.

I frowned at him. "Of course—what do you mean?"

"We can just go downstairs, have a drink," he said slowly. "Relax a little. Because if we go in there and drag her out, it's not gonna change anything. If the kid's determined to get herself in trouble, she'll do it. You can't stop her."

I clenched my teeth. Part of me whispered he was right—after all, it wasn't like I'd been able to change Amber. My cousin hadn't started out as the kind of person who'd shoot up heroin in front of her twelve-year-old daughter.

But I wanted more for Jessica. Better.

"Should I knock on the door or should you?" I asked him, determined. He shrugged, then rapped hard against the wood.

"It's Pic."

"Yeah?" a man shouted, his voice hoarse. I could imagine why, too.

"You got a girl in there named Jessica?"

I heard muffled voices, then another man spoke again.

"She says no, but she looks guilty. Give us a sec."

We waited for what couldn't have been more than a couple of minutes but felt like an eternity as I heard rumbles and thumps coming from the room.

Two male voices. Then Jessica's, raised in argument. Dear God, why did she do things like this?

Hayes leaned back against the wall the whole time, crossing his big arms and studying me like a trapped mouse. Then the door opened, revealing a tall, dark-haired young man with rumpled hair. I looked past him to find a very plain room with an ancient, sagging bed. Jessica stood at the foot, her face full of fury. Behind her was another man, this one with short, spiky blond hair. He wasn't wearing a shirt, just a pair of jeans loosely fastened, and he pulled on heavy leather boots with a look of profound annoyance.

There were smears of lipstick on his chest, trailing down across his stomach.

Holy hell.

"You have no right to be here," Jess hissed at me. My eyes flicked back to her. God, she looked awful. Ragged, torn tights, uber short skirt, and two tops layered in a way that somehow covered nothing while still giving the appearance of clothing. Her eyes were smudged with thick, dark black liner, her hair was tangled and wild, and the slash of red across her mouth matched the trail she'd left on the man behind her.

"Jess, it's time to go home," I said, and suddenly I felt every minute of my thirty-eight years. The blond pulled on a shirt then brushed past her and out the door, practically growling in his frustration. Hayes stepped forward and slapped his back as they exchanged a look I couldn't begin to read.

"I hate you!" Jess snarled.

"For fuck's sake," Hayes said, his voice annoyed. "Get your ass out here, you little shit. I don't have time for this and neither does London."

"Screw you. I'm an adult. I can do whatever I want, and I want to stay here with Banks."

The young man holding the door—presumably Banks—gave an incredulous snort. Hayes didn't do anything, but somehow the air changed. Darkened. Jessica had made a very serious mistake and suddenly I felt scared for her. I reached over, catching his arm without thinking, my fingers curling into his warm skin as I whispered, "Please . . ."

Hayes glanced down at my hand, then caught my gaze, holding it captive.

"You owe me," he said. "Because that little bitch doesn't talk to me like that, you got it? Never again."

He turned his attention back to Jess, whose face had started to reflect some concern. Maybe she was finally realizing this wasn't a game?

"You get your ass out here and apologize to your cousin," Hayes said, his voice so quiet and low I felt it all the way down my spine. "Then go downstairs and get in her car. You're gonna drive home and you're never coming out here again. You do, I'll teach you a lesson you won't forget—and don't think for a second that smiling and flashing your tits will make a difference. I've seen it all before. We clear?"

Jessica nodded, eyes wide. She stepped out of the room, moving instinctively to stand behind me, as far from the Reapers' president as she could get without making an obvious break for freedom.

"I'm ready to leave now, Loni," she said quietly.

"Okay. Let's get out of here."

I turned to leave, but Hayes's voice cut like the slash of a whip.

"Stop."

We turned back slowly. His stare flayed me, stripping through my defenses, and I realized he was much, much angrier with Jessica than I'd realized. Somewhere down in the depths of my brainstem the monkey screamed in fear, absolutely convinced a predator was about to eat us.

"Banks will take her down," he said. "You and I aren't done."

The boy stepped out of the room quickly, pulling on his Reapers vest before catching Jessica's arm and dragging her down the hallway. If you'd seen them from a distance, you'd almost believe they were a young couple holding hands . . . In reality, he was more like a guard escorting a prisoner.

"Thank you very much for helping me," I told Hayes once they were gone, forcing myself to breathe steadily. Show no fear. "What did you want to talk about?"

"I want you at my place on Monday at three," he said.

"We can work you into my schedule," I said slowly. "But I don't have my calendar with me. Can I get in touch with you tomorrow, when I'm not so tired?"

Definitely the best idea. Maybe I'd even find a way out of this, because I knew darned well going to his house by myself wouldn't be safe. Not after seeing him like this—if anything, the man was more dangerous than all the rumors combined. He smiled at me wolfishly.

"No, I'll see you at three on Monday. Bolt will give you the address. That'll cover our original deal, but have you forgotten you owe me more now?"

"Huh?" I asked blankly.

"I just gave your girl a damned big pass," he said slowly, taking a step toward me. I backed up warily. "But someone has to pay for what she did."

Hayes took another step forward, and I felt my back hit the wall. Not good. His face was cold, eyes full of ice. He towered over me, hands coming to rest on either side of my head.

"What exactly do you mean by pay?" I whispered.

"It's my birthday," he said slowly, his chest grazing the tips of my breasts. My nipples hardened without permission. "And instead of getting my dick sucked by a stripper, I just cock-blocked two of my brothers for you."

I felt myself starting to panic.

"You did get . . ." I cleared my throat nervously. "You *did* have oral sex. I mean, if you want to be technical about it. You just didn't finish."

"I'm aware."

His hips pushed down, demonstrating just how aware he was. I swallowed as I felt his hard length press my stomach. Heat rushed through me, twisting down between my legs, because no matter what else Reese Hayes might be, he was incredibly sexy. His mouth lowered toward mine, and then his nose brushed up and along the length of mine. I felt his warm breath whisper across my cheek. His lips hovered a fraction of an inch over mine and I closed my eyes.

"Just a taste," he whispered. I nodded. I couldn't help myself.

His mouth brushed mine as one of his hands slid into my hair, loosening the bandanna. His tongue traced the crack of my lips, wordlessly asking to come inside.

Sighing, I let him.

The kiss was surprisingly gentle in its intensity. His tongue reached deep, exploring in a game of hunt and chase that sent tendrils of desire all the way down to my toes and back up again. Without thinking, I pressed my breasts against his chest, startled and thrilled by just how good he felt around me. His hips moved in a slow, steady grind as he slipped a knee between mine. I felt a hand grip my rear and then he boosted me effortlessly, pinning me against the wall as my legs wrapped around him oh so naturally.

Reality hit.

Reese Hayes's penis nestled right up against my opening, and as my body strained toward his I realized we were perilously close to the point of no return.

I pictured Nate's smiling face and forced myself to pull away from the kiss. Hayes released my mouth, holding my body firm, resting his forehead against mine and breathing heavily. I pushed my spine back into the wall, adrenaline surging, but there wasn't anywhere to go. Not that the kiss had been violent or rough or even that passionate . . . I'd just never experienced anything quite like this man's quiet intensity.

And I'd never wanted anyone more than I wanted Reese Hayes in that moment.

"I need to go," I whispered. "Jessie is waiting for me."

"Stay."

"Can't. She needs me. You're a parent—you understand. I know you do."

"You can't fix her," he whispered into my ear, the heat of his mouth brushing against the lobe. "She's a big kid and she has to make her own decisions. Sooner or later we have to let them grow up."

"Is that what you did with your girls?" I asked. He stilled, then shook his head with a low laugh.

"Fuck no," he admitted. "I tried everything I could to protect them and keep them safe. Didn't do a damned bit of good in the end. Kit's running wild, and Em's shacked up with a bastard I'd give anything to put in the ground."

"Then you know why I have to leave now."

He lowered me slowly and we studied each other for long seconds, sharing a kind of understanding that I'd never have believed possible ten minutes earlier.

"I'll walk you to the car," he said.

"Thank you."

A strange mixture of awareness and tension followed as we walked down the stairs and passed through the club's main lounge. Speculative gazes touched us, which I ignored.

I could ignore the humming of my body, too—I'd accomplished my goal.

Outside, a very subdued Jessica waited next to the van in the parking lot, Banks standing near enough to watch her but not close enough to talk comfortably. He looked bored but alert, clearly determined to follow his president's orders.

So much for young love.

I unlocked the van with my key fob and Jess slid in as I reached for my own door. Hayes caught my shoulder, turning me toward him.

"Three o'clock Monday afternoon."

"I'll check my schedule."

"You do that," he said with a slow, sly grin, because we both knew damned well I'd be there, on time and ready to work. I had a feeling he'd hunt me down if I didn't. I opened the van door and climbed in, sliding the key into the ignition.

Jess refused to look at me, which worked out well because I really didn't feel like dealing with her. We'd made it halfway home before she broke the silence.

"Mom would never embarrass me like that."

After all that, she was going to throw Amber at me? Something ugly inside me snapped.

"Nope, she would've charged them to screw you because she never gives anything away for free."

Jessica gasped and I immediately felt horrible. It might be true, but I had no business tearing down Amber to her daughter. I knew better . . .

"I'm sorry—"

"Fuck you," she said, her voice cold, dark, and so full of hate I flinched. "I want to go live with her. My *real* mother."

I slowed the van to pull over, because I'd messed up and I knew it. Jess turned away.

"Just drive. I don't want to talk. You're not my mom and you're not my boss. I'm an adult. Fuck you . . ." she repeated, but this time she didn't sound strong. Nope. It was a pained whisper. My heart tore in half, because no matter how damaged Jess was, it wasn't her fault. From the instant of conception she'd been bathed with chemicals in her mother's toxic womb, and now she had to live with that the rest of her life.

In the privacy of my mind, I allowed myself a second curse for the night.

Fuck you, Amber.

CHAPTER THREE

MONDAY
LONDON

"Have to admit, I thought you might have a problem with this . . ."
I said, running a finger around the rim of my water glass. We were
supposed to have a date that night, but Nate had called earlier saying he'd been scheduled to work, so we'd met downtown for lunch
instead.

He stole one of my fries, and I smacked his hand playfully. I'd
missed having a man around, as much as I hated to admit it. Looking at him across the table, I felt a wave of warmth, because being
with him always made me happy. He was so strong and sexy in his
deputy's uniform . . . Like something out of a romance book. Nate
even had the tousled hair and dimples to complete the package.

The memory of Reese Hayes's kiss flashed through my mind, and I
flushed. I hadn't told Nate about it. We weren't officially exclusive . . .
or at least we'd never discussed it.

The implication was certainly clear, though.

"I'm not thrilled," he admitted. "Hayes is a criminal and we all know it—but he's not under investigation for anything right now. I do question his motives in asking you to come out personally."

Yeah, I wasn't going to touch that . . .

"Well, it should be interesting," I said.

"How's Jess?"

"Same as always, I guess. I'm trying to get her job hunting. She needs to be thinking about her future, and she says she doesn't want to do any more school. It's frustrating."

"Must be," Nate said, his voice sympathetic but noncommital. He'd made it clear from the start that whatever went on between me and Jess was our business. Totally hands off, which I found alternately reassuring and frustrating, because I was in over my head. "You think it's safe to leave the house for a night? I'd love to take you up to Sandpoint this weekend. There's a beautiful B&B I think you'd like."

I flushed, because we both knew what he was really asking. Was I ready to spend the night with him? For some reason I'd been stalling, which was strange, given how sexually frustrated I was. I couldn't think of a single good reason *not* to sleep with him . . . Might as well just do it, I decided. Rip off that bandage, get back in the saddle.

Great. Now I was thinking in cliches.

"I don't think I can leave overnight," I replied, offering him a smile. "I'm afraid she'd have a party and burn the place down or something. But that doesn't mean we can't take some time for ourselves."

His face brightened.

"You sure?" he asked. Nate never pushed, which was one of the things I loved about him.

"Yeah, I'm sure."

He reached across the table and caught my hand, pulling it up for a gentle kiss. I heard a little sigh and glanced over to find our waitress watching raptly.

I leaned forward and whispered in his ear.

"I think she's waiting for you to propose," I said, giggling.

"Not this time," he replied, turning his head just enough to allow his lips to graze my jawline.

Did he just say what I thought he said?

Oh, wow . . . I knew Nate wanted to get married again. He'd been divorced for three years and had been clear he was looking for a serious relationship. Still, seemed a little early to say something like that.

I tugged away, staring down at my food.

"Hey, don't worry," he said lightly. "You think too much, Loni. Just enjoy the moment, okay?"

"Okay. So . . . Maybe we should make a plan. How about I come over to your place on Friday? We could fix dinner and maybe watch a movie or something."

"I like the 'or something' option," he said, eyes sparkling.

I stirred my ketchup with a fry, pretending I had to consider the suggestion carefully.

"Yeah, that'll work."

He leaned forward to kiss me properly, right in the middle of the restaurant. Our silly waitress started clapping. Ugh. Had I ever been that young and romantic?

No. I hadn't.

Amber had been the romantic, always chasing her dreams, right up to the point where she fell down a rabbit hole and never found her way out. I'd been trailing after her ever since, doing damage control.

Maybe it was time for me to chase some of my own dreams. Starting with Nate.

I deserved a little happiness.

Why the hell am I here?

I stood on Reese Hayes's porch later that afternoon, questioning my sanity. Jessica would just get herself in trouble again—I hadn't solved anything, just delayed the inevitable. The relaxed glow I'd carried from my lunch with Nate had evaporated the minute I pulled up to the house, replaced with a sort of horrible anxiety and excitement about seeing Hayes again all mixed together in my stomach.

Of course that could've just been the fries I'd eaten for lunch.

Yeah. Right.

The big biker met me at the door with a lazy smile guaranteed to melt the panties right off a girl. Faded jeans hung low on his hips and an old T-shirt did far too little to hide the bulk of his muscles. Those ice blue eyes of his missed nothing, sweeping down my figure to take in the baggy shirt and hole-filled jeans I'd deliberately chosen to wear this afternoon. Possibly the least sexy outfit in human history and that was no coincidence.

There would be no repeats of the weekend's unfortunate events in the hallway.

Reese's mouth quirked and his face held none of the intimidating coldness of the last time I'd seen him. Nope, today he was pretending to be a seminormal human being, but only partially succeeding. I knew what was under the surface—a hard man who wouldn't hesitate to do whatever he needed to do to get his way. Unfortunately, my lady parts stopped listening to my brain right after the "hard man" part, because they were less focused on the work ahead and more focused on remembering how his mouth had felt on mine.

"Glad you could fit me into your schedule," he said slyly as I stepped inside. I bit my tongue. Literally. I couldn't afford to make him mad for any number of reasons, not least of which was the fact that the MC was my best-paying client. If I got the strip club contract, they'd be the biggest, too. All cash. I might not be suffering for work—but there's work and there's *work*. The club wasn't afraid to pay well in exchange for good service, and they didn't cheap out when it came to getting what they wanted. Expanding to take on their account would be worth the hassle.

But business aside, I was also pretty sure that if Reese got angry enough, bad things might start happening. Stabby, shooty things. I based this on the impressive display of collectible knives and guns hanging over the mantel in the living room.

"Nice weapons," I muttered, eyes wide. He laughed.

"Most of those were my dad's," he said. "Although I've picked up a few along the way myself, too."

Lovely.

I turned to face him, offering my most businesslike smile.

"Can you show me around the house?" I asked. "I'd like to get a feel for the place, see how much work I have ahead of me. I have five hours before I need to pick up Jess."

"She doing okay?"

Hmm . . . How to answer that? I met his gaze, wishing his eyes weren't so bright and blue. It wasn't fair for a man to have muscles like that *and* such gorgeous eyes. And those lips, all framed in just a scruff of beard . . .

"She's angry at me and angry at the world," I said finally. "And I said something stupid to hurt her feelings, which didn't help things. Hard to know what direction we're going."

"You wanna talk about it?"

That startled me. I coughed, looking away. Why on earth would he offer to talk to me about Jessica? Second man to ask today, I realized, thinking back to Nate at lunch. Great. I was surrounded by sexy men and all they wanted to do was discuss my shitty parenting techniques.

"No. Let's just get this done, okay?"

He raised a brow, holding up his hands in amused surrender.

"Works for me," he said. "C'mon."

We started by going up the narrow stairs to the second floor, which had three bedrooms and a bathroom. The place was old, a farmhouse built at least a hundred years ago, and wasn't anything fancy—just comfortable and homey. Colorful rag rugs covered wooden floors, and two of the bedrooms obviously belonged to his daughters. The third held a guest bed.

I figured it said something positive about him that he hadn't boxed up their things or redecorated when they moved out.

Guess nobody is *all* bad.

The homey vibe continued downstairs, despite the display of weaponry in the living room. The dining room held a china cabinet full of things that must've been Heather's. Pictures covered the walls and there were even some plants, although they weren't looking particularly healthy at the moment.

I wondered if his daughter had been the one to take care of them?

The plants weren't the only things suffering from neglect. Dust had settled on most of the surfaces, water spots covered the faucets, and the kitchen garbage seemed to be full of paper plates and old carryout containers. A few unwashed glasses sat in the sink . . . no other evidence that any cooking had taken place in the past month.

"I take it you eat out a lot?"

"Busy life. Bedroom is back here."

The bedroom.

Don't be a dork, I told myself. *You've cleaned hundreds of strangers' rooms over the years and it's no big deal.*

"I need to get my supplies," I said, chickening out. I'd look at his bedroom later, after I got the rest of the house whipped into shape. Thankfully it shouldn't be that hard a job—there might be a lot of dust, but the place wasn't filthy. I got the impression he didn't spend much time there at all, which had to limit the mess.

"You need help carrying anything?" he asked, trailing me to the door.

"Nope. In fact, it will be easier for me if you go away for a couple hours."

He studied me speculatively, and I rolled my eyes.

"What do you think I'm going to do—steal your guns? I don't even like guns. It's going to be noisy and dusty and you'll be in my way."

Hayes gave a startled snort, and I realized he was holding back a laugh. Okay. That was better than him menacing me.

"I'll be out in the shop," he said. "Come find me if you have any questions."

"Sure thing," I replied, taking another quick look around.

The sooner I got this done the better.

Nearly three hours later I'd scrubbed, dusted, wiped, and washed the entire house. Not deep cleaning—no windows—but the surfaces were dirt-free and sanitized, the carpets were vacuumed, and the dust bunnies had been executed for crimes against humanity.

Now all that remained was the back addition where he slept, which I'd saved for last. Why? I have no idea. I guess it just felt too intimate, and I didn't want to get any closer to him than I needed to. This was crazy, because I'd cleaned bedrooms through the years and never felt more than mild curiosity about their residents.

Get over yourself.

Walking into his room was like entering a different world. It was all new construction, so that was a big contrast right there, but the place was sparse and barren, too. Modern furniture, and not much of it. A dresser and an entertainment center with a giant flatscreen on it. Mirrored panels covering big double closet doors. A slider opened out the back, hung with heavy, dark curtains that weren't quite black but weren't quite anything else, either.

And the bed? Wowza.

Reese Hayes had a bed big enough for six people, and I wouldn't be surprised if he'd had that many in here a time or two. The image of him lying back on it, naked and beckoning took my breath away for an instant. *Down, hormones!* Silky black sheets covered it, another modern touch deeply out of sync with the rest of the house. It felt like some sort of dark den, which I supposed it was. He'd obviously erased any hints that his wife had ever slept in here.

"Now that's depressing," I muttered softly to myself.

"What's depressing?"

I jumped, adrenaline spiking as I whirled to find the man himself watching me. He leaned against the door frame, his big arms crossed, which flexed the muscles in a way that sent a thrill down my spine.

"Don't sneak up on me like that!"

Hayes cocked a brow, and I realized I'd yelled at him.

"Sorry," I said quickly, remembering how he'd responded to Jessica's blowup. I didn't have any reason to believe he'd be dangerous, at least not under these circumstances. That didn't mean I should feel comfy and safe around him, though.

"I didn't mean to scare you," he said quietly. "But what did you mean by that comment?"

Love that deer-in-the-headlights feeling. I tried to think, come up with some kind of safe lie, but the truth came out instead and it was horrible.

"It's depressing because it's obvious that you removed every trace of Heather from your room."

He froze, and for the first time I saw something like real emotion on his face. He looked . . . stunned. Like he couldn't believe I'd actually said that.

Fair enough. I couldn't quite believe it, either.

"I'm sorry," I whispered. He turned and walked out, slamming the door behind him.

Well played, London. Kick the widower in the emotional balls. Classy. What the hell was wrong with me?

I turned back and set down my supply bucket. Might as well get to work, because there was no way I'd be leaving this room any time soon. I didn't think I'd be able to face him for a while . . . I walked into the bathroom and flipped on the light, looking around. *Oh, dear God.* It was disgusting. Not moldy or anything, but really obvious that it hadn't seen a good cleaning in weeks, maybe even months. Much worse than the bathroom upstairs had been, but I guess that made sense. Nobody lived up there anymore.

He'd have plenty of time to forgive me before I'd get out of here, I realized. My phone buzzed.

JESSICA: Getting done an hour early and need ride.

I rubbed my temple, frustrated. I'd never finish this in one shot, and now I had even less time, unless I made Jess walk home from the community center. Knowing my luck, she'd pick up a bunch of new friends along the way and bring them back to the house for a party . . .

Wonderful.

President Friendly and I would need to schedule at least one more session, which meant more time spent with him than I'd ever imagined when we struck our deal. And that was *before* I insulted him about his dead wife in their bedroom.

Jessie is worth it, I reminded myself. *This is nothing. Just get to work and keep your mouth shut. Think about Nate and Friday night. With any luck, you'll go back to seeing Reese Hayes once or twice a month from a safe distance.*

Just the way it should be.

I was only partially finished with the bathroom when my phone timer went off, reminding me to pick up Jess. I packed up my supplies and looked around in dissatisfaction.

At least the toilet was clean.

Walking past his freshly changed bed, I tried not to think about how soft and comfortable that silky fabric would feel against my skin . . . I suspected it would be fabulous, especially if his body was covering mine and I got to taste those lips of his again. My cheeks warmed, and I wondered how—exactly—I'd gone from being a sensible, responsible woman to one who could lust after two men in one day.

I tried to think of a way to blame that one on Jessica, but not even I could pull it off. I had to own up to the facts—I'd become a perv. I guess all those articles about women hitting their sexual peak in their thirties hadn't been exaggerating.

When I entered the kitchen, I heard voices from the living room. Hayes and a woman. I smelled food, too. Pizza. The hot-cheese-and-tomato scent wafting toward me was heavenly. I'd worked up an appetite, which I guess was one good thing about my job. I burned plenty of calories on a daily basis, no question of that.

As I approached the living room, I could see the back of Hayes's head from where he sat on the couch. A woman straddled him, facing me. For one horrid, wretched moment I thought I might be about to walk in on him having sex again. She glanced up at me, curiosity written all over her face, saying something to him I couldn't quite make out. He pushed her off gently. Thankfully, she was fully clothed.

"So," I said, walking into the room, feeling unspeakably awkward. An open box of pizza sat on the coffee table, along with two open beers and a couple of empties.

Hayes stood, his thick thighs and heavy arms even sexier than I remembered, which seemed rather unfair. His companion gave me a friendly smile. She was young, cute, and apparently nice, too. Girls like that are the worst. I had a feeling I looked disgusting, and knowing my luck, I probably didn't smell too good right now, either.

Oh, and old. I felt old.

"I'm almost done with your bathroom," I said, realizing I should apologize for what I'd said earlier. I just didn't know how. "But not quite. I'll need to come back."

"I can be here tomorrow afternoon."

"I can't. But I can come on Wednesday."

"Wednesday isn't good for me. Tomorrow."

"No, I can come on Wednesday," I repeated. "I have to take Jess over to the hospital in Spokane tomorrow. She has an appointment with a specialist and it's not like you can just reschedule those."

He frowned.

"What does she need to see a specialist for?"

"That's her business," I replied, straightening myself. "I appreciate your help the other night, but that's not a license to invade our privacy."

The girl's eyes went wide.

"I need to go get something out of my car," she said quickly. I started forward, deciding retreat was the better part of valor, but Hayes stood in my way. The man was like a brick wall. A really frustrating brick wall. I tried to slip past him, but he wrapped one big hand around my upper arm, stopping me. Shoot. I'd forgotten to be afraid of him.

This was a mistake, because he could turn on scary just like that.

"What's up with your girl?" he asked again, his voice soft. "I know she's a wild kid, but this sounds like more."

I stared at his broad chest, refusing to meet his eyes. He wore a torn T-shirt that had seen better days, and it didn't do much to hide the latent strength of his muscles or just how easily he could hold me here indefinitely. Not only that, he *smelled* good. So unfair.

"I really don't want to talk about it."

His eyes narrowed.

"Do you need help, London?" he asked. "You work for us now. If there's a problem, you should tell me. Even if there isn't, I should know if you've got something big going on. Everything that touches the club is my business."

I snorted. *Now* he was interested in learning more about our lives?

"It's nothing important," I replied, forcing my voice to stay smooth, because it *wasn't* nothing and never would be. "We just need to get her checked out. But I can come back on Wednesday right after lunch. Would that work for you?"

He studied me a moment longer, then slowly rubbed his hands up and down my arms before letting me go. This was fortunate, because I'm pretty sure I got goose bumps and the last thing I needed was him figuring out how I reacted to his touch.

"I won't be here on Wednesday," he said. "But I can program in a code for you to use. I'll text it to you in the morning, sound good?"

"Fantastic," I said, feeling almost desperate to get away. "You're busy, I don't want to keep you. Night!"

I darted out the door before he could respond, then stopped on the porch. Shit. As much as I wanted to get the hell away, I needed to apologize. What I'd said about his room and Heather had been so wrong on so many levels . . . I turned to face Reese, meeting his eyes directly.

"That comment about your bedroom? That was wrong. I have no right to say anything about your home or your room—or your wife. I'm sorry. It was thoughtless and hurtful."

Reese didn't respond right away, just studied my face. Then he nodded his head slowly. Good enough for me, so I turned and moved quickly toward my van. The woman I'd seen inside leaned against her car, smoking and watching me with openly concerned eyes.

"You okay?"

"Fine," I said. "No worries."

She shrugged, throwing down the butt and twisting it under her foot. She walked back to the house as I loaded my supplies. Out of the corner of my eye I saw her go to Reese. He guided her into the house, shutting the door behind them. I started to climb into my vehicle, then glanced over at the butt on the dirt.

Leave it.

I couldn't. Being a neat freak is a curse sometimes, but darned if I could just drive away and leave that nasty little thing lying there. I gave the house a quick glance to make sure I was all clear before stomping over to pick it up. Clutching it carefully between two fingers, I carried it around the side of the house to the trash can.

It took two seconds to toss it in, and then another for a quick squirt of hand sanitizer from the little tube in my pocket.

Better.

So what if I couldn't control Jessica and I felt awkward and uncomfortable around Reese? At least that particular cigarette butt wouldn't pollute anything today. I decided to count it as a victory.

"She has a gift, you know."

I glanced over at Maggs, the new volunteer coordinator at the community center.

"Jess?"

Maggs nodded, her messy blonde hair styled exactly the way I'd tried to get mine that unfortunate time that I'd cut it all off. She looked sort of like Meg Ryan at her cutest. I'd resembled a horrific clown who'd been attacked with scissors. I glanced across the room at my little cousin, watching her crawl around on the floor with a little girl.

"I haven't seen her before," I said, nodding toward the child.

"She's new, only been coming for a couple weeks now," Maggs said. "Family just moved to the area. She's got a shunt—congenital hydrocephalus. Jessica has taken a special interest in her."

My breath caught. Of course she had . . .

"Jess is hell on wheels, but she's a good volunteer," I said, which was the truth. No matter how crazy everything else got, Jess never missed a shift at the center. "She loves working with the kids."

"Has she considered going into early-childhood education or a related field?"

I laughed.

"I don't think she's considered anything beyond her next party."

Maggs cocked her head.

"That's unfortunate," she said. "Because she'd be really good at it."

"I know," I replied, smiling. "Hey, Jess! You ready?"

Jess looked up at me and smiled, hopping up and offering the kid her hand for a high five. The little girl jumped up to smack her, obviously thrilled to get such attention from a big girl.

"See ya on Wednesday," Jess told her, then loped across the game room floor toward me. "Sorry, I lost track of the time. Hey, they're having a party for the kids and their families on Wednesday night. I signed you up to bring chicken and dumplings. They want it here by six."

"Thanks for asking first," I replied, my tone dry. She grinned at me.

"Would you have said no?"

I shrugged and she giggled, sounding young and carefree.

"Ha! I know you too well. You always come through."

That was the truth . . .

"So, I thought you were going to be done early today? Seemed like you weren't quite ready to leave after all."

"Yeah, I planned to get out early, but then we got caught up in a game," she said, shrugging. "I do want to go home, though. Mellie's coming over. We're going to a movie tonight out in Hayden—she's got her mom's car. You said you'd pay for a movie with her this week, remember?"

"I remember," I said, figuring Mellie deserved something nice after what she'd been through last weekend. Jess had blown up at her for calling me, although they'd made up again by Sunday night. That's the thing with Jess. For better or for worse, she doesn't hold on to things. Every once in a while that worked out so the good guys won.

"Do you have plans for dinner?" Jess asked casually as we started across the parking lot. Too casually. What was she up to now?

"Not really. I was thinking we could have soup and sandwiches."

"How about pizza?" she asked, and my mouth watered. I hadn't gotten the smell of the pizza at Reese's house out of my mind since I'd left. So I'd been intimidated by him . . . but I'd also been hungry.

"Not sure that's in the budget," I said slowly, mentally calculating where we were in the month. Between the mortgage and the medical bills, there wasn't much extra.

"Who said you're paying?" Jess asked, pulling out a wadded green bill from her pocket. She stretched it out and waved it triumphantly in my face.

A fifty.

My eyes widened.

"Where did that come from?" I asked, stunned. Dear God, was she picking pockets now?

"It was a thank-you gift," she said, grinning broadly. "You saw that little girl I was playing with? Well, her mom talked to me last week and she really likes how I'm working with Ivy. She's behind the other kids developmentally, and it's hard for her. I know how that feels, so I've been spending extra time with her. Today her mom gave me this and thanked me. She asked if I do babysitting, too!"

"Jessie, that's fantastic!" I said, pulling her in for an impulsive hug. She tugged away from me immediately, scowling, but I could see the pleasure in her eyes. This was a huge win for her.

Maybe an opportunity, too.

"You know, Ms. Dwyer said you have a gift with the kids," I told her. She radiated pride even as she kicked a rock, pretending not to care. "She thinks you should go into early-childhood education. You're really good with them, especially the special-needs kids."

"I like them, that's all," Jess said. "But I don't want to do more school. I already told you that—I don't like school. It's too hard for me."

I sobered.

"I know it's hard for you. But when you take the time, you do a really good job. You graduated with a 3.1, and that's nothing to be ashamed of."

She grunted.

"That's just because I took all the easy classes. I'm a retard and we both know it."

I stopped dead and grabbed her, turning her toward me. Catching her gaze, I studied her face. What I saw there killed me. She believed it. No matter how many times I told her otherwise, she still couldn't forget what those little bitches in middle school had starting calling her. Not even changing schools had helped.

"I never want to hear you say that word again," I told her, the words slow and forceful. "A learning disability doesn't make you stupid—it just means you have to work harder. You have a perfectly normal IQ. I'm incredibly proud of you, Jess, and when I suggested you go to more school it's only because I know you can handle it."

She rolled her eyes, and I fought the urge to shake her.

"Jess, listen to me. Ms. Dwyer said you have a *gift*—and you know what? You *do* have a gift. Would you call the kids you work with here retards?"

Jess's eyes narrowed and her face flushed.

"No. I would never say that and you know it."

"Then why the hell would you say it about yourself? You'll either go to more school or you won't, but don't for one minute tell me that it's because you aren't smart enough. You're smart, Jess."

She stilled, and I practically saw the wheels turning in her head.

"You said 'hell.'"

"Yes," I replied, feeling suddenly sheepish. "I guess I did."

A slow smile crept across her face. Then she leaned forward, catching me up tight in a hug.

"Thank you, Loni," she said. "I know I drive you crazy, but I love you. Thank you for always being on my side."

I hugged her back, tears filling my eyes. Why couldn't Jess be like this all the time? *This* was the girl I'd given up so much for. Imperfect and frustrating, but worth all the sacrifices and then some.

"You gonna buy me pizza or what?" I asked finally, pulling away.

"First one to the car gets to pick the restaurant," she said, then took off across the parking lot, long legs pumping. I started after her, but I never had a shot. The girl was six inches taller than me with the stride to prove it.

Good lord, I loved that kid, and every time I started to forget why, she'd do something beautiful to remind me.

CHAPTER FOUR

REESE

Wednesday was the shits.

One of the girls working at The Line OD'd right after lunch, right on the stage. They called the ambulance and Gage started CPR, but she didn't make it. We'd all known Pepper was using, but not how much, and apparently she left behind a son, too. I'd banged her the weekend before, but she never said a word about having a kid. Not that I'd given her the chance to talk much, or would've listened if she had tried.

I hated myself a little bit for that.

Now social services would step in and I hoped to hell she had family somewhere. We'd probably do a little fund-raiser for the boy, which would change exactly nothing because he didn't need money—he needed a mom.

Fucking sucked.

Then we got word out of La Grande that they'd intercepted a major cartel shipment, which was farther north than we'd realized they'd started running product. This also fucking sucked, because it meant things were heating up faster than we'd anticipated. I guess technically we'd been at war with them for six months, but it wasn't an active war. More of a wait-and-see while making plans for payback.

Clearly the waiting game was over.

To top it all off, I'd smashed my thumb at the shop fixing my bike because I'm a fucking dumbass. Now my thumb hurt like hell and the bike still wasn't up and running. On the bright side, watching me cuss and punch the walls in frustration seemed to entertain the guys.

Nice to provide some comic relief, I guess.

When I pulled up to the house, all I wanted was a hot shower, followed by a cold beer and maybe some TV. We'd already had church that afternoon—just a quick meeting to cover events down south—but there wasn't anything else going on tonight and I needed some time to myself. Normally I'd bring some bitch home for a fuck after a crap day, but Pepper put a stop to that. She'd been the last girl in my bed.

Pretty sure she shot up in my bathroom, too, now that I thought about it.

That's when I saw the goddamned minivan in my driveway. Shit. The Ice Princess had said she'd be out by early afternoon, and I wasn't in the mood to listen to her prissy voice while staring at her off-limits boobs.

"God damn it," I muttered, slamming my hand down on the steering wheel for emphasis. That sent a wave of pain shooting up from my swollen thumb and I stiffened, groaning.

Could anything go right today?

When I walked into the house I froze, disoriented. I smelled food cooking—*good* food. Some kind of savory chicken thing filled the air and my stomach growled. What the hell?

"London, you in here?" I called, throwing my shit down on the couch and moving toward the kitchen. No answer . . . but up on the kitchen counter I spotted the biggest Crock-Pot I'd ever seen full of whatever the hell smelled so good. I looked around for her, then moved toward my bedroom. The bathroom door was closed and I heard the shower running.

Still cleaning. I decided I'd forgive her for being so late, seeing as she'd cooked. I went back into the kitchen and pulled the lid off the Crock-Pot, taking a deep whiff.

Holy fuck, that was amazing.

Thirty seconds later I had a giant bowl of bubbling chicken and dumplings in one hand and a beer in the other, 'cause I don't believe in fucking around when it comes to food. I went back to my room and sat back on my bed, leaning against the pillows she'd artfully arranged over the comforter. I hadn't even known I had that many pillows.

The shower was still running. Interesting. I swapped the beer for a remote and flipped on the set. Then I took a bite and actually moaned, because the food was that fucking good.

Christ, I'd needed this. I had no idea what'd compelled her to fix me dinner, but the woman was a goddess and I regretted every nasty thing I'd ever thought about her. The shower turned off, and I heard her singing softly to herself. My dick perked up as I took another bite.

Fuck it, because I really didn't regret any of the nasty shit I'd thought about her . . . at least not the screwing-her parts, which had been the nastiest of all. The only thing better than eating this food would be if she fed it to me naked.

After a minute the bathroom door opened and London stepped out, a towel wrapped loosely around her body. She saw me and screamed, which made her tits jiggle in a way that was nothing less than outstanding.

She'd been taking a shower. In my room. Naked.

I set the bowl down and rose to my feet, stalking toward her. Clearly London operated a full-service business.

Beautiful.

LONDON

Crazy day.

Not one single thing had gone right . . . No, that wasn't true. The doctor's trip yesterday had been great. All good with Jess, no signs of complications and no need to come back in for another six months unless she had symptoms. It was easy to lose perspective on how far we'd come over the years, get impatient with her for doing stupid things. The fact of the matter was she'd been born a miracle baby and now she was a miraculously healthy adult.

I needed to remember that.

That morning I'd been scheduled to finish at Hayes's house, but I'd gotten called to the hospital instead. One of my girls was pregnant and she'd gone into preterm labor at four a.m. It looked like she'd be on bed rest for the duration, which wasn't exactly good news for me but at least she was doing okay. Fortunately I'd gotten six applications in this week, and I'd already set up interviews with two of them. Hopefully one or both would work out—they both looked good on paper.

That left me in a bind with Hayes. I had to bring food for the potluck at six, and there was no way I'd be able finish up at his place and get back home in time to fix it, let alone make myself presentable, so I'd thrown the chicken into a Crock-Pot and grabbed the ingredients for biscuits to take with me. I figured I could clean, throw together the biscuits, and then take a quick shower before grabbing the pot and running out the door.

Was it appropriate? Not even a little, but beggars can't be choosers and it's not like he was paying me. Fortunately he wasn't even home, so it seemed to be a non-issue. The last of the cleaning went smoothly enough, and showering at his place was a treat. The house might be old, but he'd gone all out in the addition and the bathroom was luxe.

Beyond luxe, actually. It was big, almost as big as one of the little bedrooms upstairs. There was a sunken tub built for two and a large, glassed-in shower stall with one of those fancy adjustable shower heads that go up and down. I'd lowered it for myself, making careful note of where he'd had it set. I'd make sure it was back where it was supposed to be when I finished, but it was still a pleasure to use a shower that was actually the right height for me.

By the time my hair was all washed and I stepped out, I was in a pretty good mood. I couldn't wait to see Jessica in her element at the community center again. Life with her was a series of ups and downs, but I had a good feeling about tonight.

Maybe she could even get a job down there, because for all her faults she really did have something to offer those kids that a more typical young woman wouldn't bring to the table. Maggs Dwyer might be new, but she was smart. When she looked at Jessica, she saw the same potential that I did.

My mood stayed good as I toweled off my hair, and then I looked around for my backpack and realized I'd left it in the bedroom. Humming brightly, I opened the door and screamed.

Reese Hayes was sitting back on his bed holding a bowl of food, eyes trailing down my figure speculatively. A slow, predatory smile crossed his face and he set the bowl on the bedside table, pushing to his feet.

Run! my brain screamed, but my feet didn't move. Seriously. No movement at all, just like in one of those dreams where a giant dinosaur suddenly appears in the grocery store parking lot and you can't seem to start running away or even throw a package of chicken thighs to create a diversion, no matter how hard you try.

Chicken thighs? Where did that come from? *Why couldn't I focus?*

Hayes stalked toward me, and then one of his fingers slid down the front of my towel, right between my breasts. My nipples perked up, acting against orders. He tugged gently at the fabric, and finally my body started listening to me. I clamped down my arms against the towel, holding it firm as I took a step back.

He let me go, a strange smile teasing his lips.

"Don't be shy," he said. "Wet and naked's a good look on you. Gotta say, between this and the food you've turned my day right around."

Food?

I glanced over at the bowl, then realized he'd been in the chicken and biscuits. Crap. I loved it when the biscuits formed a perfect, unbroken layer across the top while the broth bubbled up along the edges. Now there'd be a gap. Of course, I couldn't exactly begrudge the man some dinner, given that I'd essentially taken over his house without permission.

In retrospect, I think I might have subconsciously set myself up. From the beginning he'd fascinated me . . . He scared me, too, but he'd also gotten under my skin like a bur. Maybe if I hadn't been so out of practice, I'd have figured it out sooner.

Holding the towel firmly, I gave him a tight smile.

"Sorry. I got delayed this morning. One of my employees is in the hospital, and I have a potluck after this. I figured you wouldn't mind, seeing as I didn't even charge you for the cleaning . . ."

A flash of pain crossed his face.

"Had an employee in the hospital this morning myself," he said. "Hope yours turned out better than mine. If you aren't gonna take off that towel, then you should get dressed now, I think."

"That's the goal," I said dryly, deciding not to follow up on the hospital comment. It didn't sound like a happy story.

I didn't want to get involved.

"Can you hand me my bag?" I asked, nodding toward the backpack I'd left sitting near the door. He walked casually over to grab it, and I couldn't help but watch the movement of his legs under those jeans. His thighs were thick, and not with fat. He had a tight butt, broad shoulders, and a back that I wanted to rub my cheek against.

When he turned back toward me, my eyes widened. I have a thing for muscular men, no question, and his body pushed every one of my buttons. Broad chest, thick arms and thighs . . . And his stomach? Holy cow, I just knew that under that tight black shirt would be the perfect six-pack. The man's body was ideal—not like a twenty-year-old's, though. No, he had the solidity that only comes with age and endurance and maturity.

My eyes had just drifted lower, below the belt, when he spoke.

"How important is this potluck thing?" he asked softly. Huh? I blinked, then glanced back up at his face. Oh, wow. He'd totally caught me checking him out. He liked it, too. I saw heat in his eyes, the kind of heat that only means one thing. *This is why I shouldn't be let out in public*, I decided. I just couldn't be trusted to handle myself.

"Why?" I asked, my throat ever so slightly dry.

"Because if you look at me like that for even one more second, I'm gonna throw you down on that bed and fuck every part of you, starting with your tits. Unless that's on the menu, you need to grab your shit and leave while you still can. This is the only warning you'll get."

I gave a strangled gasp, because there was absolutely no question he was dead serious. I reached out for my pack, which he handed over wordlessly. Then I turned and bolted back into the bathroom, slamming the door shut and locking it. I heard him laugh behind me, but there wasn't even a hint of humor in the sound.

"Don't think a lock could keep me out, sweetheart."

Ha. No danger of me feeling safe in his home anyway. Five minutes later I was dressed and ready to go. I'd planned to wipe down the bathroom after I finished, leave it perfect so he'd never know I'd taken advantage of the situation. Unfortunately that ship had well and truly sailed, so I decided escape was probably more important than preventing water spots.

Like he'd notice them anyway . . .

Thankfully Hayes wasn't in the bedroom when I cautiously stepped out again, and I didn't find him in the kitchen, either. Perfect. I took my damp towel and wrapped it around the Crock-Pot, preparing to haul it to the car.

"We need to talk," he said behind me.

I froze. Was the man a ninja?

"I think we've talked enough. I've finished the job for you and it's really time for me to get going."

I heard him step forward, then felt his heat surround me. Big hands came to rest against the edge of the counter on either side of me and his breath whispered across my ear.

"You should come back here next week," he said, his voice low and growly. It slithered down my spine, sending tendrils of heat swirling through me.

No, I definitely shouldn't come back. Not even a little bit.

"I don't think that's such a great idea," I said quickly. "You probably don't remember, but I actually have a boyfriend. We're starting to get serious."

"I didn't mean you should come back to fuck, although I'm all over that idea, too, if you change your mind. Don't give a damn about your boyfriend, either, that's between you and him. Nope, I want you back to clean again, maybe make more of that food. It's really fuckin' good, and tonight I realized just how much nicer it is to come home to a house that smells like people actually live here."

My brain froze.

"I don't do houses," I said. "I mean, this was a special deal. But I run a commercial business and I use crews. I manage things and fill in—I'm not interested in being someone's housekeeper."

"Two days a week," he murmured. I felt his lips brush and it took everything I had not to moan. "You come here two days a week and I'll make it worth your while."

He leaned into me, and I felt his hardness touch my rear so lightly I wondered if I'd imagined it. This was *not* a legitimate business proposition. I needed to tell him where to go. Unfortunately my mouth wouldn't work. It was too busy imagining what licking his nipples would feel like.

Bad London!

"Your crew came in and did cleanup after that last big party at The Line, remember? Did a real good job, too."

I nodded, still unable to speak.

"I think Gage mentioned we might be looking for a long-term contract," he continued. "Something more regular so we don't have to count on the waitresses to shut down at night."

"You should really consider it," I answered quietly. "A business like that needs to be cleaned thoroughly every day if you want to keep it up right."

"Contract's all yours if you do my house, too. You cook two meals a week and you'll do some grocery shopping. I'll make it worth your while."

Then he whispered a number that made my eyes widen. That was pizza money and then some.

"That per visit or per week?"

He laughed, and we both knew he had me.

"Per visit," he said. "But you work around my schedule. I can be flexible, but I don't want you out here cooking on nights I won't be around."

"Why don't you just get one of your club girlfriends to do it?" I asked, wondering if I'd lost my mind. But having my crews seven days a week out at The Line? That would add up fast . . . The club paid top dollar, and like I said—they paid it in cash.

"Because they're little girls with dreams and plans and bullshit," he said, a hint of humor in his voice. "You're a grown-up. You know this doesn't end with wine and roses, whatever happens between us. When I don't need you anymore, you keep the shifts at The Line so long as things stay drama-free. Got me?"

"Nothing is going to happen but cleaning and cooking," I said quickly. "I have a boyfriend."

Hayes pressed forward into me, and I felt the hard heat of him all along my back, so hot I thought my spine might melt. His erection dug into my bottom and I bit my lip to distract myself—otherwise I'd start grinding back against him like a cat in heat. Then he kissed my neck, tongue tracing along my jaw, and his teeth caught my ear. I moaned, desire twisting up from between my legs, swelling my breasts and hardening my nipples.

"Unless you plan on skipping your potluck, time to go," Hayes whispered, giving his hips a slow twist. "And next time you see your boyfriend? Tell him I said hi."

FRIDAY NIGHT

"Everything okay?" Nate asked, softly ending our kiss. We were at his place and I'd had a couple of glasses of wine, along with the very nice steak dinner he'd cooked for me. Now we were out on his back deck, me on a lounger and him on me, legs tangled together in the warm summer air.

This was it. Tonight we'd be having sex.

Why wasn't I more excited about this? Guilt.

"I guess so," I said, running a hand up and around his neck. Studying his face, I tried to smile but it felt all off.

"What's wrong?" he asked, pulling away.

"Nothing."

He snorted, then flopped down on his back next to me.

"You can't lie for shit, Loni," he said. "Just spit it out, okay?"

I sighed, but figured if I really wanted to build something with this man, I owed him the truth. "I felt very attracted to someone else this week and now I feel guilty and horrid."

I don't know what I expected—maybe that he'd be upset? Nate didn't even blink.

"Did you do anything about it?"

"No," I replied. "I didn't. But I wanted to."

"Who was it?"

I swallowed.

"Reese Hayes," I said slowly. "And he wants me to keep coming out to his place to clean. He offered me a really good cleaning contract for the MC's strip club, too."

Nate frowned, but he didn't blow up at me. In fact, I couldn't read him at all. Rolling over, I leaned up on my elbow and reached down hesitantly to trace the lines of his face. He seemed lost in thought, and I wondered if I'd ruined everything.

I hoped not.

Nate was perfect for me—sexy and smart with a good job and plans for the future. And I wanted him physically, there was no question about that. We'd been making out for ten minutes and my panties were soaked, but lying was no way to build a relationship.

"C'mere," he said, sitting up. Then he caught my hand and pulled me to my feet, gesturing toward a deck chair. I sat as he handed me my glass of wine. He sighed, running a hand through his hair.

"I really blew it, didn't I?" I asked hesitantly. I felt moisture prickling my eyes. Why had I been so stupid?

"I don't know," he said slowly. "Did you? You say you didn't do anything."

"No, I didn't," I said. "I got the hell out. But I don't feel right sleeping with you unless I'm honest."

"Do you actually want to sleep with me? Or do you want Hayes?"

"I want to sleep with you," I said firmly, because it was true. "I think maybe I've gone so long without sex it's making me crazy. I like you a lot, Nate. I can see us together in the future and it's a good thing. I don't want to mess that up before it even starts. But I'm not sure where we even stand. Are we exclusive? I realized this week that we've never even talked about it. Maybe we should."

His gaze pinned mine, eyes assessing.

"We aren't exclusive," he said finally, and my heart clenched. "So I don't have any right to say you did something wrong. But I'd like to be exclusive. What would you think of that?"

"Have you been seeing anyone else?"

"Not for the past couple weeks. But I won't lie—up to that point I was still going out on the occasional date. And I think it's normal—even healthy—to experience attraction toward other people. Just because you're in a relationship doesn't mean your body turns off."

Well, that wasn't exactly romantic. I'm not sure why I felt so let down . . . It wasn't like I'd expected a declaration of undying love. In fact, it should've made me feel better, because obviously I hadn't done anything too heinous. Not if he'd been seeing other women up until two weeks ago.

"So where do we go from here?"

Nate laughed.

"Bed, hopefully," he said. "I want to be with you, Loni. Exclusively. But only if you want that, too. We're both adults here, and I'd like to think we've outgrown our romantic delusions. Being with you makes me happy and I can see a future for us. If that's how you feel, I'd love to be with you."

Now my heart clenched in a good way. I smiled at him and he grinned back, reaching forward to catch my hand. Lifting, he kissed my palm.

"Of course, if you insist on just using me for sex, I'll make the best of it."

I burst out laughing as he pulled me up and caught me in a long, hard kiss. This time it felt right, like a bubble had popped and whatever lingering guilt and weirdness I felt about Reese evaporated. I dug my fingers into Nate's beautiful hair and gave myself over to the sensation of his tongue exploring my mouth.

So what if Reese was utterly lickable in every way? He wasn't real, not like Nate. Reese wanted a quick roll in the sheets, no strings. Nate wanted a partner.

My boyfriend was perfect. I didn't need—or want—anyone else.

Parenting sucks.

My phone started blaring Jessica's ringtone thirty seconds after we fell into bed, Nate's leg thrust between mine and his hands burrowing under my bra. I ignored it because she was eighteen years old and she could darned well survive on her own for an hour or two.

Then the phone rang again.

Nate groaned.

"I can't believe I'm saying this, but maybe you should check it?" he said. "Could be an emergency."

"She better be dying," I said with a scowl, reaching out for it blindly and almost knocking over Nate's bedside lamp in the process. I found the phone right as it went to voice mail, flopping back on the bed and staring at the little screen in disgust.

Then Nate's phone went off.

"What the hell? I'm not on call this weekend. If I have to go in to work, someone's getting shot tonight," he muttered, climbing over me as he grabbed for his shirt, digging through the pockets.

"Guess that's what we get for trying to have a real date," I said, feeling a deeply inappropriate laugh fighting to escape. Nate just looked so . . . frustrated. Poor man.

"I wonder if I can get disability for blue balls?" he said, grabbing the phone and answering it. "Evans here."

He stalked off to the bathroom as I looked back at my own phone. Might as well see what fresh trouble Jessica had gotten herself into. There were two missed calls, one from Jess and one from Mellie. No messages. Great. I hit the callback button and Jessica answered.

"Loni, I need you to come and get me," she said, sounding defiant. Fantastic—I recognized that tone. Jess had gotten herself into trouble and she didn't want to admit she'd made a mistake, so she was going on the attack.

"Where are you?"

"Out at the Reapers clubhouse."

I froze. "What are you doing out there?"

"Just come and get me," she said, hanging up the phone. I closed my eyes and took a deep breath. Nate stepped out of the bathroom, his face a mixture of annoyance and apology.

"I have to go in," he said. "Apparently we had two guys on work release from the jail walk off this afternoon. Not violent offenders, but it'll be a PR nightmare if the paper gets hold of it before we've got them back in custody."

"Jessica's got herself in trouble again, too," I said, sighing. "Some date. We can't catch a break, can we?"

He shook his head, and then I started giggling. He glared at me, a reluctant smile crossing his face.

"I think the universe is determined to keep me from getting laid," he said finally.

"Would love to say you're imagining that," I told him, pulling on my shirt. "But I think you might be right. Call me tomorrow?"

"Yeah," he muttered. He ran a hand through his hair. "Sorry. Shitty timing tonight."

He stepped into me and I wrapped my arms around him in a long hug. It turned into a kiss that didn't exactly help the situation. Nate might not be Reese Hayes, but he was here and he was mine and I wanted to have sex with him. Instead I tugged free and reached for my jeans.

Like I said, being a parent sucks.

• • •

My mood was ugly as I drove out to the Reapers clubhouse for the second weekend in a row. Sure, Nate and I had managed to end our date with a laugh, but I'd just about had it with Jess and her games.

Reese Hayes pissed me off, too.

He'd promised Jess wouldn't be allowed back into the clubhouse, and I'd scrubbed his stupid toilets to seal the deal. Apparently his promises didn't mean shit, because here we were again. That's when my phone rang again. I grabbed it, answering without even looking to see who it was.

"Got your girl here," Hayes's voice purred in my ear. "I'm taking her over to your house. She says you're on a date. Think you can ditch lover boy long enough to meet us?"

"You don't need to do that," I said, frowning at myself. Of course he'd call being all helpful right after I'd been thinking bad things about him . . . "I'm headed out to the Armory right now. I'll grab her there."

"Already in the truck," he said. "We're having a nice little chat along the way—I'm explaining what the words 'stay the hell away' mean. See you in a few."

He hung up on me and I groaned. Jessica would pay for this. I. Was. Done. *Done.* I couldn't keep fighting her—if the girl was truly determined to destroy herself, I couldn't stop it.

The realization hit me so suddenly that I swerved the van and nearly went off the road.

I couldn't control Jess and I needed to stop trying.

Holy cow. That changed everything.

My job had been to raise her and I'd given it my all, but the little brat was actually right about one thing. Legally she was an adult. I could offer her advice and make sure she had access to health care, but I really couldn't stop her from destroying herself.

The thought was both terrifying and liberating.

Implications swirled through my brain as I pulled up to my little house, which was located right on the edge of town, near Fernan. I could be free now . . . Free to move on with life. Free to stop living my entire life around one young woman's whiplash hormones and emotions and crazy mood swings.

Shivering, I wondered if that made me a horrible person, because my overriding feeling on this was relief.

I parked next to Reese Hayes's big black truck. Light blazed through the windows of my place, a 1950s cinder block with three tiny bedrooms, one bath, and zero character. I'd grown up in it with Amber, who'd come to live with us when her mom went to prison. In some ways it was more Jessica's home than mine, because she'd been there on and off since birth. I'd only moved back in six years ago when Mom had passed on. She'd had a heart attack, right after Amber's near-fatal overdose. Suddenly I'd been left alone with a child who needed a real parent, one who knew what she was doing.

Instead she got me.

I heard voices as I approached the door, which was open a crack. (The frame had swollen up last winter and never quite gone back to normal, so you really had to fight to close it all the way. It was sandwiched on the repair list between fixing the car and replacing the oven.)

"Your cousin deserves better than this," I heard Hayes saying, and I couldn't help but smile. Glad *someone* noticed my efforts. "If she's smart, she'll kick you out."

"She'll never kick me out," Jess declared, and her voice sounded a little smug. A little slurred, too . . . Had she been drinking? Probably. "She'd feel guilty. She'll always take care of me because she has to—you don't know shit about us."

He snorted.

"You think she takes care of you out of guilt?" he asked. "Nope— she loves you, although I can't quite figure out why. You need to decide what you want to do with your life, because you can't just drain her dry forever. Sooner or later she'll be done with you."

His words sounded so close to my own thoughts it was almost creepy. It also made me feel guilty, because the statement was so cold and hard. *Not to mention true.*

"It's none of your business."

"London is my business, little girl," he said, and his tone was anything but nice. "I have plans for her, and they don't include her crying over your bullshit. Don't piss me off."

Yikes. I pushed through the door.

"Hey, Jess," I said, spotting my young cousin. She'd flopped back on the couch, one arm draped melodramatically over her eyes like a silent movie heroine. Clearly, her life was simply too dreadful to tolerate.

"Make him go away," she muttered. I glanced over at Hayes, who leaned against the little bar separating the living room from the kitchen. His eyes heated when they touched me, and I wondered what exactly he meant when he said he had plans for me . . . No, I took that back. I really *didn't* want to know what he meant. I just wanted him gone.

No, you want him in bed, my brain insisted. *You want more kisses like the one he gave you at the Armory.*

Unacceptable. I ignored Jess, walking over to him, determined to take control of the situation.

"Thanks for bringing her home," I said, forcing myself to be polite even though—like usual—he simultaneously scared the crap out of me and turned me on. I also resented the fact that he'd invaded my space, which made no sense at all considering he was only trying to help out. Of course, it could be the fact that I was still a little worked up from my makeout session with Nate. Hayes was just so big and rugged . . . Every time he moved, his arms flexed, and I wanted to wrap my hand around his bicep and feel those muscles working.

Snap out of it!

"I've got things from here," I told him.

He jerked his chin toward my teenage drama queen.

"You sure about that?" he asked. "Kid needs a wake-up call."

"I got it," I repeated. "Let me walk you to the door."

He snorted, then pushed himself off the counter.

"Gee, thanks, Pic, sure nice of you to bring her home. You wanna sit for a bit, maybe have a drink?" he muttered sarcastically as I pulled the door open. I rolled my eyes at him.

"I've already got all the drama I need," I said, unable to stop a rueful smile. He didn't smile back. Nope. He just looked at me for long seconds, something heavy and tangible growing in the air between us. I could almost see the wheels spinning in his head. Then he shook his head slowly, as if making a decision.

"I don't do drama, sweetheart."

Hayes stepped toward me and I bit back a startled squeak as he stalked across the floor, the ancient carpet allowing him to move silently, like some kind of great predator.

Please go out the door. Please go out the door. Please go out the door!

He didn't go out the door. He came to a halt about two inches from me, then reached over and caught the back of my head, burrowing his fingers into my hair. Then Hayes tugged me toward him, fingers tightening almost painfully. I stopped breathing as he lowered his head to mine.

His lips brushed across my cheekbone and I shivered. I swear to God, if he'd touched me between my legs it couldn't have felt better than that slight whisper of sensation.

I wanted him more than Nate, I realized. A lot more.

"You have fun on your date?" he asked, his voice low and heated. "Jess gave me all the details on the way back. She thinks your deputy boyfriend is a douche. Have to say I agree. Nate Evans is a pissant little shit."

"I know you're talking about me!" Jessie yelled, startling me so much I jerked in his hold, hair pulling painfully. I'd sort of forgotten about her playing Camille on the sofa. "Stop telling lies about me. I'm going to my room."

She threw herself off the couch and stomped down the hallway, snorting and shaking her head. Probably just as well—she was self-absorbed enough that she obviously didn't even notice what was happening between me and Hayes. Best to keep it that way.

His other hand wrapped around my waist, tugging me deep into his body. His hips pushed into mine suggestively and I felt the coiled strength in his arms. My nipples hardened (traitorous little bitches) and my eyes widened.

Hayes offered a knowing smile.

"Your girl told me he's no good for you," he said. "Of course, that might just be because he arrested two of her friends last week. Let one of them off, booked the other. Girl who walked free was real pretty, too. He tell you about that?"

"Why would he?" I gasped as his hand slid down my rear, fingers cupping and tightening on me. He tilted my head as casually as if I were a doll, studying my mouth. *Nate*, I reminded myself frantically. *Less than an hour ago you were in bed with your boyfriend. Good guy, not a thug, unlike some.* "He arrests people all the time."

"You know the sheriff's a good friend of the club?" he asked, his voice mesmerizing. I shook my head as much as I could, wondering where he was going with this. "He and I like to get together every week or so, share a beer. He's got lots to say about your boy."

"Nate's not a boy."

Hayes's lips ghosted across mine, and then he sucked my lower lip into his mouth. My legs clenched and in that instant I wanted him far more than I'd ever wanted anyone else. More than Nate, more than my ex . . . more than my high school boyfriend who took my virginity in a frantic, pawing frenzy when I was seventeen years old at a party out at Hauser Lake. I wanted that big, hard weapon of his deep inside me, spreading me open and pinning me down and making me scream until my voice broke.

I needed to get rid of him and go talk to Jessie.

Call Nate.

Be a good girl.

"He says Deputy Dick has problems following the rules," Hayes murmured, pulling free of my mouth. His lips traced along my jaw, nipping and sucking. I couldn't move. I couldn't do anything, because all I could think about was ripping off his clothes and jumping him.

No! Bad London!

"He also says there's been several complaints about him harassing young girls. Nate ever mention any of that to you? How about Jessica? She have any problems with him?"

His words hit me like a slap across the face, waking me up.

"Shut your mouth."

He pulled back, his eyes cool and calculating . . . The hard length against my stomach stayed hot, though. And the hands still holding me captive against him?

They burned.

"Maybe you should learn a little more about your boyfriend before getting too involved."

"Like you have any room to judge?" I hissed, thinking of the girls I'd seen out at the Armory. "Jess doesn't like Nate because she doesn't like me having any kind of life outside of her. Just an immature teen being selfish—it doesn't go any deeper than that."

"I don't fuck anyone unless they want me to," he said, slowly shaking his head. "You sure Natie-poo can say the same thing? You seem to think I'm the enemy, but I've always been straight up with you. I'm straight up with everyone I stick my cock into."

"You aren't sticking your . . ." I clenched my teeth, because I didn't let myself use words like that. I wouldn't let him win by tempting me to, either.

"*Cock*," he said, relishing the word. "I want to stick my cock into your pussy. Don't worry—I'll get you nice and ready first. Open you up with my fingers, make sure you're so wet and hot that when you wrap around me, it'll feel like I'm fucking a goddess because you're goddamn perfect, London. I can't wait to feel your cunt squeezing me. Lick your clit, taste you . . . It'll be good between us. You know it will."

My knees weakened—like, weakened for *real*. Not just a figure of speech. I literally wanted Reese Hayes inside me so badly I had trouble supporting my own weight, which was a huge problem. Then his hand squeezed my butt almost spasmodically, and I saw a hint of sweat start to bead on his forehead.

If Reese Hayes wanted me even half as much as I wanted him . . . *Stop thinking about it!* I needed him out of here. Now. Before I did something really, truly insane like drag him back into my bedroom and ride him until I completely forgot about Nate.

The man I'd almost had sex with less than an hour ago.

Oh. My. God. When had I become such a faithless slut?

I put up my hands and shoved against his chest—hard—until he let me go. Reese stepped back, holding up his hands, a mocking smile on his face. He obviously saw right through me. My eyes darted away, which was a huge mistake because they caught on his jeans instead. The giant bulge in his pants made me feel even more unsteady, everything melting and mixed up deep inside.

How could this be? Why could a man I didn't even like drive me crazy like this? Make me doubt Nate, who'd never done a thing to make me suspect him?

You. Have. A. Boyfriend.

I rubbed my face with one hand, leaning back against the wall for support.

"Just go," I told him, refusing to meet his gaze. Instead I stared at the door, pointedly. "Thank you for bringing Jess home."

Hayes laughed harshly, the sound a rough rasp along my spine.

"Sleep tight," he said, tapping the tip of my nose with his finger. Then he casually strolled out the door to his truck, as if he owned the place. I watched him, completely unable to look away from that beautiful butt of his. Why was he so helpful and hateful at the same time? *And who was he to imply nasty things about Nate?* I didn't believe it for a minute—Nate was a total gentleman, and if the sheriff wasn't happy with him, he could just fire him. Hayes was a tainted source. Nobody even *pretended* the Reapers were on the up-and-up, so why he thought he could get away with making accusations like that I couldn't imagine.

I shoved the front door shut hard, wood scraping as it settled into the warped frame. Loud music burst suddenly out of Jessica's room, pushing me over the edge. Stalking down the hallway, I grabbed her doorknob.

Locked.

I pounded on the door and yelled at her, "Open up, Jess! We need to talk."

Long seconds passed and the music got louder. Oh my God, was she really doing this? I thought my head might explode, I had so many conflicting emotions swirling around inside. Enough. I prowled through the kitchen and out the side door. The electrical panel was mounted on the wall right next to it. I ripped the small metal door open, slamming the breakers to the side.

Instantly the house fell dark. And silent.

Hah!

I probably shouldn't have enjoyed it quite so much, but it was the first thing that'd gone right for me that night. Then I stomped back in, bashing into the stove top with my hip. *Ouch.* I rubbed the small hurt as I jerked open the junk drawer. Slight miscalculation, I realized, peering down at it in the darkness. I should've grabbed the little flathead screwdriver I'd need to pop Jessica's lock *before* cutting the power. I dug my phone out of my pocket, flipping on the flashlight app. There it was.

I snatched the tool and stomped back to Jessica's room.

"You going to let me in?" I asked.

"No!" she yelled. "You can go to hell! You have no right to tell me what to do! I'm an adult!"

My blood pressure rose. "My house, my rules. Open the damned door."

"Fuck you!"

I growled, sliding the tiny screwdriver into the hole in the knob, popping it open easily enough. Wasn't the first time I'd had to break into her room.

I opened it to find Jess glaring at me by the light of a candle.

"I asked you not to burn things in here," I said, even more frustrated than I'd been before. She'd nearly set the place on fire a couple of months ago. "I don't want to die in my sleep because you like candles."

"Fuck. You."

"No, fuck you," I snapped back at her. Jess froze, because I didn't cuss. Not that I couldn't—I'd just made a conscious decision when I first took custody of her not to set a bad example with my language. So much for that. "I'm about done with your shit, Jessica. You think you're an adult? Fine. Starting this month you pay rent. You follow the rules or you're out on your ass. How's that for treating you like an adult?"

She gaped at me, then quick as a snake she grabbed a picture frame off her dresser and threw it at me. I ducked as she started screaming, darting out of the room and slamming the door behind me.

What the hell had just happened?

Another crash hit the wood behind me and then another. The kid must be tearing apart her room. I heard yet another shriek, then the door flew open. Jess stood there, bag in one hand and her phone in the other.

"You can go fuck yourself," she hissed, pushing past me to stomp down the hall. "I don't need you."

I followed her, a detached part of my brain observing that she really needed to expand her vocabulary.

"And how—exactly—do you think this will play out?" I asked her, crossing my arms in determination.

Jess ignored me, jerking open the front door and marching out across the porch. Then she started down the driveway, frantically texting as she kicked the occasional rock out of her path.

Just like her mother, I realized. *I should go after her, make her stop.*

No.

I should make sure that candle was out and then I should go to bed. Why keep fighting? She'd come home sooner or later. *She wants to be an adult? Let her figure it out for herself. She just saw the doctor, she should be safe enough . . .*

So instead of chasing down the girl I'd spent the last six years raising, I poured myself a glass of wine and drank it, pondering how I'd lost control of my life.

Nate. Reese. Jessica and Amber.

Right now I didn't want to see or talk to any of them.

Defiantly, I poured a second glass, followed by a third. Then— feeling warm and giddy and relaxed for the first time in forever—I called my college roommate, Dawn, and we talked for two hours, laughing like we were still twenty years old. By three in the morning I still hadn't heard anything from Jess, but for once I didn't care. I just collapsed into bed, reveling in the peace and quiet.

It was fantastic.

You know, there's a party game I've played before, where people try to decide where they'd go or what they'd do if they could travel back in time. Some people say they'd go back and meet Jesus, or kill Hitler, or talk to Albert Einstein . . . But if I could go back and change one thing, it'd be the fact that I went to bed that night without finding my girl first.

Instead, I'd use my time machine to smash that damned wine bottle and chase Jessica down the road. Stop her. Find some way to convince her that she deserved better—*more*—than following her mother's path.

But did I do it?

No, I went to sleep and didn't get up until nearly noon on Saturday. Then I went to the gym, following my workout up with a pedicure. I felt all empowered about it, too, because I knew she'd be back.

Only Jessica never came back.

CHAPTER FIVE

REESE

I spent my weekend horny and pissed off.

London's mouth, her smell, those amazing tits . . . I wanted those lips wrapped around my cock, I wanted those hands buried in my hair, and I wanted my dick in her cunt. Maybe her ass. Hell yes. Then I'd fuck her boobs because I wouldn't want them to feel left out, now would I?

Instead I jerked off and tried to remind myself of all the reasons getting involved with her would be a massive mistake.

Then I'd picture her touching Nate Evans. Nearly sent me over the fuckin' edge, because I'd actually *smelled* him on her Friday night. Like gangrene.

Gave serious thought to killing him for touching what was mine.

But London wasn't mine. The thought drove me crazy, because I had zero desire to claim a woman, at least not for longer than a night. Still, my gut insisted she *should* belong to me, which scared me shitless. Wanting someone like that leads to needing them, and loving them leads to . . . hell.

Heather died slowly.

I remembered everything about that day—worst fuckin' hours of my life. Her frail body, nothing more than pale skin stretched tight over bones gone brittle. Our daughters drifting in and out of the room, crying and begging while the light in her eyes faded. Then the beautiful girl I'd fallen in crazy love with my senior year of high school left me.

Forever.

Never wanted more than one woman and then I had to put her in the ground, cold and alone. I'd sworn that day to never let myself care like that again.

Couldn't risk it.

But London filled my head until I couldn't hardly think straight. Apparently I wasn't a joy to be around, either, because by Sunday afternoon the guys actually kicked me out of the Armory. Said I could come back when I stopped being an asshole, and that situation wasn't looking promising.

I'd stomped around the courtyard, yelling at the prospects until Bolt took pity on me, dragging me up into the National Forest lands behind the clubhouse to harvest some firewood. We'd make the prospects split and stack it for seasoning once we got back, but there's something very primal and satisfying about felling a tree and cutting it up with a chainsaw. Gotta love power tools and destruction. Not quite as good as getting laid, but better than losing your mind imagining a very unavailable cunt squeezing some other man's dick.

Never cared for the good deputy. Taking him out would be a public service, right? But ultimately not even I could justify taking out a lawman over a woman. Maybe I should just steal her out from under him, maybe rub it in his face. Yeah. That'd work. I liked that idea a lot, and the more I considered it, the more it grew on me.

Now Bolt and I were out in the middle of nowhere and things were coming clear. I felt sweaty, tired, and more sane than I had since leaving London's place, thanks to my club brother's timely intervention. Nobody ever really understood me like Bolt and I'd missed the hell out of him while he was doing time these past three years. He was more than a solid vice president—he was the man I trusted more than anyone else on earth.

He'd come back different, though. Harder, more cynical than I'd ever seen him before. I guess getting locked up for a crime you didn't commit changes a man.

Didn't help that his old lady, Maggs, had ditched his ass.

Sore subject, and not one he liked to talk about. She had her reasons and I guess from her perspective leaving him made sense. But a man inside does whatever it takes to get by. Bolt hadn't had any allies to protect him during that final stretch, so he'd done what he had to do. She never quite understood that.

Shit happens, I guess.

"What's the plan for tonight?" I asked him as he tossed the chainsaw into the back end of the truck. Between it and the trailer, we'd cut and loaded nearly two cords. Good haul for an afternoon's work.

"No plans," he said, opening the crew cab and digging into the cooler. He pulled out a beer and cracked it, offering one to me. I turned it down, grabbing a water instead. "Thought I might head over to The Line."

"Been spendin' a lot of time there," I said casually.

"Nothin' quite like pussy," he replied, pulling up his shirt to wipe the sweat off his face. He'd acquired some new ink inside, of varying quality. "Went a long time without, gotta make up for that."

I nodded, although it wasn't entirely the truth. He might not've gotten the one he wanted, but he hadn't gone without, either. Got me thinking.

"How's the baby?"

Bolt snorted.

"What baby? Startin' to doubt it was real."

Damn.

"So Maggs left you over nothin'?"

"No, she left me because I cheated on her. Now that cunt Gwen says she lost the kid—assuming she was actually knocked up in the first place. I don't know what to believe about that anymore."

I stilled.

"You think she wasn't really pregnant?"

"Does it matter?" he asked, taking another drink. "At least I'm rid of the bitch, so I guess that's something. And tonight I'll get laid, so life is good."

I nodded slowly, knowing life was anything but good for my club brother. He missed the hell out of his old lady. We all did. She'd been solid the entire time he was gone, stood by him when he went down in the first place and then worked day and night to bring him home again. Women like that weren't easy to find.

"You wanna come with me?" Bolt asked. "Get laid. Clear your brain."

"Yeah." Bolt was right—The Line was a great place to find no-strings snatch, which was exactly what I needed. If I spent one more night jerking off while imagining London, I'd have to shoot myself. Couldn't stop thinkin' of those tits, the way she'd melted under my touch.

Did she have pink nipples or brown?

Maybe Evans was sucking on them right now. Fucker wasn't working this weekend. Already checked, even tried to get Bud to call him in, but the bastard had taken personal leave and not even the sheriff could cancel that. Not without a state of emergency.

Probably spending that time with London. *Comforting* her.

Maybe even fuckin' her right at this minute.

I imagined slowly strangling the man, watching his face turn purple and his eyes bulge while his legs kicked and bucked in desperation. Nothin' fucked up about that, right?

Christ, but I wanted inside that woman.

Knew from the minute I'd seen her six months ago she'd be the end of me. Put her off bounds that same night, although I'd been hell-bent on staying away from her. Women like that were trouble—definitely not club whore material, which meant she'd probably get all pissy about a one-night stand, and not in the market to be an old lady, either. Nope, women like her wanted picket fences and nine-to-five husbands so pussy-whipped they forgot their own names.

Add in the fact that she was the first reliable cleaner we'd found in nearly three years? Recipe for disaster.

Now I'd hit uncharted territory, because I'd tasted her and the taste wasn't going away—time to face reality. Sooner or later I'd take her, and that fuckwad of a boyfriend wasn't going to get in my way. Hell, if she knew all the games he was playing, she'd get down on her knees and beg me to step in.

The image of her down on her knees . . . now *that* was a thing of beauty.

Maybe I should blow off The Line, track her down. Evans was the biggest problem—so far as she knew, he was still Prince Charming. I'd planted the seed, but now I had to step back, wait for him to fuck things up.

He would, of course.

Man like that could only pretend for so long. London needed to see his shit for herself, otherwise she'd always wonder, which would be damned inconvenient for me.

Fuck me . . . Why should I give a shit about her regrets?

Losing my damned mind.

"I'll hit the strip club with you," I told Bolt. "See if the brothers want to join us. Been a while since we all went out."

Bolt grunted and we climbed into the truck, big diesel engine roaring to life. I felt the weight of the trailer tug at the rig as I started cautiously down the mountain. By the time we hit the halfway mark my phone came to life, pinging as the messages and texts I'd gotten while we were out of range downloaded.

"Shit, sounds like Grand Central," Bolt said, raising a brow. "You think we got a problem?"

I slowed the truck to a stop in the center of the narrow logging road, grabbing the phone for a quick look. First up was a text from Horse saying we needed to talk—maybe news from the south? Seemed like we heard new stories about the cartel every day now. They were plowing through the Devil's Jacks' territory way too fast, which was very bad news for the Reapers. The Jacks were our buffer zone, the first line of defense against the southern gangs.

But Horse's message wasn't what really caught my attention.

Nope.

The fact that London Armstrong had called three times and left two voice mails stopped me dead in my tracks. I hit the button.

"Hello, Mr. Hayes," she said, voice strained but still full of that strange formality she used to distance herself. Fuckin' ridiculous—I'd sucked on her lips and dug my fingers into her ass. Time to start using first names. Instead of pissing me off, though, it kind of turned me on. 'Course everything she did turned me on.

"It's London. I have a favor to ask—do you think you could ask around about Jessica? See if maybe she's gotten in touch with anyone in your club? She was pretty angry Friday night after you left. In fact, she took off. I thought she'd come back by now, but she hasn't."

She hesitated, then spoke again, her voice shaking. "I'm starting to get worried."

Fucking great. Not enough that the little brat got herself into constant trouble—now she had to go running off, too? I seriously doubted that she'd talked to anyone at the club. They all knew she was hands off, not than anyone gave a shit. Girls like her came and went, and nobody paid much attention. If one disappeared, there was always another to take her place.

London was in a different class and I didn't like the idea of her worrying. Woman had enough shit to deal with already. I hit play on the second message, which she'd only left about half an hour ago. This time she dropped the pretense of formality.

"Reese, I'm really worried about Jess. Can you call or message me? I know things are . . . awkward . . . between us, but I'd like to rule out whether she's with someone from the club. Nobody has seen her."

"Fuck," I muttered, then glanced over at Bolt. "Give me a sec?"

He nodded and I stepped out of the truck, hitting the callback button. She answered on the fourth ring.

"Reese?"

Her voice was tense, but I still liked the sound of my name on her tongue. Of course, it'd sound sweeter if she was screaming it into a pillow while I pounded her from behind. Funny how that worked.

"Got your messages, sweetheart," I said. "I'll check with the brothers, but if she'd shown up at the Armory, they would've told me. They know she's not supposed to be out there."

"You don't think she could've gone to someone's house?" she asked, her voice tentative. "Maybe one of those men we found her with the other night?"

"No way. Painter and Banks wouldn't touch her, not after I put her off-limits. Hate to break it to you, but she's nothing special. Not worth a fight at the club."

"I see," she said, although she probably didn't. Outsiders never did.

"What does Deputy Dick have to say? He helpin' you out?"

She made a strange, strangled noise, which she tried to cover with a cough.

"Nate told me kids her age take off all the time and not to worry about it. And no, he's not around. I've only talked to him once—he didn't return my calls yesterday, and he's working this morning. I guess they've got a lot going on this weekend. Mandatory overtime."

Lying asshole. What kind of game was he playing with her? My inner caveman decided it didn't matter. Fuck safety, and fuck picket fences. London Armstrong obviously couldn't take care of herself, which meant someone needed to step in and fix this shit. If that meant claiming her, so be it. As for Evans, I'd put that fucker in the ground a hundred miles from the nearest town with a clear conscience the next time he decided to play games.

Proud of you, baby, Heather murmured.

I growled, because my dead wife didn't get a vote. If she really cared about me, she wouldn't have died. And London? I'd had enough of her shit, too. That bitch was gonna be mine and I didn't share.

You do realize you're crazy, right?

At least crazy worked for me. Always had.

"Reese? Are you okay?"

Shit. Poor woman was scared and alone, and now I was growling at her because I'd lost my fucking mind, apparently. I rubbed my chin, thinking quickly. I needed to play things smart, nudge her in the right direction if I wanted to do this right. All Evans really needed was enough rope to hang himself. He'd do the rest for me . . .

"There's some truth to what he said," I said, trying to sound somewhat sane and sympathetic. "Although it's not exactly a comfort. Is there anything I can do to help?"

"I don't think so," she said. "I've already talked to all her friends. I can't imagine where she went."

"She's probably holed up with some boy somewhere. Jess is a pretty girl—wouldn't be hard for her to find someone to take her in."

"She would've told one of her friends, though. None of them have heard from her."

I sighed, rubbing the bridge of my nose, torn between laughter, frustration, and a hint of crazed exaltation. Christ, but London was naive. No idea how she'd pulled that off at her age, but there was no question the woman was clueless. I wondered if that cluelessness extended to her sexual experience, too. Might be fun to teach her new things. Of course, if she already had some tricks, that'd be nice, too.

"They won't tell you, honey. They'll cover for her because that's what teenage girls do."

"Maybe most of them, but not Melanie," London said. "She's the one Jessica relies on the most, and she's completely freaked out. Said she got some weird text from her about heading south."

"What's down south?"

"Nothing that I can think of," London said. "I mean, the last time I heard from her mother, she was living near San Diego, but I can't imagine she'd lift a finger for Jess, let alone invite her to come and stay with her. Amber is a selfish bitch who doesn't want the men in her life to know she's old enough to have an adult daughter. Jess doesn't have the money to get down there anyway."

"You want me to come over?" I asked her, and in that moment my intentions were almost decent. Didn't like her being scared, and not even I was such a dick that I'd use her little cousin running away to fuck her. Probably. Maybe.

Who was I kidding? Of course I would.

"Why?"

"So you aren't alone," I said. "I have daughters, remember? They're good kids but sometimes it's hell—that's when things are going right. I'll grab some food and we can hang out for a while, help pass the time. Unless you have other plans?"

"I was planning to pace and look at my phone," she murmured. "It's a bad idea, I think."

"You can pace and look at your phone while we eat. I'll be over around seven, need to unload my truck and get a shower first. Sound good?"

"I don't know . . . I don't want anything happening between us, Reese. Seriously."

"I'll behave," I told her. *Unlikely.* "And try calling your cousin, see if she's heard anything. Never hurts to check."

"Okay," she said, sounding defeated.

I hung up and climbed back into the truck, considering the situation. No idea where the kid was, but Nate Evans was sure as hell making things easy for me.

Fuckin' idiot to leave his woman open and ripe for the taking.

London needed sympathy, someone to take care of her. Dumbass should've picked up on that. Of course, Deputy Dick didn't have a reputation for being the most sensitive of guys. He'd put the pressure on more than one of our dancers during late-night "traffic stops" before we'd come to an understanding about his behavior.

We'd come to an understanding about London, too. Soon.

"All good?" Bolt asked.

"Good enough," I told him. "Gotta bail on tonight, though. Something came up."

"Business or pleasure?"

"Both. Stopping by to see London Armstrong."

Bolt grinned. "I knew you were into her."

"Not exactly a secret I'm lookin' to fuck her."

"That what you'll be doing tonight? Fuckin' her?"

I laughed, because I honestly had no idea. Last time I'd felt this way, I'd been eighteen years old and crazy over Heather.

"Depends. She's havin' a shitty weekend. Not sure what the best strategy is just yet."

"Usually your strategy involves getting them naked and then pushing them out the door."

"The situation with London is a little more complicated than that," I admitted.

"Is this the point where I sing the little song about Pic and London sittin' in a tree?"

"Only if you want the tree shoved up your ass."

"Might be worth it," Bolt said, his voice sly. I flipped him off, suddenly in a very good mood.

No fool like an old one, I guess, but damned if I didn't feel like I was eighteen all over again.

LONDON

"I'm her mother—she belongs with me," Amber declared, her voice smug with triumph. I'd called her knowing Reese had to be wrong. Jessica would never go to Amber, even if she was furious with me. She knew better . . . But apparently she didn't.

Nothing made sense anymore.

"I thought you didn't want your boyfriend to know you're old enough to have a grown daughter?"

"He knows I got pregnant young."

"You got pregnant at twenty-two, not twelve."

She sniffed.

"Did she at least take her health insurance card with her? You have to keep a close eye on her—things can go south so fast. I really think you should send her—"

"Shove it up your ass, Loni," she said, just like we were in middle school again. I could almost see her rolling her eyes. "I'm sick of your lectures and bullshit. Go back to your boring life cleaning up other people's shit. I have a maid now, you know. My boyfriend hired her for me. Guess you were wrong about how I'd turn out, hmmm?"

"Can I at least talk to her?"

Instead of replying, Amber hung up. I sighed, studying my phone with mixed emotions. Jess was safe. Somehow she'd gotten a flight down to San Diego, something I would've said was impossible. The last time we'd spoken, my cousin made it clear she had no interest in seeing her daughter. None.

It didn't add up.

I decided to call Nate again, because the more I thought about it, the more suspicious I got. I knew he was working, so I figured I'd have to leave a voice mail. When he answered, it took me off guard.

"Hey Loni—what's up?"

"I found Jessica," I told him.

"Well, that's good news," he said "Where is she?"

"Down in San Diego with her mother. I didn't actually talk to her myself. She still isn't answering her phone."

"Well, that's a relief."

I sighed, rubbing my temple. Nate just didn't seem to feel any urgency about the situation, and it frustrated me.

"Not much of a relief," I told him. "It doesn't make sense. Amber is living with some rich boyfriend and she doesn't want him knowing she has a daughter Jessica's age. I tried to take Jess to visit her last summer and she wouldn't let us come. I think Amber is up to something."

"Hon . . ." he said, and his voice was patient, loving, and condescending as hell. "You sound crazy."

"I'm not crazy," I snapped.

"I know you're not," he replied soothingly. "And that's why this *sounds* so crazy, because it's not like you. I know you've given everything for Jessica, but kids pull shit like this all the time. She's with a family member. At least you know she's safe, so maybe you should just enjoy the fact that she's finally out of your hair."

"She's not a normal eighteen-year-old," I insisted, walking toward the kitchen. I found the wine I'd picked up at the store earlier and grabbed my corkscrew. "Her brain doesn't work right, you know that. And she has health issues. She doesn't even have a doctor down there."

"Nobody who's eighteen years old has a brain that works right," he said. "You know that—we all know that. Kids are wonderful but they do stupid shit. Sooner or later she'll call you, ready to apologize. Until then fighting with her is pointless."

I took a deep swig straight from the bottle, because a glass just seemed like extra work at this point.

"Is there anything you can do to check on her?" I asked, frustrated by his lack of sympathy.

"What do you mean?"

"Well, don't cops have ways of finding people? Like, calling in favors from old friends or something? I don't know."

"I think you've been watching too much TV," he said firmly, his voice going from condescending to annoyed. "We could call in a welfare check, but that's a waste of time and resources because you already know she's fine. You have to let this go and I have to get back to work. We've started something good here, babe, but I'm not interested in drama. Time to get over this shit."

He was probably right, but he didn't need to be a jerk about it.

"Okay," I said, frowning. "I'm sorry I bothered you at work."

He didn't answer for a moment.

"It's all right. But don't do it again, okay? Not unless it's a real emergency. It sucks that things aren't going like you hoped, but this doesn't qualify and I've got shit going on. I'm hanging up now."

"Do you still want to try to get together sometime this week?" I asked hesitantly.

"I don't know—are we going to pick up where we left off on Friday?"

The question startled me.

"Probably . . ."

He sighed.

"Loni, I like you a lot and I've been a good guy, but I'm tired of this. You're so caught up in Jessica that you don't have the energy for me. I'm exhausted, I'm grumpy, and I'm not in the mood. Let's talk later, okay?"

"Wow, so sorry that my family obligations are getting in your way," I snapped. "But I actually give a damn about Jessica. She's my responsibility. That doesn't just go away because she turned eighteen."

"I can't believe we're still talking about Jess," he muttered.

Then he hung up on me.

What the hell?

Nate hadn't been himself the past two days, not even a little bit.

He'd always been so concerned and supportive of me, even over the smallest things . . . and he'd never pressured me for sex. But now that I needed him, he'd checked out. I couldn't wrap my head around it.

You sure you really know him?

Reese's nasty little insinuations burrowed through my thoughts. I shouldn't leap to judgments, though, not while I was this upset— my perspective was all messed up. I wasn't thinking straight.

Still, I'd expected a *little* more sympathy from Nate. Isn't that what boyfriends do?

I sucked down another mouthful of wine, contemplating my unpleasant conversation with Amber. Apparently Jessica had flown down there yesterday, although it hadn't occurred to either of them that this was information I might like to have. I had no clue where the money for the plane ticket had come from, either.

Selfish, both of them. And Nate was selfish, too . . . although maybe he was right in his own way. For better or worse, Jessica was an adult and she'd made her decision. I should probably just accept it and let it go, because all this stress and worry wasn't accomplishing jack shit anyway.

At least the wine was still on my side.

An hour later I'd finished the bottle and things were looking up. For example, with Jess gone, I wouldn't be stuck at home every weekend. I could go places, do things . . . Sleep with Nate any time I wanted.

Assuming I still *wanted* to sleep with him.

But the more I thought about it, the less interested I was in following up on that. Sure, it wasn't like we were engaged or anything, but what's the point of having a boyfriend if he blows you off the first time you need him?

On the other hand, finally getting laid would be nice . . .

I'd completely forgotten about Reese until the doorbell rang just after seven that evening. By that point I was halfway through a second bottle of wine, which was half a bottle firmly over my limit. I

opened the door to find him standing on my porch with a bag of
Chinese in one hand and a six-pack of beer in the other. I ran my
eyes up and down his strong form, deciding he looked *fantastic*.

I wanted to bite him.

Yeah, definitely over my limit on the vino—I'd had more to drink
in this one weekend than the past two months combined. Too bad I
couldn't bring myself to care.

*Biting Reese Hayes wouldn't be a problem if you ditched the
boyfriend*, my brain whispered insidiously. I decided my brain was
right. If Nate gave a shit about being in a relationship with me, he
wouldn't have been such a dick.

Oooh, and now I was cussing in my head. Fun!

"C'mon in," I told Reese, suddenly starving. That bag of little
white cartons smelled fantastic and I couldn't wait to rip into them.
His eyes widened.

"You seem to be in a good mood," he murmured. I held up my
wine bottle for him to see.

"I decided I needed a distraction," I told him bluntly. "I called my
cousin Amber. She's a bitch and I hate her . . . Also Jessica is with
her. She's fine, perfectly safe. Flew down there yesterday and they
didn't bother to tell me. I'm washing my hands of both of them."

I tried to rub my hands together like I was washing them and
dropped my bottle in the process. Reese lunged, catching it midair.
The motion set me off balance and I fell on my ass, laughing. He
stared at me, a slow grin crawling across his face.

"You're drunk," he said.

"No shit," I told him. "Feels great, too."

"Do you have to work tomorrow?"

"I'm the boss," I informed him proudly. "I make my own schedule."

"I see," he murmured, then reached down to catch my hand, pulling me to my feet. I lurched into him, rubbing my face against the
hard muscles of his chest.

"You smell really good," I told him. "Reeallly good."

"You got a coffeepot?"

I blinked up at him, running my hands up and over his shoulders. They were nice and hard, like silk stretched over . . . something hard. I giggled because I couldn't think of the right word.

"Coffeepot?" he asked again.

"Why?"

"Time to sober up, I think. What the hell is that smell?"

I beamed at him, feeling pleased with myself.

"The self-cleaning cycle on the oven. I like to clean when I get frustrated, and there's nothing quite like a sparkly oven. You just turn it up to a million degrees, bake it, and then vacuum it out. Gas does all the hard work for you. Very cathartic."

"You're gonna kill me," he muttered, running a finger down my cheek. "Let's get some coffee in you and eat. No more wine."

I pouted, because wine was my favorite. Then I forgot to pout because he smelled all yummy, and I wanted to see if he tasted as good as he smelled.

Now if I could just catch his lip and find out . . .

REESE

This was officially the most fucked-up dinner date I'd ever had in my life.

London—

Everyone calls me Loni, Reese, but I hate it. I like how you use my real name . . . Can I touch your stomach?

—was drunk off her ass, and I had a very bad feeling that if I fucked her, things wouldn't end well. Not normally a factor for me, really. I *liked* it when things didn't work out with women. Generally that was the goal.

Unfortunately, karma's a bitch and she had a lot on me.

I stared at the TV, pretending to watch the world's least interesting movie with London passed out all over me. Her tits smashed up against my chest, her legs straddled my thigh, and her hand lay on my stomach, precisely six inches from the top of my straining dick. I knew this because exactly once every sixty seconds I looked away from the screen to make sure it hadn't ripped a hole through my pants. Then I'd start counting down again, because the counting was the only thing keeping me from rolling her over and shoving my cock so far up her cunt it hit the back of her throat. *Yeah, that'd wake her up . . .*

Why wasn't I doing this? Good question.

It wasn't because I'm a good guy or she was too drunk or any of that shit. I've never been a decent human being and didn't see a whole lot of reason to change things up at this stage of the game.

Decency isn't really my thing. This was about strategy.

London sighed in her sleep, pulling me a little closer as her hand slipped down. I groaned, and somehow my dick got harder, something I would've bet a hundred dollars wasn't even possible. It actually *hurt*, and the smell of her hair drifting up toward my nose didn't exactly help.

She smelled like vanilla cookies.

I asked myself again why I wasn't currently fucking her. I had her at my mercy—she was all over me. I should just take what she offered and enjoy it. Strategy was overrated.

She might actually make you happy, Heather told me sternly. *Don't blow it, asshole.*

Goddamn ghosts in my head.

Heather needed to back the fuck off, because I wasn't down with this shit. I hadn't actually died with her, despite the fact that it occasionally felt that way. She'd left me to raise our girls all by myself and sometimes I hated her for it.

Fortunately, thinking of my girls made me smile.

Didn't even have the words to describe how much they meant to me. Somewhere along the way I'd reengaged with life, for their sake if not my own. Biggest fight of my life, not crawling down into that grave with my wife. London was fighting the same kind of battle, in her own way. When shit hit the fan, she'd charged life head-on, taken in Jessica and fought for her, despite the fact that she had an easy out. Nobody could have blamed her for passing Jess along to social services. I respected the way she threw down for her kid, even though Jess wasn't technically hers. She understood loyalty, and that family isn't always about blood.

Much as I hated to admit it, that was the kind of strength and loyalty it took to make a good old lady . . . Then I shook my head, because I sure as shit wasn't going there. Claim her? Okay. But nobody could ever take Heather's place, let alone wear her patch.

Maybe I could find a happy medium, though, and that's where London came in. Screwing her tonight would complicate things in a way that could end with her hating me. I'm nothing if not decisive, and I don't fuck around once I've made up my mind. I wanted London and I definitely planned to keep her for a while.

That meant I should start things off right.

First order of business—remove Deputy Dick from her life without scaring the hell out of her. If I had to suck it up for a while to make that happen, I had no doubt she'd make it up to me down the line. Thus I found myself lying on a couch watching some dumbass movie with a dick harder than a diamond and no happy ending in sight.

London stirred against me again, letting out a soft snore.

Christ, her mouth was right by my nipple. I felt the heat of her breath touch me through the thin fabric of my shirt, and something like panic welled up in the back of my throat. I had to get the hell out of here, because no fuckin' way I'd be able to keep my hands off her much longer. Respect only went so far.

The brothers would laugh their asses off if they saw me now.

"Okay, sweetheart," I muttered, cradling her as I sat up awkwardly. "Let's get you to bed."

London snuggled deeper into me, making protesting noises. She really wasn't very big, despite those fabulous tits of her. I lifted her easily enough and carried her back toward the bedrooms. Her door was open, revealing a neatly made queen-size bed. The room was decorated in what was probably thrift shop furniture, but it'd been polished up and laid out in a way that looked put together and purposeful.

Nothing like my bedroom.

"Still pissed at you," she muttered as I tugged back the covers and tucked her in. Well, look at that. Sleeping Drunky was waking up, and I didn't even have to kiss her first.

"Do I wanna know why?" I asked. She frowned, eyes still closed.

"You know why, Nate. But you can spend the night anyway . . ."

Nate? She thought I was *Nate Evans*?

That fucking cockwad was *not* getting credit for this good deed.

My good intentions disappeared in an instant, brain turning off as instinct kicked in. Didn't matter that I'd decided to keep my hands off—she didn't get to dream about Deputy Dick while I held her. That was a straight-up deal breaker, something both I and my cock felt very strongly about.

"This isn't Nate," I growled, sliding my fingers into her hair, gripping her head tight. She woke with a jerk, eyes wide and confused.

"What?"

"I'm not Nate," I growled. She blinked at me.

"Reese? What are you doing here?"

Holy shit. I'd brought her food, listened to her cry, and then held her half the night—and she didn't even remember. Karma could suck my ass. I dropped down on the bed, shoving a knee between her legs, covering her with my body. My dick found her pubic bone, and I rotated my hips.

Finally.

Fucking *hell* that was sweet relief, even if it wasn't a money shot.

"Oh my God . . ." she whispered, eyes wide. "Reese, what are you doing?"

I groaned, grinding against her so hard it hurt. She bucked back, whimpering, and I completely forgot about keeping things simple. I needed inside her. Now. The rest could wait. I caught her lips with mine, nipping them before thrusting my tongue deep in her mouth. Her hips bucked again, her hands digging into my chest.

Then she bit my tongue.

"What the fuck?" I gasped, jerking away from her. Her eyes were wide and full of shock, which was right about the time I realized her hands weren't digging into my chest to rip off my shirt.

Nope.

They were pushing against it.

"I can't do this," she whispered, shaking her head. "Nate and I agreed not to see other people. I'm still with him."

"If you're with Nate, why the fuck wasn't he here when you needed him?"

London closed her eyes, taking a deep breath. Unfortunately that forced her breasts up and into my chest. I thought my cock might actually explode, and not because I blew my wad. Nope, it might split from the sheer volume of blood trapped in there.

"He and I need to talk," she said, and I growled. *Talk?* She looked almost as frustrated as I felt. I rotated my hips into hers one more time, both of us gasping in need.

"Fuck that. Your cunt wants me inside as bad as my cock wants in."

"I don't like that word."

"I don't like Deputy Dick," I growled. "But you don't see me putting a bullet in him, do you? Stop bitching and let me fuck you."

Her eyes narrowed and she shoved at my shoulders, hard. I rolled off her, chest heaving as I tried to make my brain work. Almost impossible, what with the complete lack of available blood. My cock throbbed. Literally. I felt each pulsing heartbeat hit it like a sledge-hammer.

I wanted to kill her. Fuck her, then kill her. Then kill Nate Evans for putting me through this. Teach that cocksucker to move in on a Reaper's woman.

"I'm really sorry that I got drunk and made an idiot of myself," London said after a long pause. "You didn't deserve that."

"Damned straight."

"Is there anything I can do?"

"Blow job would be nice." Throw in a fifth of vodka and a pole dance and maybe I'd reconsider killing her . . . but I wouldn't be happy until I'd split her cunt wide open. I slammed my fist down on the bed. *Fuck!*

She squeaked. Like a mouse. It was cute, which pissed me off even more.

"Anything else?"

"No, I think you've done enough," I said, closing my eyes and trying to think of something—anything—to distract me from the pain between my legs.

"It was really nice of you to come over and bring me dinner."

Nice.

Fucking bitch thought I was *nice*. If she thanked me for being her friend, it was over. I'd have to go on a killing spree.

I gotta get out of here.

Jackknifing off the bed, I stalked out into the living room, look-ing for my keys. They were on the kitchen counter, right next to the empty take-out containers. She could buy her own fucking dinner and cry alone next time.

I heard her bare feet padding up behind me.

"So I guess this probably means our deal is off?"

Her voice sounded uncertain, almost scared. Still a little slurred, too. I turned to glare at her, taking in her tangled blonde hair, the curve of her generous hips in those tight jeans, and the way her shirt drooped low enough to show plenty of cleavage.

"Not if you want to keep the club accounts," I growled, wondering why the hell I didn't just fire her ass. My cock reminded me that we weren't finished with her yet. "I'll see you out at my place on Tuesday. Make enough food for leftovers and maybe we'll have a talk about getting a crew into The Line."

"Thank you," she whispered.

"Eat shit," I said, and then slammed out the door.

Seems like a bit of an overreaction, Heather gloated as I climbed into my truck.

She could eat shit, too. Fucking women. Even dead, they stuck together.

CHAPTER SIX

LONDON

"So, where does this leave us?" Nate asked me Monday night. We sat at a table in the back of the restaurant, where the light hardly reached and the flickering of candlelight was supposed to make everything look romantic. Instead it felt claustrophobic and damning.

"Honestly? I'm not sure."

"I know you needed me and I wasn't there. Do you think you can forgive me?"

I sighed, wondering whether it mattered.

So he hadn't been there for me. I resented that. But he'd had to work, and in his defense he dealt with runaways all the time. From his perspective, this was probably a pretty good outcome. She was with a family member, not kidnapped and murdered by a serial killer.

That wasn't even the real issue, though. I'd been hot as hell for Reese Hayes, whether I liked to admit it or not. Nate and I had decided to make things exclusive—then I crawled all over another man.

What kind of person *does* that?

Not a woman who's in love. Or even infatuated . . . And if I'd fallen out of infatuation in less than two months, that was pretty much it for me and Nate. Both of us deserved better, although I hadn't decided what that should look like. It'd been fourteen years since I lived on my own. Was that why I'd been so eager to hook up with Nate? Fear of being alone?

Why was I falling into that trap?

I kind of liked the idea of doing what I wanted to do when I wanted to do it. Maybe I should try eating ice cream for breakfast for a while, or color my hair bright red. Maybe I should buy a car that didn't have a cleaning service logo on the side of it.

A red Miata. I'd always wanted one of those.

Now came the hard part.

"I don't think it's going to work out," I said slowly. Nate frowned, his hand covered mine, squeezing it tightly.

"Babe, I think you're overreacting."

"No, it's not—" I started to say, but then stopped myself. *It's not you, it's me.* Such a cliche, but in this case painfully true. Nate might not be perfect, but he was pretty great. He just wasn't the man I wanted. All I could think about was Reese and how he'd felt between my legs.

Amazing.

I wanted to feel that again. Alive and awake.

Was I actually going to sleep with him? I really hadn't decided . . . The thought definitely appealed. He wasn't relationship material, but maybe I didn't need a relationship just yet.

Maybe I just needed to get laid.

Yup. Ice cream for breakfast, color hair, get laid, buy Miata. Then more ice cream. I had a plan.

"London?"

I focused on Nate again, blinking rapidly. His face was so earnest, so full of concern.

"I think we should stop seeing each other," I said firmly, and the words felt right. Slightly painful, but liberating, too.

He frowned.

"You're breaking up with me?" he asked slowly, as if he couldn't believe what I'd just said. "Jesus, Loni. I get that I fucked up, but this seems kind of harsh."

"It's not that," I said. "I've just realized that what I feel for you isn't strong enough. I'm sorry. I wish I could change things—"

"It's about Reese Hayes, isn't it?"

I shook my head, although part of me knew I was lying.

"It's about us," I told him. "We just aren't going to work, so it's best to end it now."

"I asked you to sleep with me, not marry me," he snapped. "God, what the hell is wrong with you?"

Good question. I swallowed, because he was starting to look angry and I couldn't blame him for that. But I couldn't date someone out of guilt, either. Nope. A clean break was the only decent course of action.

"It doesn't matter," I said carefully. "There's no future here and I respect you too much to lead you on."

Nate threw his napkin on the table and leaned forward, eyes narrowed. His face was getting red and I realized I'd never seen him upset before. What Reese had told me about him ran through my mind, but I pushed it away. This was Nate. Sweet Nate. He was hurt, and no wonder. None of this was fair to him.

"What the fuck, Loni? *You don't want to lead me on?* What the hell do you think you've been doing the last eight weeks? Is your cunt made of gold? Because I swear to God, women don't pull this shit with me and get away with it."

My mouth dropped open and I gasped. Nate didn't talk like that. What on earth had happened here?

"Nate, I—"

"We're over." He stood, glaring at me. "I can't believe how much time I wasted on you."

Then he turned and walked away stiffly, rage all but radiating through the air around him.

Well. *That* was special.

I glanced around, hoping nobody had noticed our little scene. Amazingly they hadn't, despite the fact that it'd felt pretty dramatic and spectacular to me. I'd just gotten publicly dumped and it sort of hurt. Why it hurt, I had no idea. He'd done to me what I'd planned to do to him, so what right did I have to feel anything but relief?

Just be glad it's over.

The waiter walked over carrying two enormous platters of Mexican food, and I realized that not only had Nate dumped me, he'd stuck me with the bill, too. Always look on the bright side. Without Jess to feed, I wouldn't have to cook for the next week. I'd just work my way through Nate's jumbo carne asada entree.

"Can you wrap those up to go?" I asked the waiter. He cocked a brow, but wisely kept his mouth shut. I decided to give him a thirty percent tip, because someone should get something out of this date.

Then I took my overpriced takeout and swung by the grocery store, because I had ice cream to buy.

Ice cream and hair dye.

Two hours later I swirled in front of my bathroom mirror, a new woman.

Ruby Fusion.

I looked like Christina Hendricks on acid (okay, not quite as statuesque, and my boobs were smaller . . . but still very curvy!). The new hair was gorgeous. Crazy. Fun. I wondered if Reese would like it, and then decided I didn't care, because *I* liked it.

That's when it hit me.

For the first time in forever, I was doing something for myself.

It felt good.

. . .

The high lasted until about noon the next day, when I carefully sorted through my finances. Counting all my savings, the business emergency funds, and the secret vacation stash, I was still broke. Okay. So no new Miatas just yet. But if I got the contract for The Line, maybe I could revisit the idea in a year or two. Assuming Reese didn't fire me.

Powerful motivation.

I'd just have to get that contract no matter what. So what if I had to sleep with him to do it . . . I'd just call it a bonus and roll with it.

Jessica got in touch right after I went to bed Tuesday night.

"Hey, Loni."

"Hey there," I responded, biting back the "So, I see your phone still works" comment hovering on my lips. Silence fell between us, all weird and uncomfortable.

"How are things with your mom?" I asked finally.

"Things are good, I guess. I mean, she isn't here very much. She's really busy with her friends and stuff, and she doesn't like me to be around when her boyfriend comes home. I don't have a car or anything, so I've just sort of been hanging out by the pool. They've got me in the guesthouse. There are a few others staying there, but I have my own room."

"Well, I'm glad things are good," I told her. "I want you to be happy."

"I was wondering . . ."

"Yes?"

"Do you think you could pack up some of my things and ship them down? I left all my clothes up there, and Mom has been loaning me shit, but I don't feel quite right borrowing from her all the time."

I glanced toward her bedroom door, wondering if I'd be a horrible person if I said I'd set all her things on fire. Yes. That would be horrible. Pity, because a small, hateful part of me wanted to hurt her.

But even with Ruby Fusion hair, I still had to be the adult.

"Sure, I can pack some things up—but not everything. That would cost a fortune to ship. If you want more, you can get a job and earn the money to pay for it. I'll get some clothes for you, though."

"And maybe some of my books and pictures?" she asked. "You know, like the scrapbook I made of the kids at the community center? I'm kind of missing them, especially since I didn't get to say good-bye. I wanted to find somewhere else to volunteer, but Mom thought that was a bad idea."

My heart softened a little. Amber was a Class A bitch, so staying with her had to be a punishment in and of itself. My Jessie girl had some hard lessons ahead of her.

"I'll pack some things up and send them soon," I told her firmly. "But it's late and I need to sleep. I've got work in the morning."

"Okay," she whispered. "Loni?"

"Yes?"

"Thank you."

Wednesday morning I opened her bedroom door, midsized cardboard shipping box in hand. I'd come in here right after she ran away and picked up the worst of her mess from the tantrum, just so nobody would accidentally cut their feet on the broken glass. But beyond that I'd left everything untouched. Jess was a slob, and we'd come to an agreement years ago. She'd do her part to keep the rest of the house clean, and I'd stop bugging her about her bedroom.

The system had worked well for us.

Now I looked around, wondering where to begin. Most of her favorite things were strewn across the floor in dirty piles. I could either grab the things from her drawers (already clean) and pack them, or collect up what she really liked and give it a quick wash.

Well, she *had* said "thank you," which was a big step up for Little Miss Entitlement.

I grabbed the dirty clothes, tossing them into the box like a makeshift laundry basket. I carried them into the kitchen, where a washer and dryer took up one corner. Then I started sorting through and checking the pockets.

That's when I found the money.

A hundred-dollar bill, wrapped around a scrap of paper with a note on it.

Seven tonight, downtown. No bra, no panties.

What. The. Hell.

My hand trembled as the implications hit me. Jessica had some sort of secret boyfriend, the kind of man who gave her money. Enough money that she could afford to leave a hundred-dollar bill stashed in her pants.

Amber had boyfriends like that, too.

The thought made me sick, and I swayed, reaching out to clutch the counter. I stumbled into the living room, sitting down heavily on the couch, trying to think.

Mellie. She'd know what was going on.

The phone only rang once before she picked up.

"Hey, Loni," she said, sounding pathetically eager to talk to me. I felt a twinge of guilt—I hadn't given her much thought the past couple days, even though she'd spent two or three nights a week at my house over the last year.

"Hey, Mel. How are you?"

"Okay," she replied. "I miss Jessica, though. I've tried calling her but she hasn't answered. I guess she's too busy doing cool things with her mom."

Not so much, but I decided not to go there.

"Maybe. Hey, I was just going through some of her laundry and I found something strange. I thought I might ask you about it."

"What?" Mellie asked, her voice cautious. I smelled a secret. Excellent. Now I just needed to get it out of her, which shouldn't be too hard. Mellie never lied directly, only by omission.

"A note, along with a hundred-dollar bill. It's from a man, making arrangements to get together with Jess downtown somewhere. Do you know of anyone she was seeing? Someone who would have a hundred bucks to spare?"

Mellie didn't answer immediately, so I waited, letting the silence grow between us.

"I don't know his name," she said finally. "I mean, I know he's older, but I don't know any more than that. She said he was her sugar daddy. Said he took care of her."

I sighed. "And you didn't think that was relevant information to share with me when she went missing?"

"I didn't want to get her in trouble," Mellie replied, her voice miserable. "I knew how pissed you'd be, and I don't think he had anything to do with her taking off. It's not like he's dangerous or anything—not like those bikers she hooked up with. She says he's really good to her. And they didn't start sleeping together until after she turned eighteen, at least not that I know of. She says he respects her."

"Okay," I said softly. I felt like I should press her for more information, but what was the point? God, this sucked. "I appreciate the heads-up."

"Sorry," Mellie whispered. "Hey, Loni?"

"Yes?"

"Can I come over to your place sometime? I sort of miss hanging out with you."

"Sure, sweetie," I told her, feeling my eyes start to water a little. "You're always welcome here, okay?"

"Thanks," she whispered. "You know how it is . . ."

"Yeah, baby, I know how it is. You're safe here. Always. Just because Jessica left doesn't mean you aren't welcome."

"Thanks, Loni."

I hung up the phone and flopped back on the couch, wondering how I'd gotten to such a strange place in my life. I'd dumped my husband for Jess, and now Jess had dumped me for Amber. Then I dumped Nate.

I wouldn't dump Mellie, I decided.

No matter what happened, she was a sweet kid and she needed all the support she could get. I wouldn't fail her like I'd failed Amber and Jessica.

And yes, I know it was insane to think I failed them—you can't save someone who doesn't want saving. Didn't change how I felt.

The buzzer went off on the washer, reminding me that I had more clothes to push through. I needed to hit the grocery store for Reese, too. I'd go out to his place early, I decided. That way I wouldn't have to see him, because despite my bold resolutions I wasn't quite ready to confront him just yet.

I'd been through enough in the past twenty-four hours.

Reese's motorcycle sat out in front of his house when I pulled up, along with his truck and a sporty little red convertible.

A Miata. *My Miata.* I seriously considered keying the car out of pure jealousy.

Make that jealousy and frustration, because not only had I failed to avoid Reese, he apparently had company. Best not to think about whoever might be driving that pretty little car, either, because I'd bet my morning ice cream it wasn't one of his club brothers.

I sat in the driveway and pondered just turning my van around and leaving, then decided that would be pure cowardice. I'd run into him sooner or later. Might as well get it over with. It would be good for me to see him with another woman, I decided. I'd nearly slept with him the other night, and while I'd decided to break up with Nate, that didn't automatically mean hooking up with Reese was a smart idea.

It could never be more than random sex anyway. Nothing underscores the temporary nature of a booty call like seeing your intended booty calling on someone else.

You're here to work. What he does is his business.

I turned off my van, grabbed the groceries, and started toward the door. Balancing the bags gracelessly, I punched in the code and pushed through to find myself face-to-ass with the owner of the Miata.

She straddled Reese on the couch, her miniskirt pushed up around her waist, leaving absolutely nothing to the imagination—my own personal porno, front and center. Holy. Shit. I couldn't breathe. His gaze met mine over her head, and I managed to clear my throat. She froze, twisting around to see me.

Awkward.

"Thought you were coming later," Reese drawled, wrapping his big hands around her waist and holding her steady. His eyes were cold and hostile, although a mocking smile graced his face. He was still angry. Fair enough. We hadn't exactly ended things on a positive note back at my place. Miss Miata buried her head in his shoulder, obviously trying to hold back a fit of giggles. God, had he told her about me? Did they laugh together at how stupid I'd been, getting drunk and throwing myself at him?

Don't panic. DON'T PANIC.

I panicked. I felt the grocery bags starting to slip, so I tightened my grip and forced myself to inhale slowly. Exhale.

Think of calm things. Oceans. Clean ovens. Don't let him see how this hurts you.

Wait. Why should this hurt me? So I had the hots for him, but that didn't mean I *cared* about Reese Hayes. Had I been celibate so long that I'd forgotten what mindless lust felt like? I'd kicked *him* out of *my* bed, not the other way around.

I coughed, and realized I had to take control of the situation. *Break the tension. Make a joke.*

"Sorry to interrupt," I said, wondering if my voice sounded as shaky as it felt. "Do you want me to reschedule, or can you move to your bedroom? I generally frown on cleaning around people while they're having sex. All sorts of potential OSHA violations."

Hayes's eyes widened and his smile shifted from mocking to genuine. He shook his head slowly.

"You know, I want to stay pissed at you, but you're just too cute sometimes," he said finally. "I don't think I've ever met anyone like you, London."

I'd never met anyone like him, either, I thought somewhat hysterically. Maybe I'd led a sheltered life, but most of my friends liked to have sex in private. I decided now wasn't the time to discuss our cultural differences, all things considered. I'd go right ahead and keep focusing on breathing, because somewhere deep inside it felt like I'd been stabbed in the gut, which wasn't right on about a thousand different levels.

"Um, still here," Miss Miata said, lifting a hand and waving it in front of his face. "Unless she's joining us, I think we should relocate. I only get off on performing for appreciative audiences, and I think we're scaring this one."

"I'm not joining you," I stuttered.

Her eyes swept up my figure.

"Too bad."

That was my signal for full, unconditional retreat.

"I'll just put away the food," I said, walking quickly past them into the kitchen. I dropped the bags on the counter. Then I leaned forward and forced myself to inhale and exhale some more, counting to ten each time. *What the hell was going on with me?* So it was weird walking in on people having sex. Yes. Definitely weird. But not full meltdown weird.

Shit.

This was all about my stupid crush on Reese, which was apparently even stronger than I'd realized. I didn't have the right to feel hurt or possessive, yet here I was, trying not to hyperventilate in his kitchen. Not me at all. Desperate times . . .

I opened a cabinet and pulled out a mug. Then I opened the freezer and grabbed some vodka. I poured myself a nice shot, drank it, then quickly disposed of the evidence. Cold fire slid down my throat, clarifying things.

So I had a problem—Reese was beautiful, I had a crush on him, and he was currently fucking another woman in the living room. *His* living room. A place he had every right to use for sex or anything else he felt like using it for. Kind of shitty that I walked in on it, but I'd come out to his place early, too. Time to face some hard facts:

1) Reese slept with lots of women.
2) He wasn't betraying me, and so far as he knew, I was in a relationship with another man.
3) I wanted to curl up into a ball and die.

Curling up in a ball and dying seemed a little extreme, so I'd just have to pull up my big girl panties and fucking deal with this shit. First up—I had frozen food melting in the van, and it needed to be put away. Because I'm only human, I ducked out the back door to grab the rest of the bags, avoiding the spectacle out front. By the time I came back, they'd left the living room. More giggling and sex noises drifted out from his bedroom and I winced. Maybe I'd just go upstairs for a while. Vacuum. That should drown them out.

Forty minutes later there wasn't a speck of dirt or dust anywhere to be found upstairs. This wasn't a huge surprise, given how clean it was from the last time I'd been there and the fact that the rooms weren't being used. There was no getting around my unfortunate reality—I had to go back downstairs.

My feet wouldn't move, though.

I just couldn't do it. Instead I sat down on the top step, leaning forward on my knees to think. This cleaning gig wasn't going to work out after all. I couldn't handle seeing him with another woman, because no matter how I colored my hair, I wasn't sophisticated and modern enough for booty calls. I would just have to tell Reese I couldn't clean for him and let it go. Preferably by text. I really didn't need a new car or that sweet contract out at The Line.

Except . . .

Now that Jess had taken off, it really was the perfect time to start expanding my business. The strip club would be a hell of an account to do it with. I could just suck it up, right?

Yes. I'd be damned if I'd walk away from that much money.

Does that sound mercenary?

I didn't care.

So what if Reese Hayes was pretty and I wanted to have sex with him? I wanted a million dollars and a house on the lake, and that wouldn't be happening any time soon, either. Reese had all kinds of women lined up to sleep with, ten a day if he wanted that many. He'd probably lost interest in me already, and I should be happy about it. Clarified things. Didn't mean I shouldn't do my best to get and keep the club accounts.

You have to separate business from pleasure if you want a Miata.

Exactly. That's what I'd do. Pull my act together and—no, pull my *shit* together and send Jessica her clothing with a smile. I'd be a support to Mellie and be empowered and self-sufficient. I didn't need a man, but if I wanted one I'd take him and use him and then pass him along without a second thought, because I'd become a sophisticated, modern woman if it killed me.

Sure.

And I would lose ten pounds and age backward, too.

Right after I learned to fly my invisible jet.

Thirty minutes later the roast was in the oven and I was setting out frozen rolls to rise. I'd had a second, strictly medicinal shot of vodka, and while I wasn't exactly buzzed, I *was* feeling a little more balanced about things. Of course, dumping yellow food coloring in the back of the downstairs toilet tank and pouring vinegar in his milk helped restore that balance . . . I also loosened the lid on the salt shaker.

Why did I do these things?

Probably best not to examine that too closely.

Reese emerged from the back addition to lean against the door frame. He wore a pair of faded jeans and nothing else, his big, beefy arms crossing his chest with casual laziness. I refused to let my eyes linger on his muscles, although I did let myself check out his feet.

There's nothing sexier than a big, tough man walking around barefoot. I'd always had a thing for it.

"Sorry about that earlier," he said, although I could tell from his tone that he wasn't sorry one little bit. "I had no idea you'd come out to the house so early. I thought I had a couple more hours."

Wow, he sounded almost sincere.

"I was planning to get done before you got home from work," I said, turning away from him to fuss with the rolls. "What are your hours?"

"Irregular," he said. "I'm the boss, remember? I work when I'm needed or when I want to."

I sensed him moving toward me, so I turned away from the rolls and headed over to the fridge to put some space between us. Pulling open the door I studied the interior, trying to figure out what I should do next. Sadly, the beer, ketchup, and jar of pickles facing me had no insights to offer.

Turning and looking at him wasn't an option.

I wasn't sure if I wanted to scratch him for screwing that other woman or jump his bones. Either way I'd have to scrub him down with bleach, just to be safe, because he was all covered in her cooties.

"Let's put together a schedule," I suggested, studying the expiration date on a container of yogurt as if my life depended on it. "So I won't run into you here at the house."

"Scared?" he asked, and his voice was right behind me. He reached around and shut the fridge, resting one hand on either side of my body, trapping me. Every instinct I had said I should create a diversion and run like hell, but I turned to face him instead.

I didn't want to let him think he was right, no matter how hard that might be.

Professional. You are a professional and you don't play games.

I offered a bland smile and focused on a cabinet handle across the room, exactly two inches above his broad right shoulder.

Perfect.

"I just don't want to get in your way," I said evenly. "I know things are awkward between us after the other night. But I want you to know how much I appreciate your support. It was a bad weekend for me. I'm fine now."

He cocked his head and his lip curled in a sneer.

"Deputy Dick kiss it all better?"

"My personal relationships have nothing to do with my work here."

"No, I guess they're only relevant when you crawl all over me, rub your tits on my chest, and then kick me out the door after I take care of your drunk ass all night. You started it, sweetheart. I was just following through."

I closed my eyes, praying I wasn't flushing bright red.

"Let's forget that happened, okay? I was emotional and had too much wine. I almost made a horrible mistake, and I'm sorry if I used you. But that doesn't mean sleeping together would've been a good idea."

"Sounds like a damned fine idea to me," he whispered, leaning down and sniffing my neck. "I'd make it good for you."

I caught a whiff of perfume on him.

"Miss Miata is still in the bedroom," I said tightly. "Better back off or she'll see you. Then you'll be in trouble."

He laughed without pulling back.

"Miss Miata?" he asked. "Now that's a new name for her. At the clubhouse, we call her—"

"If you say something nasty, I'm going to kick you," I snapped. "Is it really worth it?"

"Define 'nasty.'"

"Anything less than complimentary about the woman you just had sex with," I told him. "Because it sounded like you were going to insult her. Just remember, anything she did, you participated in. You're equally guilty."

He gave a low laugh.

"At the clubhouse we call her Sharon," he said softly. "Which I've never considered an insult, especially given that she's named after her grandmother. But you feel free to interpret it any way you like."

I closed my eyes and counted to five.

"Just go away."

"Pic, you know where my shoes are?" Sharon said. She walked into the kitchen and I expected him to pull away, to turn to her with an explanation. He stayed put.

"Think they're in the living room, babe," he said, reaching up to run his fingers through my hair, tugging my head just enough to force me to meet his eyes.

"Thanks," Sharon said, passing by us to hunt for her footwear.

"Isn't she pissed off that you're talking to me instead of her?"

"Apparently not," he said, shrugging. "Think she already got what she wanted."

"Let me guess, this is where you tell me how many times you made her come?"

He smirked.

"No, although if you want details, I guess I could give you some," he said. "I like how you think. Dirty. But what she wanted was cash. She's a nice girl and she's in a bit of trouble. I'm helping her out, so she decided to help me out."

That took me off guard.

"Is she a . . . prostitute?"

He shook his head. "She's a person. Try not to be so judgmental—it's not nice to objectify women like that, London. Don't you know better?"

His tone mocked me, and I snorted.

"Let me go."

"Give me a kiss."

"We already covered this," I said, feeling my chest tighten because I wanted him to touch me. How did he do that? Here he was trying to kiss me right after having sex with another woman, and for some reason I hadn't kicked him in the balls yet. What was up with that? Probably the vodka, I decided. *Definitely* the vodka. "I don't think it's a good idea."

"Oh yes, you're still seeing the good deputy," he said, his voice a low growl. "You sleep with him yet?"

"I'm not, actually. Seeing him. I broke up with him yesterday."

That caught him off guard, and he pulled back, studying my face. "No shit?"

"No shit," I said firmly, taking advantage of his surprise to slip under his arm and flee across the kitchen. "I've got a roast in the oven. When the timer goes off, you can take it out and throw in the rolls for fifteen minutes. There's a salad waiting for you in the fridge and I'll invoice you for the groceries. Good-bye."

"You really think I'll let you drop a bomb like that and just walk out of here?"

I shrugged. It'd been worth a shot.

"I have work to do, Reese. I broke up with Nate because it wasn't right between us. That doesn't mean it's right with you—if anything, it just means I need to be on my own for a while. Jessica hasn't even been gone a week. That's a lot of change and I don't feel like talking about it with you or anyone else."

"This isn't over."

I laughed.

"It never started," I told him bluntly. "I'm not like you. I can't just have casual sex."

Sure you can, the slutty side of my brain whispered. *Just try it!*

Miss Miata hasn't even left the house yet, I reminded my brain firmly. *Don't be such a slut!*

"How do you know you can't have casual sex?" he asked. "It's fun. When's the last time you tried it?"

I glared at him.

"Seriously, when was it?"

"None of your business," I snapped.

"Well, if you change your mind, you know where I am," he told me. Sharon came back inside and smiled at me, wrapping her arm around Hayes's waist. She whispered something in his ear, then gave him a lingering kiss before looking at me.

"Nice to meet you," she told me with a genuine smile. "Maybe I'll see you out at the clubhouse sometime?"

I shrugged, because saying I'd rather eat broken glass didn't feel quite appropriate. How was she so friendly under the circumstances? It seemed wrong.

Stop being so judgmental . . . Reese's words echoed in my head.

"Okay, I'm out of here," she said. "Oh, and Pic? I think there's something wrong with the toilet, just a heads up. That roast smells fantastic, London. I'm watching my carbs, so good thing those rolls aren't baking yet!"

With that she gave me a perky finger wave and left, humming brightly.

Of *course* she was watching her carbs. Girls like her always were.

"That was just weird," I muttered.

"*That* was someone who's comfortable in her sexuality and not worried about overthinking things. You should try it. It's more fun than pouting. Less work, too."

"I really have to go now."

"I'll see you on Thursday," he said. "Let me know what time to expect you and I'll try to have clothes on . . . Unless you change your mind?"

I didn't bother responding as I marched out of the kitchen, and his laugh followed me through the door.

Someday I'd be the one making him uncomfortable, I decided. I wasn't sure when or how, but I looked forward to it. Seemed only fair, all things considered.

CHAPTER SEVEN

My phone buzzed as I dumped out the bucket of gray mop water. It was nine the next morning, and my crew had one more hour to finish cleaning the strip club. Hayes had kept his promise, and according to Gage—the big Reaper who managed the place—we would be getting the contract long term if he liked what he saw.

I was there to make damned sure he liked what he saw.

That meant scrubbing every inch of the place. Not that we'd have to go that far every time we came, but I wanted to start things off right. I pulled out the phone, startled to see it was Jess. Wow . . . Getting up her up before noon practically took an act of God.

JESSICA: Hey Loni. How are you
ME: Fine. Working, tho. Whats up?
JESSICA: Do you have time for a phone call? I want to talk to.
    Things arent so good here

I frowned, my throat tightening.

ME: Just a sec

Setting down the bucket, I walked out of the janitorial closet and across the empty club floor. In the distance I heard the whine of the vacuum as my crew worked their way through the VIP rooms in the back. Gage sat at one of the tables, looking up as I passed with a question on his face.

"Just a quick phone call," I told him, pushing out the front door and into the parking lot.

The phone rang three times before Jessica picked up.

"Loni?"

"Hey, baby, what's wrong? Do you need to see the doctor? You left without your insurance card, but I can send all the information right now if you need it."

"No, it's nothing like that," she said quickly, and I felt myself unclench a little. "I had a little fever last night, but I think it's just the flu. I've been coughing."

"Be careful," I warned her, as if she needed the reminder. She knew darned well—*damned* well—not to play around with infection. The last time she'd wound up in the ICU for three days on an antibiotic drip, with a surgical follow-up just for fun.

"I am," she replied hesitantly.

"What is it?" I asked, careful to keep my voice neutral. "You can tell me."

"I think you might've been right about Mom," she said quietly. "Last night they had a big party. A lot of guys came over and they weren't very nice."

"Not nice in what way?"

"Two of them cornered me in the guest house," she whispered. "I'm not exactly a virgin, but this was different, Loni. I've never had anyone treat me like that. They didn't do too much, but only because I ran off and locked myself in a closet. It was horrible."

She fell silent. I wanted to demand more information but sensed she was about three seconds away from falling apart completely.

At least she'd called me.

"Do you want to come home?" I asked, forcing my voice to stay calm and steady. "I know we've had our differences, but you'll be safe here. Maybe we can figure out a way for you to live on your own, where you can be independent and safe at the same time."

She gave a snuffling sob, and I realized she was crying.

"I'm so sorry, Loni," she whispered. "I didn't want to believe you. I was really stupid."

"Let's not worry about that right now. I can fly down there this afternoon, pick you up, and bring you home."

"You don't need to do that," she said. "But if you buy me a ticket home, I'll find a way to pay you back. I can get a cab to the airport, I still have a little cash. But not until tomorrow. Mom said she wanted me to go out with her today, shopping or something. She's going on a trip, I guess. I'd rather leave when she's not around. I don't think I can handle a big fight with her—she's not going to like it. She's been acting really strange."

I desperately wanted to leap into full rescue mode but forced myself to back off. Just calling me for help was huge—Jessica didn't need any more pressure. God, I hated this. All of it.

"Okay. I'll get you a flight home tomorrow, first thing?"

"Maybe around noon?" she asked quietly. "That would be better. She'll be gone by then. There are all these guys around here . . . Some of them have guns, Loni. I think her boyfriend might be a drug dealer or something. He's really rich, but I can't figure out how he earns his money."

I closed my eyes and took a deep breath.

"Entirely possible," I said. "She's never had the best taste in men.

Don't go asking questions, all right? You don't want to do anything to catch attention from people like that."

"Are you mad at me?"

How to answer a question like that?

"I'm more worried about you," I said finally. "I want you to be safe and happy. You didn't pick the best way to accomplish that, but I'm incredibly thankful you're all right. Let's leave it at that, okay?"

"I love you, Loni."

"I love you, too, baby. Take care today and text me every couple of hours, got it? Just stay in touch and let me know you're all right. And keep an eye on the fever, too. If anything feels off, call nine one one and get an ambulance. Don't worry about the bills or anything. Just take care of yourself."

"All right," she whispered. I ended the call and rubbed the back of my neck.

"Fucking great," I muttered, resisting the urge to throw my phone across the parking lot. I wanted to hit something, or punch a car. Instead I leaned back against the wall, banging my head on it a couple of times, just enough to center myself.

"You doin' okay?" Gage asked, stepping out the door. His pose was casual, but his eyes were sharp. I shrugged.

"Just the usual," I said. "Family drama, that kind of thing. Don't worry—it has nothing to do with the business and won't impact our ability to perform."

He nodded slowly, then held the door open for me. I smiled at him and walked through, ready to go inspect the back rooms. I might not be able to control anything else in my life, but I could control cleaning this strip club.

Too bad I'd already cleaned my oven.

Maybe Reese's oven needed a good scrub? I could go out there later and check . . . Might as well text him and see if a schedule change would work, because I'd be out at the airport tomorrow afternoon anyway. If he wanted me to come out a second time this week, he'd just have to be flexible.

Family first—even a big, dumbass biker like Reese Hayes would understand that, right?

REESE

"Your girl did good today."

Gage's words echoed in my head as I drove home. I wasn't quite sure if London qualified as my girl or not, but I wanted her—and not for a quick fuck. She'd been pretty damned upset yesterday and I couldn't blame her.

I'd rubbed Sharon in her face like an asshole.

But the thought of London and Evans rolling around naked together had lodged in my head like a virus. I'd wanted to break shit every time I pictured it, and I couldn't stop picturing it . . . A little petty revenge had seemed fair at the time, given I'm a fuckwit. Then she announced she'd broken up with him. Blew me away, because apparently London wasn't the kind of woman to play men off each other. I'd sort of forgotten what that felt like. Now I respected her even more and felt like a tool in comparison. Screwing Sharon had been juvenile and stupid.

London was turning me into a dumbass kid again, and not in a good way. At least it seemed to go both ways—she wasn't winning any maturity awards for that toilet prank . . . Laughed my ass off when I finally figured it out, though. Heather used to pull shit like that, too.

I needed to call London. Or maybe I should just show up at her place, because she probably wouldn't take a call from me. This sucked. All of it. I liked one-night stands—clean and simple, not some high school bullshit where we danced around each other instead of getting down to business. Couldn't help but wonder what other complications there might be, either. Would she even be able to handle me in bed—the real me? I wasn't used to holding back, and if women couldn't take it, I cut 'em loose.

Fuck it.

If I got my hands on London, I'd be damned if I'd let her go just because things got intense.

I turned around the final bend and spotted the cleaning service van in the driveway. *What the fuck?* I had a brief, intense fantasy that she'd decided she couldn't go one more day without my cock deep inside, and that I'd find her naked and waiting in the bedroom.

Yeah, right.

More likely she was in there injecting my toothpaste with strychnine.

I parked my Harley next to her vehicle, studying it. She only had the one rig, and driving it had to suck. Like piloting a particularly shitty barge. I wondered if she'd ever been on a bike before, whether she'd like it. There was something about her—the restraint, the sense of duty that never seemed to fail . . . She didn't take much time for herself, and I'd be willing to bet she didn't get to let go often enough.

Get her on the back of my bike, bet she'd cream her panties.

Well, that or run screaming. Either could be worked . . . Yeah, I definitely needed to take her for a ride, and now was the time. I'd just gotten it up and running again that morning after way too long stuck in the shop. Huge relief, because when I couldn't ride, I couldn't breathe. Winters seemed to last forever some years, and by spring we were all a little crazy.

Nothing quite like that first ride of the year.

I pulled out my phone—sure enough, she'd called. Fucking great, must've missed it during church. These days all we talked about 'round the table was the cartel, which had been moving in on our territory for close to a year now. They'd hit several of our clubhouses and killed the president of the Devil's Jacks six months back. For a while we skated the edge of a full-on shooting war, but things had quieted down recently, at least on the surface.

I knew the Jacks had been down south taking out select targets.

The Reapers had been doing their part, too, because nobody fucked with us and got away with it. All the houses had full security systems now, and we'd been rolling up select probationary members from the support clubs.

Sooner or later, that shooting war was gonna hit.

We'd be ready for it.

The weekend coming up would be a huge part of that getting ready—patch holders from the Jacks, the Silver Bastards, and the Reapers were coming from all over the region to talk strategy, hopefully put together a joint offensive. We couldn't just sneak around forever, or wait for them to bring the fight to us.

I flipped through my phone, finding the text she'd sent when I hadn't answered the phone.

LONDON: Change of plans. I'll be out at your place this afternoon. Something came up for tomorrow.

Something was comin' up for today, too. My dick.

Christ, next I'll be making fart jokes.

Juvenile as fuck.

Standing outside my front door, I smelled that acrid, horrible stench I remembered from her house last weekend. I turned the knob and stepped inside to find London standing on a stool in the living room, angrily dusting the weapons collection over the fireplace. She wore cutoff shorts and a black tank top—straight out of a wet dream . . . except for that god-awful stink filling the air.

She rose onto her tiptoes, one hand braced against the mantel as she reached higher. Her shirt pulled up, exposing a narrow band of skin, and I held back a groan.

God damn. I needed to either fuck her or fire her, because this in-between shit was *not* workin' for me. 'Course Gage wanted her crew working out at The Line permanently, so I guess that meant firing was off the table.

Okay, then. I'd take one for the team and fuck her.

"I'm cleaning your oven," she announced loudly, turning to face me, hands on her hips. The stance was pure challenge. Spoiling for a fight. Why, I couldn't imagine, but it was a good look on her—fire in her eyes and all that shit.

I'd screw the fire right out of her. My cock took note, tightening just enough to be uncomfortable, and I decided what the hell. No time like the present.

"What crawled up your ass?" I asked. London scowled.

"I'm just trying to do my job. I was supposed to come tomorrow, but I'll be at the airport instead. Jessie is coming back home."

Interesting.

"You don't seem too happy about that," I said, sauntering across the floor toward her. I came to a stop about three feet away, which put my eyes level with her boobs. She sniffed, then turned and lifted her arms to reach one of the higher knives with her duster. It made her tits jiggle under the tank, a sight my cock appreciated greatly.

"My cousin's boyfriend is apparently some kind of criminal," she said tightly. "I guess the place is crawling with scary goons. A couple of them cornered Jess last night, terrified her. She says she's safe until tomorrow, but I wanted her to come home tonight. She said she'd text me but she hasn't."

I stilled.

"You know anything about these guys?"

She turned back toward me, shaking her head. A smudge of dirt ran across her forehead and her bright red hair flopped around like she'd just gotten out of bed.

Not a bad look on her at all.

"Nothing, but I know I want to hurt them. She said I shouldn't fly down there. Probably a good thing, because I don't need to spend the rest of my life in jail and that's where I'll end up if I get my hands on these assholes."

"So you came out here instead? Not sure how to take that, sweetheart."

She put her hands on her hips.

"I won't be around tomorrow, and I don't want you accusing me of backing out of our deal."

Yeah, right.

"So you think I'm such an asshole I won't let you off the hook to pick up your cousin from the airport?" I asked, trying not to smirk because I had her cold. She'd come here because when shit hit the fan, she wanted to be near me. Might not be ready to admit it, but that didn't change what was really going on.

"You're enough of an asshole to have sex in front of me."

"Yeah, I'm a real piece of work—a single man fucking a willing partner in the privacy of my own home. Sometimes I cry myself to sleep, I'm so ashamed of my actions."

"Are you saying the timing was a total coincidence?" she demanded.

I laughed.

"You're the one who showed up early," I reminded her. "But yeah, I'll give you that. I'd already decided to keep Sharon around all afternoon, make a point of her bein' here. Didn't plan to screw her in front of you, but I wasn't disappointed when you walked in and saw it, either. I was fucking pissed off, London. I was there for you when you needed it, I took care of you, and then you called me another man's name. One of my least favorite men, for the record."

Her eyes widened and her mouth opened, then closed.

"You're a jerk."

"No, I'm an asshole. You wanna fight like a grown-up, start using grown-up words."

"Fuck off," she hissed, and I swear her hair started levitating a little like Medusa. Okay, so it might've just been how she shook her head, but either way it was hotter than hell. The fighting had been fun, but we'd wasted enough time. Time to get inside that tight cunt of hers, check out whether it felt as good wrapped around me as my imagination suggested.

I wrapped an arm around her waist and lifted her off the chair, hoisting her horizontally against my side as I started toward the bedroom.

"What are you doing?"

"Enough foreplay. Time to get down to business, babe."

"I'm not your babe. Put me down!"

"Not gonna happen."

She started kicking, which would've been a lot more effective if her legs could've reached any part of my body from that position. Not my first rodeo. Then she slapped at me, prying at my arm around her waist.

"Careful, don't want me to drop you."

"God! How can you be doing this? It's not fair—you're too strong for me. I hate you!"

I decided how I could be doing this was fucking obvious, so it didn't need answering. Good thing, too, because she dug her fingernails into my arm so hard I think she drew blood.

"Stop playin' around, London." We passed through the kitchen. My bedroom door was open. I kicked it shut behind us, then reached around to lock it because I'd be damned if I'd put up with any interruptions at this point.

Then I tossed her on the bed.

London scuttled back like a crab, bracing herself against the headboard with wide eyes.

"What's wrong with you?" she demanded breathlessly.

"I'm horny," I said, my voice matter-of-fact. I sat on the edge of the bed and pulled off my boots. I grabbed my T-shirt and drew it up and over my head, tossing it over to land on top of my dresser. Then I stood and went for my pants.

London squeaked again.

"Door's right there," I said. "Locks from the inside, so not like you're trapped here. If you want to leave, go. Otherwise take your clothes off."

I stood and shoved down my pants, cock springing free to smack against my stomach. She gasped and I smiled, because I knew the view was generally considered a good one.

"Clothes?" I reminded her.

She sat up, then sort of pulled her dignity around her like a heavy cape, as if that could protect her.

It couldn't.

"Let's talk about this," she said quietly. "We should set some rules, figure out where we're going."

"We're going to fuck. Then I think we'll probably do it again. After that I'll buy you dinner, but only if you're nice."

"I brought dinner with me," she muttered.

"Christ, you'd be perfect if you didn't have such a stick up your ass."

I crawled forward on the bed, grabbing her ankles and jerking them down abruptly. She squawked, but she didn't fight when I caught her hands and pressed them back into the bed, over her head. Then I lowered my mouth to catch hers—had to see if she actually tasted as good as I remembered.

She did.

I thrust my tongue in deep, closing my eyes as I savored finally getting inside her body. At first she lay passive. Then her tongue started playing with mine, a game of chase and follow I could've kept up for hours if my dick wasn't on fire. Kneeing her legs apart, I settled down between them, realizing the hard way I was in serious danger of denim burn on my cock.

I pulled back and smiled down at her. Her cheeks were flushed, her eyes were bright, and that shiny red hair of hers lay across the pillow like a lava flow.

"I like that color on you," I said, shifting to the side so I could slide my hand down to her stomach. The button of her jeans opened easily enough, and her hips surged upward to meet my fingers as they found her clit.

Wet as hell. Beautiful.

"Thanks," she muttered. "I didn't think you'd noticed. You didn't say anything the other day."

"Oh, I noticed."

"Holy crap, that feels good . . ." she whispered.

"I do my best."

Her breasts rose and fell rapidly as her breathing increased. I slid my fingers up and down, dipping into her pussy and then pressing in and upward as my thumb kept the action going outside. Finally I pulled back and she whimpered, protesting.

To hell with this slow shit.

"You're wearing too much," I said. "Take something off, because otherwise I'm going to start ripping things."

LONDON

Take something off, because otherwise I'm going to start ripping things.

I nearly had a heart attack.

Reese would let me walk out the door if I asked. I knew he would . . . But if I walked out, I might never come back, and in the past five minutes I'd come to the clear realization that I wanted to come here in every sense of the word.

He shoved up my shirt, exposing the red satin bra I'd decided to wear while cleaning his house for no particular reason I cared to acknowledge. Reese's mouth caught my nipple and I forgot all about taking things off.

This was unfortunate. He hadn't been kidding about the clothes. Apparently sucking me through the fabric wasn't good enough, because seconds later he caught the center fastener of my bra and snapped it in half. My breasts spilled free and then I felt the heat of his mouth pulling me back in, deep. His fingers burrowed down into my shorts, finding my clit and rubbing it hard enough that it should've hurt. Instead it just felt really, really good.

Need grew out of my center, sending tingles through my entire body. I couldn't think, but I could sure as hell feel. It felt good. *Real* good. Better than I remembered sex, and I remembered sex as something very nice indeed.

Reese switched to my other breast, and somehow I regained enough awareness to reach down between us and cup his hard length.

His *cock.*

I liked the word, I really did. I liked it a lot and I liked the fact that I was free to use it as much as I wanted. I wanted to see more of it, too.

"I want your cock," I managed to whisper, and Reese froze.

Then things changed.

Before he'd been restrained, if not gentle. Yeah, that was over now. Within seconds he had me flipped over on my stomach, and then I felt my shorts ripping down my body. I'm not quite sure what happened to my panties, but a heartbeat later his hand came under my stomach, lifting me to my knees.

I barely had time to catch my breath before I felt the head of his erection at my entrance. Not for long, though. He thrust in—hard—which was more than a little startling because I hadn't seen any real action for years.

"Holy crap," I grunted, and he stilled, letting me grow used to the feel of him deep inside. I felt pinned, impaled . . . vulnerable. "Oh my God, I can't believe you just did that."

"Believe it," he muttered, fingers finding my clit again. He toyed with it and I squirmed, squeezing down on him every time he found just the right spot.

"Fuck . . ." he groaned. Then his hips pulled back and he started moving in me. He wasn't gentle and as he hit home I gasped, because the man was big and it sort of hurt but in a weirdly good way.

Did I mention it'd been a while?

Fortunately, Reese "Picnic" Hayes had magic fingers, because by the third time he filled me, I'd lost all sense of time and space. All I could feel was the pressure building through me, centered on my clit and the delicious friction of him pushing deep against the front wall of my vagina.

My vibrator just couldn't compete.

Then I had a horrible, horrible thought.

"I'm not on birth control."

"Got a condom," Hayes grunted. "And a vasectomy."

Huh. How had I missed him suiting up? I couldn't feel it, either, which was probably because I was so damned wet. Reese caught my clit in his fingers, almost pinching at it, which should've hurt like hell but was quite possibly the most amazing thing anyone has ever done to me.

It was enough to push me over.

I gasped, my muscles clenching down hard on him as I came. He groaned. Then his hands caught my hips, which was a good thing because my entire body ceased to function and I collapsed.

Reese ignored my mental and physical crash, lifting my ass up high for his penetration, pumping into me faster and faster as he got close to his own release. Then I felt a renewed tingle of sensation, and realized that I might be capable of achieving the Holy Grail for all women—multiple orgasms.

"Up on your hands," Hayes told me harshly. Somehow I pushed myself up, startled I had the strength. His hand caught my hair and jerked back. I screamed and reared back on my knees, bracing my hands against the bedstead.

"Oh my God," I gasped, wondering if it was possible for eyes to literally roll into a person's head from the intensity of an experience.

This time I came hard, no long buildup of sensation or gentle warming. Nope. Just an explosion of lust and satisfaction braced like an animal in the home of a man I wasn't even dating.

Glorious.

Reese pulsed deep inside me as he came. Then he stilled, my butt pulled tight against his groin, his fingers digging into me hard enough I figured I'd find bruises later.

The thought made me giggle.

I might have a *sex injury*!

Reese let me go, pulling out and catching the condom. I collapsed onto my stomach, still panting, wondering if I could just go to sleep for a while. Pretend the outside world wasn't real, and that Jessica wasn't in the shit yet again.

His thick, muscular arm came around me, pulling me back into the cradle of his body.

"That was very nice," I murmured, eyes closed.

"Nice? I think I'm insulted," he replied, although he sounded smug as hell. His hand cupped my breast, casually playing with my nipple as we lay in silence.

"I'm going to be sore tomorrow . . ." I said, yawning. "But totally worth it."

"Sore? I wasn't that rough."

"No, just been a while."

"How long?"

"Well, my ex-husband left six years ago, when I got custody of Jess, so . . . six years."

Reese's hand stopped moving.

"You haven't had sex in six years?" he asked, his voice incredulous.

I frowned. "You don't have to say it like that."

"Like what?"

"Like I'm a freak."

"You're not a freak, sweetheart," he replied. "But gotta admit, I'm surprised. You're gorgeous."

I sighed.

"Single moms who run businesses don't have fabulous social lives, Reese," I told him.

"Well, glad you picked me to break the dry spell," he said finally. "You're not half bad for a chick who's out of practice. I'd give you a six out of ten."

I smacked his arm playfully and he squeezed me tight.

"Okay, make that nine out of ten," he whispered, kissing the top of my head. "I'm holding out the last point in the hopes you'll give me a blow job next time."

"Dream on."

He chuckled quietly, and then I felt his breathing grow regular as he drifted off to sleep. Letting my thoughts go, I fell into the darkness, wrapped tight and protected in his strength and warmth.

Perfect.

CHAPTER EIGHT

My phone woke us up early in the evening.

I couldn't figure out where I was at first, or why there was a heavy arm holding me prisoner. I tried to grab the phone and Reese tightened his grip, grunting.

"It might be Jessica," I told him, shoving at the arm until he let me catch the call.

It wasn't her.

Of *course* it wasn't her . . . Just because she'd realized things weren't so sunny down in San Diego didn't mean that she'd magically turned into a responsible person. I managed to push Reese off and lean up onto my elbow to take the call anyway, because Caller ID said it was Melanie, and I'd sworn I wouldn't ignore her.

"Hey, Loni," she asked, her voice hesitant and a little shaky.

"Is everything okay?"

Reese reached out and caught me again, pulling me back into the crook of his arm. I found my face pressed against his chest while his fingers started running through my hair. I couldn't believe we'd actually had sex. S. E. X. For real. Wasn't sure how to process that. On the one hand, I felt incredible . . . Warm and full of endorphins that still gave me a full on glow. On the other, I knew I needed to protect myself because Reese was a Grade A man-whore, and I couldn't let myself get attached to him.

Fun to play with but not a keeper.

Then again, keepers weren't part of my new, improved plan to be a free and independent woman. Unfortunately, neither were hurt feelings and picking up Jessica from the airport tomorrow afternoon. The plan wasn't off to a good start.

"Loni?" Mel asked. I blinked.

"Yes?"

"Aren't you going to answer me?"

Oh my God, I'd done it again. I'd forgotten about Mel—while I was on the phone with her, no less. I was such a shitty person. Ugh.

"What was the question again?"

"Can I come over to your place tonight?" she asked, her voice full of hope. "Dad's in a real bad mood. I have some news . . ."

Uh-oh.

"What is it?"

"I think my mom took off," she whispered. "That's what Dad told me, and I haven't seen her for two days. He's been skipping work. He's really drunk right now—I'm kind of scared. Do you think I could stay with you for a couple days?"

I closed my eyes, feeling a rush of hot, righteous indignation. How *dare* that asshole do this to Melanie? She was a sweet girl, a good girl who worked hard and deserved happiness.

"Oh, baby . . . Of course you can. Go let yourself into the house. You can get anything you want out of the kitchen, just make yourself comfortable. Settle yourself in Jess's room, okay?"

"What time will you be home?" she asked in a small voice. I burrowed into Reese's side and felt his hand sweep down to cup my bottom. He caught my knee with his other hand, pulling it up and over his leg until I sort of straddled him in a weird, lying-down kind of way.

His erection stirred to life, and I looked down through the faded light to see it. Still couldn't quite believe that thing had not only gone into me, but made me come twice in a row.

Shitty to be me, because Mellie needed me more than I needed Reese's dick.

"I'll be home in twenty, thirty minutes." Hayes snorted, and I smacked his chest to shut him up.

"Thanks, Loni. You know . . . Sometimes I wish you were my mom."

A lump grew in my throat.

"Well, you're part of my family," I told her. "Don't worry, we'll figure something out."

"Thanks . . ."

I ended the call and then dropped the phone, nestling into the muscles of his strong chest.

"Everything okay?"

"Define okay," I said, feeling a bitter smile spread across my face. "Jess has a friend named Melanie. Her home situation isn't so good, so she spends a lot of time with us. I think I just invited her to move in with me."

"Nice of you."

"She's a good kid," I said, sighing. "And she's nearly nineteen—older than Jess. They graduated in the same class but Mel had a late birthday and Jess had an early one. They probably should've held her back a year along the way."

"Sounds like this girl can do all right, you give her a fighting chance," he said. "But I want you to stick around a while longer. I'm not finished with you yet."

At that, he caught my hips and tugged me up and onto his body. My legs tangled with his and my breasts crushed into his chest, all of which made me wish to hell that Mellie's dad had chosen another night to get drunk. Of course, he was drunk every night, thus her mom's decision to take off. Nicole should've left his ass years ago—but she should've taken her daughter with her.

Selfish bitch.

Mellie was so eager to please and easy to be around. I couldn't imagine why her mom would pull this shit. Thinking about it made me feel sick. That's why, when Reese cupped my bare ass with both hands and pulled me into him, I shoved against his chest.

"I have to go."

"I'm sensin' a pattern here," he muttered, frowning at me. "Every time I get you horizontal, you run away. Not a fan, sweetheart."

"If one of your girls needed help, you'd be out of here so fast I'd find myself on the floor."

He sighed and I knew I had him. Then one of his hands slid slowly up my body, catching me around the back of my neck. I let him kiss me, amazed that such an intense man could be so gentle. His tongue flirted with mine and his fingers tightened on me. His penis—no, his *cock*—kept getting harder and I felt a restless ache stir between my legs.

I have to get the hell out of here, I realized. *Otherwise I won't make it.*

The kiss ended and I pulled back, staring down at his face. The man was beautiful, no other way to describe it. His short brown hair was sticking up all around his head at the moment. His eyes were bright blue, like aquamarine birthstones shining in the center of his face, and the scruff covering his chin held just a hint of gray. Not enough to make him look old. Just . . . mature.

And the arms holding me?

I'd never met anyone with such strong, safe arms.

You're not safe, my brain hissed. *He's a dangerous man, you have no idea what he might be involved with.*

My brain made a good point—I knew damned well that the club

had business interests that weren't totally legitimate. Everyone knew it. That's why they paid so well—they weren't just buying cleaning services, they were buying silence.

"I'm going home," I whispered, kissing his cheek softly. Then I tried to roll off him, stand up. He held me tight for a second longer.

"You sure?" he asked. "If you're worried about Melanie's dad, I can send one of the guys to watch her."

I shook my head. "Her physical safety isn't the problem. She's a young woman whose mother just abandoned her and she's terrified. She needs hugs, not a bodyguard."

Reese grew very still, and his fingers dug deep into my flesh.

"You didn't mention her mom before," he said, his voice deceptively calm, but with an undercurrent of strong emotion I couldn't place. What was that all about?

Then it clicked. Heather. She'd had to leave their girls behind. Totally different circumstances, but that didn't change the end result—young women without a mother, forced to grow up too early.

"Her dad is a drunk," I said, deciding five more minutes wouldn't make a difference. I let my head fall down on his chest, and he loosened his fingers, running them through my hair again. "I think he was beating on Nicole. She's Mellie's mom. I tried talking to her a couple of times but she didn't want to hear it."

"And now she's taken off and left her kid behind? Fuckin' cunt. He treats her like that, he'll treat her girl like that, too."

Wow, that was harsh . . . but fair. Nicole *was* a cunt. She abandoned her daughter to a drunk who liked to hit women. If she didn't fit the word, I wasn't sure who did.

"Don't worry—I'll take care of Mellie. She's like my own."

He looked thoughtful, then nodded.

"Okay, let's get some shit straight and then you can head out."

Great, here it came. The Talk. Fortunately I was ahead of him for once.

"Don't worry, Reese. I know this was just a one-off for you, and that you don't want a relationship. That's what I needed, too, so in a way it's perfect. No harm, no foul. We can just pretend this never happened."

A scowl covered his face. "What the fuck are you talking about?"

"Us. Or rather, the fact that there isn't an 'us.' I get it—you like to sleep around. I had a good time, but I'm not expecting a ring or anything."

His eyes widened, and I smirked.

"Although I'll be around if you want another booty call," I added slyly.

Yay me! I'm a sophisticated woman who knows the difference between love and sex.

Reese's scowl grew deeper, and then suddenly he moved and I was under him, pinned down against the bed. He pulled my hands up, holding them prisoner above my head.

"Are you fucked in the head?" he demanded harshly. "You get laid for the first time in years, it's phenomenal—"

"Well, aren't you the modest one?"

"It's *phenomenal*," he repeated, emphasizing the word heavily. "And now you're just going to ignore me? I am not fuckin' down with that."

Now it was my turn to be startled.

"I see you with women all the time," I said, confused. "I know how you operate. Strictly sex. I'm not looking to change that."

"The fuck?" he muttered, shaking his head. It was like we were having two completely different conversations, because I had no idea why he was acting this way. "You're so fucking stupid I could strangle you. Don't know exactly what we're doing here just yet, but it's not just sex. For one thing, I'm not okay with your seein' anyone else, especially Deputy Dick."

"Right, and I suppose you're planning to be true and faithful? I don't buy it. You're a known man-whore. Also, you *ever* call me stupid again and I'll dump paint stripper on your bike. That isn't a threat, it's a promise."

He looked me straight in the eyes, his face grim and serious.

"I have no plans to fuck anyone but you, at least for now."

"I don't believe you," I told him, feeling almost wistful. "And you don't need to be saying things like this, because I'm not interested in tying you down."

"Listen. To. Me," he said, his face growing colder, which I wouldn't have considered possible ten seconds earlier. "I'll admit it—I've slept around since Heather died. Slept around a lot, but none of them ever felt real to me. There's something about you, London, something that's *real* in a way I can't even begin to explain. I like it and I want it and you dumped your boyfriend and came to me when you were hurting. Guess that means you want it, too. So far as I figure, that makes you mine."

"I don't understand," I whispered. "We hardly know each other."

"And we won't get to know each other if we're out there screwing other people, so I think we're gonna have to stop doing it. Should be easy enough for you, under the circumstances."

"So you're saying you want to be in an exclusive relationship with me? I thought you didn't do that. What about Heather?"

"Heather is dead. I'm not. Now I'm gonna kiss you and you're gonna kiss me back. Then I'll let you go home because it's important and I respect that. Tomorrow you'll go get your girl at the airport and I'll give you the evening together, but come Friday night you're with me. Havin' a party out at the Armory and I want you there. You got a problem with any of that?"

I shook my head quickly, relatively certain that "havin' a problem with that" wasn't really a solid option at this point.

"Great. Let's get started."

Then he kissed me, and not in a laid-back kind of way. His mouth took possession, head slanting as his tongue pushed in. It wasn't a seductive kiss, or even a comfortable one. Nope, this was his body telling mine we had unfinished business. I didn't even notice I'd spread my legs for him until he pulled away long enough to slide on a fresh condom. Then he was deep inside, claiming and conquering me yet again.

Turns out you can improve on phenomenal. Go figure.

Half an hour later, when Reese gave me another kiss, it was a quick peck through my van window.

"Sure you don't want someone keeping an eye on your house? If her daddy's a mean drunk, might not be a bad idea."

I shook my head, which jiggled my chest. He'd destroyed my bra, unfortunately—and I was a big enough girl that going bra-less wasn't the best of options.

"Mel's spent at least two nights a week at my place for the past three years. Not sure what the long-term plan will be, but I'll get her set up. Unlike Jessica, she's got a job and she's planning to start classes at NIC in August. They've got student housing."

He smiled at me, reaching out and tucking a strand of my bright red hair behind my ear.

"You know, this is sexy as fuck," he said. "But you were gorgeous as a blonde, too."

"Thanks," I whispered. Then I pulled away and turned the key in my ignition.

The starter turned over, but the engine didn't catch.

I frowned, and tried again. "It's not starting."

"Your check engine light is on."

"I know," I said absently. I pushed on the gas pedal and tried again. The starter whined in protest. "It goes on and off all the time."

"Sweetheart, you do realize that when the check engine light comes on, you're supposed to check the engine, right?"

I shot him the Look of Death, and he laughed.

"Want a ride back to your place?" he asked. "I can figure this out for you, but I'm thinkin' if you want to be with your girl while she's all upset, now isn't the time to start tearing apart your rig."

I closed my eyes and sighed.

"Thank you," I said. "That would be great. I can't believe it's not working. What am I going to do about picking up Jess tomorrow? Shit, now I'll have to rent something and it'll be a fortune and—"

"London. Honey. Settle the fuck down. One of the perks of datin' a man who owns a repair shop is that shit like this is no longer a crisis. I'll find something for you to borrow while I take care of it, okay? Now get your ass out of there and over to my bike. I'm takin' you home."

He pulled the door open and I stepped out. He held out his hand.

"What?"

"Keys, babe. Gonna need keys if you want me to fix your car."

"Don't fix anything without checking with me first," I said, my voice serious. "If it's really bad, I may need to go out and find something new. This van is nearly twelve years old, not sure how much life she has left in her."

"Keys?"

I pulled off the van key, which I kept on a little dealie that snapped off my main keychain for situations exactly like this one.

"Great. Now get your ass on the bike."

I stepped toward the big Harley, which was black and silver, with the Reapers symbol painted on the gas tank. The seats were black leather, the chrome was shiny, and the whole thing looked ginormous now that I was actually standing right next to it. Hayes handed me a helmet. I studied it, bemused. It'd been a strange day and now it was getting stranger—the president of a motorcycle club was giving me a ride home.

After fucking me.

And he planned to fuck me some more.

Wow.

It took everything I had to bite back a little *squee* of excitement, because there's not a woman on earth who doesn't secretly want to ride off into the sunset with a bad man on a bike . . . Especially after having excellent sex with that man.

I glanced up at the sky. Sure enough, it was streaked with pinks and blues and gorgeous clouds, glowing as the very last of the day's sunlight kissed the north Idaho mountains.

"It goes on your head."

I blinked, confused.

"The helmet," Reese said, slowly and distinctly. "It goes on your head."

Then he smiled at me and I think I might have blushed, which is kind of crazy considering I'm thirty-eight and well past the blushing years.

"Where do you go when you drift off like that?" he asked. I laughed and gave a shrug.

"Everywhere, I guess. I've always done it. Used to get in big trouble at school for it, because they thought I was ignoring them on purpose. But things just catch my imagination and then I'm off. I'm sorry—I wasn't trying to be rude."

"Doesn't bother me," he said. "Just curious. Let's go make sure your girl Mellie is all right. Come mornin' I'll get one of the boys to run a car over for you."

"Thank you," I said, wondering if any of this was real.

"Just remember, Friday night is mine."

"Friday night is yours," I repeated.

Then I climbed on Reese Hayes's bike, wrapped my arms around him tight, and let him carry me off into the sunset.

It was full dark by the time we reached my place.

I didn't want to get off the bike and step back into reality . . . there was something incredibly thrilling and powerful about riding with Reese, and I wanted to enjoy it while I could. Whatever he might have said earlier, I wasn't exactly holding my breath that this would turn into a real relationship. The odds weren't in our favor. But until things fell apart, I'd let myself savor the moment—giving up control and trusting him to keep me safe was the most liberating thing I'd done in six years.

When he turned off the Harley, I couldn't seem to make my hands let go of him. This didn't seem to bother Reese. He caught them in his own and pulled me tighter against his back. I smelled the leather and felt his strength between my legs. Surreal.

Then he let go.

I climbed off the bike and back into reality. The porch light came on and the front door opened to reveal Mellie. She stopped dead when she saw Reese, and her jaw actually dropped.

Fair enough.

Last time she'd seen me, I'd been dating a deputy sheriff. Now I'd come home with an outlaw biker, and I'd be willing to bet that anyone seeing us would know we'd been together. There was an intimacy between us that hadn't been there before. I felt it in the way he put his hand on my back protectively, and the way I found myself leaning toward him.

Oh, and it probably didn't help that I'd lost my bra—the night air was cool enough to nip me out in a big way.

Mellie had always been shy, so I was surprised when she stepped off the porch and started walking across the lawn. The kid must've been even more upset than she sounded on the phone. I'd just started toward her when a horrific burst of sound and heat and light exploded out of the house. Reese tackled me to the ground, covering me with his body.

Everything fell perfectly, utterly silent.

What the hell had happened?

Reese lay on top of me for long seconds. I couldn't hear his voice but I felt the vibrations of his yelling through his body. Why couldn't

I hear him? After an eternity, he rolled off me and I looked up to find an inferno where my house had been, flames licking up toward the sky.

I realized my house had exploded.

My house had fucking exploded!

An instant later I remembered how close Melanie had been when it went up, and my heart stopped.

"Mellie!" I yelled, grabbing Reese's arm, jerking him toward me. "We have to find Mellie!"

He yelled something back at me, but I couldn't tell what it was. Then he was on his feet, running across the lawn. I staggered upward, trying to figure out what the hell was happening. Neighbors were pouring out into the street all around us. Slowly sounds took shape—mostly an unpleasant ringing—and I realized the force of the explosion had temporarily deafened me.

Reese was a dark silhouette against the fire, searching through the debris. He stopped suddenly, and I saw him lift Mel's still form, carrying her toward me. Then he was laying her in the grass and noises started filling my ears again. I fell to my knees next to her body.

Oh God. Mellie . . .

She looked dead.

"I'm calling nine one one!" someone yelled behind us, startling me. I was still stunned—I couldn't seem to *think*. I needed to check her pulse, make sure she was breathing. Old training kicked in, and I could have cried in gratitude for the CPR classes I'd taken over the years. I found her pulse. Weak, but definitely present. Then I leaned my face into her mouth and nose, praying I'd feel her breathe against my skin.

Air tickled my cheek.

"She's alive," I whispered. Tears rolled down my face.

"Thank fuck for that," Reese muttered, pulling me into his arms as one of my neighbors knelt next to Melanie, covering her with a blanket. The wall of safety came crashing down around me and I started to shake.

My house was gone. I'd almost lost Melanie . . . What the hell could possibly explain this?

The wailing howls of emergency vehicles filled the air. I heard a car screech to a stop, and out of the corner of my eye I vaguely noticed that a man in a sheriff's uniform had stepped out, speaking into his shoulder radio urgently.

Then a fire engine rumbled down the street. Firefighters ran past me, dragging their hoses with them, and EMTs swarmed Mellie's still form.

To my relief they weren't doing anything that looked serious and scary like you see on TV—no chest compressions or IVs or shocking her with shiny paddles. Instead they monitored her vitals, voices calm as they methodically got a neck brace on her before rolling her onto a backboard. Seconds later they lifted the entire apparatus—backboard and all—onto the rolling gurney and started back toward their vehicle.

"That board won't do much good if you already paralyzed her. Should've left her where you found her," I heard a familiar voice say. I looked up to find Nate standing over me, his voice full of venom. I pulled away from Reese and stood slowly. Nate reached a hand down to help me, but Reese caught my arm.

"Stay the fuck away from my woman," he growled. Nate's eyes went wide.

"Guess that cunt's not made of gold after all?" he commented. Reese lunged toward him and without thinking I jumped between the two men.

"I don't have time for this," I shouted, staring them down like two little boys who needed a time-out. "I need to check on Mel. Reese had to get her away from the fire, Nate. If you'd been here, you'd have done the same thing. She was practically on top of it. And

Reese? What happened between me and Nate is between me and Nate. I'm a big girl and I can fight my own battles. I'm going to follow Mel to the hospital, and you better fucking behave yourselves because I'm not in the mood."

Both men gaped at me. I didn't care—these weren't normal times and I could give a fuck about their little pissing match. I decided to ignore them and follow Melanie.

"Is she all right?" I asked the EMT, who was busy securing the gurney in the ambulance. She glanced over at me but didn't miss a beat.

"Dunno," she said. "They'll check her head at the hospital. Looks like she hit something hard. You have any idea what happened here?"

"None," I said, my voice grim. "But we're really damned lucky to be alive. She was just coming out of the house when it exploded."

"Definitely lucky," she said. None of this added up.

"Houses don't just explode. Do they?" I didn't realize I'd asked the question out loud until the woman answered me.

"I've seen stranger things," the EMT said. "Are you a family member? We're headed toward Kootenai. There's another bus coming, they'll be able to check you out—she's higher priority and we need to get her in. I'm going to close the doors now. Step back, please."

"I'll meet you there," I said anxiously. I turned to find Nate and Reese still in their standoff, staring each other down in the flickering light of the flames. My neighbor, Danica, walked up to me and wordlessly wrapped a blanket around my shoulders.

"You okay?" she asked. "Can I do anything?"

"Can you give me a ride to the hospital?" I asked, the words broken by a sudden, harsh cough. "I need to make sure Melanie is okay."

"Of course," she said. "Do you want to check in with the police first? I'm sure they'll want to talk to you, probably have a ton of questions they need to ask."

"The answers will still be the same after I make sure Mellie is okay," I said tightly. "Just get me out of here."

"You got it," she said. "Car's parked behind the house, back in the alley. Good thing, too, because everyone on the street is blocked in. Um . . . I couldn't help but notice that big guy over there was with you. And that the other one used to be with you. You want to touch base with them before you leave?"

"I don't think so," I said, shaking my head, frustrated. "They can play caveman without me. All I care about right now is getting to the hospital."

CHAPTER NINE

REESE

"Here's what you need to know," I said to Evans, clenching my fist because I've never wanted to hit a man more in my life. I wasn't exactly used to holding back. "London is with me now. You don't talk to her, you don't touch her, you don't think about her. Otherwise we'll have another discussion, and that one won't happen where you have a thousand cop buddies to save your ass. Got me?"

Evans studied me and shook his head slowly, the flickering light of the fire throwing his face into shadow.

"I don't want her. I could give a shit about London Armstrong."

Yeah, and my next bike was gonna be a Honda.

"Then you won't mind staying the hell away from her," I said. "Things won't get ugly and I won't find myself diggin' a hole down in the Bitterroots."

His eyes went big.

Yeah, fucker. You heard that right.

"Just to be clear—you just threatened a cop with murder? Not smart, Hayes."

I laughed.

"You got a great imagination," I told him. "I think we're finished here."

His expression turned ugly, and I thought I saw a glimpse of something like hatred in his face. Fair enough—feeling was mutual. Then the sheriff himself stepped between us, smacking me on the back before gripping my shoulder meaningfully.

"You okay, Pic?" he asked.

"Still here, Bud. Kind of concerned about my woman's place, though. Houses don't usually blow up," I said, holding my gaze fixed on Evans. "Not too impressed with your boy, either. He called London a cunt. For the record, she's the owner of this property."

"Evans, get back to your car," Bud snapped. Deputy Dick gave him a mock salute, then ambled off. "Goddamn but I hate that man. I think he's gonna run for sheriff next election, too."

"He can run," I said, my voice cold. "He ain't gonna win."

"Not so sure about that," Bud replied. "My Lavonne met up with Jennifer Burley at the casino last week. Jen said that Nate's dad has already started talking about mounting a campaign for the boy. Fund-raising."

"If you had any balls, you'd fire his ass."

"I fire his ass, the commissioners will have mine," Bud said bluntly. "You know that. I don't think there's a politician in the county his daddy doesn't have something on."

"Well, maybe you should've been more careful," I told him, losing patience. "Might be time to throw yourself on your sword, you ever consider that? He'll do a lot more harm before he's done."

Bud's eyes narrowed and I shrugged off his hand. Fucking coward. I'd had just about enough of this shit.

"So that your woman's place?" he asked, jerking his chin toward the burning house. "Falls under my jurisdiction. Just outside the city line limits. Anything I should know?"

"Yeah, that's my woman's place," I said slowly, the words feeling strange in my mouth. "But we're a new thing. This wouldn't have anything to do with the club, even if it wasn't accidental. What's your gut read?"

"Probably a gas leak and buildup," Bud said. "That's what the firefighters think, and they got good instincts about this kind of shit. Nobody'll say anything official until there's a full investigation, of course, but all the signs are there. We're damned lucky it's not full of crispy critters. She have a gas stove?"

"She did," I said, shrugging. "Last time I was here, I smelled it. She said she was cleaning the oven. No big deal."

"Looks like a pretty big deal to me."

"No shit."

"Off the record, EMTs think the kid'll be fine. Wanna check for internal bleeds, spinal trauma, all that shit. But it's just routine. We'll need to talk to both of them, of course."

"Of course," I responded, noticing for the first time that Mellie was gone. Damn, where was London?

"She went to the hospital," Bud said dryly, clearly reading my expression. "Saw her leave while you were pissin' over her with Evans. Somethin' to consider next time you feel like fighting over a woman instead of taking care of her."

I turned on him, my face grim. How had I missed her taking off? And since when did Bud have the balls to lecture me? Then I realized the bastard was right.

Fuck.

I was out of practice with this relationship shit, but the pissing matches were all but hardwired into my DNA after so many years in the club.

"Headin' to the hospital," I told him shortly. "She'll be upset, confused. I want updates, but you won't question her until tomorrow, got me?"

"Yeah," Bud said, nodding. "No real reason to, so far as I can tell. Nothing that can't wait. That'll change, we find any evidence this wasn't an accident."

"You find any evidence it wasn't an accident, you call me," I told him, my voice cold and serious. "First call you make. You scared Nate Evans's daddy'll go after your job? I'll go after your fucking *family*. We clear?"

Bud smiled, his mouth tight.

We were clear.

LONDON

It was around ten p.m. when Reese sat down next to me in the hospital waiting room, handing over a cup of coffee without saying a word. Wasn't sure how I felt about him being there. Sure, we'd had great sex. But the whole showdown with my sort-of ex? I was a grown-up. I didn't need that kind of complication, no matter how fabulous he was in the sack.

On the other hand, he *had* thrown himself over me when the house blew up. He definitely got points for that.

"You over your snit with Nate?" I asked him, rubbing the back of my neck.

"I think we cleared things up," he said. "You hear anything about Mellie yet?"

"They think she's probably all right," I told him wearily. I'd had a hell of an adrenaline rush, but it was starting to wear off. "They're doing some scans to make sure, but sounds like a mild concussion. Might keep her overnight."

"Her dad show up?"

I snorted.

"Her dad was too drunk to understand me when I called him," I admitted. "I think he said she wasn't welcome at his house but it's hard to tell. He wasn't making a whole lot of sense. I can't let her go back there. She can stay . . ."

Shit.

That's when it hit me—I had nowhere for her to stay . . . or for me. I had to find somewhere to live. Immediately. I remembered someone saying something about the Red Cross and a hotel room, but the details were blank. Reality hit me all at once—I looked at Reese, eyes wide.

"I'm homeless," I whispered. "Oh my God, I don't have anywhere to live. Jessie is flying back home tomorrow and there's no *home.*"

He reached out and took the coffee he'd just given me, setting it on the little table in front of us. Then he pulled me over onto his lap, wrapping his arms around me. One hand caught my head, pulling it down against his shoulder and stroking soothingly.

I resisted at first—I didn't like the idea of being dependent on him, or him thinking I needed him for anything . . . but maybe just this once.

"Just let me be strong for you for a minute, okay?" he said softly. "You've held on for a long time, sweetheart. Nobody can say you haven't been strong. But it's been a hell of a night, so why don't you let me hold you and help you right now."

It took me a minute, but then I nodded because he was right. I'd been strong for a very long time and now I'd have to be stronger. Oh, God. What was I going to tell Jess?

"You'll come back to my house tonight," he said. "And if they let Mellie go, she can sleep upstairs in Kit's room. Tomorrow you'll pick up Jessica and she can stay at my place, too. Fuck, I'm used to having a house full of girls. That'll give you the time to figure out what your next step is. I'm assuming you had insurance?"

Insurance. I'd forgotten about insurance! *Woo-hoo!*

"Of course," I said, sitting up so quickly I almost fell off his lap. "I have insurance. I need to call my agent—I think it even pays for an apartment or something."

"Okay, that's a start," he said, then smiled at me. It hit me hard, the way those bright blue eyes crinkled at the corner, and I felt a very inappropriate wave of lust sneaking up. Even if the house had blown up, it didn't change the fact I'd finally gotten laid and it kicked ass.

Something stirred under my butt. Guess I wasn't the only one in lust.

Leaning forward, I whispered, "I feel sort of like a pervert."

He laughed, rubbing his nose along my cheek.

"Ms. Armstrong?"

I looked up, full of that sudden, guilty, caught-in-the-headlights sensation I remembered from the time the PE teacher at my high school caught me making out with Troy Jones behind the bleachers. We were supposed to be running laps.

See? I wasn't *always* a good girl.

"I'm London Armstrong," I said quickly, standing up and smoothing my clothes—a pointless task if one ever existed, because they were muddy and disgusting from Reese's protective tackle earlier. My hair wasn't much better, although I'd managed to get the dirt off my face in the bathroom sink.

"Melanie's done with her scan now," the ER nurse said, a hint of humor in her eyes. Glad someone could appreciate the situation. "She'd like you to come back and wait with her."

I started to follow, Reese one step behind. The nurse paused and frowned.

"She didn't mention him," she said. "Are you family?"

Reese shook his head.

"I'm here with London," he said. "If Mel doesn't want me in there, I'll leave. No arguments. I don't want to make her uncomfortable . . . but I'd like to talk to her if she's okay with that."

The nurse looked skeptical, but she nodded.

"If she doesn't want you in the room, you're out."

"No worries."

Then he caught my hand in his, giving it a quick squeeze as the nurse used her card to buzz us through the big double doors separating the ER itself from the waiting area. We passed room after room until she stopped outside one at the end of the hallway, giving the door a quick, crisp knock.

"Yes?" Mellie called, and I sighed in relief. She didn't sound full of energy and giggles, but her voice was steady and calm. The nurse opened the door for us.

Mellie's eyes went wide at the sight of my new . . . whatever the hell he was. Boyfriend? Seemed a little too cutesy, somehow.

"You want him out?" the nurse asked bluntly, which I thought was pretty brave of her considering Reese was twice her size and looked scary enough when he wasn't covered with dirt and soot.

Mellie glanced at me, and I nodded encouragingly.

"This is a friend of mine," I said. "A good friend. But if you don't want him here, he's gone. Reese is the one who pulled you away from the fire."

"He can stay," she said hesitantly.

"Just push the button if you need anything," the nurse said. "The doctor will be in as soon as we have your scan results."

She left the room and we stood there, Mellie trying not to stare at Reese and failing miserably.

"I'm Reese Hayes," he said, his voice gentle—far gentler than I would've dreamed possible. "London and I are together now, and she's told me all about you. I have two daughters, just a few years older than you. Told London she could come out to my place while she gets things straightened out. You're welcome, too. I hear home's a little uncomfortable these days."

Mellie's face crumpled, and she sniffed.

"Thank you," she whispered. "I'm so sorry, London. I didn't mean to burn down your house. I can't believe you're still talking to me."

Oh shit. Like Mel needed more trauma and guilt? I moved quickly toward the bed, taking her hands into mine.

"You didn't do anything wrong, baby," I told her. She shook her head, then tears burst out like a dam had broken.

"I was using the stove," she gulped between sobs. "I checked to make sure the burners were all off, but I guess I missed one. It's my fault."

I frowned.

"I don't know what happened," I said slowly. "But I sort of doubt that leaving on one gas burner for a short time would be enough to blow up the whole house. Even if it was, it's okay. It's just a house."

Huh. I'd said it to make her feel better, but it was the truth, too. It really was just a house. The sadness and shock I'd been fighting faded, replaced with relief. Not that I was happy about losing my home, but I was mostly just thankful that Mellie hadn't been hurt. That *I* hadn't been hurt.

"I can buy a new house. Or build one . . . I don't know. Nothing that really matters is gone."

The door opened, and a woman stepped in. She looked way too young to be a doctor, but she had all the right props—white coat, stethoscope, hair pulled back in a bun.

"Hi, I'm Dr. Logan," she said. "I've got your test results, Melanie. Would you like to talk with me privately?"

"No, they can stay," Mellie said, her hands tightening on mine.

"Well, I think you're going to be just fine," the doctor said with a reassuring smile. "You've got a concussion, so we'll keep you overnight to keep an eye on things, but I don't think you need to worry. There's no sign of bleeding, no serious trauma to the head or spine. You got lucky."

Relief filled her face. Then she glanced at me.

"Do I have to stay at the hospital?" she asked quietly.

"I think it's a good idea. You can go home first thing tomorrow, if there aren't any complications."

"I'll come and get you," I told her, feeling suddenly exhausted. "But the doctor's right—better to be safe. You were unconscious for several minutes."

"All right," Melanie agreed, and I smiled, leaning over to tuck a strand of her hair behind her ear. Such a sweet girl. Whatever else Jessica had gotten wrong, she'd definitely hit the jackpot the day she dragged Mellie home with her.

An hour later we had Mel all tucked into a room upstairs, and she was starting to drift off into sleep. Reese walked me downstairs, where I was startled to see several of his club brothers waiting for him, including Gage and both of the prospects I'd met that night I'd driven out to the Armory.

There were also the two men I'd seen with Jessica that same evening. Painter and Banks? Hard to remember their names, although I'd never forget the sight of them in that little room with her. Hateful night.

I smiled at them weakly but opted not to say anything. I didn't have the energy.

"I'm takin' London home," Reese announced. "Painter, you're with me."

"I'll come out, too," Gage said. "We should talk."

"Everything okay?" I asked, wondering what could possibly be more important than sleep at this point. A giant of a man with shoulder-length dark hair gave me a quick, charming smile. The patch on his leather vest said "Horse." Funny name.

"All good, babe," he said. "No worries. We'll talk to the boss and then get out of your hair."

I shrugged, because I was past curiosity. We all walked out to the parking lot, where Reese carefully helped me onto his bike. I wrapped my arms around his waist and leaned my head against his back, utterly spent.

The sun kissed the mountains through the darkness as we pulled out of the parking lot, sending pink streaking through the sky for my second ride with Reese. Same colors as last night—this time it was sunrise, the start of a new day.

My whole world was changing faster than I could keep up with, and it scared me a little. I hugged him tighter, thankful that in the midst of all this mess I had someone solid to anchor me.

Wishful thinking?

Probably. I didn't care—all I wanted were his arms around me while I slept. Warm. Strong.

Safe.

REESE

I sat at the head of my dining room table, wondering how many times over the years we'd had meetings in here just like this one.

Too many to count.

Back in the day, Heather always kept the fridge fully stocked with beer and snacks for when the guys came over. My girl Em had done the same as she grew up, although not as efficiently.

Now I took a deep, cold drink of the beer London had gotten at the grocery. Hadn't asked her to do it, she just noticed what I liked and then bought more of it when I got low. Felt good to have a woman in the house, even if she only took care of me because I hired her to do it.

I wasn't paying her to fuck me, though.

Thinking about her in my bedroom right now, wrapped tight in my sheets, waiting for me? That gave me a satisfaction and sense of rightness that I hadn't even realized I was missing.

Dangerous.

"So, what's the report?" I asked Gage. Ruger, Horse, Bolt, and

Painter sat back, waiting patiently. I had a feeling they'd had this discussion at least once already, probably in the hospital parking lot.

"They'll be checking it out, and whatever goes in the final report gets run by us first," Gage said slowly. "Off the record? Fire investigator told me it might not be an accident. Houses explode sometimes, of course. Faulty valves let the gas build up and then when something touches it off, boom. But he doesn't think it fits the pattern of an accidental explosion."

"Interesting . . ." I murmured. "Bud said he thought it was an accident. Said that's what the firefighters were sayin'. He full of shit?"

Gage shrugged.

"Could be. He's gettin' a lot of pressure from the Evans family. They're out for blood, and this shit with London dumping the crown prince for you puts us in their sights. But I think what's really happening is they're cuttin' Bud out of the loop. Everyone knows he's on borrowed time, so they're pickin' sides. Fire department is with us, always has been. They'll report to us first, then tell him what he needs to hear."

Painter grunted in agreement, his young face grim. Once upon a time, I thought he might end up my son-in-law. Still couldn't decide how I felt about that. He didn't love Em, not the way I wanted her loved by her old man—that meant he wasn't the right one for her. But now she was living with Hunter Blake, a nomad with the Devil's Jacks. Hated that fucker. I'd come to respect him, but that's where it ended. Too much bad blood between us.

"I talked to Jeff Bradley," Painter said. "Went to high school together, he's one of the firefighters who was there tonight. He's pretty new, but one of the older guys told him it looked wrong for an accident. I think we need to at least consider that this was a planned hit."

"But why London?" I asked. "Wasn't 'til today that I finally nailed her. Not like she's an old lady."

"No, but she belongs to the club," Ruger said thoughtfully.

"Works for us, been comin' out to your place. From the outside, probably looks like you've been bangin' her for a few weeks now."

He raised a good point.

"So we assume it's a strike at the club until we learn otherwise. Thoughts?"

"Wait and watch," Horse said. "Smells like the cartel to me—they love blowin' shit up. See if they tip their hand moving forward. Let the cops play with it for now, see how it goes."

"Yeah, I'll keep London out here with me until we know for sure," I said. "Want her safe."

"So it's like that?" Ruger asked.

I shrugged. "Dunno what it is. But I know that I don't want her caught in the crossfire, assuming this is about the club. I got a bad feelin' about this shit tonight. Way too coincidental, doesn't add up. Whatever happens between me and her, don't want her hurt because she caught my eye."

"Since when do you care?" Painter asked, his eyes sharp. "You in the market for an old lady?"

Tension filled the air, because the older brothers knew better than to suggest I'd ever replace Heather. I'd laid good men out for less. Somehow the question didn't piss me off like it normally would. Probably because this time it made sense. I'd never moved a woman into my place before—he had a good reason for asking. I realized they had all stilled, waiting for an answer. Might as well clear it up.

"I'll never have another old lady," I said carefully. "I like London. She's a good fuck, handy around the house. Cute. But that doesn't mean I'm keepin' her long term."

"Just don't fuck up so bad she drops the cleaning accounts," Gage said, his voice serious. "I got high hopes for her at The Line."

"No shit," Bolt chimed in. "Best thing that ever happened to the pawn shop."

"Since when we do let business come before pleasure?" I asked, cocking a brow.

"Since the night I had to scrub the fuckin' toilets because the old cleaners were stealing shit and I had to fire them," Gage said bluntly. "Not a fan, Pic. Anyone can suck your dick, but a woman who stays on top of the toilets is a goddamn treasure. I'd protect her from whoever blew up her place on that basis alone."

I snorted, shaking my head because he was right. Gettin' my dick sucked on a regular basis wasn't exactly a challenge, but London was a fuckuva lot more than that.

And not just because she cleaned.

I liked having her under my roof. Sooner or later she'd talk to her insurance agent, maybe look into getting an apartment. To my surprise, I didn't care for that idea much at all.

"Okay, so we'll keep an eye out," I said. "And I'll keep her out here for the duration. She's got a couple kids in tow, too—the girl who was at the house tonight and her little cousin. Guess they'll be sleepin' upstairs until we get this worked out."

"Admit it. You hate living in a house that isn't full of girls screechin' and fighting over the bathroom, you fuckin' masochist," Horse said, evil glee in his eyes. "Em and Kit are gone, so you're auditioning replacement daughters. Seek professional help, bro. Or at least go for a son this time. Somethin' wrong with a man so eager to get pussy whipped."

I rolled my eyes and flipped him off, standing up.

"Okay, we're good here," I said, glancing pointedly toward the door. London was waiting for me, which meant fightin' with Horse wasn't exactly a priority.

"Painter stays out here tonight," Gage said. "Don't want to step on your toes, prez, but you need backup. If that really was the cartel, we can't leave you uncovered."

I sighed, because I knew he was right. As sergeant at arms, it was Gage's job to worry.

"Okay, kid," I said to Painter. "You take the guest room. Tomorrow you head home, grab some shit. Might be stuck here for a while.

If Jessica comes back from California, the hands stay off. Don't care how convenient it would be. Got me?"

Painter gave a sharp nod, and then the meeting was over. Shitty night, but at least I'd be bedding down with London soon. Not sayin' I was happy her house had blown up, but I guess there's always good with the bad. Probably best not to share my theory with her under the circumstances, though.

Women get all touchy and shit sometimes.

LONDON

I woke up in a man's arms for the second time in twenty-four hours. Reese. His body surrounded mine, and I wore a T-shirt that was far too big for me. Not mine. Why was I here?

Then it came back to me.

My house was gone.

My clothing, my pictures, my books . . . All of it. Gone. For no good reason. I lay still in the early-morning light, wondering what the next move should be. What I really wanted to do was cry and feel sorry for myself, but I've always been practical. With my life, I've had to be—no point in wasting time whining when there's work to be done.

First up, I needed to call Jessica.

I rolled over to grab my phone and felt Reese's arm tighten on me. He pulled me back into his hips, the press of his morning erection sending tingles radiating up between my legs to my nipples.

"I need to make some phone calls," I told him softly. He nuzzled the back of my neck and I squirmed, because I couldn't just lie down and pretend last night hadn't happened.

He sighed and loosened his grip.

"I'm here, babe," he said softly, kissing my shoulder. Three little words, but they felt so good. He was here, with me. For once I wasn't on my own, and while I wasn't fool enough to think his presence changed anything in my big picture, just waking up in his arms meant more than I could have imagined.

"Thanks," I whispered. Then I took my phone and pressed my finger to Jessica's number. Surprisingly, she answered on the first ring, her voice alert, almost strained. Had Melanie called her already?

"Hey, Jess," I said softly. "I have some bad news for you."

"What's that?" she asked.

"I don't know how to say this . . ."

"Just spit it out," she snapped. I heard a cracking noise and then she coughed suddenly, gasping.

"You all right?" I asked quickly.

"Yeah, I'm fine," she replied, her voice more subdued. "Sorry, just dropped something. What's going on?"

"The house blew up."

Silence.

"Excuse me?"

"The house blew up," I repeated, the words sounding unreal even to me. "I don't know how or why. Probably a gas leak. I'll talk to the police later today, but it all burned down. There's nothing left."

"Is Melanie all right?" she asked, her voice full of dread. I paused, wondering how she knew about Mellie.

"She got out. They took her to the hospital because she hit her head. I'll go get her in a bit, but I stayed with her long enough to know she's going to be just fine. Nothing serious. You should know that her mother—"

"I know about her mom," Jess said softly. "She called me last night after she got to our place. I've been thinking of her."

"I'm just thankful she's okay . . ." I said. "And I have a place for us to stay, at least until I get the insurance worked out."

"With Nate?" she asked quickly. Awkward question . . . I hadn't actually told her about the breakup. Oops.

"Yeah, I should probably talk to you about Nate," I said, feeling

Reese tense behind me. I decided not to worry about him for the moment. "I'm not actually with him anymore. I'm seeing Reese Hayes."

"That's fantastic," Jess said, surprising me with her enthusiasm. She'd never approved of me dating anyone before. Huh. "You'll be safe with the Reapers."

"And I wouldn't with Nate?" I asked, biting back a startled laugh. She didn't respond. "Well, anyway, I'm with Reese now. I'm out at his place—he was actually with me when the house blew up. He took care of me last night and he said we can stay with him while we get things figured out. He's got a room upstairs for you."

"You don't need to worry about that," she said quickly. "I was planning to call you anyway. I changed my mind. Mom and I just had a little fight, nothing big. I was exaggerating things. You know how I get all worked up. It's no big deal."

I stilled. Reese started rubbing my back soothingly.

"It *was* a big deal," I said slowly. "You were scared of those men. I heard it in your voice."

"You must've imagined it," she said brightly. "Really, it's all good here. You should just hang out and take care of yourself, get the housing situation figured out. I have to go now."

"Babe," I started to say, but she cut me off.

"Seriously, London, you need to let it go. I had a bad night, okay? I got a little homesick, but that doesn't change the fact that I'm happier here. Mom has lots of money and she doesn't have to work all the time. You need to make your own life instead of trying to take over mine."

With that she ended the call. I stared down at the phone, completely confused. Then I flopped back down and burrowed into the crook of Reese's arm.

"I will never, ever understand teenage girls," I said slowly. He snorted.

"No shit. They're all fucked in the head. Doesn't get better when they hit their twenties, either. What's the story?"

"She says everything's okay and she doesn't want to come back to north Idaho. I don't get it. She was scared, Reese. This doesn't make sense."

He reached up and ran his fingers into my hair. I snuggled deeper into him, wondering how and why my world had gotten so strange so fast.

"You're really a nice guy," I said. He groaned.

"Don't say shit like that. I'm not a nice guy, sweetheart. Trust me, I'd know if I was."

"Well, you're being nice to me."

"I have ulterior motives. I like fucking you."

I laughed. "Whatever the reason, thanks for last night. I suppose I should get to the hospital and check on Melanie. Pick her up. I'll get us out of here in a day or two. I know I'll have to talk to the cops, and then get hold of the insurance agent. I can't remember exactly what my coverage is."

"Don't worry about that for now," he told me. "Worry about Melanie. Later I'll take you out and we'll find you some clothes and shit. Until we know what happened with your house, you're with me. Nice and safe here. Nonnegotiable."

That caught my attention and I rolled onto my elbow, looking down at him with a frown.

"You think I wouldn't be safe somewhere else?" I asked quickly. "That sounds like you think my house wasn't an accident?"

He shrugged.

"I got no idea what happened to your house," he said. "Probably just a gas leak. Just like the idea of keeping you around for a bit, letting shit settle. Probably hasn't totally sunk in what happened just yet—you need to figure things out. This is a good place to do it. That's all I meant."

I relaxed.

"Sorry, guess I'm a little edgy."

"I take it that means you aren't up for wake-up sex?"

I closed my eyes, then shook my head.

"I don't think I'm up for anything at all," I muttered. "I have whiplash. Too much happening too fast."

"Fair enough. Let's get to the hospital, go check on girl number two. See if they'll let us spring her."

An hour later we stood outside the hospital, Mellie gripping my arm as she took in the sight of Painter's motorcycle.

"I sort of thought you meant a car when you said you'd give me a ride home," she whispered, eyes wide. I nodded, more than a little startled myself by the transportation situation. Reese had insisted on us riding his bike that morning, saying Painter would meet us at the hospital to give Mellie a ride if she needed one.

I'd assumed that mean a ride in a *car*. Not so much.

"She *did* have a head injury," I pointed out. Painter stood tall next to his bike, his blond hair in short spikes. He frowned at Mel.

"Then call a cab," he said, his voice challenging. "Don't have my car with me."

Reese rolled his eyes.

"Sort of thought the car was implied," he muttered.

Painter shrugged.

"You didn't say and it's not like she's really hurt or anything. You got a headache?"

Mel frowned, looking nervous and a little excited all at once.

"No, I don't actually," she said. "Although they said no sudden movements."

"So you'll have to hold on tight," Painter replied, smirking at her. "I don't mind."

"Oh, for fuck's sake," Reese said. He reached into his pocket and pulled out his cell. "I'll call someone else."

"No, it's okay," Mel said suddenly. "I'll try riding the bike."

She smiled hesitantly at Painter, and my mom radar exploded to life. This was the same kid who'd been screwing Jessica. He was tall, with lots of tattoos and muscles and cute in that way only bad boys can be . . . My Mellie was a good girl, not the kind of girl to get involved with someone like this Painter. Shit. Was she blushing?

I turned on Painter, whipping out my Parental Voice of Authority like a sword.

"You watch yourself with her," I snapped. "I don't want anything bad happening to that girl. I see right through you, little man."

Reese, Melanie, and Painter all froze, their faces full of shocked surprise. Then Painter started laughing.

"Fuckin' priceless, prez," he said, smirking at me. Then he glanced at Mel. "You comin' or not?"

She nodded quickly, hopping up on his bike while I glared at them both. Painter kicked his Harley to life and then roared out of the parking lot, leaving me alone with Reese.

"Kid's survived prison, you know that?" he asked me slowly, shaking his head. "Bigger than you, too. Really think talkin' to him like that is a good idea? You're kind of small."

I put my hands on my hips and glared up at him.

"Then why the hell did you let him ride off with her?"

"Because he'll do what I say," he told me. "And I told him to take her out to my place and keep her safe. He'll die before he lets anything happen to her. He's my brother and I trust him."

"I don't care if he's an Orthodox rabbi," I said, my voice cold. "He'll keep his filthy hands off Melanie or he'll answer to me."

"Just because he fucked Jess—"

"I don't want to have this conversation," I said tightly. "I'm protective of her. Unlike Jessica, Melanie works hard to avoid trouble. I hear you're protective of your girls, too, so I bet you know exactly how I'm feeling right now."

He laughed.

"Yeah, babe, I get it. Just remember—he's a big boy and he

doesn't have to take any lip from you. Bein' with me doesn't give you the right to say shit to him, so be glad you made him laugh instead of pissin' him off."

I stepped forward and threaded my hands up and around his neck. Then I gave him a sweet, sugary smile, staring deep into his blue eyes.

"I didn't do it because I'm with you," I said softly, my voice deadlier than arsenic. "I did it because that child's mama ran off yesterday and I'm her emergency backup mother. It's a job I take seriously. Don't fuck with a mama bear, Reese. Doesn't end well for anyone— not even big, bad bikers."

He burst out laughing, then shook his head.

"I guess it doesn't." He leaned down and gave my nose a quick kiss. "I'll be careful not to piss you off in the future."

"You do that. I'm small, Reese, but I'm persistent. Like a rabid ferret. Don't make me bite you, because my teeth are very sharp."

"Didn't know you were into that," he whispered. "You keep surprisin' me, London."

I started giggling, sounding more like Melanie than myself. But Reese made me feel that way. Young and vibrant and alive. I'd forgotten just how much fun it felt to fall in love.

Wait.

I was falling in *lust*. Possibly infatuation. Love was something else entirely. I needed to pull my head out of my ass before I got hurt.

"Everything okay?"

I nodded.

"Yeah, it's fine. Let's get going, though. I've got a lot to do today—Oh, crap. I don't have a car."

"We'll stop by the shop, pick up that loaner."

"I can't—"

"If you say you can't accept any help, I'm going to strangle you."

I stared at him, shocked. Reese shrugged, holding out his hands.

"It's a guy thing," he told me. "We like taking care of our women. You don't let me help you, the other boys'll make fun of me and then I'll have to cry. Are you trying to make me cry, London?"

He blinked at me like an innocent puppy, and I couldn't help it. I started laughing, and we both knew he'd won.

"You suck," I told him.

"You like it."

He was right—I totally did.

CHAPTER TEN

LONDON

Thursday passed in a blur.

We started out with a quick trip by Target so I could grab something clean to wear. I'd rebuild my wardrobe down the line, but for now just having fresh panties and jeans that weren't covered in dirt and soot was a huge improvement—not to mention a new bra. Reese seemed a little disappointed by that, but he'd get over it. The girls liked their support.

Then I met with the cops and the fire investigators. Reese made some phone calls, and a lawyer I didn't know sat in on the meetings with me, which seemed a bit excessive. Then again, what did I know about exploding-house procedure? Not that it mattered. The suited assassin (seriously—this lawyer wore a black suit and looked exactly like a hit man) just listened with a blank face, occasionally cutting off a line of questioning for reasons I never quite figured out. The official types didn't seem overly concerned by this, so I decided not to worry about it, either.

I was more worried about how I'd pay the guy but apparently it was a non-issue. According to Reese, "He's on retainer with the club, babe. Part of his job. Don't think about it."

The sheriff—Bud Tyrell—and the fire investigator wanted to know about my history with the house (long), whether I'd ever had issues with the oven (occasionally), and if I had any large, outstanding debts (always).

The latter got the most attention from them, because despite the fact that business was thriving, I was always a step behind financially. It wasn't that I blew money. Not at all. But there were six years of medical bills built up from Jessica's ongoing surgeries and treatment, which added up fast even with insurance.

When they asked for specifics, I couldn't tell them anything. All my records burned up in the fire. They'd see plenty if they pulled my credit report, though. Maybe I could use the insurance settlement to pay off my debts? Tempting . . .

That's when I realized having a lawyer in the room might not be such a bad idea after all.

It's all about motive, right?

Meeting with the insurance agent was easier. I'd never really paid attention to my coverage, but he'd been my mother's agent for years and he'd known what he was doing when he set everything up. Not only did I have fantastic coverage to rebuild the house, but I had coverage for living expenses for the duration.

I could move out of Reese's place any time I wanted.

The idea was less appealing than it should've been. I mentioned looking for an apartment and he shut me down, so I figured that was an argument I'd tackle tomorrow. The thought of one more night in his bed wasn't exactly unappealing under normal circumstances—as things stood, I was more than happy to stay put for a couple of days.

• • •

Thursday night Reese took me and Melanie out to dinner, with the ever-present Painter tagging along for good measure. I glared at him every time he talked to Mellie, which seemed to give him perverse pleasure, and when I complained about him to Reese after we locked ourselves in the bedroom, he rolled me over and shut me up with his mouth.

It was an impressive argument in favor of silence, all things considered.

In the midst of all this, they called on Friday to let us know my van was ready. I drove the loaner over to the shop, where I was handed my keys by a gruff, overweight man who ignored me when I asked about a bill. He wouldn't even tell me what'd been wrong with the vehicle, which seemed a bit excessive. I would've been pissed if I weren't so thankful that it was up and running without me having to blow my savings completely. Sure, I had insurance money coming. Theoretically. But I'd need that to rebuild, and those medical bills were always waiting for me.

Now it was Friday evening, and I was about to experience my first real biker party out at the Armory. I wasn't sure how I felt about this—before all the drama with the house, I'd promised Reese that he could have Friday night and I wanted to keep my word. On the other hand, I'd watched my house blow up and I didn't have anything to wear.

Reese laughed at me and suggested I go naked.

I went shopping instead, both for clothing and for several large containers of baked beans and fruit salad, because exploding house or not, I'd be damned if I'd show up to a potluck empty-handed. The gravel parking lot outside the Armory was about half full when I pulled in, with the same two young prospects I'd met on my first trip out there directing traffic.

Did those poor guys ever get a break?

This time they didn't question me as I walked toward the building, just waved me through a side gate in the wall. I followed a narrow passage between the wall and the looming mass of the fortress itself, leading to a large courtyard in the back. It was a mixture of pavement, open grass, and outbuildings that had to cover a good acre or two.

It felt like being inside a castle courtyard, but instead of knights and ladies there were big, scary guys with beards and more cleavage than I'd ever seen outside a girls' locker room. People bustled around everywhere and they all seemed to know each other or have a job to do. Feeling awkward, I glanced around for Reese. Maybe coming out here had been a mistake. Then a tall, curvy woman in tight jeans came up to me, smiling broadly. She looked about my age and very friendly.

"Hey, I'm Darcy," she said, reaching out to take the container of beans from me. "I'm Boonie's old lady. He's president of the Silver Bastards. I don't think we've met before?"

"London Armstrong," I said, putting on my game face. "I'm friends with Reese Hayes."

"Picnic?" she asked, looking startled. "Um, don't take this the wrong way, but you don't look like his usual type. Are you . . . together?"

A heavy arm came down around my shoulders, startling me so much I squeaked. I looked up to find Painter grinning at Darcy, a hint of the devil in his pale blue eyes. His white-blond hair was newly spiked and he wasn't wearing a shirt under his leather cut. Made me feel kind of pervy to notice, but between the muscles and the tattoos he was actually very attractive. He smelled good, too.

Oh, I *definitely* needed to keep his handsome ass away from Melanie . . . Boys like this one were dangerous, and not just because of the whole prison thing.

"London's playing house with Pic," he said blandly. Darcy's eyes opened wide.

"You don't say?"

Painter nodded.

"Yup, they're shacked up," he said. "Expectin' him to get down on one knee and propose soon. It's all so beautiful we could just cry."

Her mouth dropped and he burst out laughing.

"Fuckin' priceless," he said, shaking his head and dropping his arm. "She's his newest piece of ass. Seems to be sticking more than the usual, but we all know how he is. She doesn't like me much for some reason, do you, babe?"

I glared at him, trying to decide whether kicking him in the nuts on Reaper property was a bad idea.

Probably.

"Reese and I are dating," I said to Darcy, pulling my dignity around me like a queen. "I had a problem with my house, and he graciously offered to let me stay as his guest until I get things worked out. Anything else is *baseless speculation*."

With those words I scowled at Painter for emphasis. He held his hands up in surrender, a look of blatantly fake empathy taking over his features.

"Wow, guess I'm not wanted here. I'll go. You bring Melanie with you? I'd love to show her the clubhouse."

I growled and he burst out laughing again before swaggering off.

"I see . . ." Darcy said slowly. "Well, you must be something special, because Pic doesn't *date* women. He fucks 'em and dumps 'em. I should know. Enough of his leftovers have shown up at my place crying over the years."

"Well, that's very interesting," I replied, because what else could you say? Darcy shook her head, frowning.

"I'm so sorry. I wasn't thinking—that was so rude and I didn't mean it that way. We must seem like the strangest people you've ever met."

I didn't respond to that, and she shrugged sheepishly.

"Don't worry. Painter"—she paused to glare at him across the courtyard—"just has a strange sense of humor, and I'm sure he didn't mean to offend you. And I know all the other old ladies will be thrilled to meet you. This is a special party, because we've got people coming in from five different states. Montana, Idaho, Oregon, California, and Washington. Three different clubs. You'll have a great time, although you might want to stick close to either Pic or one of us, seeing as you don't have a property patch."

"What's a property patch?"

"Wow, you really are new," she said, eyes widening. "It's when a man marks you as his, so the others know to keep their hands off. See mine?"

She turned around and for the first time I noticed she was wearing a leather vest, just like one of the guys. On the back it read "Property of Silver Bastards. Boonie."

Once again, I had no idea what to say. She seemed proud and pleased with it, although I couldn't quite imagine calling myself property. Of course, I couldn't imagine my house blowing up, either. Sometimes life throws you a curve. Darcy turned back toward me, eyes assessing my face carefully.

"In club culture, being a man's property is like being married to him," she said. "It means he's my old man, and that's a special bond. The others respect it."

"I see . . ."

She laughed.

"No, you don't, but you're being polite and I like that," she told me. "More polite than I was. Here, come on over and meet some of the other girls. You'll like them, and while you may not be Pic's old lady, you're obviously someone special. Otherwise you wouldn't be sleeping over at his place. Don't listen to Painter—he's just fuckin' with your head, okay?"

I shrugged, because I hadn't planned on listening to Painter anyway. I liked Darcy, though. She was a little different, but she seemed genuine and kind. That went a long way in my book.

She started walking across the cracked concrete, and I followed her, studying the scene. There was a largish group of women arranging food on long tables back against the building. They all worked together smoothly to put together the meal, and I got the impression that every movement was well rehearsed—they must do this a lot.

That sort of surprised me, although I'm not sure why. I guess I'd pegged the parties as one hundred percent debauchery, but even sex fiends have to eat. At least my baked beans and fruit salad fit right in, because this spread wouldn't be out of place at a church social. Apparently some things are universal, and potlucks are one of them.

Off to the right was a big fire pit built out of curved concrete landscaping blocks. The blackened smoke streaks and enormous pile of firewood stacked behind it made it clear the club used it often and well. Past that was a long patch of grass that I wouldn't call lush, but it seemed to be holding its own despite the presence of a big wooden play structure complete with swings, slide, and rope bridge to a treehouse. The latter had been built into the branches of an enormous tree with a trunk that had to be nearly six feet wide. Old growth. Probably predated the building.

"Ladies, this is London Armstrong," Darcy said as we reached the tables, which was surrounded by bustling women wearing property patches like Darcy's. "She's with Picnic."

Several of the women stilled, studying me with sudden intensity. I glanced around, wondering what I'd done. A small brunette with riotously curling hair stepped forward, grinning at me. I'd met her before . . . What was her name? Marie. That was it. She'd shown me around Pawns the first night my crew had come in.

"Hey, London," she said brightly. "Good to see you again! Sorry if it looks like we're acting weird, but Picnic doesn't usually bring women around here. Well, not the kind of women who bring fruit salad with them."

I rolled my eyes, because I knew exactly what kind of women he liked to hang out with, and I'd be willing to bet some of them weren't old enough to know how to make baked beans. *You didn't make the beans, either,* my brain pointed out caustically. *Jealous much?*

Well, I could have made them if I wanted to, I insisted right back.

"Um, London? You okay?"

Oh, crap. I'd zoned out in the middle of a conversation again. I really, really needed to stop doing that. I smiled brightly and pretended I wasn't a giant dork.

"Reese and I are dating and he wanted me to come to the party," I told her, holding out the plastic bowl like an offering. "And I don't believe in coming to parties empty-handed. Now how can I help?"

Marie looked impressed, and I realized I'd passed some sort of invisible test. I didn't know what it was and I didn't care. It was just nice to be surrounded by friendly faces, because despite the fact that the Reaper men had been good to me—for the most part—they were still scary.

"I'm Dancer," said a tall woman with long hair, dusky skin, and a slow smile that screamed sexy. "I'm Bam Bam's old lady. Horse is my brother, and we practically grew up in this club."

"I met Horse," I told her, smiling. "But I don't think I've met Bam Bam."

"He'll be here tonight," she said, her voice soft with something I couldn't quite read.

"Horse is my old man," Marie chimed in. "He's a handful, but he's a good guy. Most of the time, at least. Pic give you a gun yet?"

"Excuse me?"

"Has Picnic given you a gun yet?" she asked, as if it were a perfectly reasonable question. I shook my head, wondering if I'd somehow missed half the conversation.

"Just sort of seeing where things stand," she said, smirking. That made no sense at all, so I decided to ignore it.

"Hi, I'm Em," said a young woman with brown hair and Reese's eyes. I recognized her immediately from the photos around his house and felt a sudden burst of nerves. This was his daughter. The one who'd moved to Portland last year, leaving him with an empty nest.

Why did I suddenly feel like I was in a job interview?

"Hi," I said. "I've heard all about you. I didn't realize you lived close enough to come to a party, though. I thought you were in Portland with your . . ." I fumbled for the right word, because she didn't seem old enough to use the term "old man." But I was pretty sure he was more than a boyfriend, and they weren't married. Awkward, trying to figure out how to say things.

"My old man is Hunter," she said, her eyes sparkling as she said his name. "He's here for the meet. Bunch of clubs coming together, but that doesn't have anything to do with us. Your only job here is to have fun, okay? Let's go find you a drink and we can talk. I want to get to know the woman who's moved in with my dad."

"I wouldn't say we've moved in together . . ."

"Have you slept there more than one night?" she asked, her voice challenging. I nodded. "Well, that's more than he's done with any other woman since my mom died."

Damn. No pressure there.

Em took my arm and pulled me over past the tables to where several plastic garbage cans held silver kegs surrounded by ice. She grabbed a red Solo cup.

"Beer?"

"Sure." Not that I'm a particularly big beer fan. Usually I drink wine, but it seemed the polite thing to do and I could nurse it through the evening. I pulled out my phone while she primed the pump, wondering why Reese never answered my message. He'd told me to text him when I arrived. Nothing.

"You waiting to hear from my dad?" Em asked, holding out the cup. I shoved the phone back into my pocket, nodding. "He's probably welcoming the other officers who traveled here. It's important—otherwise I'm sure he'd be out here with you already. As the president, he has certain things he needs to do at events like this, but he obviously trusts you to handle yourself. Want to sit down?"

"Sounds good," I said, noting that she hadn't gotten a cup of beer for herself. Hmmm . . . Should I have accepted her offer? Maybe it wasn't considered appropriate to have a drink so early? A quick, surreptitious glance around told me other people had already hit the beer.

I decided I was overthinking things. Sometimes people just don't feel like drinking, and if I kept worrying about doing something wrong I'd go crazy. We found a spot at a picnic table near the playground, and she sat down, straddling the bench to face me.

"So, this is different," she said, and while her tone was friendly, her eyes were serious. "Since my mom died, Dad hasn't exactly been dating women. Half the bitches he screws are younger than me and none of them have brains. I hear you own a business and while I'd never say you're old, you're definitely in the right age range for him. What gives?"

I smiled weakly.

"Not sure how to answer that," I said, wondering why the hell I'd let him talk me into coming out here tonight. If he wanted me to meet everyone, he should be introducing me to them. Instead he'd thrown me into the deep end without a warning, which was sort of a dick move. "Your father and I are sort of seeing each other, I guess. Officially, just a couple days ago, although it feels like longer. It's complicated. I've worked for the club since last February, and he hired me to clean out at his place. We hooked up and then my house blew up. It's not a typical relationship."

Her eyes widened.

"No, I guess not," she said thoughtfully. "Why did your house blow up?"

"Good question," I said, shrugging. "Gas buildup, so far as I can tell? Maybe the oven—in the past year or so, gas started leaking if you bumped the controls wrong. The fire investigator is looking into it. I guess for my purposes it doesn't really matter why the place blew. All that matters is I don't have a house . . . That's really what I'm focused on at this point."

"So he moved you into our place," she mused. "And he moved in your daughter, too? Did I hear that right?"

Taking a drink of my beer, I tried to figure out the best way to answer that question.

"Melanie isn't mine," I said. "In fact, I don't have any children of my own. I've been raising my cousin's girl, though, and Melanie is her friend. Jessica is down in California right now and I don't know if she'll be coming back or not, but Mellie needed a place to stay. We're actually really lucky she wasn't hurt in the explosion—she was in the house right before it went up."

Em's eyes widened.

"Interesting . . ." she said, and I wished I could read her thoughts. "You realize this isn't normal for my dad at all. Is Melanie out here tonight?"

"No," I said, shaking my head emphatically. "She's already got a crush on that Painter jerk, and the last thing I want is her out here spending more time near him."

Em snorted.

"Let's not talk about Painter, okay? Hunter and I will probably sleep out at the house tonight, so maybe I'll meet her in the morning. We weren't sure we were coming until the last minute. Things are sort of up in the air, but we usually stay with him . . ."

I caught a hint of question in her voice, and I realized she must be wondering if my presence would change things out at her dad's place. I took a deep swig of my beer, because the longer this conversation continued, the more awkward it got. Where the *hell* was Reese?

"I'm sure he'll want you to do whatever you normally would," I told Em. "Please don't let us get in your way. You'll like Melanie— she's a sweet kid. And she deserves better than what she's got going on back home. I really appreciate your dad's kindness."

A funny look came over her face, and she shook her head.

"'Kind' is not a word women use for my dad."

I shrugged, because he'd been kind to me.

He'd also been overbearing, scary, and pushy . . . But once a man throws his body over yours to protect you from an explosion, I guess you tend to overlook the little things.

My plan to slowly sip one drink over the course of the evening fell apart pretty quickly. For one, I was nervous as hell and the booze soothed me every time I started feeling panicky. Ideally he would've met me at the gate, introduced me to people, et cetera. But I also understood he was a host, and it made me feel kind of proud that he trusted me enough to simply throw me into his social circle on my own.

My "slow sipping" plan also fell apart because the Reaper women knew how to drink and they weren't shy about encouraging me to join them. Before I knew what was happening, Dancer had lined up a row of tequila shots in front of us, issuing everyone salt and limes before declaring, "Drink up, bitches! If God wanted us sober, he wouldn't have made shot glasses so cute!"

We all licked our hands, poured our salt, and sucked the shots down like a line of good little soldiers.

All but Em, that is.

"What's up with that?" Dancer demanded, shouting to be heard over the music and growing noise of the party. She nodded toward the younger woman's water bottle. "You love shots. You used to sneak them in my bathroom with your sister. Don't tell me you've given up alcohol?"

Em shrugged.

"Not in the mood, I guess. Is there a law that says I have to drink?"

The women stilled and Dancer leaned in, studying the younger woman with owlish eyes. She held up a finger, waving it back and forth in the air like a divining rod, biting her tongue in concentration. Then the finger moved down, pointing toward Em's stomach.

"You got somethin' in there we should know about?"

My eyes went wide, darting toward Em's tummy, which was covered by a loose T-shirt. She blushed and looked away. Dancer and Marie burst out in screams, jumping up and down, and suddenly we were surrounded by big men wearing leather and concerned facial expressions.

I was glad to see them, too, because so far as I could tell, the women had lost their minds.

"What the fuck, babe?" Horse demanded, catching Marie and pulling her into his side protectively. A young, tall, muscular man wearing black leather with red accents came up behind Em and tugged her back into his arms. He let his hands rest over her stomach and he grinned.

"Told you they'd figure it out," he said, not looking particularly upset. I glanced at his patches and decided this must be Hunter. With his hands over her stomach. *Holy shit—Em must be pregnant!* Wow. I wondered how Reese would feel about that?

Grandpa Hayes.

"Fuck me," muttered another man. He was tall and built and had a pierced eyebrow and lip. His vest said his name was Ruger, which I recognized, although I'd never met him in person. This must be Sophie's old man—I'd met her earlier with the other girls, although she'd wandered off toward the kitchen to grab more cups a few moments ago.

"Pic know about this?" someone asked. Em shook her head.

"When's the due date?"

"Early next year," Hunter said. "She's a little more than three months along, but we wanted to keep things quiet for a while."

Someone snorted, and I realized it was Darcy.

"Good luck keeping things quiet around here," she declared.

"Congrats," a familiar voice said, and I looked up to find Painter staring at Em, his face utterly blank. Everyone stilled.

Interesting.

"Thanks," she said, but she didn't look at him. Instead she turned her head toward Hunter, who took the opportunity to press a deep, intimate kiss on her. I blushed, because if she hadn't been pregnant before that kiss, she would've been after. Nobody else seemed to notice or care, though. Nobody but Painter. He turned and stalked off.

Obviously there was a story here. Not that I'd pry . . . but it was only human to feel curious, right?

Then something in the air changed, and I felt that sense of tension and anticipation that only came when Reese was nearby. I looked around for him, spotting him coming out of the Armory's back door. His eyes found mine and he smiled. I melted, any lingering annoyance about being left on my own disappearing because just seeing him made me feel special and wonderful.

Ruh-roh.

I really shouldn't be falling for him this quickly.

He came striding up to our group, throwing an arm around my neck casually, tugging me into his big body with an air of primitive possession that sent a thrill racing through me.

"Emmy Lou," he said in greeting, and I felt the love in his voice. "Hunter."

Not so much love for him. Lots of stories I hadn't heard, here . . .

"Pic," Hunter said, nodding. His grip on Em tightened, and that's when Reese spotted Hunter's hands folded protectively across Em's stomach. I felt his entire body tense.

"What's going on here?" he said, his voice deceptively casual. "I heard screaming, which usually means we're under attack. Of course, it could also mean that Marie and Dancer found a new nail polish color they like."

Em smiled at him hesitantly, and swallowed.

"Daddy, you're going to be a grandpa."

He stared at her blankly.

"I'm pregnant."

"Well, I'll be damned," Reese muttered, and I couldn't quite read his tone. Neither could anyone else, apparently, because we all froze. Finally he spoke again. "Congratulations, baby. Hope you're ready for it. Kinda like the idea of some little muppet givin' *you* hell for a change."

"Means you're stuck with me, Pic," Hunter said, his voice full of satisfaction. Em tugged free and smacked his arm. Then she came toward Reese, who let me go so he could give her a deep hug. I stepped back, not wanting to interfere with their moment.

People scattered, giving them space, and I tried to figure out what to do with myself. Looking around, I noticed that the tables were littered with empty plastic shot glasses and beer cups. Reese and Em were still talking quietly to each other, so I figured I might as well clear up a bit while they shared her big news. Not every day a man learned he had a grandchild on the way.

It was on my third trip to the garbage, arms full of empties, that I spotted Painter out by the big old tree in the back corner of the enclosure. He'd been a jerk to me, but there was something about his body language that caught my attention. For once he didn't look cocky.

I walked toward him, then put a hand on his shoulder.

"You okay?" I asked, my voice soft. "I don't know all the history, but to an outsider, it seemed like that was a rough thing for you to hear. Anything I can do?"

He looked at me, and if I didn't know better I'd say his eyes looked suspiciously watery. Then he shook his head, throwing that casual arm around me once again, pulling me in for a quick hug. Not mocking this time—genuine.

"I'll leave her alone," he said quietly. I glanced up at him, confused.

"Melanie," he clarified. "I won't bother her, so don't worry about it."

I nodded, wondering if he was telling the truth. Reese's words came back to me—these guys had so many women falling all over them that one more wouldn't matter, right?

"Thanks," I whispered. "She's had a really hard time."

"Yeah, I get that."

"Okay, then," I said, patting his back awkwardly. "You want a drink?" He shook his head and let me go.

"Naw, think I'll go for a ride," he said. "Clear my head a little. You go find Pic, help him celebrate. He should enjoy tonight. Things'll fall to shit soon enough around here. They always do."

Alrighty, then . . . I glanced back toward the party, then spotted a cluster of empty cups that had been left on the play structure. They offended my sense of order and cleanliness, and that's when I realized something wonderful.

I had something to offer these people.

I'd been feeling out of place ever since I'd gotten here, and while the women were definitely friendly and the drinking was fun, I hadn't quite known what to do with myself. But this—making sure things got picked up, or keeping an eye out for stragglers like Painter? I could do this and help Reese in the process, because despite the fact that it was a social event, you'd have to be an idiot not to see he was under a lot of pressure here.

Better yet? I could do it and still drink.

I felt my stress drop away and I nearly laughed out loud, because I had a job to do, helping the man who'd gone out of his way to help me.

Life was good.

CHAPTER ELEVEN

I was still high off my little revelation when arms came around me from behind, catching the cups I'd been holding and setting them on the table. Then Reese turned me toward him, looking down at me in satisfaction.

"You throw yourself right in, don't you?" he asked, and I smiled, puzzled. "You're picking up, helpin' the girls. I even saw you talkin' to Painter despite the fact that he's been sort of an asshole to you. You like takin' care of people, don't you?"

I rolled my eyes, feeling all smug.

"I'm just being polite," I said. "Who sits around at a party ignoring a mess like this? I've had fun hanging out with the other women, too—they seem like a good group. They're really friendly, and they've told me all sorts of interesting things about you."

"Really?" he asked, smirking. "Why don't you fill me in."

With that he drew me away from the table, catching my hand and leading me past the bonfire toward the same corner of the courtyard

where I'd talked to Painter earlier. The giant tree sheltered everything, and behind the massive trunk you couldn't really see the rest
of the party. It formed something like an outdoor room back here,
with the corner of the courtyard wall ensuring privacy.

Reese grinned at me, then sat down and leaned back against the
trunk. I tried to sit next to him, but he caught my leg and tugged it
over his waist. I fell off balance and then I was straddling him, hands
braced against his shoulders. His own hands caught my waist, pulling my pelvis down and into his.

Oh, very nice . . . Like always, being near him filled me with tension and longing, a feeling I knew was mutual because his penis was
getting harder and harder. It pushed up at me through our jeans, and
I couldn't help myself. I just had to wiggle around just a little.

Reese groaned, then his fingers dug into my ass hard, dragging
me up and down along his length.

"Christ, feels like forever since I've touched you. Been stuck yap-
pin', instead of hanging out with my girl."

"I was a little upset with you earlier," I admitted. He leaned forward and started sucking on my neck. Not hard enough to make a
mark, just enough to heat me up and start driving me crazy. The
space between my legs was hot and empty. I wanted him up inside,
filling me, stretching me . . . We'd been together enough now that I
knew it would be good, but not so much that the mystery was gone.
This position, for example. I realized that I'd never been on top with
him before.

So much potential.

I caught my hands in his hair and jerked his head back, then
kissed him hard, reversing our usual roles. My tongue plunged deep
and he reached between us, unhooking the button on the front of my
pants. Then his hands slid down my ass, under my jeans and under-
wear, cupping me hard as our mouths fought with each other.

Finally I pulled back, out of breath, panting. I felt how much he
wanted me—his dick was harder than a rock, and that wasn't an

exaggeration. Like a pillar of granite. I wanted to taste it . . . Yes, I definitely needed to taste him now that I'd finally gotten him alone, because who knew how long it would be before someone found him and needed something? Knowing my luck they'd spot us any minute.

Well, if they did, they'd get a show because I was tired of waiting. *What? Sheesh, how much have I had to drink? That isn't me.*

But why couldn't it be me? I'd been stuck doing the right thing, being a good girl, my whole damned life. Fuck that.

"So you still pissed?" he asked.

"What?"

"You still pissed at me?" he asked again. "Right before you kissed me, you said that I'd upset you. What's the problem?"

My head shook, and I smiled at him, feeling dazed.

"You told me to come out here and then you weren't around," I told him. "At first it bothered me, because I felt like you abandoned me. But it kind of worked out. I had to reach out and introduce myself. I don't think I would've met nearly so many people if I'd been with you. I like your friends—at least, I like the women. The ones wearing the property patches. I didn't really talk to the others."

He smirked.

"Probably just as well," he said. "You probably wouldn't like the stories they have to tell nearly as much. Biker groupies and club whores. Nice girls, a lot of them, but they aren't part of the community the same way the old ladies are."

I frowned.

"You seemed pretty comfortable with that Sharon chick. I thought she was part of the community. Now you tell me she isn't?"

"It's complicated. Sharon's a good kid," he said, hands kneading my ass in a slow rhythm that nearly made my heart stop. I struggled against the lust, trying to turn off my brain and listen to him. "But she's still a club whore."

"You told me she wasn't a prostitute."

"It's just a term," he said, shrugging. "She isn't getting paid or anything. Just means she likes to hang around, and in exchange she'll sleep with whoever wants her. She's under our protection."

He slipped a hand around to the front of my body, then reached down and found my clit with his fingertip.

"You really wanna talk about Sharon right now?"

I shuddered, and shook my head, burying my face in his shoulder as he started working my clit harder. My hips twisted over his, grinding his cock down hard as the tension built inside me.

"Ladies first," he whispered, then used the hand still on my ass to lift me just enough for him to shove three fingers down deep inside. *Holy crap.* I don't know how he pulled it off logistically and I didn't care. All that mattered was the way he filled me up and ground down on my clit at the same time. My heart was beating too fast and I felt dizzy with need and desire and pleasure that wound so tight I thought I might explode.

Oh, God . . . please explode!

Then it hit, and I bit his shoulder so I wouldn't scream, waves of ecstasy shattering me. My body went limp over his, and he pulled the hand that'd tortured me free. Then it was at my mouth, pushing inside until I tasted myself all over him as he gripped my jaw in a soft but firm hold.

"You ready to suck my cock?"

I nodded so fast it made me dizzy. Then he let me go and I slithered down his body, ripping at his jeans and pulling his belt free. He lifted his hips to help me, his erection springing free to slap up against his belly. I'd seen it before, of course, but never up quite this close and personal. We hadn't had a normal courtship, and I realized with a shock that we'd only had sex three times, total. Wow. Felt like so much more than that.

A little frisson of excitement raced up my spine—there was so much more about him I couldn't wait to learn. I giggled, giddy, and he grinned down at me, wrapping his fingers tight into my hair.

"I feel like a kid when I'm with you."

"I do, too," I whispered back at him. "It's fun."

"Yeah, it is. Why don't you suck me off like we're in the backseat of a car and you've got ten minutes 'til curfew," he said, winking.

I leaned down and licked his full length, root to head, in answer. He groaned and dropped his head back against the tree. My tongue wound around his cockhead, tracing the smooth ridge dividing the head from the shaft. Then I found the little notch on the bottom and pointed my tongue, wiggling across it.

Reese groaned again, shifting his hips as his hands clutched my hair. He tugged at my head and I knew what he wanted.

Not yet. I wasn't done playing.

I sucked and nipped my way down the shaft, letting my teeth brush him just enough to let him know they were on the job, so he'd better behave. I'd always loved giving head. I don't know why . . . Maybe the power of it, the way a man will do almost anything if you offer to touch his dick with your mouth? I found his balls and reached up to catch them in my hand, squeezing them gently before sucking one into my mouth.

Oh, he definitely liked that.

I pulled my head away and looked up at him through my lashes, letting my tongue slide along my lower lip.

"You ready for it?"

He nodded, something close to desperation in his eyes. His thigh muscles were rock hard under my hands, and while he might look relaxed against the tree, I knew that was a lie. If I pulled away right now, he'd probably stroke out. Fortunately, I'm a benevolent kind of woman, so I opened my mouth wide and sucked in his cockhead like a Popsicle.

Bobbing up and down, I took him a little deeper each time. He hands came up to clutch my head, fingers tightening in my hair with restrained power. He could force me if he wanted to. Just shove me down over his erection, slamming it into my throat.

The hint of danger turned me on and I felt myself getting wet again between the legs.

By the fourth or fifth stroke I'd gone as deep as I could without gagging, which thankfully seemed to be plenty good for him. He grunted and groaned as I sucked him hard, bringing my hands up to catch and squeeze the lower part of his shaft with every stroke of my mouth.

Then he started swelling in my mouth, and I realized he must be getting close. His length twitched and he gave me a little tap on the side of the head, a warning to pull away. A real gentleman. But I wasn't feeling ladylike, not at all. I sucked him down harder, and when his shaft throbbed and he started spurting I swallowed hard as he groaned and shuddered.

Finally I pulled away, catching the edge of his shirt to wipe my mouth. My lips felt sore, almost bruised, and when I spoke my voice rasped.

"I'm not an experienced club whore, but I hope that was okay with you?"

He stared down at me, blinking, then gave me that sexy smile of his again.

"Fuckin' amateurs compared to you, babe. You got a real talent for that," he muttered. "Shit, how long since you had sex again? Six years? That include givin' head?"

I rolled my eyes.

"Six long years," I said. "But I think my dry spell is over. I want to brush my teeth, though. You got a toothbrush around here? Or is that too much to ask?"

He laughed, then dragged me up his body, holding me close.

"If we don't, I'll send a prospect to the store to buy you one," he muttered. "Fuck, babe. You can have whatever you want."

I squeezed him tight, because I already had what I wanted.

Him.

This.

Us.

Unfortunately, fantasies are for children and I was a grown woman. I should've known it wouldn't last.

REESE

I lay in the darkness on my office couch, eyes closed, mind drifting.

London was passed out on top of me, her soft curves molding against me. She gave a tiny, ladylike snore. Adorable. I let my hand slide down to her ass, cupping it as I considered all I had to get done in the next twelve hours.

Big meeting today. Big decisions, and I had a feeling that within the next couple of weeks we'd start to see the bodies pile up. There'd been more drama in the south, more cartel bullshit. My daughter's old man was in it up to his ass.

I had mixed feelings about that situation.

On the one hand, I wanted Hunter dead for all he'd done to Em, not least of which was stealing her from me and knocking her up. On the other, the last thing I needed was some cartel fuckwad pulling the trigger on him. If anyone put that bastard in the ground, it would be me.

Yeah, right.

Like I'd do that to my little girl. Or her baby. *Shit*. Couldn't quite wrap my head around that—my little girl was gonna be a mom. She didn't seem old enough, although I'd been several years younger than she was right now when I planted Emmy in Heather.

God help Hunter if he treated her wrong. He'd be on his knees praying for death before I ended him.

London stirred against me, the perfect distraction. Couldn't wrap my head around her, either. I still couldn't believe how much fun she was. Her house exploding had turned into something of a bonus, at least in terms of keeping her in my bed. Not like I was happy about her losin' everything, but I was more than willing to take advantage of it, given the opportunity.

She'd talked to her insurance agent Thursday, mentioned moving out into an apartment. Wasn't gonna happen—at least not any time soon. I liked her way too much. Sure, having Mellie around was a pain in the ass, but kids always were. She'd move out by the end of summer anyway. Planned to start college, and I knew she'd signed up for housing. All good there.

Now my brothers? They weren't too sure about me and London. They liked her plenty, but they also knew I was a player and they didn't want me fucking up the cleaning contracts.

Fuck 'em. What's the point of being president if you can't pull rank every once in a while?

Someone knocked at the door and I glanced at the clock. Almost nine in the morning, though you'd never know it seein' as the office didn't have a window.

"You in there, prez?" Bolt asked.

"Yeah," I said, keeping my voice low. London stirred, then slumped back down into sleep.

"Girls got breakfast going," he said. "Shade says he wants to start church before ten. We got a lot to get through."

"'Kay," I muttered. I shook London, who grumbled and muttered at me to go away. Biting back a smile, I rolled her to the side, sliding her off my body and down into the fabric of the couch. Her butt stuck up in the air and her hair covered her face. She gave another little snore.

I stood and stretched, reaching for the little light on my desk. I found it and flicked it on, sending a soft green glow through the room from the banker's shade covering the bulb.

You have fun last night? Heather asked.

I glared at her picture on the file cabinet.

Yeah. You got a problem with that?

She laughed, and I imagined her shaking her head.

I told you to be happy, baby, she seemed to whisper. *I like this one. She makes you smile and she pitches in. The girls like her. I know you don't want another old lady, but maybe you need to pull your head out of your ass.*

Fuck that. Happenin' too fast. London grunted and rolled onto her back, making a smacking noise with her mouth. It wasn't the sexiest thing I'd ever seen, but the sight of her tits flattening out across her chest was right up there. She'd seemed too sweet, too soft when I met her. She'd never survive in the club, I'd known it in my bones.

Then she'd sucked my cock like a pro in the courtyard, and the fact that any one of a hundred people could've walked up on us at any moment didn't seem to bother her at all. Earlier, when I'd gotten stuck talking to my national president and left her hangin' for hours with a crowd of strangers, London did great on her own. The woman wasn't a coward.

Not only that, she brought food to the party and she wasn't scared to stand up to Painter. She pitched in to keep things tidy, made sure everyone had enough to eat. Hell, she didn't even freak out when her house exploded, which would've been totally fair, even in my book.

Old lady material.

You don't want her, maybe you should pass her along to a man who does? Heather suggested, her voice sly. *Don't waste a good old lady—bring her into the club. Doesn't have to be you claiming her. We need women like this one . . . Bolt's lonely as hell these days.*

"Bolt touches her, I'm shootin' him."

London stirred, then opened her eyes.

"Did you say something?" she whispered. I shook my head.

"Must've been someone in the hallway," I grunted.

"You mind if I sleep some more?"

"Not at all," I told her. "You rest. I think later on the girls are goin' out, getting their toes done or some such shit. You should go with them."

London's eyes were already closed again.

I gave Heather the finger and slipped out the door.

"It's time," Hunter declared, looking around the big game room on the second floor of the Armory. We had men from three clubs here—nowhere near enough room in the chapel for all of us. "We've been playing defense against the cartel for too long. The Jacks are standing strong, but we don't have the manpower to hold out much longer. We're already losing territory. They're gettin' more powerful and soon they won't be satisfied with anything less than open war. We think it's better to attack them before they come after us with full strength, but we can't do it alone. We need the Reapers and the Silver Bastards to join us, along with your support clubs. This may be our last chance to stop them."

I sat back in my chair, wishing I didn't dislike Hunter quite so much. Hard to listen to him making such sense and reconcile my respect for his opinions with him fuckin' my baby girl and putting a baby in her. Shade, the Reapers' national president, gave Hunter a respectful nod. The younger man sat back down, making way for Boonie—the president of the Silver Bastards—to speak.

"I agree," Boonie said, surprising me. The Bastards had the most to lose in a war at this point. They were smaller than us, and so far as I knew, the cartel wasn't directly interfering with their operations in the Silver Valley, which meant they were only here out of loyalty to the Reapers. I knew Boonie would lay down his life to save any one of us, but there's a big difference between standing by a brother and following him into war. "The Jacks can't hold—no offense meant by that, it's just numbers. And when they fall, the Reapers will fall and then it'll be too late for the Bastards. If we're going down, I want to do it with my gun in my hand while there's still a chance we can win."

"So we agree?" Shade asked, looking around the room. "I know there are details to be worked out, but if I'm hearing right, all three clubs are on board with an offensive?"

I raised a hand, and Shade gave me a nod. I stood.

"I'm not sayin' we shouldn't go after the cartel," I started. "But I think we need to be damned careful how we plan it, because even with the support clubs behind us, we just don't have their firepower. Straight-up confrontation won't work. This needs to be a smart attack, take out their head and then smack them down before a new one pops up. That should buy us some space, at least for a few years. I don't think anyone here is naive enough to think we can destroy them completely."

"Wouldn't matter if we did," said Duck, the oldest man present. He'd been through Vietnam and had watched more than one MC president rise and fall. Normally only officers spoke at a meet like this, but Duck had earned the right ten times over. "You take out one, another one comes. But we *can* defend our territory and make a difference if we hit it right. Just remember this—they've probably got the CIA behind them. Not that I have any proof, but there's plenty of evidence the feds have fingers in the drug trade. Goes all the way back to 'Nam. But those spooks aren't loyal, which means if we weaken the cartel enough, they'll pull out their backing and it'll fall apart. Could buy us years of peace. Maybe more if we strike a truce with whoever comes along next."

Men grunted in agreement, and I sat back, deep in thought. Duck had been goin' on about the CIA for decades, and it used to be we tuned him out. Recent years had proved him right, though. Time and again they'd been caught out doing business with the cartels, until I hardly noticed when the news reported another incident. I guess their theory was pick a partner and back them against all comers, because some influence over the drug trade was better than none?

Throw in legalization and things got even weirder.

"It settled, then?" Shade asked. "We go in together, take out se-lect leadership targets in a coordinated attack. Anyone got a problem with that plan?"

Silence.

"Then we got some other business to discuss," Hunter said, star-tling me. Given we'd been in here talkin' for the past four hours, seemed like there wasn't much potential left for uncovered ground.

"What's that?" Shade asked.

"It's about London Armstrong."

I sat up and caught his gaze, jaw tensing.

"Christ, not enough you're fuckin' my daughter?" I asked. "Now you gotta climb into my bed, too? Not club business how I handle my woman, so back the fuck off."

Hunter shook his head slowly, eyes holding mine, not giving an inch. God damn, but I should've killed him when I had the chance. Probably too late now, what with the baby and all . . .

"Not when it's part of this war," he said. "And she's right in the middle of it."

"That's a serious charge," Duck growled. I felt Gage behind me as he pushed off the wall, coming to stand next to my chair.

"I'm not sayin' she's a spy," Hunter started. "But I did some dig-gin' on her. There's things about her you don't know, deep shit. Could be she's an innocent woman in the wrong place at the wrong time. Could also be you're sleepin' with the cartel. Needs to be addressed."

Gage put a hand on my shoulder, squeezing it tight.

"Since when are you interested in who I'm sleepin' with?" I asked. "Thought we were allies. You spyin' on me?"

Hunter shook his head.

"Your daughter loves you for reasons that occasionally confuse me, so I'm tryin' to show a little respect," he said slowly. "I know this shit with you and London is recent, but there've been rumors for a while now. Heard you let her walk into the Armory and pull out a girl, all with your blessing. That shit's not normal and it got me thinkin'. Did a little background work on your girl. You aware that her cousin is shacked up with the cartel's number two man north of the border?"

I froze.

"Explain," Shade snapped.

"She's been with him for more than a year now," Hunter said. "Guess he's married to some poor bitch down in Mexico, but he won't let her come north to enjoy the good life. Not while he has his pretty girlfriend to play house with . . . And guess who's living with him now, too? The daughter. That Jessica kid London's so protective of is in his house, eatin' his food and probably tellin' him all about Auntie London and how much the president of the Reapers comes runnin' when she calls. Then suddenly—right after you finally close the deal—her house blows up and she needs a hero to rescue her. Now she's livin' in your house with full access to whatever the hell you might have hidden there. Still sure she's innocent?"

I shook my head.

"No way," I said. "She's got no clue."

"You aware that Nate Evans is on the cartel payroll?"

"That's a fuckin' joke," Ruger said quietly. "Nate Evans answers to his daddy, nobody else."

"I disagree," Boonie said, which shocked the hell out of me. "We've been hearing things in the Valley. The Evans family gets their money from the White Baker mine, and according to the union, it's near played out. They're tryin' to keep it quiet, but you can't fool the men underground. The ore's no good. Means Natey-boy needs a new backer if he wants to run the show around here."

"That's a game changer," I said slowly. "Not that I think London's in on anything, but I had no idea the Evans family was short of cash."

"Think about it," Hunter said, his voice quietly intense. "You got an out-of-the-way mountain pass, one the feds don't watch too close. Cartel wants Montana, the Dakotas—hell, anything between here and Chicago? They gotta get through the mountains somehow and there's not many places better than right here. Straight shot east, straight shot north. It makes sense strategically, and if they control local law enforcement, they've got it made once they take us out. It all starts with you, Pic. London may be a victim who's in the wrong place at the wrong time, or she may be one of them, but either way she's dangerous as fuck. You gotta cut her loose."

I stood so fast my chair fell over backward.

"Not gonna happen."

Silence fell over the room. Shade sighed.

"Okay, so we got that information," he said. "It's on you, Pic. You and the Coeur d'Alene brothers. Now you know, so you use it the best you can. Hell, might be a good thing. You feed her bad intel, see if it gets through. If it does, then we have a way to fuck up their game. Doesn't really change anything in the end, so long as you keep your shit tight. Might not be a bad idea to put some extra security on her, though. Rest of the women, too, seein' as things are gonna heat up fast. We all gotta cover our asses."

I nodded tightly.

"Anyone else?" Shade asked. Nobody spoke. "Okay, then. Hunter, I know you're standin' in for Burke, so take time to consult with him if you need to."

Hunter shook his head.

"Burke's on board," he said. "So's the rest of the club. We're under fire already—can't hold out much longer. We want blood."

"Okay, adjourned," Shade announced. A quiet murmur broke out, and I felt my brothers surround me. I looked to Ruger.

"Double-check the cousin," I told him. "I don't want to believe Hunter, but we gotta know what we're lookin' at here."

"She's not in on it," Bolt said quietly. "She didn't even meet Evans until a couple months ago. I did a full background on her before she started at Pawns."

"You missed the cousin," I said.

"She's a distant relative livin' a thousand miles away," he said. "I tracked down all of those, we'd never finish a background check in under ten years. But no way I'd miss a boyfriend, or even a fuck buddy. She met Evans for the first time at a fund-raiser two months ago—talked to one of the bitches on her cleaning crew about it. Listened to her go on about him through the closed circuit one night. She had no idea I was even there."

"Okay," I said, rubbing the back of my neck. "But if they've got Jess, they've got a hostage she won't be able to ignore. Let's confirm where the girl is, okay?"

"You got it," Ruger said. "Shouldn't take too long. I'll make some phone calls, see what I can come up with."

"And Evans?" Gage asked. "What about him? You think he's in bed with the cartel?"

"No idea," I said slowly. "It's possible. He's got no morals, no sense of loyalty to the community or the job. You might start thinkin' of ways to get him off alone, maybe think of a permanent solution to our problems with him."

Ruger's mouth tightened, but he nodded.

"Thinkin' that's gonna be how it goes," he said. "Fuckload of trouble, takin' out a cop."

"Yeah," I answered. "We'll talk about it more at the next church. Gotta say, if it comes to puttin' a bullet in his brain, I won't cry. Gage, look into extra security for the girls, too—at least until we know what caused that explosion."

"Pic, you got a minute?"

I looked up to see Boonie, his face thoughtful. A young man stood next to him—prospect. Had a real hard edge to his face, although I wouldn't peg his age much higher than nineteen or twenty. Old eyes.

"What's up?"

"Wanted to introduce you to Puck," he said, nodding toward the kid. "Been prospectin' with one of our chapters out in Montana.

Things got a little hot for him out there, so he's moved into the Valley for now. Thought he might be helpful to you."

I sized him up. Kid was tall with short, dark hair. Built like a fuckin' Marine, but his tats were all biker. Both arms covered in full sleeves, and a scar running across his face that made him look like an ax murderer.

"What's your story?" I asked him.

"Grew up in the club," he said, holding my gaze steadily. "Dad was a patchholder. Dunno if you ever met him? Went by Kroger."

I nodded my head slowly, because damned straight I knew Kroger. He'd been killed on a run down to Cali, three years back. At the time we assumed it was cartel, but no real evidence.

"Feelin' motivated, are we?"

"Something like that."

"We'll find something for you," I told him. "Might come out of it with a patch, you do good enough."

His eyes flickered with something I couldn't quite read, and he nodded. Boonie and I exchanged back slaps, and I started downstairs. Lotta guys would be heading home this afternoon, but others would be spending another night. Needed to check on food, make sure everything was ready.

Hunter caught my arm on the stairs. I paused and stared down at his hand, because he had no fuckin' business touching me.

"Think me and Em are gonna head out this afternoon," he said.

"What, not enough to move her four hundred miles away from me, now I don't even get to see her for the weekend?"

He frowned and shook his head.

"Not like that—she's got cramps, feelin' sick. It's been smooth sailing so far, but I want her home and in bed."

I felt something tighten in my chest.

"Let's take her in to the ER," I said. "Better not to fuck around with this shit."

Hunter snorted.

"Yeah, that's not gonna happen. I already suggested it and she laughed at me. She says she's fine, she went off to get a pedicure with the rest of the girls, but I think she needs to rest, maybe go see her midwife on Monday. We stay here, she'll wear herself out tryin' to do everything with everyone."

"I hear you," I said, although I hated him for it. "Better be safe. Keep me posted, okay?"

"You got it."

"Thanks."

He started down the stairs, the Devil's Jacks colors on his back taunting me. Asshole.

Asshole who takes care of our little girl, Heather reminded me.

I had to give her that one.

Still didn't like him.

CHAPTER TWELVE

LONDON

"Admit it," Em said, narrowing her eyes at me. "I was right about the color."

I looked down at my feet and wiggled my toes, which were now painted hot pink. I wasn't a hot-pink kind of person, and the toe bling was almost beyond my comprehension . . . but I had to give her credit.

"You were right," I admitted. "It looks fantastic. I always go for the traditional look. Never would've tried it if you hadn't *bullied* me into it."

She grinned and I laughed, taking a drink of my iced coffee. Me, Darcy, Em, Dancer, Marie, and Sophie had all taken off for the mall after breakfast in search of the perfect pedicure. Surprisingly, Maggs Dwyer had met us there—apparently she'd been Bolt's old lady for years but had dumped his ass recently. I got the distinct impression he'd done something horrible to her. The women were all clearly pissed at him, but they didn't offer any details and I didn't ask. Ignorance is bliss and all that, because I still had to work for the guy at Pawns.

I wasn't totally comfortable with my brightly painted nails, but if nothing else they were fun and playful. My toes looked like they'd been dipped in a vat of flamingos. Make that flamingos on fire, with bright red accents and brilliant sparklies.

Shiny.

"Ladies, this has been fantastic, but I'd better get going because I have to work this afternoon," I said reluctantly, standing up from the table we'd taken over in the food court. "I just hope I don't gack my nails while I'm at it."

"Pisser," Em said, pouting prettily. "I was hoping we could go shopping until the men finish their Top Secret Important Biker Business."

"Maybe tomorrow?" I asked, flattered that she'd invite me along. Em sighed.

"It'll have to be another time," she said. "I think we're headed home this afternoon. I've been cramping a little—no big deal—but Hunter's all worked up about it. He's terrified I'm going to break or something."

She rolled her eyes and we all laughed. Then I waved good-bye and headed out to my van.

The first hint something was wrong was the open driver's-side window. I never left my van open. (Not that I had anything valuable in it, but I carried enough equipment and cleaning chemicals in the back that I worried some little kid might get in there and get hurt. My insurance agent had spent forty-five minutes three years ago explaining the concept of business liability to me, and I'd been irrationally nervous ever since. The man was a sadist. He should've worked as a high school guidance counselor, because not one of those kids would've been brave enough to have sex after a sit-down with him.)

The second red flag was a business-size manila envelope sitting on the seat. A white mailing label had been stuck to the front, but instead of an address, one word had been printed in large, black letters.

"Open."

In a movie, this is where the bomb squad gets called out. But it didn't look big enough for a bomb, and I lived in Coeur d'Alene, Idaho. We'd already used up our entire town's annual drama quotient on my house. I reached down, my fingers trembling, and picked it up. A black smart phone slid out.

It came to life—a Skype request for videoconferencing.

I fumbled for a minute, then managed to press the accept button. Jessica's face appeared on the phone, her eyes swollen with tears. A purple bruise darkened her cheek. *Oh shit oh shit oh shit . . .*

"Loni?" she asked, her voice tight and strained. I leaned heavily against the van, my legs turning to Jell-O.

"Jessie, what's going on?"

"I'm in some trouble," she whispered. "Mom's friends are here with me and they want to talk to you. Please listen to them. I think they're going to hurt me more if you don't."

With that, someone grabbed the phone out of her hand and jerked it away. The image swayed, giving me glimpses of concrete and men wearing dark masks. Then it stilled, focusing on Jessica's arm. A man's gloved hand held it down, spreading out her fingers across what had to be a butcher block. Then a giant knife came into view— no, that thing was more like a machete. It flashed down and then Jessica's screams came pouring through the phone's tiny speakers.

A terrible fist clutched my chest, cutting off my breath and stopping my heart.

They'd sliced off her little finger.

I could see it sitting right there on the block, and *it wasn't attached to her body anymore!*

Blood was gushing and Jess was screaming and somewhere in the background a man laughed, but my eyes would only focus on that little pink hunk of flesh, complete with sparkling gel nails that had recently been filled. I had a sudden, discordant vision of Jess and Amber getting manicures together. Laughing. Maybe grabbing something to eat before they came home and Amber *handed over her beautiful daughter to a fucking psychopathic madman!* I had no fucking doubt this was Amber's work.

What kind of animal cuts off a child's finger?

The picture abruptly disappeared, switching to audio. I put the phone to my ear, wondering if I'd imagined the whole thing. My body felt distant and shaky. Shock? I needed to *breathe*. I managed to climb into the van's seat and drop my head down over my knees as a man started speaking.

"Next time it'll be her hand," he said, the heavily accented words laced with menace. "Then maybe I'll cut that tube right out of her head, see what it looks like. Always wondered how they wire up retards to make them look normal. She's cute, so I'll probably fuck her before I kill her."

"What do you want?" I whispered. "Please, she's just a girl—let her go. We won't tell anyone about this."

"If you want to keep her alive, you'll do exactly what I say, because I *own* you now," he said, his voice dark and low and radiating so much evil I could cry. Wait. I *was* crying. "I want you to go through Picnic Hayes's house and find papers for me. Anything you can that looks like it might be business related. Lists of names. Schedules. Take pictures with this phone and I'll access them. You'll do the same at Pawns and The Line. You've got until Tuesday to get it done, but I want to see progress along the way. If I don't get something from you every day, her hand's back on the block. We can cut off a lot of pieces before she dies—it's all on you."

I swallowed, wishing I could afford to play dumb, do something to buy time, *change* it somehow because this couldn't actually be happening, could it?

"She's more susceptible to infection than other kids," I said desperately. "That shunt keeps her alive, and if it gets blocked or infected, it's very serious. It could even kill her. Please—if she spikes a fever, get her to a doctor. She might need surgery if things go wrong. I saw a bruise on her cheek, which means someone hit her. Jessica can't take trauma like that. She's not a normal kid, it could kill her."

"You should worry about *me* killing her. But if you do a good job following my directions we won't have to hurt her any more. Start going through the house. Text me if you find something and I'll download it. Be careful, because if he catches you, he'll shoot you and then Jessica will die, too."

"What about Amber?" I asked quietly, wondering if I really wanted the answer. "Does she know what you're doing to her daughter?"

He snorted.

"That cunt's dead. Unfortunate accident, couldn't be helped. Let's hope we don't have any more of those, sound good?"

"Sounds good," I whispered, closing my eyes as he ended the call. Wow. Just . . . wow . . . How was this happening?

Amber. It always came back to Amber. I wanted to strangle her, but then a wave of guilt hit me because she was already dead. God, I'd hated her so much over the years, but I loved her, too, and the thought of her bloodied body being dumped somewhere filled me with agonized sorrow.

Detach. DETACH. You can do this. You have to do this. Doesn't matter how much you like Reese, he's just a man and your girl needs you. Life is about choices.

I knew what my choice had to be—the same one I'd made six years ago.

Jessica was a child of my family.

Saving her had to come first.

Things got weird after that.

There's an understatement for you.

I considered calling Nate. I considered telling Reese. I considered driving to California with a gun and shooting people until they gave me back my little girl.

In the end, I decided to do what he told me, because Jessica's life was at stake. End of story. There wasn't anything I wouldn't do to save her. I'd beg, borrow, steal, kill . . . I'd give every one of those men the best blow job they'd ever had, if I thought it would make a difference.

But they didn't want *me*—they wanted Reese's papers, and I'd find them if it killed me.

I'd do it because I was Jessica's *mother*. The only real one she'd ever had. *Fuck you, Amber. Fuck you all the way to hell.* I'd become Jessie's mother the hard way, cradling her tiny body in my arms in the NICU, holding her as she cried after her first boyfriend dumped her.

Dragging her out of the Reapers clubhouse in the middle of the night.

Jessica was a pain in my ass and she'd screwed up plenty, but this? This was all on Amber. Beyond that first burst of involuntary pain, I refused to let myself grieve for her. That bitch was lucky she was already dead, and that's the fucking truth.

Because life is surreal, I still had to work that afternoon or people would've gotten suspicious. This turned out to be a good thing. There's nothing like hard, physical labor to clear your mind. One of my crew leads had the day off, so I found myself cleaning a local attorney's office downtown. Unfortunately, he wasn't the assassin who worked for the club. I'd bet there were all sorts of interesting papers in that guy's office, ones that might buy Jessica some time.

We also cleaned Pawns that night.

Usually Bolt was in the back room—so far as I could tell he slept on a cot in the storeroom half the time. I'd assumed he was just crashing there out of convenience, but based on our conversation at the mall, Maggs had thrown him out.

He wasn't actually at the store that night, but I decided it would be stupid to break into his office and search for papers. The whole place was probably wired up with cameras—it was a pawn shop, for God's sake, which meant it was full of valuable, portable merchandise. The real question wasn't whether the cameras were there, but whether they would still work if the power was cut.

Something to think about, because if I fucked up, they'd chop off another piece of Jessica.

Reese had asked me to come back out to the Armory that evening after I finished my jobs, but conveniently I didn't get done until after ten. That meant I wasn't lying when I told him I was too exhausted. I drove out to his house instead, fingering the black smart phone thoughtfully. If I got lucky, I'd have most of the night to search. I couldn't imagine he'd be home any time soon—maybe he'd even crash at the Armory. God, I hoped so. I wasn't sure I could look him in the face without giving anything away.

We'd slept on the couch last night, the same couch where—

Shit. If he slept at the Armory, who would he be sleeping with? Could I really trust him not to cheat on me with so many willing, available women running around all the time? A wave of jealousy hit me, but I squashed it because that was fucking crazy. I was doing my best to betray him and the people he loved most to an evil stranger who liked to cut fingers off young women.

So far as I could tell, that sort of trumped the jealous-girlfriend bit.

God, I would miss him . . .

If we both lived through this, I'd be lucky if he didn't kill me himself. Not an idle concern, either. I'd heard the rumors—I knew what the Reapers were capable of. But I'd also heard that they didn't take out anyone who didn't deserve it.

Unfortunately, from their perspective I'd probably deserve it. They wouldn't be entirely wrong about that, either.

Shitty to be me.

• • •

The Hayes house blazed with light when I pulled in the driveway, and two bikes were parked out front. One looked familiar. The other I'd never seen before. Neither belonged to Reese.

I let myself in the front door to find Melanie sitting next to Painter, his arm draped loosely across the back of the couch over her shoulders. She was buried in a quilt with only her eyes showing. They were glued to the TV screen, where a chainsaw-wielding man was about to cut a woman's hand off.

I threw up a little in the back of my throat, grasping the door frame for support.

Another young man leaned back in the lounge chair, feet propped casually on the end of the coffee table. He had short dark hair, heavy stubble, and eyes so cold and dead he could've been holding the chainsaw. It was hard to see in the dim light, but it looked like tattoos completely covered his arms. Handsome and unnerving—a very dangerous boy, I decided.

Painter paused the movie, standing up slowly. I glanced between him and Melanie, shaking my head. Couldn't believe I'd fallen for his shit—apparently this was International Fuck Over London Armstrong Day.

"London," he said quietly.

"Painter," I replied, wondering if we were starting some kind of standoff. I guess we were, because he'd promised to stay away from her, yet here he was. Although to be honest, my perspective on that whole issue had changed in the past twelve hours, what with watching Jessica's finger get cut off. Somehow Melanie's virtue wasn't seeming quite as important in comparison.

"We'll talk in the kitchen," he told me, then jerked his chin toward the scary young man. "This is Puck. He's a prospect with the Silver Bastards. Pic asked him to stay out here tonight. Said it wouldn't hurt to have some extra security, given how many people are in town right now."

Panic closed my throat. Extra security? That didn't make any sense—they must know something. Painter was going to take me into that kitchen and kill me for betraying the club.

Shut up! My brain snapped. *Chill the fuck out, because there's no way they could find out so fast.*

Good point. I took a deep breath and tried smiling at the young prospect. He just studied me, crossing muscular arms in front of his chest. He really was extremely attractive. Black hair, dark eyes, dusky, thick eyelashes—near perfect, except for the scar running up one cheek, along his nose and into his forehead.

Damn. Looked like someone had tried to cut his face off.

Not that it hurt his looks at all. If anything, it kept him from being too pretty. Dark skin said he came from a mixed background. Maybe one of the local tribes? Or Latino . . . Hard to tell, and not really any of my business anyway.

"Nice to meet you," I said, then looked back at Painter. "I assume you got him settled upstairs?"

"It's covered," Painter replied. "Let's talk in the kitchen."

I nodded, pausing to give Mel a quick squeeze on the shoulder. She seemed to be operating on the theory that no murderers or monsters would be able to get her so long as she stayed under the covers. Clearly she wasn't willing to risk that safety for a hug, which made me smile sadly.

I was learning the hard way that nothing can protect us from the real monsters.

"What's up?" I asked Painter once we reached the other room. He caught and held my gaze, his expression focused.

"I didn't lie to you about Melanie," he said. "I won't do anything to hurt her. She was just scared of the movie. Puck and I had no idea she'd be so frightened, and she didn't say anything ahead of time. Otherwise we would've watched something else. Pic didn't want her out here alone, and I knew you'd be pissed if I took her back to the Armory."

I would've felt extremely relieved to hear that if I hadn't been so completely focused on keeping Jessica alive.

"Good to know."

"I've fucked up before," he continued. "I'm a dick and an asshole. But I promise you—I'm not gonna screw her over. Okay?"

"Okay."

He nodded, as if something important had been decided. I wasn't even close to understanding what was going on behind those eyes of his, and it didn't matter. All that mattered was saving Jessica.

"You wanna watch the rest of the movie with us?"

I have my own horror movie playing on a loop in my head. But thanks for asking.

"No, I think I'll get to bed," I told him, smiling weakly. "Nice to meet your . . . friend? Brother? I don't know what to call him."

"Call him Puck," he said, giving me a charming grin. "You might want to get used to him, too. I think Pic plans to have him stick with you for the next week or so. Security."

Well. That was inconvenient. I decided I'd think about it tomorrow, because I'd burned through the last of my energy when I'd come home to find the living room full of young bikers I was pretty sure were capable of killing me without blinking.

Painter—apparently oblivious to my terrible tension—ambled toward the fridge and pulled out a beer.

"Want one?"

I shook my head.

"No, I'm going to bed. Ready for this day to end in a big way."

Nothing.

I lay sprawled in the center of Reese's bed, staring up at his bedroom ceiling and trying not to cry. It was four in the morning. He'd texted me at two saying not to wait up for him, so I'd made the most of the opportunity, going through every drawer, every box, every inch of his bedroom looking for anything that might be valuable to the sadists down in California.

Not a goddamned thing.

Although I knew a lot more about Reese now. For example, I knew Heather had written him a beautiful letter saying good-bye right before she died. She told him to be happy. She said that when her girls got married, she wanted him to give each of them a diamond pendant, set in silver, from her. She called them "something new" for the big day.

She also told him she didn't want him to grow old alone.

According to Em, I was the first woman he'd really let in since Heather died. "Guilty" just wasn't strong enough to describe how that made me feel, given my current plan to betray him. At least I didn't need to worry about him knowing I'd searched the room. I'd been incredibly careful, taking pictures of his things before moving them, so I could put them back exactly where they'd been before. Realistically, there wasn't any more that I could do, but I couldn't sleep, either.

I rolled over and turned off the light, wishing I were better at praying. Now would be a real good time for it . . .

Big hands slid under my shirt.

I sighed and shifted, confused. Reese caught my breasts and squeezed lightly. Then I felt his lips touch my stomach and I squirmed, heat pooling between my legs.

"Missed you last night," he said, his voice low. I opened my eyes, but the room was still dark. Must be very early morning, right before dawn.

Then I remembered. Fuck. Oh, *fuck*. Jess was in danger, Amber was dead, and I had to screw over the first man who'd made me feel anything real in years. Maybe ever.

"Sleepy," I murmured, which was true. It was also a great way to get out of conversation, because I hadn't had a chance to figure out the proper etiquette one uses when destroying a man's life. His fingers burrowed under the fly of my jeans, and then I felt him opening them. Wow. I hadn't even gotten undressed last night.

I didn't remember falling asleep at all.

My jeans opened and then he tugged at them, murmuring for me to lift my hips. I obeyed without thinking. He slid them down, along with my panties, and tossed my clothing across the room.

Then I felt his lips on my stomach again.

Instead of teasing me, this time they moved steadily downward, and then his hand caught at my inner thighs, pushing them apart. His tongue felt like fire on my skin and I shifted restlessly. A finger slid along the edges of my labia, pushing in just enough to collect some of the moisture growing there. He rubbed upward, finding my clit as it started to swell, circling it and teasing. I wiggled under him.

"Did I mention I missed you?" he whispered. "Probably a hundred bitches out there tonight, half of them ready and willing, but all I could think about was getting home to this."

"Do you really have to call them bitches?" I asked, trying to focus. "Seems kind of ugly."

"Just a figure of speech, doesn't mean anything," he said. Then I felt him shake his head, and he laughed. "No, guess you got me on that. We call 'em bitches because they aren't that important."

"Sharon seemed important enough to you," I muttered, wondering if I was losing my mind. Why would a woman interrupt a man about to go down on her—or at least I assumed that's what this was leading up to—to argue about what he calls someone else?

"You wanna talk semantics or get your clit sucked?"

Hmmm . . .

"That second thing," I said. His mouth opened on my stomach and he made a huge raspberry noise. I squealed because it tickled, and then he was tickling me with his hand, blowing raspberries on my stomach over and over until I screamed.

"Stop! You have to stop it!"

He stopped, sliding up to cover me with his body, holding my hands prisoner on either side of my head.

"Now give me a kiss and let me know you're happy to see me," he said. "You wanna talk about other women, we can do that tomorrow. Right now's about you and me."

I lifted my head and met his lips. Despite the tickling and playing, this wasn't a teasing kiss. It was hard and fast, nipping and dueling until I felt faint from desire.

Or maybe that was lack of air?

He pulled away, and we both gasped.

"Now. What would you like me to do?"

"Um, you could . . ." I trailed off, squirming. I still wasn't so great at the explicit talk in front of him. Why I felt so inhibited I couldn't imagine. I'd always assumed that I'd have things figured out by my thirties. Not even close.

"What did you say? I don't understand," he asked. I couldn't see his smirk in the darkness, but I knew it had to be there.

"You could go down on me," I said, the sentence ending on a squeak. "I think I need more practice talking about sex. It feels really weird."

"Yeah, sort of picked up on that," he whispered into my ear, nuzzling at it. "Kinda hot when you get all embarrassed."

"I'm not embarrassed," I insisted. "I just don't have a potty mouth."

He stilled.

"Did you seriously just use the phrase 'potty mouth'?"

I giggled. "I think I did."

"Okay, let's try this again. Tell me what you want me to do."

"Will you suck my clit, Reese?"

"Why, yes, London. I'd be happy to suck your clit for you."

"Gracious of you," I muttered, but at least he was moving back down my body. His fingers found my folds again, and then his mouth caught me, hot and wet and completely amazing as he attacked my most sensitive place.

Within minutes I was moaning and squirming under him. When he started thrusting two fingers inside me, sliding up and along my inner wall, I lost the power of speech. Fortunately that didn't matter, because I didn't need words to scream when I blew apart into a thousand pieces.

I also didn't need words to express my approval when he pushed into me hard and fast a minute later. Instead I wrapped my arms and legs around him, savoring the feel of him deep down inside because it was beautiful.

He was beautiful.

And he was wrong about using dirty words, too, because this wasn't something dirty and it wasn't fucking.

We were making love.

Under the circumstances, I'd rather fuck. The only thing worse than destroying the man you care about is destroying him after he makes heartbreakingly beautiful love to you.

I was still going to do it, though.

I didn't have a choice.

CHAPTER THIRTEEN

"It's not good enough," the man whispered in my ear. "I told you to find me something or I'd cut off another piece of her. Did you think I was joking?"

No. I really, really didn't think he was joking.

I don't know which grip was tighter—my hand holding the phone or the one holding the steering wheel. Thankfully I'd been driving when he called, which was the only time I'd gotten any privacy since Saturday. Now it was Monday and Reese's minion, Puck, was following me everywhere in the name of "extra security." Fortunately, when I'd very politely told Reese that the minivan was off-limits, Puck quickly volunteered to ride his bike instead.

I could've cried with relief.

Puck scared the hell out of me. I knew he was young—probably only nineteen or twenty—but he had the eyes of a killer and that scar across his face wasn't exactly reassuring. For once I was happy to have Painter around, because Puck was also weirdly sexy and I suspected Melanie would've fallen for him in a heartbeat if she weren't already sighing heavily every time she saw Painter.

God, when had *he* become the lesser evil?

"There's nothing else for me to find," I said to the man on the phone, willing him to believe me. "I've looked everywhere I can. There's always a prospect with me, or Reese. Even at work they follow me."

"Why?" he asked. "Have you given yourself away? If that's the case, you aren't useful to me anymore and neither is this little teenage shit. Might as well kill her now."

Oh God oh God oh God oh . . .

"No, please," I whispered. "I'll figure something out. There has to be a way."

"One more day," he said. "Then it's over. Want to talk to her one more time? This'll be the last if you don't get me something I can use."

"Please . . ."

"Stop whining. Nobody likes a whiny cunt."

I heard a rustling sound, as if he'd put his hands over the mic. Then Jessica came on the line, her voice soft and weak.

"Loni?"

"Jess, how are you?"

"It hurts, Loni," she said. "It hurts all the time. My hand hurts so bad and I have dreams and I want to come home . . ."

"I'll get you home," I promised, although I had absolutely no idea how I'd pull that one off. Maybe I should just shoot Bolt and raid his office. So what if they killed me? All I needed to do was get Jessica free—after that? Whatever.

"I need you to come get me," she whispered. "I'm so scared, Loni. They hurt me. Last night they . . ."

She paused, and my mind raced, filling in the blanks.

"That's enough," the man said, his voice muffled in the background. The call stopped and I nearly drove into the ditch because I couldn't stop the tears filling my eyes. Couldn't see for shit.

I took a long detour heading home, wondering how I'd explain that to Puck, and then deciding I didn't care what he thought. I'd just tell him I got distracted and didn't notice I'd gone down the wrong road, or something like that.

He didn't ask, though.

When we pulled up to Reese's place, he just parked his bike and got off, following me into the house. Reese sat at the dining room table, flipping through a motorcycle magazine and drinking a beer.

"Hey, sweetheart," he said, looking up at me. "Come here, sit on my lap for a while."

"You need me for anything else tonight?" Puck asked, his voice bored but his gaze focused, taking in everything. That's what unnerved me about him the most—the fact that if I made even the slightest mistake, he'd catch it.

"You're free for the night," Reese said as I came to a stop next to him. He caught me by the waist, lifting me easily to straddle him across the chair. His hands lifted and framed my face, those brilliant blue eyes of his seeming to stare right into my soul.

What did he see there?

"You can talk to me," Reese said, and my heart stuttered. He knew. He had to know. Why else would he say that? "Whatever it is, if something's wrong talk to me, babe. It's the only way I can help you."

I felt like my face was cracking, but I managed to smile at him.

"What brings this on?"

"One of the girls down at The Line," he said. "She got herself in some trouble a couple days ago, and instead of talking to us, she decided to sell us out."

I closed my eyes, trying to force my pulse to slow down. Could he feel it racing under his fingers?

"What'll happen to her?"

His eyes darkened, and he didn't answer. I felt his hand slide around and into my hair, fingers combing through it lightly, and then he caught it up, twisting it around his wrist until it just almost hurt.

He tugged my head back, exposing my throat. Then he wrapped his other hand around my neck lightly, caressing me.

"You don't want to know," he whispered. His hand tightened in my hair painfully and he tilted my head, taking my mouth in a hard kiss. It shouldn't have turned me on. I was scared of him, scared of the men in San Diego.

Scared of everything.

But his dick was hardening between my legs and I wanted him so bad it hurt. When he let my mouth go and cupped my butt in his hands—lifting me and carrying me back into the bedroom—it never occurred to me to protest.

I wanted him way too much.

All of him.

His smell, his strength, the way he'd thrown himself over me when my house blew up. The love in his eyes when he saw his daughter, and the fact that I'd found two stunning diamond pendants in blue Tiffany boxes next to the letter his wife had written him, right in the top drawer of his dresser.

None of that would ever be mine . . . But for tonight, I'd take what I could get and pretend my world hadn't ended.

"What did you find for me today?"

That voice. It haunted my dreams. I think it would've been easier if he yelled at me, or even if I sensed that he enjoyed hurting Jessica. But we could've been talking about the weather or what I'd eaten for lunch. The guy was like an exterminator, and I could tell he'd shoot Jessica and then go home and put up his feet, maybe watch a TV show.

We weren't even human to him.

I drove on slowly, Puck following me on his bike, wondering if I should just turn out along the highway and head for the high bridge. Then I'd drive off the side. End of story. Suddenly I heard the bloop of a police siren, then caught the flash of blue lights in my rearview mirror. At first I couldn't tell if they were after me or Puck.

Then he pulled over and the cop stopped behind him. Thank God for that—no way I could deal with the police and this phone call at the same time. Puck might've just saved Jessica's life by distracting the cop for me, I realized. Was her existence really hanging by a thread that thin? Yes, it probably was. Sweat broke out on my forehead.

"London? I'm waiting."

Catching the phone between my head and shoulders, I reached up to swipe at the moisture with the back of my hand.

"I don't have anything," I admitted. "Reese didn't want me cleaning today, so I didn't even make it inside. He said they were shutting things down. Security situation. Same excuse he gave for having someone follow me around. I think he knows what's going on—"

"Who's following you?" the man asked, his voice casually curious.

"A prospect named Puck," I said. "He's with the Silver Bastards. He's not following me right now, though. The cops just pulled him over and I'm still driving."

"Interesting. Why not a Reapers prospect?"

"How should I know? Maybe they're watching the other girl-friends and old ladies. Things are really tense right now. I talked to Marie this morning and she said that even Maggs had someone with her, and she's not part of the club anymore."

"So why would you think they know about you?" he asked. "All the women are under guard. Things are tense, and you don't even know why. Unless Hayes has been talking to you?"

I shook my head, then realized he wouldn't be able to see it.

"No, he doesn't talk about anything important. Not about the club or business or anything. He said a girl at The Line sold them out, but I don't know the details."

It was his turn to be silent.

"He give the girl's name?"

"No," I whispered.

"So, you're on your own right now?"

"Yes."

"Good, I've got a new job for you. Do you have a gun?"

"Why on earth would I have a gun?"

"This afternoon you're going to get one," he said slowly. "And tonight you're going to kill Reese Hayes. If you do that for me, I'll let Jessica go."

The van swerved. I slammed on the brakes and skidded to the side of the road, wondering if he'd actually said what I thought he said.

No.

Not possible.

"I can't kill him. I can't kill anyone," I babbled. "I don't even know where I could get a gun—I don't know how to use one."

"You have all afternoon," the man told me, his voice calm and patient. "I'm going to give you an address. You'll go to your bank and pull out six hundred dollars. Then set your GPS for that address and follow it out there. Someone will meet you, and you'll buy the gun he offers. You won't discuss me with him and he won't say anything to you. If you try to say something, he'll leave without giving you the gun and Jessica will die. Are we clear?"

My tongue wouldn't work. I couldn't kill Reese—I didn't kill people. Real people didn't have things like this happen to them.

This couldn't be happening.

"London, are you paying attention?" he asked me.

"Yes," I whispered.

"I don't think you're taking this seriously enough. Maybe you need some encouragement."

The phone pinged, and suddenly a video request came through. I stared at it for a second, then closed my eyes, took a deep breath, and hit accept.

Screams filled the air.

Jessica faced me on the screen. A large, muscular hand held her by the hair, which gave me a nasty sense of déjà vu because Reese had held my hair almost exactly the same way last night. Jess wasn't sitting in anyone's lap, though.

A second hand flashed through the air, hitting her so hard that she ripped free of her captor and slammed to the ground with a sickening thunk, her head literally bouncing from the impact against the concrete floor. Someone started laughing. The man who'd been holding her opened his fingers, chunks of her hair drifting down across her body. I clutched my side, my vision going dark, and for long seconds I wondered if I'd lose consciousness.

"Jess?" I finally managed to whisper. She didn't respond. A man kicked her in the stomach, and then I heard some muffled Spanish in the background. Her body jerked, quivering for about ten seconds before falling still again.

Seizure. She used to get them as a child, but I hadn't seen one in years.

"You need to take her to a hospital. That kind of head trauma can damage the shunt. She'll die. You can't let her die!"

The video died, transitioning back to audio only. I raised the phone slowly to my ear, hand shaking so bad I almost dropped it.

"After you kill Hayes, we'll dump her in front of a hospital," the man said. "I'll need proof. Homicide report will do nicely. Call nine one one yourself if you want things to move faster, I have people monitoring the police scanners up there. They'll tell me when it happens."

I swallowed. I couldn't imagine killing anyone, let alone Reese.

But Jessica was dying—hitting the floor that hard would be bad for anyone. But with the shunt her risk was so much higher. One slip, one tear, one tiny blockage . . . The fluid would start building in her skull and it wouldn't stop until it squeezed the life out of her brain completely.

It might be happening already—I'd seen the seizure.

I'd do it. I'd shoot Reese, then I'd call the police. Maybe I'd wait for them to get there, or maybe I'd try to get away first. Jessica would need someone to take care of her if they did another surgery . . .

Pulling up the edge of my shirt, I wiped my face hard to get rid of the tears rolling down my cheeks. Then I grabbed the mirror, tipping it down so I could see how I looked. Red eyes. Nothing I could do about that, and it wasn't like crying was illegal. I put the van into reverse, then did a three-point turn across the road. I had close to four thousand dollars in the bank. I'd need all of it in cash, if by some miracle I survived the evening, because one thing was for sure.

If the Reapers caught me, I was a dead woman.

When I passed by Puck and the cops, they had him lying facedown on the side of the road, hands behind his back. A second cruiser was just pulling up. Perfect—hopefully it would give me enough time to do what I had to do.

Two hours later I owned a gun.

The man who'd sold it to me wasn't a gun dealer—he was just a guy in a car with a gun. I met him alone in a field halfway to Bayview, which I found using the GPS on the smart phone they'd so helpfully provided me. I paid him the money and he'd handed me the weapon, a box of ammunition, and what appeared to be an extra bullet holder. I stared down at them blankly, wondering how the hell I'd even load a gun, let alone shoot it.

My confusion had to be obvious, because he reached for the weapon again and when I handed it over, he demonstrated how to pop another bullet holder out of the gun's handle like magic. He also showed me how the bullets could be taken out, then had me put them back in again.

The he showed me how to shoot it.

It was surprisingly easy. All I had to do was unhook the little safety switch, pull the trigger, and BOOM. The shell casing popped out and then it was ready to go again. My hand hurt a little after the third shot, but the gun didn't really have much of a kick or anything. After that, the man got in his car and left without saying good-bye . . . or anything else. I'd bought a gun and learned how to use it all without either of us talking. Surreal. Fucked up. I could almost pretend it'd been a dream if it wasn't for the extra weight in my purse.

So. Now I had a gun. I just had to stop off and get some groceries before killing Reese. Oh, and maybe some gas.

You can do this, I told myself. *Just take it one step at a time.*

I made it halfway back to town before reality hit me. Had I lost my fucking mind?

Killing Reese wasn't an option.

Letting Jessica die wasn't an option, either. There had to be a solution. That's when it hit me—Nate. I'd call Nate. If the kidnappers wanted a police report, Nate could make that happen. I supposed I'd probably end up in jail, but that was the least of my concerns at this point. Jail was nothing to me. Hell, it'd be a vacation compared to this.

I grabbed my phone and found his number.

"Get tired of fucking the biker?"

Did he have to be nasty about everything? How had I ever been attracted to this asshole?

"Nate, I really need to talk to you," I was working hard to keep my voice even. "It's an emergency."

Silence, and then when I'd almost started to wonder if he'd hung up on me, he spoke again.

"What is it?"

"I need to talk to you in person. It's . . . complicated."

"Where are you?"

"I'm just coming up on Hayden," I told him.

"I'm not too far away. Meet me at the cafe across from the flooring place, down on Government Way."

"Thank you, Nate."

"Don't thank me yet. God knows if I'll help you. Right now I'm tempted to tell you to fuck off."

I swallowed my pride.

"Thanks for hearing me out. You're the only person I know who has the power to change the situation I'm in."

God, I hated sucking up.

"I'll listen," he said after a pause. "No promises."

"Just having you hear me out means the world to me."

I ended the call, leaned out my window, and threw up. *Remember, you need him*, my brain reminded me. *Play nice.*

The restaurant wasn't too busy, thank God. Nate was already waiting for me, sitting in a booth in the back corner. I smiled at him weakly as I walked over. My purse felt too heavy, the strange, hateful weight of the gun throwing my whole world off balance.

So wrong.

"You look like shit," he said as I slid into the seat. "Your eyes are all red and puffy, like you've been crying. Lover boy not as wonderful as you thought?"

I shook my head—now wasn't the time to fight or defend myself. If Nate found a way to help me, he could say whatever the hell he wanted.

"I have a big problem," I replied slowly, wondering just how exactly I was supposed to explain all this to him.

"Coffee?" a waitress asked, smiling down at Nate. He flashed her a flirty grin, reminding me so much of the night I'd met him that it might've hurt, if I still had the capacity to experience more pain. Lucky me—I'd already topped up on suffering for the day.

"Decaf," he said. "London?"

"Just water, please."

She nodded, although I could see a look in her eyes that said she didn't appreciate me taking up table space if I wasn't going to order anything.

Shitty to be her.

"I don't know how to say this, so I'm just going to spit it out," I told him. "There are some bad guys down in California who have Jessica, and they're going to kill her unless I commit a murder for them."

I expected to startle him, maybe have him question whether I'd lost my mind. Instead he just smiled.

"Yeah, I know."

It felt like someone had hit me in the stomach with a baseball bat. Guess I could still feel more pain after all.

"What?" I whispered.

"I know all about it," he said casually. The waitress came back and handed him his coffee.

"You want anything with that?" she asked.

"Slice of pecan pie would be great," he said, winking at her. "With a scoop of ice cream?"

"You got it," she said, glancing over at me again. "Hey, are you sick? You don't look so good."

I managed to shake my head.

"No," I said, my voice hoarse and weak. "I'm fine. I just . . . need to talk with the deputy, okay? Can you leave us?"

She sniffed, then strutted off, smacking her little order pad down on the counter as she passed into the back.

"Now you pissed her off," Nate said casually. "If she spits in my pie, I'm making you pay for it. In fact, I think I'll let you pay for everything anyway. So was that all?"

"Was what all?"

"Was that all you wanted to talk about? If that's it, you should probably get going. Sounds like you got your work cut out for you. Good luck with that."

"You're a police officer," I said, still stunned. "What's wrong with you?"

"Nothing," he replied, taking another sip of his coffee. "Well, I guess I'm a little bored right now, but I love pie. I should eat up, sounds like it'll be a long night. Crime scene to process and all that."

"I can't believe you—what's wrong here? Is this some kind of joke to you?"

Nate smiled, so much hatred in his eyes that it scared me. Had I ever known him at all?

"No, Loni, this isn't a joke. You've got a job to do, and if you want that little cunt Jessica to survive, sounds like you better stop dickin' around and get it done. Oh, now don't look at me like that. It's not like I want her dead—kid's fuckin' great in the sack. Wouldn't mind another run at her."

I reeled. My brain seemed to shut down, incapable of accepting any new data.

"You were sleeping with Jessica?"

He rolled his eyes.

"God, you're stupid," he muttered. "Someone had to give her enough money to get down to Cali when you had your little fight. This whole thing was a lot of work to set up, but I have to admit that screwing her tight little ass was the fun part. Christ, you didn't actually think I was into you, did you? You're too old, used up . . . And now it's time for you to go and take care of your business. Don't bother trying to call the cops before it's done, either. Nobody's going to help you."

Somewhere in the middle of his little speech, I shut down. I could still see everything, hear everything . . . but it all felt distant and unreal.

"You're an evil person," I whispered.

"I'm a man with a goal," Nate replied, his voice serious and his eyes hard—nothing like the person I thought I'd known. He leaned forward, his words precise and clipped. "I know what I want, and I'm willing to do anything to get it. I fucked your girl and convinced her to go to San Diego, Loni. I rigged your house to blow so Hayes would take you in. Now you're right where I want you, and you'll fucking dance because I told you to. No more questions."

"Here's that pie," the waitress said, walking toward us.

"Thanks, hon," Nate replied with a smile. She leaned in to him just a little, her body language making it clear she had more than pie to offer.

They ignored me when I pushed up and out of my seat, trying not to stumble as I walked out of the restaurant and back to my van. I sat in the driver's seat for several minutes, trying to process what the hell had just happened. But some things don't make sense no matter how you look at them, so I turned my key in the ignition and pulled out of the parking lot, because I still needed to hit the grocery store. I had a list of things to buy and I was running out of time to get dinner on the table.

Why was I fixing dinner? I don't know.

What I do know is that by the time I paid for the food, my side hurt where my purse kept thwacking me as I walked—the gun threw it off balance, I guess. I ignored the small pain as I drove home to cook dinner for Reese. Not like killing a man is less awful if you've fed him first, but what else was I supposed to do for the rest of the afternoon?

God damn Nate Evans to hell, and God damn me for falling for his shit. God damn the men holding Jessica, too. If there was any justice in the universe, Amber was burning in a fiery pit surrounded by demons right at this minute. I hated all of them.

Mostly, though, I hated me.

REESE

"Why bother playing it through? She's got a gun in there and she's gonna shoot you with it. Not many ways to spin that and get a happy ending," Puck said, holding my gaze steadily. "I spent almost two hours gettin' harassed on the side of the fucking road while she plotted your death. How much more proof do you need?"

The kid had balls, talking to me like that. Still, he'd been thrown into deep shit, headfirst, and he'd rolled with it and done his job. Nobody wants to be the one telling an MC president that his woman's fixin' to kill him. The Silver Bastards prospect had showed me respect without fucking around.

I still hated him for what he'd discovered.

"Hate to say it 'cause I like London, but I'm with Puck on this one," Gage said. He sat back in an old office chair I'd hauled down to my shop a few years ago. Right now it was positioned in front of a long, low table with two monitors set on top of it. They each split into four screens, playing a live feed of different rooms in my house. Ruger had a gift for electronics, no question.

I'd have to make sure he didn't forget to take any of those little fuckers out after this was all over, too. Last I needed were eyes on what went on in there on a regular basis. Been damned fuckin' hard to act normal this week, knowing the brothers were watching everything I did.

Make that *almost* everything. I didn't let them put anything in the bedroom, because fuck that shit.

We'd spent a good part of the afternoon down here—Gage, me, Ruger, Horse, Painter, Bam Bam, and Duck. Bolt was off at Maggs's place. Not sure what drama was goin' down with those two. Hopefully I'd never find out. Couldn't even manage my own woman, didn't need to worry about his.

"Christ," I said, watching London bustling around the kitchen on the monitor and sighing. I'd fallen for her, I realized. Not just fucking her, but *her*. Comin' home to her felt good, and havin' her with me at the party? Hadn't felt like that since Heather was alive.

I'd never hated the cartel more than I did in that instant.

We might not have the full story here, but didn't take a genius to see they were using Jessica to manipulate her. Was that an excuse? No. London should've come to me, let the club handle things.

"She's got no fuckin' clue what she got herself into here," I muttered. Bam grunted.

"That's how they work. Nobody sets out to get controlled and used by a fuckin' cartel. They're like parasites, workin' their way in and then taking over until you can't pull them out without killing the host. Lost cause at this point, Pic. She's made her choice and it wasn't you. Those weren't blanks I pulled out of her purse—so far as she knows, that gun is still loaded and she's obviously plannin' to use it."

I sighed, torn between wishing he wasn't so damn blunt and thankful my brothers weren't afraid to give it to me straight.

"So why are we still waiting?" Gage asked. "We go in and find out what's going on—she won't be able to hold out on us long. We can make a decision about what to do with her after that."

"Because he's hoping she'll change her mind," Duck muttered. He sat on a shop stool, eyeing all of us cynically. "Fuckin' pussy thinks that maybe true love will conquer all, and then she'll climb onto his bike and they'll ride away into the sky on a rainbow while we all throw rose petals at them."

Puck snorted, quickly turning it into a cough.

"Just 'cause you're old doesn't mean you can talk to me like that," I told Duck, my voice like ice. He shrugged.

"Call it like I see it," he said. "Whatever you do, let's do it soon. If you want it to go all the way to the end, that's fine with me. Just get moving because I'm hungry. Whether she tries to shoot you or not, that food she's cookin' will still taste good."

"Jesus, Duck," Painter muttered. Then he caught my eye. "If this is really goin' down, I should grab Melanie. She's upstairs, and I don't know what London's planning to do about her witnessing things. We don't need her seein' this shit. No more collateral damage than necessary, right boss?"

"Go get her," I said. "Take her to dinner and a movie, or some such. Make it a date. That'll be a good alibi for both of you if anything happens. I'll keep you posted and if things go to hell you can dump her with one of the girls, sound good?"

"Yeah," Painter said. "I'll take her out and then tuck her in safe once you give the all clear. Good luck, Pic. Hope it works out okay."

He leaned over and gave me a rough hug. I slapped his back, and the rest of us settled in to watch as he drove his bike around the back side of the hill, pulling into the driveway like he'd come directly from town.

"So, you find anything interesting in her purse besides that gun?" I asked Bam.

"Well, there's the phone they've been usin' to talk to her, but that's nothing new."

"Still fuckin' pissed about that," Ruger muttered. "Shouldn't be so hard to crack the bastard, but still haven't been able to tap it. Ninjas or something."

Despite everything, I had to smile. Ruger wasn't used to being beaten by technology.

"Finally met your match," Duck grunted, his voice satisfied. "I keep tellin' you, we can't just count on electronic shit to cover us. Nothing like human intel combined with real firepower. Beats one of your little bugs any time."

"Without my bugs, we'd have no idea what we're walking into," Ruger said. Duck rolled his eyes.

"You still got no idea," he muttered. "We know she's got a gun somewhere and we're pretty sure she's planning to shoot Pic. Has somethin' to do with that kid of hers. Hard to know more without hearin' both sides of the conversation, but it doesn't really matter. We haven't learned one damn thing about the cartel that's new or useful in all of this, and I'll bet she can't tell us shit, either. This is the sideshow—the main event's gonna be in Cali, not here."

"We know they want Pic dead," Ruger said.

"Yeah, 'cause that's a big fuckin' surprise," Horse said. "And here I thought they loved him, up to this point. Who knew?"

"Dick."

"Asshole."

"Christ, you're like two-year-olds," I muttered, glaring at him and Ruger. "You need a fuckin' time-out?"

"Painter's in," Gage said quietly. We watched on the tiny screens as he went upstairs to talk to Melanie, who apparently needed some time to get ready. This wasn't a huge surprise to me, seeing as I raised two daughters. Painter went down to the kitchen and chatted up London while Mel was primping, then guided her gently out of the house to his bike.

"I think Painter's got a little crush," Horse said. "Isn't that sweet? We should all congratulate him on that, make real sure he knows we're pullin' for him. He'll love that."

Puck snorted again.

"Shut the fuck up, prospect," Duck said. "No respect."

"I'll take that as my cue," I said, rubbing the back of my neck. "Horse? You come with me, along with Puck and Bam. Ruger, I want you keepin' an eye on things until we finish with her. Then get your ass down to the house and tear it all down. Tonight. No more fuckin' cameras in my shit. And I want everyone ready to leave for Portland by midnight, got me? No point in makin' things easy for the bastards if they're spying on us."

"You got it," Ruger said. "Sooner we get this done the better. Make our move before someone in the Devil's Jacks decides they don't want to play nice with the rest of us."

"Unlikely. They're fucked," I said. "So are we, come to think of it. This is it, brothers—we either smack these cartel cocksuckers back now or we get ready to start followin' their orders. Not a whole lot of ground in between."

For once, neither Horse nor Ruger had a joke.

"Ready for a beer?" London asked brightly as she opened the door for me. I studied her face for a hint of something—guilt, evasion . . . Hell, even hostility.

Nothing. She was like a pretty, blank blow-up doll going through the motions. Completely checked out.

"Thanks, sweetheart," I said, reaching out and catching the back of her neck, pulling her in for a kiss. She didn't respond, which wasn't exactly a surprise under the circumstances.

"I've got chili cooking, and some corn bread," she told me when I let her go. "Why don't you make yourself comfortable in the dining room? Food'll be ready soon, I'll bring it out to you."

As she walked me toward the table, I decided there'd never been a more incompetent assassin in history. I hadn't really believed she was deliberately working with the cartel from the start, but now I had proof. Nobody who knew what they were doing would be this stupid about it.

She'd set a magazine out for me in front of the chair at the head of the table. Facing away from the kitchen—wasn't that convenient? That way she could just walk up to me and shoot me in the head.

"I'll just check on the corn bread," she said without meeting my eyes. I watched as she drifted away. Fuck. Guess it'd been too good to be true.

Sorry, baby, Heather whispered.

Yeah, whatever.

I grabbed my magazine and walked around to the far side of the table. Knowing my luck, she'd ditch the gun and go after me with a rolling pin. Never turn your back on a woman with a weapon—I'd learned *that* from Heather. Come to think of it, she'd tried to kill me at least three times over the course of our marriage . . . 'Course, only one of those was serious.

Ten minutes later London came back into the dining room, something heavy pulling down one side of her sweater. Christ, but she was clueless. It would've been funny, but pretty fuckin' hard to laugh when the woman you love tries to kill you.

Love?

Now that was probably takin' it a bit far, I mused. But whatever I felt for her, it was a step up from lust. Pisser, because that was a gun in her pocket, and from the determined look on her face she was definitely planning to use it against me. I decided to throw a Hail Mary anyway.

"Something you want to talk about?" I asked her. Her mouth twisted as she bit her lip, clearly startled to find me in a different place than where she'd left me. Yeah, 'cause I always made it as easy as possible for people to kill me. I'm a giver that way.

Last chance, London.

"No," she said quietly, sticking her hand down into the pocket with the gun. She caught me watching, and her face actually turned white.

"Babe, you look like you could use a day off," I told her, wondering if there was a way to get through to her. Couldn't decide how I felt about that . . . Duck had been right. I wanted things to end happy, for her to fall into my arms and let me take over and fix everything. But I was also fuckin' pissed, because I could no longer deny that this woman truly meant to kill me. Hard not to take that personally. "Have you considered hitting the spa? Maybe get a massage?"

"That costs too much," she said automatically. I frowned at her, wondering how such a smart person could be so stupid. *Talk to me before it's too late.*

"I wasn't suggesting that you pay for it."

"I don't want your money—"

"Yeah, I know, you're totally independent and you like it that way. Blah, blah. Just let me do something for you, for once."

She looked like she might throw up, and then her eyes started turning red. Tears. London knew what she was about to do was wrong, and she knew she didn't want to do it . . . yet it *still* didn't occur to her to reach out for help. I got that she had to protect Jessica—I'd do the same for Em or Kit. I even got that she was confused and frightened. But what really sucked in this situation was that she didn't trust me to save her.

Had it been anything but sex for her?

No. Time to face reality. I was just a booty call to her, proving once and for all that karma's one hell of a bitch. And so was London.

Fuck.

"The food won't be ready for another ten minutes. You look sort of tense. Want a neck rub?" She started to walk around the table toward me, clearly planning to blow out my brains. Now I felt a wave of fury hit. How dare this cunt use me for sex and then try to shoot me in my own home? I'd have done anything to help her, but she couldn't even bother asking.

"I think you should stay back." *Otherwise I might strangle you.*

"What do you mean?"

"Well, I'd hate to make it too easy for you, sweetheart."

She smiled weakly. I wanted to slap the smile right off her lying face.

"I don't understand."

Yeah. You understand. And now you'll understand what it means to be afraid.

"I'm assuming you're planning to shoot me in the back of the head," I said, forcing myself to stay calm. "That's a bad idea. You shoot that close, you'll be all covered in blood spatter. Means you'll risk tracking more evidence out of the house or taking time to clean up. Either way, complicates things."

That clear enough for you, bitch?

She pulled out the gun slowly, raising it carefully to aim at my head. Little idiot. A gun like that wasn't exactly a sniper's weapon. Even at this close range, she should be going for the biggest target— my chest.

"Go ahead, do it," I said, smirking at her. I wanted to scare her. Hurt her. Make her pay for not trusting me . . . "Show me what you're made of."

"I'm so sorry," she whispered, and those tears building in her eyes started spilling out, running down her cheeks. Behind her I saw Horse step up quietly, waiting. Puck and Bam Bam would be in the kitchen, and I knew they'd do whatever I needed, up to and including disposing of London's body for me. "You'll never know how much I wish this weren't happening."

"Then don't do it," I told her, catching and holding her gaze because I'm a fucking fool. Even now I'd forgive her if she just opened her mouth and told me what was going on. *Trusted* me. "Whatever it is, we can work through it. I'll help you."

"You can't . . ."

I sighed, because that was it. Over. Goddamn waste, tryin' to connect with a woman. Heather had been one in a million—I'd already had my time.

Fuck it.

I gave Horse a tip of my chin, letting him know wordlessly that I'd had enough of this shit. London would have to pay for what she'd done, which was just too fuckin' bad. That's what you get for tryin' to kill the man you're sleepin' with.

"It's over, babe," Horse said. I saw shock all over her face, but I had to admit, the bitch had balls, because she pulled the damn trigger.

I sighed again as Horse reached around the woman I'd fallen for, grabbing her wrist and squeezing hard as he threw her down on the table face-first. London dropped the gun, crying openly. I stood and strolled over to her, dropping down on my haunches to study her. Her eyes caught mine, expression full of pain and despair.

Appropriate, because she was well and truly fucked.

"You'd really benefit from one of the handgun classes down at the gun shop," I told her quietly. "Learn all kinds of good stuff there. For instance, they'd teach you to check and make sure nobody's tampered with your weapon when it's out of your control. They'd also teach you to check and make sure it's loaded."

She closed her eyes and bit her lip.

I'm a sick bastard, because the sight of her laid out on that table, held down and crying? That should've bothered me. It turned me on, though. Even now I wanted to fuck her.

"Are you going to kill me?" she asked, her voice a hoarse whisper. Horse shot me a glance, and I considered the question.

"Haven't decided yet," I finally admitted. "First we're going to get information from you. I'd suggest you cooperate, because otherwise we'll have to convince you, and the fact that you've been in my bed isn't going to help you out of this."

She closed her eyes and nodded. The life had gone out of her completely . . . But just when I wondered if she'd roll over and die, she opened them again, forcing herself to reengage.

"You need to know something," she said quietly.

"Yeah?" I asked, waiting for her to start going on about love or some other bullshit, trying to save her ass.

"They have Jessica."

"Yeah, we kind of figured that out," I told her, my voice dry. "Forgive me if I don't give a shit. I don't care why a person tries to kill me. I'm all about the end result."

"Jessica is going to die if she doesn't get help," she said, ignoring my sarcasm. "Like, help in the next twenty-four hours. She's got a shunt, Reese. Born with hydrocephalus."

"The fuck?" Horse asked, frowning at me.

"Water on her brain," London said. "Her cerebrospinal fluid doesn't drain right, which means she has a little tube running down from her skull through her neck to drain the fluid. If that tube gets

blocked or infected, she's dead. Head trauma is particularly dangerous for people with shunts—I watched them throw her down. Her
head hit the concrete and then she had a seizure. I know I messed up,
and it was wrong to try to shoot you, Reese. But please—if you have
any mercy at all—please try to find a way to help her. It's over for me
and I'm fine with that, but you have children. You'd do anything to
keep them alive, wouldn't you? Please . . ."

With that she seemed to fold in on herself. I glanced at Horse.

"You know about this?" he asked.

"Knew the kid had medical issues, not the details," I said slowly.
"Bills came up on the background check. This shunt shit is news,
though. Fuck, London—why the hell didn't you tell me she had a
tube in her head?"

"Jessica doesn't like people to know," she whispered, her voice
miserable. "She says it makes her feel like a freak, so we don't talk
about it."

"None of this matters," Puck said, stepping into the room.

"How do you figure?"

"It's over for your girlfriend. We all know it—sucks for the kid,
but there's nothing we can do for her. You can't let her get to you."

"You're a cold fucker, aren't you?" Horse asked. Puck shrugged.

"Practical. It is what it is. You can't let the woman who tried to
kill the president of the Reapers MC get away with it."

Horse and I exchanged quick looks. London stayed silent.

"Let's get her out of here," Horse said finally. "Figure out what
to do with her back at the Armory—we don't even know how useful
she might be to us yet. Burn one bridge at a time, brother."

CHAPTER FOURTEEN

LONDON

Relief.

That's what I felt, more than anything else.

I think I was supposed to be afraid, maybe cry and beg for mercy. Instead I wanted to cry with relief just because it was finally over. Jessica would live or die, but there wasn't a damned thing I could do about it at this point.

The instant I pulled the trigger, I'd known that I'd made the worst mistake of my life. They say God shows mercy on drunks and fools. That I believed, because despite my resolve, the gun didn't fire. I wasn't entirely sure why and I didn't care—if they killed me, so be it.

It was a strange realization. Reese and I hadn't even been together a full week. I didn't truly know what kind of man he was, ultimately. But I knew he had people who loved him. He'd been crazy about his wife, he'd raised two children by himself, and he'd protected me with his own life.

I had no justification to shoot Reese Hayes, no matter what was at stake. Period.

Let it be.

During the short ride to the Armory I drifted, thinking about everything and nothing . . . They'd bundled me roughly into the back of my own van, which I supposed would have to disappear along with my body. I wondered how they'd explain things to my employees, then figured it didn't really matter. None of them knew anything that could get them in trouble. They'd just have to find new jobs.

On the bright side, job hunting is rarely fatal.

Horse and Bam Bam drove me, with Gage in the backseat by my side. They'd cuffed my hands in front of my body, which was fairly considerate under the circumstances. I sort of expected a burlap bag over the head before being stuffed in a trunk. This seemed luxurious, all things considered.

After what felt like hours and still no time at all, we pulled up to the Armory and they opened the gate into the back courtyard. The pale sunlight showed a very different picture from the way it'd been the last time I was here. The tables had been put away, and instead of laughing people, a grim circle of men wearing Reapers colors stood waiting for us.

Reese wasn't among them.

I opted not to meet their eyes when Gage opened the sliding door and caught my arm, dragging me out of my seat. He pushed me roughly across the pavement toward a sunken stairwell at the back of the building—a basement entrance, leading down into darkness.

You know, I'd been nervous the first time I walked into the Armory. It's an intimidating place and the men are rough and scary looking. Now I kept waiting for the numbness to lift and the fear to set in.

Nothing.

They hustled me along a barren, dimly lit concrete hallway lined with doors that looked like prison cells. One of them stood open, and

I saw a small cot with a nasty little mattress. Definitely a prison cell. I wondered what'd happened to the last person in there, then decided I really didn't want to know.

I'd tried to make death quick for Reese, and as painless as possible. I could only pray he'd do the same for me.

Gage shoved me through a door farther down the hallway. Two bare-bulbed work lights hung suspended from rusty hooks in the ceiling. A rope hung down, too—it'd been strung through a metal loop bolted into a massive support beam. Gage nudged me forward, looping the rope around the chain between the handcuffs.

Bam Bam caught the other end and pulled it, stretching my arms up and over my head. Shit—were they going to hang me from the ceiling? I'd just reached the point of discomfort when he stopped. Bam tied off the rope to another loop bolted to the wall. Horse watched me the entire time, as if he expected me to say something. Were they waiting for me to beg for mercy?

They'd be waiting for a while. The thought made me smile, and Gage finally broke the silence.

"Are you on something?"

I looked at him, startled. "What do you mean?"

"You're way the fuck too calm," he said slowly. "Did you take something? If you're about to OD, tell me. Drowning in your own puke isn't the way you want to go."

I shook my head.

"It's just that this is a huge relief," I said. His face showed the first emotion I'd seen. Surprise. That struck me as funny, and I started laughing—not gentle, dignified noise. These were real, genuine belly laughs. The kind where you snort your drink out your nose because it catches you by total surprise, and then your friends make fun of you and everyone catches it and you're all laughing like crazy people. You know what I'm talking about.

But these men weren't my friends and they weren't making fun of me. They were staring at me like I'd lost my mind. Maybe I had.

"Christ, she's falling apart," someone muttered. That was even funnier. I snorted again, then choked a little bit on my own giggles. I laughed so hard my throat hurt and tears streamed down my face.

A wall of cold water hit me, shocking me into silence.

I shook my head, blinking rapidly. Reese stood in front of me, an empty bucket in his hands. His eyes were cold and there was so much coiled tension in his body I could *feel* it, like electricity crackling through the air during a storm.

The bucket fell to the floor with a jolting clatter, and he kicked it out of his way.

"Shut the fuck up."

Eyes wide, I shut the fuck up because this was Reese, but not a Reese I'd ever seen. This couldn't possibly be the same man who'd laughed with me, made love to me . . .

I couldn't find my Reese in this man's face.

That first night at the Armory, he'd scared me. Then I'd fallen for him, and while my brain remembered he had darkness inside, my body convinced me it wasn't true. Now I realized I'd never seen the real Reese at all—I'd only seen hints of his true capacity.

Holy God.

This was the reality of Reese Hayes, and it was darker than I ever imagined.

He terrified me.

Expressionless, Reese stepped toward me, reaching down and slowly wrapping his fingers around the hilt of the big hunting knife he wore strapped to his leg. The thing was huge, and it'd freaked me out the first time I saw it. Then I'd gotten used to seeing it and it became just another part of him.

Apparently the part he used to murder people.

The wicked blade glinted as he brought it up, testing the edge with his thumb.

"You're going to kill me," I whispered, feeling my own mortality wrap around me like a suffocating blanket.

He didn't answer. Nope. Just started walking around behind me, circling out of my line of sight. I glanced toward the other men, wondering if they'd stop him or say anything, but their eyes were dead, and I saw my own end clearly reflected back at me. One of these Reapers would bury my body later tonight. Nobody would ever know what happened to me, and I would never learn what happened to Jess, either.

"Will you wait until we find out whether she's alive?" I asked hesitantly.

"Not the time to be askin' favors, sweetheart," he said with quiet emphasis. Suddenly he caught my hair, jerking my head backward hard and fast. The knife flashed, and then I felt the blade digging into my throat. A line of fire crossed my neck. This was it. Reese Hayes was about to slit my throat.

I waited to die, the sound of his breath harsh in my ear. Then he laughed.

"You don't get off that easy, bitch."

That's when I realized he hadn't severed my windpipe . . . The blade still pressed at my throat, and I felt a faint trickle of blood slide down my neck. He'd cut me, but not badly. Just enough to part the skin.

"Now tell me everything," he whispered. "Don't leave out anything, whether you think it's important or not. Got it?"

I started to nod and he jerked my hair back violently.

"Bad idea to nod when you've got a knife at your throat," Horse said casually from across the room. "Might wanna be a little more thoughtful in your movements right now, London. Just a suggestion."

"Yeah," I said, my voice so hoarse that it came out with a croak. I cleared my throat, then tried to talk again. "Um . . . you know Jess got mad at me and went down to her mom, Amber? Well, the guy Amber was living with is holding Jess prisoner. You already know she was scared of the men at Amber's house, told me she wanted to come home. That was Wednesday morning. Then my house blew up Wednesday night, and you brought me out to your place."

Reese's fingers tightened in my hair hard enough that I wondered if I'd have any left in a minute. The knife shifted painfully.

OhmyGodohmyGodohmyGod!

"So you know about that," I continued, almost thankful for the cuffs holding up my wrists. I wasn't sure I could've stayed on my feet without their support. "The next morning I called Jess and she said she'd changed her mind. That was in your bedroom, remember? Looking back, I think they'd taken her already. She didn't sound like herself, something was off. That night I came out here for the party—" Reese growled, low and deep in his throat. He jerked me into his body, still holding the knife to my throat, and I felt his cock hardening against my ass. Must've been remembering our time together out in the courtyard.

A hint of desire built between my legs, and I wondered just how much more twisted my lust for him could get. He'd made me feel free, adventurous . . . guess that sense of adventure ran deeper than I realized, if I could get turned on by him holding a knife to my throat.

In the unlikely event that I actually made it out of here alive, I really needed to look into some serious counseling. The thought struck me as funny, and a snort of laughter escaped. Nobody else laughed—guess they couldn't quite appreciate the humor?

"Your daydreamin' bullshit is only cute on days you haven't tried to kill me," Reese murmured in my ear. "Fuckin' talk or I'll cut you."

I swallowed, forcing myself to focus.

"So the next morning the girls invited me to go out with them and get pedicures. That was Saturday. We had a good time and got some lunch after. Then I left because I needed to get to work. I went back to my van and the front window was open. There was an envelope on the seat and I opened it. There was a phone, the same one you probably found in my purse. It's black."

"Didn't occur to you that maybe opening a strange envelope was a bad idea?" Bam Bam asked, his voice casual. "Your house had already blown up, and then you find someone's been in your car? Not real bright, London."

"Yeah, I'll give you that one," I said, biting back the urge to laugh again. God. What was wrong with me? Oh yeah . . . imminent death . . . "Not smart at all, but I did it anyway. They sent me a video chat request, and I answered it. Jess was there and I talked to her, and then they held her down and cut off one of her fingers while I watched."

Reese's breath hissed in my ear, and for the first time I saw the carefully blank expression on Horse's face crack a little. He looked . . . disgusted?

"So they cut off her finger and told me that I had to take pictures of papers I found in Reese's house," I said slowly. "They told me they'd kill her if I didn't, and I believed them. I think they might have done it already . . . They didn't care about hurting her, and they have no clue what they're dealing with. She's not a normal kid, at least not medically. Not with that shunt in her head. Other stuff isn't quite right with her, either—her brain doesn't process cause and effect correctly. Fetal drug effects. Amber did a lot of drugs while she was pregnant, so Jess came early and spent months in the NICU over at Sacred Heart. We'll never know if the hydrocephalus is connected to that . . ."

"Shoulda told me," Reese gritted out. "Shoulda told me about Jessica's medical shit, shoulda told me somethin' was wrong. Gave you lots of chances."

"Fuck, London," Gage said, shaking his head. "Why the hell didn't you come to us?"

"I hardly know you," I said, and for the first time I felt something that wasn't numbness or fear. Anger. "Why the hell would I come talk to you? Crazy men have my cousin and she's in danger, and all I really know about you is you throw great parties and everyone says you're criminals."

"Nice to know our time together meant so much to you," Reese whispered, and I've never heard so much menace in a man's voice before. But his cock was still hard against me and my nipples tightened in response.

Serious fucking counseling.

First thing on my to-do list, right after not dying in this basement.

"Think about it from my perspective," I said, trying to keep my voice calm. "I don't know you very well. Her life is at stake. Would you risk Em's life based on a relationship that's only a week old?"

Silence fell, so terrible I actually heard my own heartbeat.

"Babe, I wouldn't risk lettin' you flush a fuckin' toilet at this point."

"This is getting off track," Horse muttered. "Pic, hold it in. We gotta figure out the situation, then you can deal with her, bro. Hear me?"

"I hear you," Reese said. He let go of my hair abruptly, which scared the hell out of me because the sudden release pushed my throat deeper into the knife. Then the knife pulled away, and his hand wrapped around my throat instead, big fingers catching me under the jaw and pushing my head back into his shoulder.

Now I felt the full length of his body behind me, cradled in his embrace. How could this be the same man who'd held me before? I'd felt so safe in his arms. Now all I felt was terror.

Terror and unholy lust.

"So what does this mean in terms of them holdin' Jessica?" Bam Bam asked, his voice tight. "She need special drugs or somethin'?"

"No," I whispered. "But she's really vulnerable to infection and head trauma. That shunt gets damaged, it'll take her out fast. She can't be handled rough, it's too dangerous. I did what they said. I searched as much of the house as I could, although I didn't find anything."

"We know," Reese told me, tightening his hold until I could hardly breathe. "We watched you."

I closed my eyes tightly. God. I'd been so stupid.

"You knew all along?"

"Not all the details," Gage said, his voice soft. "But we knew you were working for them. That's why you had Puck on you."

"I guess that's not a huge surprise," I admitted. "It all felt wrong—I kept thinking you knew. Not that it matters. I couldn't find anything for them, and then they called me again today. I talked to Jessica, and then I watched them throw her down on a concrete floor. She hit her head and started having a seizure. He told me I have to kill Reese or she'll die. If he dies, they'll dump her at an ER. So I tried to kill him."

"Did you ever see their faces on the video?" Reese asked, his voice like ice.

"No, they only let me see Jess."

"Where did you get the gun?"

"They gave me an address and I drove there using the GPS on my phone. Up north of Hayden. It turned out to be the middle of a field, and a man met me there. He showed me how to use the gun. I didn't learn his name or anything."

"What then?"

"Then I went to Nate."

The air in the room changed. Sudden menace radiated from Reese, and his hand tightened so hard on my throat that I couldn't breathe and my vision started to swim with black dots.

"Let her go," Horse said suddenly. "You're gonna hurt her, Pic."

I squirmed, desperate for air.

"Fuck," Bam Bam said, his voice urgent. "Pic, let her the fuck go. You don't wanna do this, bro. Believe me."

Reese let me go, stepping away as I collapsed down in the handcuffs. I gasped for oxygen, vision hazy as Reese stalked around me, tossing his knife back and forth between his hands. He wasn't looking at me, though. No, he stared down his club brothers like a force of nature.

"Get the fuck out," Reese said, the words soft and calm and more terrifying than anything I'd ever heard before in my life. "Or I'll kill you."

"Fuck, bro—" Gage started. Reese shook his head slowly.

"Not playin' games," he told them. "Get out. My woman, my business."

Horse cocked his head, eyes assessing. Then he gave a sharp nod and left the room. Bam Bam followed, smacking his hand hard on the wall as he passed through the door. Gage stayed, studying us.

"Don't kill her," he said. "You'll regret it. Walk away."

"Last chance," Reese said, the words quiet and cold. Gage sighed and gave a sharp nod.

Then he walked out, leaving me alone with a madman.

He turned and our eyes met. I searched his, trying to identify what I saw there. Hate? Anger? Maybe rage or betrayal?

None of those words were strong enough to describe the air of cold menace filling the space between us. Menace, but also a flicker of awareness. There was something broken in my libido, I decided. I shouldn't be turned on by this. Not even a little bit. He started stalking toward me, lifting the knife and touching the side of the blade to one cheek.

"You went to Nate."

I closed my eyes and swallowed.

"I didn't want to kill you," I whispered. "It'd gone too far. Looking for papers is one thing, but shooting a man is another."

"Yet you pointed a gun at me and pulled the trigger."

"That's because of Nate," I replied. He lowered the knife and raised his hand, brushing a finger down my cheek. Then he caught a strand of my hair and slowly wound it around his fingers, until it pulled and I couldn't move my head. He leaned forward, brushing his nose against my cheek and whispering in my ear.

"Did you fuck him?"

The hot touch of his breath sent a thrill through me, some sort of twisted lust mixed up with fear and adrenaline, and a sick, savage pleasure that he wanted to know, 'cause nothing fucked up about that, right?

"No," I said, the word hoarse. "I met him at a diner. I told him what was happening, and what they were trying to get me to do. Then he said he knew all about it and that he's the one that blew up my house."

"Told you he wasn't a very nice guy," Reese said, sucking my earlobe into his mouth. I moaned, and he twisted my head back, forcing me to look up at him. His mouth ghosted across my skin, and he nipped at my lip. I gasped, almost expecting a kiss, but instead he asked another question. "Let me guess—he's buddies with the guy holdin' Jessica, and this was all a setup?"

"Yes," I whispered. "He said he . . . He said he had sex with Jessica. That he gave her money. Melanie told me she had an older boyfriend who bought things for her. I think it must've been him. He told me I had to kill you and that the police couldn't do anything to help me."

"So you came home and tried to shoot me?"

"Yes."

"That was very, very stupid," Reese said, his voice growing hard as he pulled back from me. "And now you're going to pay. But you're a very lucky girl, did you know that?"

"Why?" I asked, my voice a whisper.

He offered a feral smile.

"Because I still want to fuck you."

More of that sick lust tore through me, all mixed with fear as he raised his knife. Grasping the neckline of my shirt, he slowly slit the fabric in half, exposing my upper body and bra. Then he tugged the bra down, popping my breasts out the top.

I saw the pulse pounding in his neck, smelled a hint of musky sweat. It was messed up and horrible and wrong in every way, but I wanted him inside me. Desperately. That's my only explanation for what I did next.

Licking my lips, I spoke, taunting him.

"You wanna talk or you wanna fuck? 'Cause I know which one I'd prefer."

His cheeks flushed dark red and then the knife whipped upward, slashing through the rope holding my handcuffs. I collapsed instantly, and he caught me, throwing me roughly over his shoulder as he carried me out the door. I had a vague impression of bare concrete, bright white lights, and a grim-faced Gage as we found the little room with the cot. Reese slammed the door shut behind us with his foot.

I hit the bed hard, knocking the wind right out of me. Then I heard a slithering, whipping sound, and Reese was cinching my hands to the top of the bed with his belt. Seconds later my pants came down around my ankles. His hands grabbed my hips, lifting them high and I felt his cock at my entrance.

Then his eyes caught mine and he snarled.

I screamed when he slammed home, because it hurt and I was scared and it felt incredibly good and my brain just wouldn't work anymore. Reese wasn't a gentle lover under the best of circumstances, but this was brutal. He stilled and braced above me with those strong arms of his, smiling.

It wasn't a friendly or loving smile.

No. This smile was a baring of teeth, and in his eyes I saw rage, pure and simple. Rage and hate and some kind of unholy, twisted desire that cut through both of us, no matter how sick that was. Holding my gaze, he pulled back and thrust again, this time harder. It burned and I cried out, but he didn't stop. I didn't want him to, either. I wanted more—I wanted him to pin me and fill me with his come and I didn't care anymore whether that was wrong or right.

I just needed this terrible tension building between us to break. I needed *him*.

"That the best you can do?" I demanded, laughing almost hysterically. He growled and my laugh turned into a shriek as he showed me that no, it wasn't the best he could do. It was just the beginning, because Reese started thrusting into me so hard my body could hardly take it. My legs spread wide and my hips pressed back into the thin mattress and I screamed again. I had never, ever in my entire life felt anything so amazingly good as the sensation of his body tearing into mine.

This wasn't sex—this was revenge and it was *perfect*.

He pounded into me without mercy after that, our eyes glued to each other, lips snarling. There were no tender kisses, no playful giggles. Just the raw desire of two people whose lives had crashed together in the worst possible way. My orgasm didn't build slowly and wash over me. Nope. It slammed through me, ripping apart my existence until I cried out and tears ran down my face.

Reese didn't even acknowledge that it'd happened.

He just sank deep inside over and over again, driving my body toward another explosion. I think my synapses weren't firing right, because I knew I'd be raw and bruised after this. I just didn't care. I wanted to take all of his hate and pain and anger and own it because I deserved it, but instead of suffering he just kept filling me and it felt way, way too good.

Then it hit again. I blew apart, my fragile mind all but shattering with the intensity.

This time he came with me, groaning painfully as his hot seed shot deep inside. His arms quivered and his heavy frame hung over mine as I crumpled, utterly exhausted. I'd used up my adrenaline, lost the edge of fear in favor of lust, and couldn't even bring myself to think about poor Jessica. My brain had had enough, and my body agreed. Reese pulled away from me without a word, and I realized we hadn't used a condom. Oh well.

My life span probably wouldn't be long enough to worry about STDs anyway.

I heard the sound of him zipping up, and then his big hands came down around mine, pulling the belt free but leaving me cuffed. He turned and walked out of the cell, slamming his hand against the wall as he went. The door clanged shut and the bolt slid home with a thunk.

I blinked in the darkness, trying to figure out what had just happened.

Holy. Shit.

I had no place to store this in my head. I didn't want to think about what we'd done, how much I enjoyed it, or whether it meant anything. Considering this situation too carefully was scary, and I couldn't afford to be afraid right now. Not if I wanted to survive and save Jessica.

My natural pragmatism kicked in. I was alive. I had no idea how much longer that would last, but I had to make the most of it. I closed my eyes and started taking deep breaths, counting to ten on each inhale and exhale. The relaxation technique had served me well over the years, and it didn't fail me that night.

Eventually sleep crept in, bringing an entirely different kind of release than what I'd found with Reese.

The cold woke me.

I tried to reach for the covers, to pull them up and over my freezing body. Then I realized there weren't any, because I was on a cot in a cell in the Armory basement. My shirt and bra were ripped apart, my hands were cuffed together, and my wet jeans were still tucked around my ankles.

Other than that, things were great.

I rolled onto my back, bemused. I hadn't really expected to make it this far. I sort of assumed that I'd tell them everything and they'd shoot me. The end.

Finding myself alive threw me.

I tried to think, figure out what the next step should be. Nothing came—all of this was so far beyond my ability to process that my brain just spun out.

None of that changed the fact that I was cold. Maybe I could do something to fix that?

It took me a couple of tries to stand up because my legs were cold and rubbery. One of my feet had fallen asleep, too, which wasn't such a bad thing once I caught my balance. The tingling pins and needles helped me wake up and sharpen my perspective. I set about pulling my pants up, which was harder than you'd think, because they had that cold, wet, clingy thing going on that makes jeans so unpleasant sometimes.

My bra was a lost cause, but I managed to stretch my shirt across my chest. It wasn't great, but it was better than just sitting around all naked and vulnerable. I walked around the cell, testing the door with my cuffed hands. It didn't open—big surprise there, right?

By that time I was getting seriously cold. I sat back down on the bed and realized that what I'd thought was the mattress cover was actually a thin, woolen blanket wrapped over the padding—one of those striped army surplus ones from three wars back.

Crawling under it wasn't easy, but I figured the wool might help me stay warm. Theoretically, wool holds in heat even when it's wet. Practically, huddling under a wet wool blanket in a basement sucks ass, and I'm saying that as a lady who tries not to cuss. My teeth started chattering as I considered my options.

I still wasn't quite sure what to make of that last little episode with Reese. I felt sore between my legs and dirty in my soul, but I couldn't deny it'd been the best sex I'd ever had in my life. Messed up, but I don't believe in hiding from the truth—apparently scary life-and-death situations turned me on.

Or at least they turned me on when Reese was involved.

Go figure.

I supposed I could use that to try to stay alive, manipulate him somehow—I was over the whole "I don't care if I live or die" numb feeling from the night before. When the shit hit the fan and Reese whipped out that big knife of his, I had very much wanted to live.

Okay, so I had that figured out. I wasn't going to just lie down and die. Good to know.

But what was I willing to do to stay alive? Yesterday I'd decided to kill an innocent man to save Jessica's life. That hadn't ended so well for me, and I was forced to admit the truth. I really wasn't a very good assassin. This limited my options, which was probably just as well.

So what should I do next?

The answer seemed clear. I'd do whatever I could to help the Reapers fight their enemies, because despite my little episode with Reese, I knew who the real bad guys were. Nate and his drug dealer friends down south. They'd killed Amber, they were killing Jessica—if they hadn't already—and they'd almost made me kill Reese.

A knife at my throat followed by crazy monkey sex in a basement wasn't all that bad in comparison. I tried to shoot him. In exchange he'd given me two orgasms, so I guess in some ways that counted as a win?

Maybe the Reapers would be able save Jessica, although whether they'd be motivated to try was a whole different question. I certainly couldn't do anything more for her at this point, and the cops obviously weren't an option. *Assholes.* If I got very lucky, Jessica might live. If cooperating with the Reapers raised those odds in any way, I'd consider helping them my new goal in life.

And if Jessica died?

Well, then I'd spend whatever time and freedom I had left hunting down the fuckwads who'd done this to us. I might be a crappy assassin, but I was a fast learner and I had a sneaking suspicion that Reese would be a hell of a good teacher.

Sound crazy?

Probably, but what other options did I have? The only ones who hadn't lied to me or used me were Reese and his brothers, and we shared a common enemy. Wars have been won with less, so maybe we could pull something off.

Assuming they didn't kill me first.

CHAPTER FIFTEEN

REESE

"Nate Evans. Always a pleasure."

I smiled at my least favorite law enforcement officer, because some twisted part of me was almost relieved he'd finally fucked up bad enough for us to take him out. The once and future prince of the Kootenai County Sheriff's Department sat tied to a metal chair in the center of our interrogation-slash-torture room, face covered with fresh bruises.

Not a bad look on him.

Bolt loosened the bandanna gagging Nate's mouth, smacking him on the head in the process for good measure. Deputy Dick had pulled Maggs over for "speeding" once.

Bolt wasn't a fan.

"Have you lost your fucking mind?" Nate demanded. "I'm a cop. They'll be looking for me—they'll never stop. Not even you guys can kidnap a deputy and get away with it."

"I got a feeling Bud will find evidence that you were embezzling, and that you took off," I said slowly. "Sounds like a cold case to me. Ya think?"

"*You can't do this,*" he said, shaking his head in blind denial. "My family will destroy you. *This isn't how it works.*"

"I think it's safe to say that today, this *is* how it works," I told him, feeling a smile creep across my face. "You fucked up, but I have good news for you. You still got a shot to get out of here alive."

He shook his head and spat.

"You'll never let me go," he said. "You know you're fucked."

"But you said I was fucked if I *didn't* let you go," I countered mildly. "You should probably work on those threats a bit. These contradictions are confusing, and you really can't afford to have us get frustrated, now can you?"

Horse grinned.

"I think I should be the one to do it," he told me. "I don't really have anything against him. Not personally, I mean. You all have too many reasons to want him to suffer before he dies, so letting me kill him fast would really be the merciful thing."

I shrugged.

"You're probably right. You know how sloppy I get when I'm pissed off, and then the prospects will have a big mess to clean up."

Horse carefully took off his cut, folding it and handing it to Bam Bam. Then he picked up a hammer and started toward Evans, whistling a familiar tune faintly. I tried to place it . . .

"The Wheels on the Bus."

Fucked-up shit, but that's sort of what we loved about Horse.

Seconds later he brought the hammer down hard on the good deputy's right hand. The man started screaming like a baby.

"So, here's the part where I tell you I changed my mind about making it fast," Horse said, his tone friendly. "It's just so much fun, you know? Now I'm going to break all the bones in your feet so you can't walk ever again . . ."

Nate shrieked and babbled, tears running down his face.

"Oh, c'mon," Bam Bam said, his voice heavy with disgust. "You fucked that girl and sent her down there to die. You blew up London's house. Then you blackmailed her into shooting Pic. Now you're whining because of a broken hand? I thought you were hardcore and shit, but you're just a little girl with a badge."

Nate's jaw started working, and we waited patiently until he managed to form words.

"I'll do anything you want," he gasped. "Just don't hit me again. Don't kill me. I don't want to die."

"How 'bout this," I said slowly. "You call your friends down south and tell them me and London are dead. Murder-suicide, or some such shit. If they let the kid live, we'll let you live."

"How do I know you'll keep your promise? You can't afford to let me survive at this point."

I sighed heavily, rubbing my temples with a thumb and finger.

"You know, I almost don't want him to call," I told Horse. "Jessica is a pain in my ass, and if she comes back home, I won't get as much pussy. Doesn't change anything in terms of the war if we save her. Why don't you just have some fun with him, and then when you get bored we'll shoot him?"

"Okay," Horse said, shrugging.

"Wait!" Evans shouted.

I cocked a brow at him. "I thought we couldn't afford to let you live? That's what you just told me. What's the holdup?"

"While he's still alive, he's still got hope," Bam said, smirking. "So now he's gonna do exactly what you tell him, because every minute he's breathing means he could still get out of this. Am I right, Nate?"

"Get my phone," Nate said, sweat breaking out on his forehead. "I'll make the call."

"We'll dial for you, 'cause we're helpful that way," Horse said. "People don't always give us full credit for our warm, fuzzy side, but it's definitely there. We just love to help."

"Fuckin' Mother Teresa of the MC world, Horse," Ruger chimed in. "Brings a tear to my eye."

Gage snorted and tossed me the man's phone.

"Who do I call?" I asked. "Remember, if you double-cross us, you die. If Jessica dies, you die. You got a lot more to lose here than I do, because I really don't give two shits about the kid. Might be easier for me if she doesn't live. Something to keep in mind."

"Julia Strauss," he said. "That's the number."

I scrolled through the contacts, finding the name. Then I hit the call button and put it on speakerphone. It picked up, but nobody spoke.

"It's me," Nate said, eyes darting quickly around the room. I wondered if he'd warn them. Probably not. The man was too much of a coward to sacrifice himself for a cause. For once I agreed with him—the cartel wasn't worth a sacrifice, and they sure as shit wouldn't appreciate or reward one. "It's done."

There was a pause, and then a man with a deep voice and faint Spanish accent replied.

"You sure? We didn't hear anything on the scanner."

"No police report," Nate said. "London called me after she shot him, and I went out there. Now she's dead, too, made it look like a murder-suicide. I left them—we'll let someone else find the bodies. You can let the girl go now."

The man gave a harsh laugh.

"I'll authorize the transfer to your account," he said, and the line went dead.

Nate's face fell, the hope in his eyes fading.

"They're going to kill her," he said. "Always knew they would. She's a good kid . . ."

I punched him in the face so hard his chair fell over backward. His head hit the floor with a hollow-sounding thud and he started crying again. Standing over him, I cracked my knuckles, choosing my words for maximum effect.

"While she's alive, you're alive," I told him. "So if you have any idea how to find these fuckers, now is the time to talk. If we get her out because of information you give us, the deal stands."

"I thought you didn't care if she lived or not?" he asked, blinking in the glare of the work lights hanging from the ceiling. "You're going to kill me and we both know it. Why should I help you?"

Painter stepped over, nudging the man's shoulder with one booted foot. He'd only just gotten back to the Armory, after settling Melanie in at the house. Perfect timing—he had his own scores to settle with Evans.

"How's this?" he asked, the words soft and feral. "Let's throw in a little more motivation. How 'bout you help us get Jess out safe and I won't kill your parents."

I glanced at him, impressed because he'd really stepped up his game. Painter was still young, but the past year had changed him. Nate's mouth gaped and Painter laughed, reaching down to grab the front of his uniform shirt, jerking his body up—chair and all—and setting him upright again. Then he leaned down, right into Evans's face.

"I don't get off on old bitches, but I'll make an exception for your mom," he whispered. "This is my promise to you. I'll fuck every hole she has before I slit her throat, and I'll be sure to tell her it's all from you."

"I can give you an address," Evans moaned, his entire body shaking. "I don't know for sure if he's there, but he has a warehouse. I saw it once. It's the perfect place to hold her—that's all the information I have."

"Well, aren't you just the reasonable little man?" Horse asked, grinning at him. "I just knew we could work this out. Now let's take care of some more business. I think you need to call in sick to work— you just don't look quite right. Maybe it's your time of the month or somethin', so you'd best let them know. Wouldn't want 'em worrying, would we?"

"Gee, you're always so thoughtful," Bam Bam said to Horse.

"I try," Horse responded, his tone modest. I snorted back a laugh, then nodded at Painter to follow me out of the room.

"That was a new level of twisted shit, little bro," I said quietly as we walked down the hall together toward London's room. "Not that I don't appreciate it, but what the fuck?"

Painter shrugged.

"If Jessica dies, Melanie will cry."

I studied him, wondering if I wanted to go there. Nope, I really didn't.

"Fair enough. Go let the others know we're riding to Portland. Deke called in a favor, so we'll be hopping a cargo flight south from there."

"'Bout time we took the war to them," Painter replied, that feral gleam in his eyes again.

"Don't get too excited. There'll be bodies before this is over."

"Can't live forever. You decide what you're doing with London yet?"

I stopped in front of her door, frowning thoughtfully.

"No goddamn idea," I said. "Takin' her to Portland with us. We'll make a decision there. She might be useful to us down south—don't like the idea of leaving her alone here. Someone might go vigilante on her ass."

"Sounds good, prez," he said, then started toward the stairs. I grasped the bolt, sliding it open, then reached for the handle to open the door, wondering what exactly the fuck I was going to do about London.

Heather, if you're actually out there somewhere, I could sure use your advice right about now.

She didn't answer, which shouldn't have surprised me, seein' as she was a figment of my imagination. Still, bitch always chimed in fast enough when it *wasn't* convenient for me. Probably sittin' up in heaven right now, drinkin' a beer and laughing her ass off.

Fuckin' women.

LONDON

By the time Reese came back, I'd started shivering so hard my muscles and joints ached from the strain. My toes and fingers had gone numb, and while freezing to death wasn't exactly a danger, this borderline hypothermia shit bit the big one.

Then I heard footsteps outside the door, and the low murmur of voices. The bolt slid back with a thud and the door opened. Light from the hallway blinded me at first, and I blinked rapidly at the shadowy outline of what had to be Reese.

I supposed I should be scared of him, but I was just way too cold.

"H-hey," I said, the word unsteady. "A-a-any word on J-Jess?"

"What's wrong?" he asked, and I started laughing because the question was so ridiculously stupid.

"W-w-why don't we just l-list what's right?" I asked, too tired and cold to think straight. He shut the door and came toward me, sitting down on the bed.

"Shit, you're freezing," he muttered, pulling back the blankets. *"Fuck."*

Within seconds, he'd wrapped me up in the blanket and was carrying me out of the room, yelling at Painter to go find some keys or something. He hauled me down the corridor and up three flights of stairs before turning down the same long hallway we'd visited when I'd first come looking for Jessica.

Painter was ahead of us, opening up one of the rooms, and then Reese carried me in and set me on my feet. He fumbled for a minute to unlock the handcuffs, then stripped off my wet clothing with smooth efficiency. He led me to a tiny bathroom, switching on the shower and waiting until steam started rising before putting me under the hot spray.

Amazing.

The water flooded over me, and after a few minutes my shivers died down. Reese stood watching me, his face pensive, until the water started to cool. I reached over and twisted the faucet closed.

"You have a towel?" I asked, feeling self-conscious. Sure, he'd seen me naked . . . but that was *before*. He stepped out of the bathroom, returning seconds later to hold a towel out to me wordlessly. I dried off quickly, then wrapped it around me.

"You're all bruised up," he said.

I shrugged. "Shit happens."

"C'mon over to the bed. Let's talk."

"Is this like the last 'talk' we had?" I asked, my voice rasping—probably from all the screaming I'd done. "I know you're in charge, but I'm still kind of sore down below. Not sure I can handle more talking quite yet."

He shook his head, eyes serious. I walked over to him as he sat on the bed and learned back against the wall. He caught my hand and tugged me down until I settled between his legs, my back to his stomach. His arms came around me and I let myself relax into his heat and strength, wishing things had been different.

"Is there anything I can do to help?" I asked him finally, hating to break the strange sense of peace that had settled between us. "I realize you have no reason to believe me, but I'm sorry for what I did, Reese. Really sorry, and not just because it backfired on me. I know it was wrong and stupid and you'll never trust me again . . . but if there's a way for me to help you fight, I want to do it."

"Fight? What do you mean?"

"I'm not stupid. These people—these drug dealers—they're out to hurt you, and probably a whole lot of other people, too."

"They're a cartel. Big one, out of Mexico. Control the West Coast trade, up through northern Cali. Movin' upward now into Oregon and southern Idaho."

"I want to stop them. I don't care what it takes," I murmured, burrowing deeper into his embrace. My neck still hurt from the tiny cut he'd given me, but considering I'd tried to shoot him, I'd gotten off easy. At least so far. I still didn't know what they planned to do with me, but for the moment I chose not to think about the future.

Sounds crazy, but even now I felt safe when he held me.

"What about Jess?" he asked.

"I don't think they ever planned to let her go," I whispered. "I think she's going to die unless someone stops them. Kills them. They're evil."

"Wish you weren't right," he replied, and I felt his chin come to rest on top of my head. "Cartel bastards think I'm dead now. Think you shot me, then killed yourself. They still aren't gonna let her go, even though we gave them what they wanted."

Shit. I'd suspected, but hearing Reese lay it all out felt like a punch to the gut. I swallowed.

"How did you convince them we're dead?"

"Deputy Dick told them."

"Why would he lie to them? Isn't that dangerous?"

"We asked him very nicely."

Somehow I didn't think Reese was using the word "nicely" in the traditional sense. Didn't sound promising for Nate's future prospects. I considered the situation—did it bother me that the Reapers had obviously done something terrifying and horrible to make him lie?

No. It really didn't. Did that make me a bad person?

I decided I didn't care.

"He used Jess, then he sent her down to those people knowing what they are," I said slowly. "And he tried to turn me into a murderer. I don't know if it's allowed under the circumstances, but I'd like to see him before you kill him. Talk to him. I have things to say, and I'd like to see his face when he realizes he lost."

"Assuming we had him—and I'm not sayin' we do—why would we let you witness something that could be used against us?"

"I want to be an accomplice," I told him, the words spilling out of me with sudden force. "I want to make Nate pay, and I want to shut those fuckers down. I know you're planning to do something big. I can sense it—all those meetings? People coming in from all over, and extra security? There's something happening and I'm in the middle of it now. I messed everything up with you, and I know you can't trust me . . . But I'll do whatever I can to help. *Anything*. I figure there's a good chance I won't survive this situation and I'm coming to peace with that—but I really want to make Nate pay before I go, Reese. I want to look him in the eye and watch him suffer. Then I want to shoot him."

The thought made me smile, and I wondered how the hell I'd gone from cleaning lady to bloodthirsty killer. Okay, so I wasn't a very *competent* killer, but the sentiment was there . . .

"Damn," he muttered, pulling me into him tighter. "When did you turn so hard-core?"

"When I realized my girl is dying or already dead"—the words made me choke, but I forced myself to push past them—"and that Nate Evans is the reason. I had a good life before I met him. It wasn't perfect, but I had a home and a family, and he took them away from me. Fuck him, Reese. He should have to pay for what he did."

I felt Reese's lips touch the top of my head as I bit back tears. I didn't want to cry or look weak or beg for mercy—I'd made my bed . . . Now I had to own up to my choices.

"I'm sorry," I whispered. "Sorry for all of it. For trying to shoot you. For not trusting you. You didn't deserve any of this."

"Little late for that."

"I know."

Silence fell again.

"We're going to Portland in a couple of hours," Reese said softly. "Then we're heading down to California to make a strategic strike at the cartel leadership. Got our targets already, been scoping 'em out for a long time now. I'm going to try and find Jessica while I'm down there."

I felt a sudden surge of hope, then bit it back. I couldn't afford hope.

"How can I help?"

"You can't, unless you remembered something you haven't told us already?"

I shook my head, thinking hard.

"I told you everything," I said. "I wish I knew more. Will you let me see Nate?"

He didn't answer for a minute, and then he sighed.

"Yeah. But you can't shoot him. We might still need his ass."

"What's going to happen to him?"

"That's on a need-to-know basis. Somethin' you should learn about the club—we don't like it when people ask too many questions. We'll be leaving soon, and you're coming with us. Marie is bringing over some shit for you to wear."

My breath caught.

"Does she know what I did?"

"Nope," he said. "And she won't. We don't need the girls all worked up about your situation, so keep your mouth shut if you happen to see one of them."

"Thank you," I said quietly.

"For what?"

"Trusting me again."

"I don't trust you for shit."

"You trust me enough to come to Portland with you. I can't change what happened, but I promise I won't fuck up again, Reese."

"You really expect me to fall for that?"

I sighed, so many thoughts running through my head that I couldn't hardly catch them all . . .

"Just promise me one thing," I said finally.

"What's that?"

"If there's a way for me to help you stop the cartel, let me do it. I don't care if it's dangerous. You can even use me for bait, if you think it'll work. I just want the chance to fight back, for Jessica and for me."

He exhaled hard. "We'll see."

. . .

Half an hour later I was dressed in biker babe clothing just a little too small for my generous curves. Marie and I were the same height, but my chest was a little more . . . substantial. At least I was warm and dry. They'd even found me a leather jacket somewhere, which was important because apparently I'd be riding to Portland on the back of Reese's bike. This surprised me—I'd assumed he wouldn't want me around, or that his brothers wouldn't tolerate me.

Apparently the politics of biker betrayal were more complicated than I realized.

People had started gathering for the trip when Reese led me down the stairs and into the basement for a second time that night. I followed him down the hallway until we reached the same nasty, scary room where they'd hung me from the ceiling just a few hours earlier.

Things were moving so fast I could hardly keep up.

Reese pushed the door open, and I walked in to find Nate sitting in a battered metal chair, his arms and legs tied down tight. A dirty bandanna had been used to gag his mouth. Dried blood crusted his face and hair. It looked to me like one of his hands had been smashed with a mallet.

He wasn't a happy camper.

The fire I felt died a little, because imagining Nate in pain and seeing him like this were two very different things. I didn't feel sorry for him, exactly. Just sort of creeped out. I was determined, though. I wanted to personally make him pay and this was my big opportunity.

"You wanted to talk to him?" Bolt asked, and I glanced over to see he'd been waiting for us in the room. I nodded hesitantly.

"Nate, are you awake?" I asked. My former boyfriend's eyes flickered open, catching on my face.

"You want the gag off?" Reese asked, his hand at the small of my back. I still had no idea what the club had planned for me in the next twenty-four hours, but at least they hadn't beaten the shit out of me like this. Good thing, too. I had too much work to do before they killed me. Jessica needed saving and I wanted revenge, too. After that? Well, I'd probably be dead then, so I guess I wouldn't worry about it.

"No, I don't want to hear anything he has to say," I answered. Then I took a deep breath, steeling myself. "Nate, I came down here because I want you to know I see exactly who and what you are. You're a pathetic, evil little man, and I hope they kill you. I already asked Reese if I could shoot you and he said no. I found this very disappointing."

Nate's eyes widened and I smiled, understanding for the first time in my life how one person could enjoy hurting another, because for better or worse this felt kind of good.

Empowering.

I stepped closer, leaning down to examine his smashed hand.

"That's never going to heal up right," I said softly, then looked up at his face. One of his eyes was swollen nearly shut, and it took everything I had not to poke it, just to see him flinch. "So I've been trying to decide what I should do to make you pay . . . I could hit you, or poke you, or maybe just take those broken fingers of yours and start twisting them around for fun. Maybe cut them off? That's what your friends did to Jessica."

He grunted frantically and I spat in his face, which was vaguely satisfying, but nowhere near enough. I stood up, glancing around the room. In the corner was a pile of wood scraps, including a chunk of two-by-four about the length of a bat. Perfect. I walked over and grabbed it, hefting it experimentally. Felt good in my hand.

Gage gave a low, warning whistle.

"We need him alive," he said. "And able to talk."

I nodded thoughtfully, then walked back toward Nate, studying his frame. Drawing back the wood, I swung it at his right knee with everything I had. It hit with a crunch and he screamed through the gag. I felt a little sick to my stomach, but forced myself to speak.

"That's for using Jessica, and sending her down to California."

Taking a deep breath, I hit him again, this time on the other knee. He gave another piercing screech, then started a low, steady keening in pain.

"That's for fucking things up with me and Reese."

I paused to consider the situation. I wanted to hit him again. I'd planned one blow for each thing he'd done to ruin my life, which meant I still owed him for lying to me and for blowing up my house. Instead I dropped the two-by-four, because no matter how much the man deserved to suffer, a part of me realized I was sinking to his level.

Turning toward Reese, I spoke. "I'm good. Thanks for that."

He raised a brow.

"Sure? You might not have another chance."

I shrugged.

"He's like a vicious dog," I told him softly, realizing it was true. "No point in torturing a dog, even one that's a killer. Best to just shoot it in the head and dump the body."

Nate made another noise and I heard the chair scrape against the concrete floor. Ignoring him, I focused on Reese, holding those ice-blue eyes of his steadily, savoring the sight of the little wrinkles at the corners as he gave me a strange little smile. In the background, I was vaguely aware that Gage watched us curiously. It didn't matter. Nothing mattered anymore.

"You ready to go?" Reese asked me quietly. I nodded. Whatever happened next, I wasn't lying or playing games. I'd made my decision and it filled me with a weird sense of peace.

CHAPTER SIXTEEN

By the time we hit Portland, I was exhausted but still absolutely determined to do whatever I could to help the club—not only were they my best hope for saving Jessica, they were also my best shot at some sort of revenge for what those cartel fuckers had done to my life.

I needed sleep first, though. In a big way.

The short rides I'd taken with Reese hadn't come close to preparing me for this. My ass had started to hurt, growing slowly worse until finally it went numb. Even if I hadn't been sleep-deprived the trip would've killed me. Just to make things more pleasant, not one of the fifteen men riding with us would talk to me, or even look me in the eye.

Good times.

When we finally pulled down a narrow alley into a residential neighborhood, I didn't quite register that the ride was over. We stopped in front of a great big old carriage house with huge wooden sliding doors on the back. They opened slowly and the men rolled their bikes in, leaving just enough room on one side for the battered gray cargo van that had trailed us from Coeur d'Alene. They had a prospect driving it, but I had no idea what was in the back.

No way I'd be asking, either.

I'd learned my lesson about questions.

The heavy doors slid shut behind us, blocking out the light and sound. Some seriously solid walls in this place. As my vision adjusted, I looked around in the gloom to find Hunter, Em's boyfriend, watching the activities with a proprietary air.

His gaze caught on me standing next to Reese, and he strolled over to join us.

"What's the story there, Pic?" he asked quietly, ignoring me. "Not a trip for women."

Reese shook his head, face grim.

"We had an unpleasant incident yesterday," he said. "I'll tell you all about it later, but the quick and dirty is she tried to kill me. Cartel was behind it."

Hunter's face hardened.

"Sorry to hear that," he said. "We were all hopin' it would work out."

"Shit happens," Pic said. "Fuckers have her cousin—she did it to save the kid's life."

"Sounds like an interesting story," Hunter said, his jaw tightening. "So she's a prisoner?"

Reese nodded sharply.

"Haven't decided what to do with her yet, but figure the Portland prospects can babysit her just as easy as the Coeur d'Alene ones. Didn't want to leave her behind. We haven't had time to make any decisions, you know how that goes."

"I got a strong room we can put her in," Hunter said.

"We'll need that for someone else."

That caught my attention, and I glanced back at the van. Had they hauled Nate across the state, too?

"How about the storage room upstairs?" Hunter asked. "It's not as secure, but the window's high enough she won't be able to climb out and she'll have to pass through the chapel to leave the building. Should be safe enough for the afternoon."

"Sounds good," Reese answered. He gave me a nudge and I followed Hunter upstairs through a big, open space with a broad wooden table and then down a hallway to the storage room.

"Don't touch anything," he told me, his voice grim. "You wouldn't wanna learn what happens if you break something. And if you find something in here you can use as a weapon, don't. This is my place, and I don't give a damn how much Pic likes fuckin' you. You pull any shit, you're dead."

I nodded, studying the room after he closed the door behind me. Dusty boxes lined three of the four walls. The last wall had a garage sale couch pushed up against it, and above the couch was an old leaded-glass window. I climbed onto the cushions and looked out to find a fenced backyard hidden behind the carriage house. The house attached to the yard was two stories, with a high porch off the back. It looked to have been built about a hundred years ago—obviously one of those not-quite-Victorians littering the older neighborhoods in Portland.

Must be Hunter and Em's place, I realized. They probably lived in the house while his club used the carriage house out back as a base of operations. Not a bad setup, all things considered.

I could see a barbecue pit in the center of the grass, with several canvas folding chairs circling it. There wasn't much open space, though. The yard was essentially a jungle—just a mass of overgrown shrubs surrounded by a circle of mature trees providing complete privacy, despite the fact that I knew there had to be buildings on either side of us. Nobody would be able to see my window, that was for sure.

Good thing I wasn't trying to catch any attention, or escape.

I wondered how long I'd be stuck here. Considering I hadn't really slept in nearly twenty-four hours, being locked up long enough for a nap sounded pretty good. I flopped down on the couch and closed my eyes.

Bliss.

I don't know how long I'd been out when the sound of a car backfiring woke me. I took a minute to orient myself, rubbing the sleep out of my eyes and wiping off what felt suspiciously like a trail of drool.

Sexy.

The light had changed—now it streamed through the window much more brightly. I rose to my knees and looked down through the leaded glass to find Em sunning herself on a white blanket in the center of the lawn. She wore a bright red bikini that showed off a very small, very cute baby bump, and one arm had been thrown over her eyes.

The girl was obviously sound asleep. Early pregnancy. I hadn't had children myself, but I'd seen enough of my friends go through it to learn that sometimes naps weren't optional. Such a pretty girl.

God, I hoped I got my own pretty girl back, safe and sound.

Reese was a lucky man, because while I hadn't met his other daughter yet, Em was a treasure for sure. He'd done a great job with her despite losing his wife so tragically. As I watched, Em shifted restlessly and rolled to the side, dropping her arm down to clutch her stomach. Her face twisted, but she didn't seem to wake up.

Oh, fuck.

Something was very, very wrong here . . .

Bright red blood covered the blanket where she'd been lying—blood that seemed to be coming from between her legs. She must not be asleep, but unconscious. Blood smeared the backs of her thighs. Adrenaline hit, and I ran for the door, jerking at the knob desperately. Nothing. I pounded on it, yelling for someone to come and get me.

Nobody responded.

The walls were old and thick, built by hand to last.

ShitShitShitShitShit! Em might be dying out there, and obviously nobody could see it but me. I had to do something.

Running back to the window, I climbed up onto the couch and peered through the glass, trying to figure out how to get down to her. Nothing really jumped out at me, but maybe I'd be able to figure something out if I broke out the glass. I found an old, broken stool propped against a pile of boxes and grabbed it, shoving the legs through the glass. It shattered easily enough, and after three more blows I managed to knock the leading out, too.

Pulling off my leather jacket, I laid it down across the windowsill to protect my hands from glass shards, then leaned out to take a good look around. In the movie version of my life, this was where I'd find a convenient tree branch, or maybe an old trellis to serve as a ladder.

Nada.

I *did* see a great big shrub right below the window, though. Maybe if I climbed out I could lower myself to shorten the fall, then jump into the bushes to cushion myself? A quick glance at Em showed the pool of blood spreading slowly but steadily.

Shrubbery it was, then.

I climbed out and caught the sill with my hands. That's when the first thing went wrong, because instead of lowering myself down carefully, I fell off the ledge with a thump. The second thing to go wrong was the shrub itself, which had seemed rather lush and cushiony from the window.

Not so much.

I'd fallen into a forest of pointy branches, cutting through me like a thousand tiny, sharpened stakes. My right arm screamed in agony, and I looked down to see a quarter inch stick passing right through the fleshy part of my forearm. My vision blackened, and I took a couple of deep breaths, willing myself to hold it together.

Em needed me.

Painfully, I pulled my arm off the stick, ignoring the gush of blood as I shoved my way out of the bushes. My entire body was covered in smaller scratches and cuts, and I felt something warm and wet trickling down my face. At least nothing seemed to be broken.

I ran across the yard toward Reese's bleeding daughter, dropping to my knees to check her pulse. There, but very weak. *Fuck*. I saw a phone lying in the grass next to a bottle of water. A real phone, the kind that's connected to a landline. Thank God for that, because I didn't have an address to give them.

I grabbed it and dialed 911 frantically, praying it wasn't too late.

REESE

"Burke will meet us in Cali," Hunter said. "They went down to scope out targets already. Shade and his boys will be flying in this evening, and the Silver Bastards are headed south, too. Between them and our local allies, we should have close to three hundred men."

"What's scary is not even that many guys are enough to stand up to the cartel head-on," Horse grunted.

"Their soldiers are disposable," I said. "Ours aren't. We know what we're doin' and we can trust each other. Combine that with the fact that we aren't giving 'em the chance to meet us head-on, I think it'll be enough."

"So we're wheels up just after ten tonight," Hunter said. "It's a cargo plane, and things are all smoothed out with the shipping company. The pilot's a friend of mine and he's solid. When we land, we'll have brothers there to meet us and we'll bring our own hardware. Sound good to everyone?"

The room filled with grunts and nods of approval.

"Thanks for settin' all of this up," I told him.

"No prob," Hunter replied, glancing toward the man sitting next to him, who rolled his eyes. "I made Skid do most of the work, anyway. I suppose now it's time to talk about your woman?"

"It's complicated," I admitted. "Not sure what to do. Long story short, she got manipulated by the cartel. Nate Evans may or may not have planned to set her up, but when the opportunity showed itself, he took it. Guess he was fuckin' her cousin—the one who lived with her—and probably filling her head with all kinds of bullshit. Then he gave her money to run off down south, where the kid's mom happens to be shacked up with Gerardo Medina."

Hunter gave a low whistle.

"Damn, bitch aims high."

"No shit," I agreed. "Now he's livin' the high life while his wife stays tucked away in Mexico. Anyway, when Jess went down, Medina took her and used her to control London. Guess they cut off the girl's finger while she watched, and London lost it. We knew somethin' was up, so we put a man on her, and some cameras out at my place. Then shit escalated and Puck found a loaded gun in her purse. He took her ammo and gave me a heads-up. We waited until she made her move before we took her down. Wanted to see how far she'd go."

Silence filled the room.

"Any particular reason she's still alive?" Hunter finally asked.

"She didn't want to do it," Gage said, his voice thoughtful. "She hates that fucker Evans more than we do, which is sayin' somethin'. Went after him with a two-by-four. Says she wants to help us take down the cartel, and she's definitely got the motivation. We're the only shot she has to save the kid at this point."

Hunter smirked at me, and I saw the mocking laughter in his eyes. He knew I'd fallen for her, I knew I'd fallen for her, and now I had to kill her or look weak in the eyes of the Devil's Jacks.

Goddammit.

The wail of sirens filled the air, and I cocked my head. The walls in here were solid as fuck—hearing them so loud meant they had to be close. Cops? *Shit.* We had two goddamned prisoners in this barn, and about a hundred guns of one kind or another.

Not good.

Puck burst into the room, and for once he wasn't calm and collected.

"You guys gotta get down here, fast," he said. "Pic, your daughter's in the backyard and I think she's bleedin' out. London's with her, guess she called the ambulance. We got EMTs and firefighters all over the place."

Hunter almost knocked me over, he was out of the room so fast. I was on his heels, tearing down the stairs and out into the backyard.

Oh, shit, Heather murmured in my head. *That's our baby . . .*

What I saw nearly killed me.

It's probably no surprise to hear I've ended more than one person's life—I had a pretty good idea what it looked like when someone lost too much blood to live. That much blood and more coated Em's lower body, and the blanket she'd been lying on was soaked with it, too.

Hunter stood over her—frozen—as two EMTs worked frantically.

London stood to the side, her eyes full of despair. A distant part of me noted that she was covered in blood, too. It ran down her head and into her face. It even dripped off her arms—looked like her clothes had been . . . shredded?

Fucked-up shit, and my baby girl was in the middle of it.

For an instant I was almost thankful Heather was dead, because if she was still here, she'd tear the skin right off my body for letting this happen. Whatever the hell *this* was. Looked like the blood was comin' from between Em's legs, and that was a bad fuckin' sign for my grandbaby.

I'm so goddamned sorry, Heather.

Hunter turned on London, grabbing her arms and shaking her violently.

"What the fuck did you do to her? I'll fucking kill you for this, bitch!"

Skid, Gage, and Horse leapt into action, pulling him off and dragging him halfway across the lawn before the cop had time to do much more than blink.

"What's going on?" I asked one of the EMTs, my stomach sinking. I'd never dreamed London could be a threat to Em—was she behind this? *Fuck.* What the hell had I done, bringing her here?

"Looks like a miscarriage," the man said, catching my eyes. "You a family member?"

"I'm her dad."

"You need to follow us to the hospital," he said. "This is serious—she's lost a lot of blood. I don't know what the hell's going on around here, but time to cut the drama because your kid needs you. Got it?"

"Got it."

Christ. I hated this helpless feeling. It took forever for them to load Em—looked like she was dying, and there wasn't a fuckin' thing I could do to help. Out of the corner of my eye I saw one of the firefighters checking out London. She didn't look so good, either. I glanced up at the carriage house, finding the remains of the second-story window. She'd obviously smashed it out and then dropped down into the bushes. There were broken leaves and sticks everywhere.

Fuck.

"That woman saved your daughter's life," the cop said, coming to stand next to me. He obviously recognized my colors, but he didn't seem intimidated. "She jumped out the window and called nine one one. You wanna explain to me why someone would have to break out of a second-story room to get help, instead of using the stairs?"

"No idea," I said. They were loading Em into the ambulance. Shit. I needed to follow them.

"Take care of your kid," the cop said. "Don't worry about the other victim. I'll make sure she gets to the hospital and stays *safe.*"

His words caught me, and I looked at him—really looked at him—for the first time. He saw right through us, I realized. He knew London was a prisoner, and he was going to get her out of here. Of course, I had thirty brothers with me, and they'd fight to hold her if I asked them to . . . but that was a losing battle. This guy might be the only cop, but there were at least six firefighters. We tried to pull any shit, whole fuckin' city would come down on us. The cop smiled, because he knew he had me. Ignoring him, I strode toward the carriage house, jerking my chin for Skid to join me.

"They're takin' London to the hospital," I said in a low voice. "Cop knows it's not right, he's gonna talk to her. I need the brothers and the evidence out of here before that happens, got me? Just in case."

"I hear you," he said, eyes narrowing. "*Fuck*. You should've taken care of this before you left home—shut her mouth so she'd never talk."

"If we'd done that, Em would be dead right now," I said coldly. "Don't forget who called nine one one. London said she wanted to help us and she's got good reasons to keep her word. Those cops won't be able to get her cousin out. We're her only hope, so let's just wait and see what happens."

LONDON

"Reese asked me to find a box for him," I told the cop, my words deliberate and careful. "He's my boyfriend. We rode over from Coeur d'Alene last night to visit his daughter. I went up to the storage room and started looking around—then I accidentally bumped the door and it swung shut, locking me in. That's when I saw Em outside in the backyard, and after nobody heard me shouting, I broke out the window and jumped down."

"What was in the box?"

"Motorcycle parts. I never found it."

"If he's your boyfriend, why isn't he here to make sure you're okay?"

I sighed, because now he was just being stupid on purpose.

"Because his daughter was bleeding out the last time I saw her, and all I've got are a few scratches. I think she takes priority over me for now, don't you?"

The cop stared at me without speaking. We'd been through this whole story three times now. Each time he made it clear he didn't believe I was telling the truth. Each time I made it clear I didn't care what he believed.

In some ways I had to appreciate what he was trying to do—all too many police officers turned a blind eye to abuse, which was obviously what he thought was happening here. He was trying to save my life, and if staying alive were my top priority I'd be all over that.

But rescuing Jessica was my top priority, followed closely by killing the men who'd hurt her. Survival was a distant third.

"You aren't going to change your story, are you?" he asked, his voice tired.

"It's not a story," I replied softly. "It's what happened."

"Here's my card," he said. "I'm putting my personal cell number on the back. Call me if you decide to talk, or you need help. We both know something's wrong here, and sooner or later it'll come crashing down around you. Don't be afraid to reach out, okay?"

"Thanks for your concern, but I'm fine."

He shook his head and walked away, leaving me alone in the small private room they'd given us. There were lots of tissue boxes placed in strategic spots—I had a feeling this was one of those places they put families right before they told them someone had died. I hoped very much that Reese wasn't sitting in another room just like this somewhere else in the hospital, mourning his daughter. I needed to find him, or at the very least find someone who could tell me what the hell was going on with Em.

Standing up hurt, although none of my bruises or cuts were serious. They'd given me a couple of stitches on my forehead, disinfected me, and called it good. I was supposed to keep a close eye on the puncture wound in particular, and see a doctor asap if there were any signs of infection, blah blah blah.

I grabbed the bag holding the remains of my clothing and clutched it to my chest. (Although I wasn't sure why they'd bothered to give them back to me, because I'd never be able to wear them again. At least the scrubs they'd given me were comfortable.) I'd already been discharged from the ER, so I was able to just walk right out into the waiting room. No sign of Reese, but I spotted Painter. His expression was grim.

I walked over to him, scared of whatever news had put that look on his face.

"How is she?" I asked, not bothering to say hello.

"Not good," he said, standing up and facing me. "I guess the baby wasn't right. They called it an octorpic pregnancy, or some such shit."

"Ectopic?"

"Yeah, that sounds right. The baby wasn't in the right place. Instead of growing in her womb, it was in one of the tubes to her ovary, and then it busted the whole thing open. That's what started all the bleeding. They've got her in surgery right now, but she's lost a fuckload of blood, London. They said she might die. The baby never had a shot."

I swayed, and he caught me, still holding my eyes.

"Reese and Gage put me here to watch for you," he said slowly. "Gage said you were talking to the cops."

I shook my head, trying to catch my breath.

"You don't need to worry about that," I told him quietly. "I didn't give them any information. I'm not trying to get away from the MC, Painter. I want to go to California and save Jessica, and the only way that can happen is if I stick with the club. But right now I need to find Reese. He must be terrified."

Painter nodded his head.

"Pretty sure he is, though he'd never cop to it. I can take you up there . . . But I need to tell you something first."

"What?"

"Just because you saved Em, and you didn't talk to the cops? That doesn't mean you're safe with us, and Pic isn't necessarily the one who'll make that call. You need to understand what you're doing here, London. If you go upstairs and find Pic, there's still a chance the club won't forgive you. Even if they do, that trip to Cali might be one way—this isn't a game. Give me the word and I'll go take a piss, let you walk right out that door. Got about two hundred bucks on me and it's yours. That's the best I can do."

I reached my hands up and cupped his face, smiling at him sadly.

"That's one of the most beautiful things anyone's ever offered me," I said softly. "But I need to go find Reese, and then I need to go to California to find my girl. Whatever happens, happens, and I'm okay with it. Now where do I need to go—can you show me?"

"I'll point you in the right direction, but I shouldn't go in with you," he told me.

"Why not?"

"Hunter doesn't need to be seein' my face right now. We got history, me and Em. I've come to terms, but he and I aren't exactly friends. Don't wanna stress him out more than I have to."

Pieces fell together in my head, and I patted his arm, startled at how different he seemed from the young man I'd met just weeks ago. Painter put up a hell of a front, apparently.

Then again, so did Reese.

He escorted me as far as the corridor outside the surgical waiting area. I walked in, spotting Reese and Hunter immediately. Waiting with them were Horse, Ruger, and Bam Bam. There was also a young man wearing Devil's Jacks colors I didn't recognize. He was covered in tattoos and looked vaguely hipsterish with his skinny jeans.

Wow, if Portlanders could do that to a biker, they could turn *anyone* into a hipster.

Between him and Hunter sat a young woman whose face was streaked with tears and heavy black mascara. She looked like something out of a horror movie, but at least she showed some emotion. Hunter's face was completely blank. So was Reese's. I started toward them, and then stopped—across the room sat the same police officer who'd just been talking to me. Damn, but he was persistent.

He watched Em's little support group closely, eyes speculative. Shit.

We didn't need this right now. Maybe a little show would get him off our asses? I started walking toward Reese again, hoping like hell he'd pick up on what I was doing and not blow it. When I got close enough, I flicked my eyes toward the cop, then set myself down in his lap like I had every right to be there. I wrapped my arms tight around his neck and whispered in his ear.

"That cop over there is trying to save me. I told him you're my boyfriend, and that I just got stuck in the storeroom looking for something you needed, so treat me like you don't want to strangle me and maybe he'll go away."

His arms tightened around me hard, and I let myself pretend for a moment that I'd spoken the truth. That he actually *was* still mine, and that he would be relieved to find me safe.

"Thanks," he murmured. "One less thing to worry about."

"You don't trust me," I said softly. "I understand that. But I'm on your side, Reese. I screwed up and now I'm trying to fix it. I don't expect you to forgive me, or that things will ever be like they were before, but I won't betray you again."

He nodded, then loosened his grasp. Apparently I wasn't the only one aware of our audience, because none of the others showed the slightest hint of reaction to our little reunion. Hunter rose to his feet when Reese let me go, and walked over to us.

"I'm sorry," he said, his voice strained. "They tell me she'd be dead already if you hadn't saved her. I shouldn't have jumped on you like that, London. Guess I just lost it."

God, he looked so young and scared.

I put a hand on his arm, offering him a little squeeze. Easy to forget some of these bikers were essentially still kids, despite how tough they acted. This boy was scared shitless because he'd lost his baby, and he might be losing his girlfriend soon, too.

"Don't worry about it. I understood what was happening and didn't take it personally."

The girl who'd been sitting next to him joined us.

"I'm Kelsey," she said, looking me over. Her face was tight and strained, and her entire body radiated leashed tension. "I'm this asshole's sister, which makes Em my sister, too. Thanks for what you did. That took balls."

I shrugged.

"Let's just hope they can help her."

As if summoned by my voice, a doctor stepped into the waiting room and we all looked up, trying to read his expression.

"You the family?"

"Yeah," Reese said, standing to face him. "What's goin' on with my girl?"

"She's through surgery and it went well, all things considered. You already know she lost a lot of blood. We transfused her in the ER and again on the table, and I think we turned it around. Unfortunately there's no way the fetus can survive in an ectopic pregnancy like this one. Wouldn't matter how early we caught it and there's nothing she could've done to prevent it. Sometimes it just happens."

"Did you see if it was a boy or a girl?" Hunter asked, his voice anguished.

"It was a girl," he replied. "She was about fourteen weeks old. I'm very sorry for your loss. We're very lucky to have saved the mother—it was close, maybe a matter of minutes that made the difference. The next few hours will be critical, but I'm hopeful she'll make a full recovery."

Horse threw his arm around me and squeezed me tight.

"Thanks for rescuing our Emmy girl," he said softly. Ruger nodded at me, and I wasn't sure what to do or say. Reese seemed lost in his own world and Hunter's eyes had turned red.

"How soon until we can visit her?" Kelsey demanded.

"She's in recovery right now," he said. "It'll be a while before she's ready for company, and I'd like her to get as much rest as she can. Immediate family only, and the rest of you can visit tomorrow or the day after."

"I'll stay here tonight," Hunter said. "Unless that's a problem?"

The doctor smiled, although the expression didn't quite reach his eyes.

"The waiting room is all yours," he replied. "We'll keep you posted."

He turned and walked out, his mind obviously already on the next patient.

"So now what?" Ruger asked slowly. "This is fucked, but we got three hundred brothers travelin' down to Cali for a major offensive. We gotta make a plan, because we can't just leave them hanging."

"I'm out," Hunter said bluntly. He gave his friend a quick glance. "Skid can step up and take over for me. I already told Burke what's happening."

I looked at Reese, wondering if he'd say the same thing. Nobody could blame him if he decided not to go to California—but there was no way in hell I'd get a chance to save Jessica without him there. He looked at me and sighed, reaching up to rub the back of his neck.

"I'll go," he said to Hunter. "You take care of my girl for me, and I'll make sure we got your club's back."

Hunter seemed surprised, and I saw Ruger and Horse exchange a glance I couldn't interpret.

"Appreciate that," Hunter said, turning toward Skid. "You need anything more from me?"

"Naw, I got it."

"I'll head back to the house," Reese said slowly, although I could see it was killing him to leave Em. "Call me when she wakes up? I'll come back and see her before we take off."

"Sounds good," Hunter said. "And Pic?"

"Yeah?"

"I'll take good care of her. I promise."

"Gonna hold you to that."

CHAPTER SEVENTEEN

The plane touched down at eleven that night.

I'd fallen asleep on top of Reese, which was comfortable and wonderful and probably more than I deserved, but I figured I'd take advantage while I could. He seemed to want me with him, and I even felt a slight stirring of hope at one point. Maybe I hadn't killed everything between us when I pulled that trigger?

Then I wrestled my head out of my ass, because I couldn't afford to let hope distract me.

Still, there was a noticeable change in attitude toward me after we got back from the hospital. Nobody had been at Em and Hunter's place initially—apparently they'd cleared out in anticipation of a police raid.

A raid they'd expected because of me.

The combination of my silence and the fact that I'd saved Em had gone a long way toward rebuilding the club's goodwill, and nobody bitched when Reese announced I'd be coming with. That meant everything, because if they found Jessica, I needed to be there for her. If they didn't, I had other, less pleasant work ahead of me.

Now it was one a.m. and I was sitting in the dark. Waiting. We'd gone to a warehouse in the middle of bumfuck San Diego, which was apparently very similar to regular San Diego, but with more shootings and gang activity. It'd taken quite a bit to convince Reese to let me join them for the actual attack—I think he'd planned for me to hang with the women at someone's clubhouse or something.

Fuck that.

We'd compromised when I swore to stay outside in one of the vehicles (an anonymous-looking cargo van—something I was starting to think was MC standard issue) unless they called for me. Puck stayed, too. During the time we'd been stuck out here, he hadn't said anything to me. Not. One. Word. I hunched down in the darkness, praying for something to happen. Anything.

I still wasn't sure who our targets were or where the rest of the men had gone—we had about thirty in our group total, a mixture of Reapers, Silver Bastards, and some other club of locals who were apparently their allies. None of them wore their distinctive colors and everything was very hush-hush. All of them had ignored me completely, except for Puck, who radiated resentment at being stuck with babysitting duty.

Fair enough, because I was starting to resent his silent ass, too.

After what felt like hours, Puck's phone vibrated. He answered it, grunted a few times, and hung up, turning to look at me with a frown marring his handsome features.

"They need me inside," he said. "You'll have to come, too—can't leave you out here by yourself. Keep quiet and don't say, do, or touch *anything*. Understand?"

I felt like telling him that he was young enough to be my son, and I wasn't fucking stupid. Instead I said, "I understand."

Another grunt. Some day he really was going to have to learn some real words, I decided.

We stepped out of the van and started around the side of the building. Around the corner we found a door guarded by a man I didn't recognize. He opened it for Puck silently, eyeing me with suspicion as I followed the prospect inside.

The warehouse surprised me.

I don't know what I was expecting . . . Maybe some kind of big, open space with catwalks and spotlights, and an evil genius laughing maniacally in the background.

A hairless cat or two?

Instead, dim security lights showed an interior that looked less like a crime lord's fortress and more like a Costco. There were long stacks of boxes and bins and pallets forming alleys, some of them piled nearly to the ceiling. A perfectly normal forklift was parked near the door. It didn't even have a machine gun mounted on the roof or anything.

Puck pulled out his gun and started down the second row of pallets, which my active imagination immediately pointed out would operate like a cattle chute. You know, the long, narrow paths they use to guide animals to their deaths in slaughterhouses?

Not a happy thought.

He crept through the darkness and I followed him like a good girl. Then I tripped on my own shoelace, somehow doing an elaborate dance and shuffle to stay upright without making a sound.

When I was stable again, I dropped down into a crouch to fix the lace. Puck kept moving ahead, oblivious, and there was no way I could stop him without making a sound. Which was worse? Making noise or getting separated?

Making noise seemed more likely to get us killed.

Sucked to be screwing things up less than five minutes into the operation. Kneeling down gave me a whole new perspective on the situation—specifically a perspective low enough to see through a gap in the pallets that was only about two feet high, and maybe eighteen inches wide. On the other side of the gap I could just make out a . . .

Oh shit. That was a body over there—not one of the bikers, he wasn't wearing the right kind of clothes.

There was dark black crap puddled around him on the floor.

Blood?

Yeah. Had to be blood, and way more of it than had come out of Em. This guy was deader than dead, no question. Wow. This was really happening—London Armstrong from Coeur d'Alene, Idaho, was in the middle of a gang war and people were dying . . . I backed away, looking ahead to see that Puck had almost reached the end of the row, still clueless that we'd gotten separated. Wasn't that just perfect? I'd just started rising to my feet when I heard the noise.

A snuffling, whimpering cry . . . High-pitched, like a child or maybe a young woman. My mom radar went on point, because I recognised that cry.

Jessica.

She was somewhere on the other side of these pallets, which meant I could either run to the end of the long row and go around, or I could try crawling through that narrow little gap. But running around would take time and possibly make noise . . . Not only that, if I caught up to Puck, he might not let me go look for Jess, not when he had an assignment of his own to accomplish.

I'd just have to crawl through.

The only downside was Mr. McDead over there, which I had to admit was a major strike against my plan. Then I heard Jessica whimpering again, and she sounded weaker this time—no more playing around. I dropped back down and started slithering my way through the gap. It wasn't particularly fun or comfortable, but deadly raids against notorious cartels rarely are.

The first thing I discovered when I reached the other side was that Mr. McDead's blood was still warm—something I figured out by accidentally putting my hand in it. I could smell it, too. Metallic, with a hint of sweetness. I started to wipe it on my shirt, and then stopped, because *ewww*. Wondering faintly if God would strike me for defiling the dead, I leaned down and carefully wiped my hand on his shirt.

My fingers brushed a hard lump.

I froze. There was something solid under his shirt, something that had fallen down toward his left side. Giving another quick glance down the row, I didn't see anyone, so I tugged up his shirt to look.

It was a gun.

The whimper came again, and I looked around for the source. Along the wall stretched a series of doors. They were all shut, like they were offices that'd been locked up for the night . . . Except for one clearly marked as a bathroom—that door had been propped open. Was she in there, hiding?

I decided to check my new gun before going in, because I didn't want to get caught out without any bullets this time. Oh-so-carefully, I let the little bullet holder-thingy slide out of the bottom. Yup. Full of bullets, all right. Then I pushed it back up and wrapped the bottom of my shirt around the whole thing, muffling the sound as I carefully cocked the weapon.

Now I was locked and loaded, ready to go rescue my little cousin like Lara Croft herself. All I needed was Angelina Jolie's body and I'd be set. Make that Angelina Jolie's money—then I could outsource the rescuing and screw Brad Pitt. I felt an inappropriate little laugh try to bubble its way out of my throat, which I swallowed down brutally. Too much tension rattling around in my head.

Stop making jokes and go rescue Jessica.

Okay, then. I took a centering breath, edging toward the bathroom door. The shattering crackle of gunfire suddenly echoed through the building, scaring the hell out of me. Men shouted in English and Spanish, followed by more shooting. I scuttled across the floor and through the bathroom door, into total darkness. Then I tugged the door shut behind me—it might not provide much in the way of a barrier, but it had to be better than hanging with a dead body right out in the open. Trailing my hand along the wall, I made my way deeper into the room, around a corner.

The gunfire died down outside.

Now I heard someone else breathing in the tiny room. Jessica? Murderous cartel thug? How the hell was I supposed to tell them apart in the darkness?

"Can you help me?" a voice whispered, and I nearly started crying because my mama instincts had been right—I'd found my girl and she was *alive*.

"Jess?"

Silence, then a sobbed attempt at speech. "Loni? Is that really you?"

"Yeah, baby, it's me. I'm here to save you. You'll be happy to hear I left the minivan home this time."

More silence.

"Am I imagining this?"

"No, Jess. I'm real, but the warehouse is full of dead people and I touched one of them, so I think we should get the hell out now, okay?"

"They've got me handcuffed to the pipes," she whispered. "I'm on a toilet, so I won't make a mess."

Jesus Christ. I suddenly wished Mr. McDead were still alive so I could kill him again—given his position outside, he'd probably been guarding her. I assumed the bikers had taken him out, but who knew? Whoever it was hadn't found Jess, which was the only thing that mattered. Now I just needed to get her out of the cuffs, then sneak her out of the building without getting both of us killed.

Easy, right?

"Loni?"

"Still here," I said quickly. Another round of gunfire filled the air—time to get her loose and out the door before someone came in here and started killing us.

Speak of the devil . . .

Footsteps thudded outside as someone ran down the long canyon between the wall and the pallets. Then the door banged open and bright white light flooded the bathroom, blinding me. Jessica screamed as shooting seemed to explode all over the building. I scuttled backward frantically, away from this new threat, more screams filling the air. Jessica's, but also from men outside. Men in pain, or dying.

This shit was getting *real*.

My back hit a wall and I found myself under a sink, blinking rapidly as my eyes adjusted to the light. Not six feet from me, I saw a short, fat Hispanic man in an expensive-looking suit stop in front of the lone stall, gun in hand. His breath came heavy and he muttered to himself as he dug in his pockets for something.

Keys.

He opened the stall and I caught a glimpse of Jess for the first time—only a flash, but I saw dried blood and her jaw was swollen. She shrieked as he reached for her, and then I heard the clatter of what had to be him fighting to open the handcuffs. Jess kicked out and the key dropped, skittering across the floor to the far corner of the room.

"Leave me alone!" she yelled.

"Shut your mouth, cunt!" the man yelled back. Then he slapped her. Hard.

She shut up.

Outside the gunfire died off, but a new noise had started up. A shrill wailing that could only be a fire alarm.

Holy fuck. I had to end this somehow or we were both going to die like rats.

The bastard lowered himself heavily to his knees, muttering curses under his breath as he hunted for the key. His motions were desperate, and I realized I wasn't the only terrified one in here. Good. Nice to know the bad guys got scared, too. Maybe I could use that against him.

Jessica's frantic eyes met mine over his back. Her face was bloodied and bruised, and she'd obviously lost some weight. More than she could afford. To make things even more wretched, her hands were fastened behind her, and they'd left her on the toilet with her pants around her ankles.

Shouts sounded outside, and a loud crashing noise. Like a body thrown against the wall?

The man muttered under his breath, his movements growing more frantic. I couldn't figure out why he didn't just run away—was he cornered in here? If that was the case, he needed Jess alive. A hostage was his best shot to get out, although whether the club would let him go to save Jess was very much in question . . .

He spotted the key under one of the urinals and backed out of the stall, scuttling across the floor toward it like an exceptionally large cockroach.

I smelled smoke. More shouting outside.

Floor Man ignored it all, absolutely determined to get that key and unlock Jessica. I had no idea who he was and I didn't care. He had the key, which meant he was responsible for her being here and that was good enough for me.

Time to end this and get the hell out of here before we died.

I rose silently to my knees and aimed the gun, just like Disturbing Field Guy had taught me. Then I took a deep breath and pulled the trigger, the explosion shattering so loud in the tiny room that my ears started ringing. Jess screamed again as the bullet caught him in the side, knocking him back against the wall. His eyes found mine and widened in surprise. Then his hand started fumbling for something that'd crashed heavily to the tile next to him.

His gun?

Fuck that.

I shot him again, this time in the chest. Another shot, catching his arm. I started knee-walking across the floor, determined to grab that key and get Jessica out. *God.* He was *still alive.* His eyes blinked, and he held up a hand, as if he could stop me by sheer force of will.

His mouth moved but I couldn't make out the words through the ringing. Smoke started curling through the air above me, filtering through the air vent. We really, *really* needed to get out of here.

Time to end this asshole.

Holding my gun with both hands, I shot him point-blank in the center of his forehead. Blood and brain spattered everything in the room, including me. I gagged, trying not to throw up. I didn't slow down, though. I couldn't afford to, not with smoke pouring into the room, half an army waiting to kill us, and Jessica chained to a fucking toilet with her pants on the floor.

Time to find that key. Too bad it was wedged somewhere under Fatty McDeadfuck.

His body was heavy and limp, but I managed to roll it toward me long enough to dig through the gore and find the little key that'd cost him his life. Then I was on my feet and unlocking Jessica. She was just standing up when the door burst open again.

I raised the gun, ready to shoot.

Reese.

His eyes widened, taking in everything. My blood-spattered face, Jessica peeking out of the stall . . . Fatty McDeadfuck's spattered brains.

"Holy shit," he muttered. Huh. Guess my hearing was working again. Yup. More gunfire in the background, along with even louder wailing from the alarm, now that the door was open.

"Hi, Reese," I said, smiling just a *tad* too brightly. "I found Jessica."

Ruger came in behind him, followed by Horse and some bearded stranger I didn't recognize. Suddenly the bathroom was way too crowded.

"That's Gerardo Medina," Beard Man said. "He's dead . . . Holy *hell*. Who shot him?"

"I did," I snapped, waving my gun for emphasis. They all froze, and I realized waving deadly weapons for emphasis while covered with blood and brain chunks probably wasn't such a hot idea. This struck me as funny, but I managed not to laugh.

That's when I realized *perhaps* I was losing my shit a little.

"Oops. Sorry."

Reese let out a slow breath.

"Okay, give me the gun, babe," he said, reaching out for it. I hesitated—what if I needed to defend Jessica again? My thoughts were racing way too fast, I couldn't *think*. Reese considered me warily.

"I'm impressed as hell, London. You just killed the number two guy for the Santiago Cartel in the U.S., so job well done. But much as I respect your deadly instincts, I think we'll all be safer if you hand that gun over."

"I'm fine keeping it," I said, narrowing my eyes to focus on his face. Damn. Why was everything moving so fast?

"Tell me right now how much ammunition you have left."

"Why?"

"Because if you can't answer the question, you got no business carrying that thing around."

He made a good point.

I handed over the gun with the barrel pointed down carefully, startled by how hard it was to keep my balance. Then he was lifting me up and throwing me over his shoulder in a firefighter's carry. He raced out the bathroom door, smoke surrounding us and the roar of guns growing louder. Something whacked my shoulder and my arm went numb.

"Loni!" Jess screamed behind me, and I raised my head to see Horse carrying her, dangling pants and all. Then I heard someone yell "*Fuck!*" really loud, followed by "*Get the hell outta here!*"

Reese pelted toward the end of the warehouse as the whole place seemed to burst into flames. Smoke burned my eyes, and I had no idea how he was getting enough air—I certainly wasn't. Still, we barreled down the row of pallets like a herd of wild horses until I saw Puck waiting by the door we'd used to enter, waving at us frantically.

Then we were through it and out in the night air.

Reese tossed me into the back of a van and jumped on top of me, knocking the breath right out of my body. Horse and Jessica followed, and the vehicle took off, cargo doors swinging wide as we tore down the street. From my crumpled position on the floor, I saw a pillar of flame burst through the top of the warehouse roof. Then Horse caught hold of a tie-down mounted on the van's wall and leaned out, grabbing the doors and slamming them shut.

There was a giant, roaring whoosh as something blew up, and the entire van rocked violently.

"People have *got* to stop blowing up buildings at me," I muttered, trying not to giggle. Something was wrong here . . . Why wouldn't my brain work? Felt like I was looking at everything through a film of honey. I tried to push Reese off, but my arm still wouldn't work.

"I'll look into it," Reese muttered back at me.

"You do that."

He pulled me close and squeezed me, which should've made me feel all warm and safe. Instead I didn't feel anything at all. I knew I should be checking on Jessica, there was something important . . . but I was just so incredibly tired and weak.

I don't remember anything after that.

The garbled noises that woke me sounded like someone speaking underwater.

This made sense, because I seemed to be floating. I just wasn't quite sure *how* I was floating—or why—but I definitely wasn't on solid ground.

Lovely . . .

"London?"

I tried to say "go away," but it came out more like "gwo cay."
Huh.

"London, can you hear me? Try and wake up, sweetheart."

I shook my head, feeling a sharp twinge of pain. It cut through
the floating sensation in a way I simply couldn't approve of. I opened
my eyes to try to find whoever was making my head hurt. Maybe if
I bit them hard enough, they'd stop? But identifying the culprit
wouldn't be easy—apparently he'd filled my eyelids with sand, because they were all scratchy and dry.

"I've got news about Jess," the voice said, catching my attention.
Jessica. Memories started to come back. Oh, sheesh. We'd gone to
California and I'd killed a man. But I'd found Jess—that part was
important. Jessica was alive. Then another building had exploded. I
blinked, trying to focus on the face above mine.

Reese.

"Hey," I managed to croak out. "What happened?"

"You got shot in the arm and passed out," he told me. I frowned.
I didn't remember getting shot. Shouldn't I have noticed?

"How?"

"I'm assuming with a bullet," he said, voice dry. I considered hitting him, but that would've involved raising my hand, which didn't
seem to be a realistic option at the moment.

"Why do I feel so weird?"

"Doc shot you up with painkillers. Probably a little more hard-
core than you needed, but I didn't want you hurting."

Guess that explained the fog. I blinked some more, trying to
clear it.

"What about Jess?" I finally managed to ask.

"She's doin' great," Reese said. "They've done a CAT scan and
the shunt is fine. Aside from the finger, the only other thing wrong
with her is a little dehydration and some bruises. They want her to
follow up with a plastic surgeon for the hand, but otherwise it's all

good. No sign of any seizures, either. She's actually in a lot better shape than you—girl's stronger than you thought."

That was a relief. The ball of tension loosened in my chest, which was very curious. Up to that moment I hadn't been able to feel my chest at all. Probably because of the drugs, which they'd given me because I got . . . attacked by a bullet? Oh yeah. Maybe I should ask Reese about that, now that I knew Jess was safe . . .

"When did I get shot?"

"In the warehouse," he said. "Do you remember the man in the bathroom?"

I shuddered, wishing I could forget him—I had a feeling I'd be seeing those eyes blinking at me in my nightmares for the rest of my life.

"Yes."

"We think it might've been a ricochet in there," he said. "Either that or a random hit while we were running out of the building. It's a graze along your arm, but you got lucky. Didn't penetrate much past the outer layer of muscle—no nerve damage. You had so much other blood covering you that we didn't even notice until you passed out on the floor of the van. Like Em all over again. Thought I'd have a fuckin' heart attack."

I frowned. "Why didn't I feel it?"

"Adrenaline. Happens more often than you'd think."

I blinked at him, the world finally coming into focus. Reese looked tired, his eyes shadowed with dark circles, and I had a feeling I wasn't looking too shit-hot myself. My head was starting to throb—felt like a Mack truck had rolled right over me. I looked around, trying to move as little as possible in the process. I seemed to be in a child's bedroom. There was a kitten poster up on the wall and a pink canopy overhead.

"Where on earth are we?"

"At a friend's house," he told me, scooting his chair closer. "His club and the Reapers are allies, so when you needed a place to go, he offered. We've had a medic in to see you, and they stitched you up while you were out. Doc said you'll be fine, gave you a shot of pain-killers before he left. He's a friend of the club, too—won't report anything. Jessica's situation is a little more complicated, because she needed more tests. Got her into a private clinic. They'll keep their mouths shut so long as they get paid enough."

I closed my eyes again, too tired to keep talking. The bed dipped and then Reese was lying next to me. It hurt to move, but I cuddled into his arms anyway. He made me feel safe and protected.

"One more thing I should mention," he said.

"What's that?"

"Looks like Jessica was raped. Repeatedly. She'll need STD and pregnancy tests."

I closed my eyes, because I couldn't handle thinking about that just yet.

"She'll need a lot more than that."

He didn't say anything, which I appreciated. Instead he rubbed my back softly, soothing me. Why, I have no idea. I didn't deserve his kindness—not after what I'd done.

I drifted off, waking up again when someone opened the door and asked Reese something.

"No," he answered quietly, although I hadn't caught the question. *You need to pull yourself together, figure out what happens next.*

"Anything else I should know about?" I managed to whisper, the drug fog muffling me. He gave a humorlous laugh.

"Well, apparently someone hit five drug warehouses and eight safe houses belonging to the cartel last night. No idea yet about a body count, but the cops are sayin' almost all the leadership was taken out nearly simultaneously. They're tryin' to figure out who might be behind it."

"Did all of our guys make it out okay?"

"We lost three," he said, his voice lowering. "One Reaper and two Devil's Jacks. Nobody you knew. And here's bad luck for you—

the cops picked up Puck and Painter last night for speeding. Found some guns in the car, so now they're lookin' at a trafficking charge."

"Shit. By 'lost,' do you mean . . . ?"

"Dead."

"Who were they?" I asked, my voice a whisper.

"My brothers," Reese said, his voice rough. "Even the Jacks—they earned it with their blood. Now isn't the time for crying, though. Gotta get everyone home safe first. Then we'll remember them."

"What about Puck and Painter?"

"Lawyer's on his way right now," he replied. "But probably not lookin' so good for either of them. Both have priors. You owe Puck, by the way. He's the one who figured out where you were. Hadn't been for him, we might not've found you in time."

I frowned.

"Surprised he bothered. I don't think he likes me very much."

"Doesn't matter how he feels about you," Reese told me. "Protectin' club property. That's his job."

I had no idea how to react to that statement, so I decided to pretend I hadn't heard it.

"Overall it was a big win for us—it'll take years for them to recover," he continued. "The boss down in Mexico's already been in touch, askin' for a truce. They've agreed to stay south of San Francisco, at least for now, and leave the local clubs alone. In exchange, we gave 'em a little token of our appreciation."

"What was that?"

"Evans."

I stilled.

"I thought you said if Jess made it through you were going to let him go."

"No, we told him if she survived, he'd survive, and he was definitely alive when we handed him over to the Santiagos. But only an idiot thinks he can double-cross the cartel and keep breathing long term. He was dead already, just didn't know it yet."

Scary as hell, but I had to agree. Nate had made his own bed, and I didn't feel particularly sorry for him at all. I yawned. Between the drugs and the drama, I was exhausted.

Reese probably was, too . . . But I had one more question for him. An important one.

"What about me?" I asked, my voice a whisper.

"Not sure I follow."

"Has the club decided what they're going to do about me?" I repeated, the words slurring. "Now that it's all over. I'm really sorry. I know I keep saying that and it doesn't change anything, but it's true. What I did was wrong—you always tried to help me, and even after I stabbed you in the back, you still saved Jessica. I know you don't trust me and you probably don't believe me, but I'd do anything for you, Reese. For the club, too. I can't ever thank you enough for rescuing my baby girl . . ."

"Babe, I think it's safe to say you're fine with the club," he replied, and I heard a touch of humor in his voice. "You saved Em's life, lied to the cops to protect us, and then killed Gerardo Medina— all in twenty-four hours. That's impressive, honey. You know how many people have tried to take his ass out? Not only that, we all sorta got off on you kneecapping Deputy Dickhead. Don't sweat it, okay? Fuck, Heather tried to kill me at least three times over the years. We'll get through this."

"I don't think I understand bikers."

"That's okay, babe. You'll figure it out."

CHAPTER EIGHTEEN

Jess cuddled up next to me like a baby the entire flight home, tucked into my side with a blanket around us both. I hadn't quite believed Reese when he told me she was fine. She was, though. At least physically. Sure, she'd lost a finger, and I knew recovering from that wasn't going to be fun. But her shunt really hadn't budged, there were no signs of infection, and even the concussion she'd gotten from hitting the floor was healing up like it should.

We also had no idea why she'd had the seizure. Of course, we'd never really understood why she had them as a child, either—or why she'd stopped having them. One thing I've learned over the years spent with her in hospitals and doctors' offices is that medicine is an art, not just a science.

They don't know nearly as much as they want you to think.

Mentally, things were going to be a lot harder for her. She didn't want to talk about the rape or what had happened to her mother, but she flinched every time a man came near her. That was answer enough for me. Maybe she'd be ready to open up as time went on— not like a cargo plane full of bruised and bloodied bikers was the best spot for a heart-to-heart anyway.

Wasn't my place to push her.

We finally reached Em and Hunter's house in Portland early in the morning, less than forty-eight hours after we'd left it. Crazy, right? Reese pointed us toward a guest bedroom before taking off, saying he needed to visit Em. They'd talked by phone, but it wasn't enough. He wanted to see her for himself, make sure she really was going to be okay.

I felt the same way about Jessica. I tucked her in like a child and then lay down next to her, counting her breaths like I had when she was in the NICU. I should probably go downstairs, make sure everyone else was okay . . . But I was so tired. Instead I drifted off, wondering what our next step should be.

The pinging sound of a text woke me. This seemed odd, considering I hadn't seen my phone (or purse) since before I tried to shoot Reese. I rolled over, blinking quickly, trying to figure out what was going on.

"Turn it off," Jess mumbled, flopping over onto her side. "Too tired for school . . ."

Guess some things didn't change.

I looked across the room to see the purse in question sitting on top of a plain wooden dresser, next to two neat stacks of folded clothing. *Who could be texting me?*

Pushing myself to my feet was painful at best. Every single part of my body hurt, including my fingernails and hair. I was sore, scratched, cut, and shot. Astoundingly, none of these things had been fatal, or even particularly serious. I stumbled across the room and unzipped my leather bag, digging around for my phone. The battery was low, but it showed a missed call and a message from my neighbor.

DANICA: How are you doing? Still can't believe what happened. Wanted to let you know that Hugh's dad read about your house in the paper. They've got that cabin out on Kidd Island Bay road and not using it this year—was rented but the tenant fell thru. You can have if you want. Nothing special but decent. 2 bedrooms 1 bath, friends & family rate. Sitting empty and want to help.

I stared down at the text, considering the opportunity. I'd been out there a couple of summers ago with Danica and her sister for a girls' weekend. She was right—it wasn't anything special. But it would give me, Jess, and Melanie some space. Things were still up in the air with Reese, although I was starting to believe him when he said I was safe. The guys had been friendly enough on the plane, too. Well, as friendly as a bunch of exhausted men who'd just lost three of their brothers in a battle against a drug cartel could be.

That didn't change the fact that Jess flinched whenever one of those big, scary men looked at her, or that I had no idea what kind of relationship Reese and I would have moving forward.

Sure, he'd offered us rooms at his house until I figured something out . . . *before* I tried to shoot him. Not only that, no matter how happy the two of us might be together, if he scared Jessie, his house wasn't a good place for her.

Okay, then. Cabin it was.

ME: I'm interested. Call you later tonight?
DANICA: Sounds good. I'll tell him. He says you can move in any time, he knows your good for the money. I have the keys and its furnished.

So. That was solved. We had a place to live.

∙ ∙ ∙

Someone had scrounged up some clean clothing for us, including jeans that were a little too long and tight for me and a Reapers MC T-shirt. A plain sports bra and elaborately decorative thong completed the ensemble—dead giveaway that they'd been digging through the back of a closet. Probably Em's.

Stepping quietly out of the room, I found the bathroom across the hall and got myself cleaned up, brushing my teeth with my finger and some toothpaste left on the counter. I looked like hell, which wasn't exactly a surprise. Few women come through shootings looking fresh and energetic, and that wasn't even taking my plunge through the shrubbery into consideration.

When I finished, I decided to go downstairs and get an update on Em.

I found Reese, Horse, Bam Bam, and Skid sitting around the kitchen table drinking coffee. The clock over the oven said it was eight in the morning. They were all haggard, with bloodshot eyes and stubbled chins, and their faces weren't particularly perky.

"Hey," I said softly. Reese looked up at me, and something flickered in his gaze. Then he pushed his chair out just a bit and patted his knee. I went and sat on it, leaning into his comforting bulk.

"How's Em?"

"She's good," he said. "We're gonna run back over to the hospital soon. Kicked me out earlier, guess they're doing some tests or something. She wants to see you."

I hardly knew what to say.

"You okay with me visiting her?"

"Yeah, sweetheart. Seein' as you saved her fuckin' life, she's probably safer with you than with me. None of us even noticed something was wrong. Although I should warn you, her sister's there. Kit's hell on wheels and she's been asking questions about you."

Great. I'd get to meet his other daughter for the first time looking like something a cat puked out.

"How's Hunter?"

"Good enough," Skid said. "Tough on him, though, hearin' about our losses."

"Em needed him," Reese said, his voice firm. "Anyone has a problem with that, they can talk to me."

"Nobody has a problem with it, Pic," Skid replied, and I could tell from his tone that this wasn't the first time they'd discussed the issue. Alrighty, then.

"You guys want breakfast?" I asked brightly. "Do we have time?"

"Hunter said he'd call," Reese told me. Obviously it bothered him to be waiting on "permission" to see his daughter.

"Breakfast it is."

I tugged free and walked over to the fridge, inspecting the contents. Options were limited . . . But there were eggs and bread. I hit the pantry and found some syrup. Twenty minutes later I had hot French toast coming off an electric skillet, which the guys seemed to appreciate. Then everyone but Reese left the kitchen, which was either convenient or extremely *in*convenient, depending on how one interpreted things.

"So how's Jessica?" he asked, as I started washing dishes. To my surprise he came over and picked up a towel to help dry. Didn't fit the whole He-Man vibe of the past few days, but I guess even the manliest of men will pitch in if you feed him first.

"Still sleeping," I said. "I don't know how long it'll be before she opens up about what happened. You notice how jumpy she was?"

"Yeah," he said. "Not a good scene."

That was the best opening I'd get, so I ran with it.

"We haven't talked about what happens next," I said hesitantly. "Crazy, but you realize it's only been a little over a week since we first slept together?"

"Seems like longer," he said, taking a plate from my hand. "Too much shit happenin' too fast."

"Hard to process all of it . . ." I said slowly. I turned to him, cocking my head. "I need to know—are we past what I did to you? Because I don't understand how you could just let go of something like this. I've told you how sorry I am, but I can't change what happened. I'll understand if you can't forgive me."

"Let it go, babe."

"But—"

"I don't like that you did it, but I understand why and I don't think you'll do it again. Let. It. Go."

I blinked rapidly, my eyes filling with tears.

"Thank you."

He grunted, and we continued washing dishes for a few more minutes. I couldn't relax, though, because there was another piece of unfinished business—and his reaction to it would tell me a lot.

"So . . . I found a place for us to rent this morning. We can actually move in as soon as we get back—my neighbor Danica has the keys waiting for us already, and it's even furnished. That'll get me and the girls out of your hair."

Reese set down the plate very carefully and turned to face me, arms crossed. I kept washing, which was harder to do than you'd think with him standing there, his face like granite.

"You tryin' to dump my ass?" he asked, his voice low and cold. I dropped the sponge and met his gaze, wiping my wet hands nervously on my thighs.

"I don't know," I admitted. "I don't think so, but I don't know what our relationship is, either. I mean, we agreed to see each other exclusively, then I tried to shoot you, then you threatened to slit my throat, and we finished things up by going on a killing spree together. This is outside my realm of experience, Reese. Does 'let it go' mean we're still a couple, or does it just mean I shouldn't worry about you killing me and hiding my body in the woods? Right now I'm unclear."

His expression softened.

"I was kind of hoping we could move on to somethin' a little less fucked up. Maybe watch some movies, hang out and barbecue at my place? We've had a rough start, but we've covered a lot of ground

fast, too. You know, Heather and I didn't go on a killing spree together until we'd been married for a good five years. You think Jess
was a complication? Imagine shootin' up a cartel with two pre-
schoolers taggin' along."

Holy fuck.

His mouth quirked and then he reached up and gently pushed my
jaw shut.

"London, I'm joking. This shit is not normal. None of it. But this
part isn't a joke—we both got a lot to answer for, but I'm hopin'
you'll give me another shot and maybe I can do the same for you?
No reason for you to move out, sweetheart. I like havin' you around.
Like it a lot."

I studied his face, trying not to fall into those gorgeous eyes of
his. They always got to me—no man should be that beautiful. But it
wasn't just about me.

"Jess needs a place to heal up," I told him softly. "You've got the
club in and out of your place all the time, and right now she's scared
of men. I need some space, too. Things happened too fast, and I want
to be sure that we're doing this for the right reasons. Sometimes you
have to take a step back if you want to move forward."

"You sound like a refrigerator magnet," he said, his voice tight.
"I'm not gonna walk away from us, London. What we were workin'
on was different. Real. I want that and you do, too."

"Renting my own place isn't walking away from us," I replied.
"But we barely had time for there to be an *us*. We had sex on a
Wednesday and by Saturday I was spying on you. Tuesday I got kill
orders. All I want is my own space while we explore us, whatever
that might end up being. We'll take it from there."

"I don't like it."

I narrowed my eyes at him.

"Did Heather always do what you told her to do?"

He stilled, and I wondered if bringing her up was a mistake. But
he'd started it . . .

"Heather almost never did what I told her," he admitted. "In front of the club? Sure. But she also liked to keep a knife next to the bed. Always said I was free to fuck whoever I wanted, so long as I understood that the night I came home smellin' like another woman would be the night she killed me in my sleep."

I bit back a smile, looking up at him through my lashes.

"She sounds like she was a hell of a woman."

"She was. But she's dead, and you're a hell of a woman, too, London. Come back home with me."

"I'll come to visit," I said, holding his gaze. "Sleepovers, how does that sound? We can get to know each other, do this the right way. We already did everything wrong once, but if what we have is real, me having my own place won't kill it. When we're ready, we can talk about moving in together."

His arms stayed crossed, but he nodded.

"I'll give you the summer," he said slowly. "After that all bets are off."

Smiling, I reached my arms up around his neck and tugged his head down to mine for a kiss. He let me, but he didn't respond at first. I pulled back.

"Really, Reese? Pouting?"

He frowned.

"When you say it like that, it sounds so juvenile."

I didn't respond.

"Fuck," he muttered, then wrapped his arms around me, pulling me in tight. His lips caught mine and I opened for him. Need and desire flared to life, and I wanted more than his tongue inside. Good thing we'd talked before we started making out, I realized. Otherwise I'd have done whatever he asked, because kissing Reese was *that good*. By the time Horse stepped into the kitchen and cleared his throat, Reese had me up against the wall, both legs wrapped tight around his waist.

"Your daughter called," Horse announced. "She's ready for you to come and visit. Said not to forget London. Should I call her back and say you're too busy fuckin' in the kitchen?"

Reese froze, groaning as I started to giggle. Then he leaned his forehead against mine, eyes closed.

"Children," he muttered. "Shit for timing. Always."

He lowered me and I straightened my clothing. Horse didn't look away or give us even a hint of privacy. Nope. He just stood there smirking like a total creeper.

"You like to watch?" I asked him.

"Fuck yeah, I like to watch. Doesn't everyone?"

Reese glared at him, which seemed to make him smirk even harder.

"Okay, let's go see Em," I said, tugging at Reese's hand. "Just 'cause she's a big girl doesn't mean she doesn't need her daddy."

Reese rolled his eyes, then gave me a strange, almost sheepish smile.

"Thank fuck for that."

"Hi, Dad," Em said softly when we walked into her hospital room. She looked pale and weak, but her eyes were bright and she still managed to give Reese a smile.

Hunter stood next to her, his eyes watchful and concerned. He was still the badass biker I'd first met in Coeur d'Alene, but that didn't mean he wasn't devoted to his girl. He'd do anything for Reese's daughter—I saw it written all over his face.

I decided I liked him, despite the fact that he'd locked me in a storage room.

"Hey, baby," Reese said, dropping my hand as we crossed over to her bed, which was by the window. Em didn't have a roommate. I wondered if that was because she'd gotten lucky, or if Hunter had scared the nurses into giving her space.

Probably best not to ask.

Reese leaned over and kissed her forehead, then sat down on the bed next to her. I stood beside him, which should've felt awkward but it somehow didn't.

I was just happy to see Em alive and well.

"So I hear you saved my ass," Em said to me, her eyes full of gratitude. Not a hint of blame or wariness—she obviously had no idea I'd been a prisoner when I discovered her bleeding. Guess that was on a need-to-know basis, something I found very comforting. I'd just as soon she didn't find out I'd tried to kill her dad. I had a feeling she'd hold a wicked grudge.

"I did my best," I said quietly. "You scared me—thought we might lose you. How are you feeling now?"

"Weak," she replied. "Sad. They told me it was a girl. It's strange . . . I was kind of scared when I saw the positive pregnancy test, but I loved her. I wanted her. I can't believe she's gone."

"I'm so sorry."

Em nodded, a hint of red around her eyes. I glanced up at Hunter, seeing shadows written in his face. They'd obviously both wanted her. I hoped they'd get another chance . . . Ectopic pregnancies could do a lot of damage.

"You tired, little girl?" Reese asked, reaching out to catch Em's hand. "You want some rest? We can go wait outside."

"No," she said, squeezing his fingers. "I'm just glad you're here."

"Hello, Reese," a new voice said, and I looked up to see a girl standing in the door frame. This had to be Kit, the daughter I hadn't met yet. I recognized her from her pictures, although they'd all been taken before she'd adopted her current style. She looked like a Betty Page pinup, all vintage clothes, sculpted black hair, red lipstick, and tough-girl attitude.

Like Em, she was stunning, but in a completely different way.

Reese stood and walked toward her. She flung herself into his arms, squeezing him tight as he lifted her up for a hug. He'd told me she liked to pick fights with him—and I had a feeling calling him by his first name was part of that dynamic . . . But clearly when shit hit the fan, the Hayes family stood together. After long seconds he let her slide back down to the ground and she stood back, smiling at him with a hint of vulnerability in her face.

Then her eyes found me, and they narrowed.

"This her?" she asked, her voice sharp. Em sighed heavily and Hunter rolled his eyes. Time to step in and diffuse, I decided.

"I'm London Armstrong," I said in a clear, friendly voice as I walked over and held out my hand. "You must be Kit. I've seen so many of your pictures, but none of them are recent. I love your look—very classic."

She sniffed, signaling clearly that it would take more than flattery to win her over. Alrighty, then. I'd try another tactic.

"Reese, would you like me to go and get coffee for everyone?" I asked. "Let you have some family time together?"

He raised a brow, but Kit looked triumphant. Clearly she thought she'd scared me. Not the case, but I wasn't looking to butt heads with her. Em was her sister and Reese was her dad—this was about them, not me. I saw right through this girl. Under the belligerence was an undercurrent of fear and insecurity. She needed to know I wasn't here to take her father away from her, and the best way to communicate that was with space.

They could have their moment without me.

"I'll help you," Hunter said suddenly. I nodded, surprised. Up to this point, I would've bet a hundred bucks that he wouldn't be leaving this room for anything.

Interesting.

He followed me into the hallway. "Cafeteria's this way."

We started walking, falling comfortably silent. I had no idea why he'd come with me, but if I needed to know, he'd say something. I felt like my role here was to support, not question.

"They should have time together," he said finally. "They're tight, but Kit and Reese love to fight. Like two alley cats. Us being in there just gives 'em one more thing to fight about, and Em doesn't need that."

I laughed, shaking my head as it fell into place.

"They're not the easiest of families, are they?"

"You got no fuckin' idea."

We bought the coffee and carried it back slowly, but despite our best efforts the errand only took about twenty-five minutes. I knocked on the door and pushed it open carefully. Em lay back in the bed, Kit cuddled up next to her on top of the covers. Reese sat between them and the window, leaning back in his chair casually. He rested one ankle across his knee, watching over his girls as they whispered quietly to each other.

Then he looked up at me and smiled, pale blue eyes creased with warmth, obvious pride written all over his face.

"C'mon in," he said.

I glanced at Kit, but she ignored me. Em winked, patting the side of the bed. I walked over and sat down awkwardly in the tiny sliver of space, wondering what the future held for me with this family.

Only one way to find out.

"Who wants coffee?"

CHAPTER NINETEEN

ONE MONTH LATER
LONDON

I leaned forward into the bathroom mirror, carefully brushing mascara over my pale lashes. Outside the bathroom door I could hear Mellie and Jessica arguing about something—the cabin was only about a thousand square feet and I was very, very happy that Melanie would be moving into student housing in a few weeks.

Wasn't sure how much more of this I could take.

Loud music started blaring as I brushed my hair, changing abruptly to rap as I smoothed on lipstick. That would be Jessica taking control of the stereo.

It switched back again and I realized a full-on musical battle royale was starting outside the tiny bathroom. Taking one more quick look at myself—not perfect, but I'd do—I stepped out, prepared to start yelling. Before I could, the music stopped completely. Both girls stood in the living room, glaring at each other. Melanie had started standing up to Jessica in recent weeks, something I'd always wished she would do. Now I regretted that wish because I lived in a war zone.

"You're a fucking idiot," Jessica growled. I took a deep breath, prepared to tell her off. Melanie beat me to it.

"Don't talk to me like that."

"I will if it's true. I saw that letter. He's just another pussy-chasing asshole, and writing to him in jail is desperate and pathetic. You're smarter than me, so why don't you act like it?"

Mellie's mouth dropped and so did mine.

Then the doorbell rang.

Melanie stomped past me toward their shared room, leaving Jessica standing in the center of the living room, eyes bright with fury. The bell rang again and I decided they were big girls who could figure this out on their own. Grabbing my backpack, I walked over to the door and opened it.

Then I smiled because everything was okay again.

Reese was here.

REESE

Christ, but she was gorgeous.

I took London's hand and tugged her out onto the porch for my kiss, because I didn't feel like dealing with whatever girl drama was brewing in the cabin. And there was major drama brewing—after raising Em and Kit, I could fuckin' smell that shit in the air.

Fortunately, the sweet softness of London's lips more than made up for the girls and their games. My hands found her ass, lifting her up and into my body. As always, my cock was as happy to see her as the rest of me.

Rap music blasted out through the window, all but knocking us off the porch. Just as fast it turned off again.

That's when the screeching started.

"We have to get out of here," I growled, dragging London toward my fully loaded bike. Being the clever woman she was, she didn't argue. Let the girls kill each other—this was *our* weekend, and they weren't gonna fuck it up for us.

Five minutes later we were pulling off the road and onto the highway, heading north toward the Canadian border. Over the past month London had gotten more comfortable riding with me, which was great for the most part . . . Although I sort of missed the way she used to cling to me like her life depended on it. Now she felt comfortable enough to raise her hands, weaving and dancing them through the air as we flew down the road.

Things had been fucked up and tense for a while when we'd gotten back. Some of it between me and her, but mostly just getting shit settled with the club. Painter and Puck were facing jail time no matter how you looked at it, and of the three brothers lost, one had been from the Moscow chapter, ninety miles south of Coeur d'Alene. He was a good man, and I'd known him more than a decade. London had come down with me for the funeral. Our relationship might be new, but she'd earned no small amount of respect when she killed that Medina fuck back at the warehouse.

She'd handled herself well at the memorial, too, and afterward more than one brother asked me why she wasn't my old lady already.

Hard question to answer.

This weekend wasn't about answering questions, though. It wasn't about the club, the girls or anything to do with the cartel. Nope, this was about camping out, spending time together, maybe gettin' my girl drunk and takin' advantage of her. Perfect.

It was still early by the time we reached my favorite campsite up on the Pack River. Calling it a river was a bit of an exaggeration, at least this time of year. The Pack was fed by snowmelt, and by late summer it wasn't much more than a foot deep in any given spot. It meandered through a wooded valley, the central channel running across a wide bed of rounded rocks, small sand banks, and waterfalls two or three feet high at most.

Our campsite wasn't anything particularly special—tucked away off a dirt road, just a little clearing in the trees with a fire pit next to the river. I'd been coming here since I was a kid.

Had to be one of the most gorgeous places on earth. Couldn't wait to share it with London.

I set up the fire while she rolled out the sleeping bags. Still too early to light it, which was fine because I had other things I wanted to do. And no, I'm not talking about fuckin' her, although that was on the list, too.

"You ready for some fun?" I asked, and she smiled back at me.

"What did you have in mind?"

"When's the last time you shot a Super Soaker?"

She stared at me blankly.

"Water gun, sweetheart. Plastic? Pump it up, water sprays out?"

"I know what they are, Reese."

"Excellent. I couldn't carry the big ones on the bike, but the smaller ones are great, too. I'll give you a head start 'cause you're new at this."

With that I pulled out the plastic gun I'd brought for her with a flourish. It was neon orange and green, and it held about two cups of water. More than enough for a good fight, especially since we'd be in the river. Easy to reload.

Her mouth dropped.

"Did you seriously bring me up here for a water fight? I thought this was a romantic weekend?"

I cocked a brow at her.

"Sweetheart, you gotta look at this from my perspective. I shoot right, your T-shirt gets all wet and then I get to roll around with you in the water. Tell me that isn't romantic?"

London snorted, but I could see a hint of playfulness in her eyes. Yeah, she was on board. I tossed her the gun and turned away.

"You got until I hit a hundred," I told her loudly. "And you'll do better if you ditch your shoes. The rocks aren't sharp but they're slippery, and there's lots of places where you can only walk in the water. Now run, unless you want it to be a real short game. Upriver there's a pool where we can swim, and if you get there before I catch you, you win. If you hit me with your gun, I have to stop and count to ten again. If I hit you, I get a kiss. One. Two. Three. Four . . ."

Because I'm an asshole, I stopped at fifty. No reason to make it too easy for her.

Turning toward the river, I looked upriver. Couldn't see her, which wasn't a huge surprise. The swimming hole was only about half a mile away, but it took longer to get there than you'd think because of the rocks and the way the Pack twisted around. I leaned down and filled my gun, then pumped it up, ready for action as I started up the river.

Five minutes later I still hadn't seen her. There were a lot of ways to play the game—if she just booked ahead as fast as possible, she'd probably beat me. But that wouldn't be nearly as much fun, and I knew London.

She wouldn't be able to resist an ambush.

The first one hit out of nowhere. I'd just come around a bend when cold water slammed me in the side of the head. I heard her laughing hysterically, but I closed my eyes and started counting. Fast. Now I knew she was nearby and I listened carefully for the sound of splashing. When I opened them again, she was still in range, so I lifted my gun and shot her in the back.

She turned toward me shrieking.

"You cheat, you didn't count to t—"

I shot her in the face before she could finish the sentence, then started toward her through the water. Walking across the smooth, round rocks was awkward, but I have long legs, so it didn't take long.

"I counted fast," I told her smugly. "And you owe me two kisses."

She glared at me, but when I caught the back of her neck and pulled her in to claim my prize, she didn't protest. After long seconds we broke apart, gasping for air. Her wet shirt clung tightly to her tits.

Outstanding.

Then she leaned forward to kiss me this time. I closed my eyes, savoring the delicate touch of her lips and—

"Holy fuck!"

Bitch shot me in the cock with her gun, point blank.

London started laughing and took off up the river, shouting back at me.

"You count for real this time, asshole! Otherwise I'm taking your gun away from you."

By the time we reached the little pool, both of us were soaking wet, so no real point in keeping our clothes on. It was only about three feet deep and maybe ten feet across, so we couldn't really swim, either—fine with me. Instead we sort of splashed each other, then wrestled, and then the next thing I knew I was sitting under a waterfall while London rode my cock.

Best. Game. Ever.

Later that night I lay on my back, looking up at the stars, London tucked into my arm, one hand across my chest.

"I wish we could just stay out here forever," she murmured softly. "Where nobody can find us and we don't have to do anything. God, the girls are driving me crazy."

"Mellie will be gone soon," I reminded her. Above us a star shot by, then then another. "Heather and I used to come up here every year at this time for the Perseids shower. You see that? They'll be falling all night."

"Yup, I saw it," she whispered. "Do you think about her a lot?"

I considered the question, trying to find the right words.

"Sometimes. But I think about you a lot more. After she died I swore I'd never take another old lady. Just couldn't wrap my head around it, not until now. But it's right with us, isn't it? You feel it, too."

She didn't answer for a second.

"I feel it, too," she agreed.

"You ready to make it official?" I asked. She shook her head, rubbing her hair against me. Smelled good.

"Not yet. I know this sounds silly, but let's keep this ours for a bit longer. Just a little secret we don't have to share with anyone else. Everyone counts on us all the time and that's not going to go away . . . but for now, let's not give them this."

I hesitated. I wanted things out in the open, wanted everyone to know London was my woman for real. Fuckin' proud of her. But I understood, too.

"End of the summer, then? Only about two weeks left, sweet-heart."

"That sounds perfect."

"How much longer you gonna stay in that tiny little cabin when I got a whole house just waitin' for you?"

She gave a snort of frustration.

"The day Mellie moves out, I'm packin' my shit. I'm losing my mind there."

"What about Jessica?"

"She actually has plans, believe it not. I'm sort of torn about them. I want her with me . . . but I also know she won't be happy out at your place. She isn't ready to get back into life like that just yet. But I'm really proud of her for realizing she has to move forward, make her own decisions."

"Really? What's she gonna do with herself?"

"She's moving in with Maggs Dwyer."

"Bolt's old lady?"

"No, Bolt's ex," she said firmly. "She's pretty emphatic about that detail. She runs a program at the community center for special-needs children. Jess has been volunteering there for a couple of years, and she's decided to enroll in the early-childhood education program down at the college. Maggs is giving her a part-time job and a room to rent. It's perfect in a lot of ways."

"Bolt won't like that," I mused. "He's tryin' to get back with her. Havin' Jess around won't make things easier."

"Not Bolt's decision."

Fair enough.

"So two weeks and you're all mine."

She nodded, giving a yawn. "Assuming you still want me."

"Fuck yeah, I want you."

She made a happy little snuffling noise and we fell silent again. Another meteor streaked overhead. London's breathing slowed as she drifted off.

Hey, babe, Heather whispered. *Remember coming here together? Two little girls snuggled up between us, watching the stars shooting all night? You told them they were people riding up to heaven on rockets.*

Yeah, I remember.

I remembered everything, although sometimes I wished I could erase those memories because they hurt so bad. Tonight, though? Tonight they were beautiful.

She's good for you—this is what I wanted. Someday when Em and Kit have kids, you bring them up here for me, will you? Tell them Grandma Heather's watching over them . . . Then tell them Grandma London's gonna give 'em extra loves, because they're such special kids they deserve double.

I swallowed. London stirred next to me, and I took in her scent. Clean and fresh, her hair still just a little damp from the river.

I'll always miss you, I told Heather. *But it's time to let you go.*

She didn't answer.

Another star shot by in the darkness, and London raised her head.

"You okay, Reese?"

"I love you."

Silence.

"You've never said that to me before."

"Wasn't ready. I'm ready now."

"I love you, too."

She settled back into my body, and I felt right in a way I'd almost forgotten existed. Darkness surrounded us, broken only by the meteor shower. I waited for Heather to say something. Nothing.

Now it was just London and me.

Felt good.

EPILOGUE

THIRTEEN MONTHS LATER
SOUTHERN CALIFORNIA
PUCK

"Can't decide—should I get drunk first and *then* get laid, or the other way around?"

"Shut the fuck up," Puck muttered, staring at the ceiling. He lay back on the top bunk, trying to ignore the annoying mouth breather he and Painter shared a cell with. At least they *had* a cell. Given how crowded the prison was, half the guys didn't have any space of their own at all.

"Yeah, I'm gonna start with sex," Fester continued, oblivious to the threat in Puck's voice. The guy was a complete moron, but at least he was harmless. Over the past year, he and Painter had needed to fight off the cartel boys at least once a month. An annoying cell mate was better than getting shanked in your sleep. "There's this chick I saw once who—"

"If you don't shut the fuck up right now, I'll cut off your dick," Puck muttered. Fester laughed, because they'd had this same conversation at least once a day for the past six months. But today they were in lockdown, which meant Puck couldn't get away from the little shit.

Painter snorted in amusement across the room, because he knew exactly how much the man got on Puck's nerves.

"How 'bout that girl of yours?" Fester asked Painter, shifting directions abruptly. "She have anything interesting to say? I always think about her in that blue sundress she was wearin' in that one picture. You know, the one where her tits were sorta pokin' through? I swear to fuck, those were her nipples. They taste good? I'll bet they taste good."

Puck closed his eyes and shook his head. Fester had no fuckin' sense of self-preservation at all. Painter didn't like questions about his girl. This was not new territory.

"You say one more word and I'll kill you on the spot," Painter replied, his voice like stone. "She's not my girl and whatever you think you saw, you forget. You're not good enough to look at her picture, asshole."

"Sorry, Painter," Fester said quickly. "Sorry, didn't mean to bother you. You just keep readin' your letter and I'll go over here for a while. Maybe draw a picture or somethin'."

"You do that," Painter said, then Puck heard Fester move across the room, followed by the sounds of crayons dumping out across the desk. Man had the mind of an eight year old, no joke. Puck wondered how he'd survive when they got out in two weeks, but he didn't put too much energy into it. Fester was like a cockroach—he'd find a way.

"Any news from home?" Puck asked, although "home" wasn't really the right word. Painter'd gotten a packet of notes and pictures from Coeur d'Alene, all gathered together by one of the Reapers' old ladies and sent down at once.

"Not really," he said. "Looks like Bolt and Maggs are back together."

Puck grunted, trying to remember who Maggs was. Bolt he remembered, but they hadn't talked much. He'd only been in Coeur d'Alene a few days before everything fell to shit. After their first four months inside together, Painter had suggested he come prospect with the Reapers when he got out. Wouldn't be happening. Puck's dad had been a Silver Bastard, and that's who he wanted to ride with.

Assuming he ever got to ride again.

"Mellie got a scholarship," Painter added after a few minutes. "Says she's excited, because it means she won't have to work during school this year."

Puck grinned, but he didn't say shit. Painter had it bad for the girl—pussy whipped, despite the fact he'd never even gotten a whiff. He'd never fall for that, no fuckin' way. Life was hard enough without some bitch whinin' all the time.

Not only that, who wanted to pick just one?

The warning bell rang for lights out, and Fester scrabbled around, presumably picking up his crayons. Freak had a talent for drawing, strangely enough. He could draw pictures of anything, all shaded and complicated and shit. Puck wouldn't have thought you could pull that off with crayons, but what did he know?

The lights went out and Puck closed his eyes, ignoring the howls and moans of inmates up and down the block. This was the best time in prison. He might be stuck in a concrete box with Painter and their pet fuckwit, but with the lights off he could imagine being somewhere else. Outside.

Get drunk first or get laid?

Damned fine question, he had to admit. Christ, but he missed women. Specifically, he missed fucking them . . . But he also missed their softness, and the way—when he smiled just right—their eyes went all liquid and they'd do whatever the hell he asked, no matter how fucked up it might be.

Okay, laid first.

He tried to picture the girl. Blonde? Dark hair? Fuck, he didn't care. He'd start out with a blow job, and then move on to her pussy, maybe eat her out. Yeah, that'd be good. His cock twitched and he lifted his hips, sliding down his pants. On the bunk below him Fester grunted, breaking the spell—but not for long. Puck ignored him, palming his dick and squeezing tight.

Just like that.

But her mouth would be hot and wet, and the thought of her pussy was so sweet it made his teeth hurt. And he'd find one with a sweet pussy for that first night outside. No nasty old bitches for him. Nope. Nothing but the best, because it was his fantasy and he'd damned well do what he wanted in it.

His cock swelled as he pictured sliding it into her slowly from behind. Favorite way to do it, looking down at their asses, all heart shaped and pretty. Jacking his hand slowly, he tried to decide what he wanted. Pale skin? Dark? Maybe some freckles, or just all creamy smooth? Hell, he'd order one of each, find a new one to play with every night.

Speaking of asses, he'd hit that, too. Yup. Mouth, cunt, ass. Then he'd get drunk and start all over again.

Fuckin' beautiful. Too bad she wasn't real. Frustration filled him, but Puck jacked harder, lust for his imaginary girl clashing with the cold, hard reality that a man's hand just wasn't enough. Not after thirteen months.

But his hand would have to do.

Fluid started seeping from his tip, and he caught it, slicking his way as he kept going. His heart pumped faster now, matching his rhythm. Sweet, tight, and hot. Young. Pretty. Maybe long hair, so he could hold on to it while he fucked her, because riding rough worked for him in a big way.

Oh yeah . . .

He liked the idea of pulling her hair, maybe giving her ass a little smack. The vision was so intense he practically heard the slap of his hand against her flesh, the way she'd tense around him when he did it. *Fuck,* that was good. The pressure inside grew tighter and he knew he was close. So fucking close.

His vision shifted—now she knelt in front of him, looking up with big, deep brown eyes as she wrapped her pink lips around his cock. Holy hell, that was perfect. Puck's arm started to ache, but he didn't slow down. Probably making enough noise for the others to hear and he didn't give a shit. Painter was his brother—might not be with the same clubs, but brothers just the same. They'd done time together, forged a bond that couldn't be broken. Shit like this meant nothin'.

And Fester?

He didn't count.

The girl in his head pulled her mouth free of his cock, and glanced up at him playfully. Then she reached out with the tip of her tongue, poking the slit at the end of his length.

Puck exploded.

Jesus.

So *fucking* good. Fucking *perfect.*

For a moment he just lay in the dark, free in that instant. What a joke.

Too bad his little mama wasn't real. And she wasn't. Because here he was, stuck alone in the dark with two other men, one of whom was half in love with some bitch he'd probably never touch. Nope. Painter wouldn't make a move even after they got out. Precious Melanie was too pretty and perfect up on her pedestal to get dirty, Puck figured.

As for Fester? He liked to eat his own crayons.

Pathetic. Both of them. Puck needed to get out, sometimes thought he'd go crazy if he didn't get *out.*

Two weeks.

Fourteen days.

Puck wiped off his hand and pulled up his pants. After tonight, only thirteen days left.

"Those was definitely her little titties pokin' through that dress," Fester whispered.

"God damn it!"

Painter was out of bed and across the room in a heartbeat, dragging dumbass out of bed so hard that Puck's bunk shook.

"Don't do it," Puck snapped. "You fuck him up, could mess with our parole."

Painter stilled.

"You don't talk about her," he said finally, dropping the other man to the floor. Fester gave a high, nervous giggle.

Two weeks.

Fourteen days.

Mouth. Cunt. Ass.

AUTHOR'S NOTE: *Many readers have asked me to write about what happens to various Reapers and their ladies after their stories have been told. This bonus epilogue gives a sneak peek of the club's future without revealing any spoilers for the books ahead. That being said, it also ends with a bit of a tease for a storyline that won't be addressed or resolved in the next book. I let the readers on my fan page vote on whether I should share it with you, and they were overwhelmingly in favor of including it. Read at your own risk.*

BONUS EPILOGUE

NINE YEARS LATER
JESSICA

"Jessica Amber Armstrong."

I took a deep breath and stood up, my advisor at my side, her brightly colored academic robes fluttering like flags in the light breeze. We climbed up onto the outdoor stage, and I looked out to see London, Reese, Mellie, and all the others watching me, pride written all over their faces. When they'd come in—full Reapers colors on display—everyone had gotten out of their way quick. Worked out well, too. Now they had the front two rows all to themselves.

Reese caught my eye and winked. I smiled back, then turned toward my graduate advisor, lowering myself so she could put the academic hood over my head. Right up to that point I was doing great—just one more step in the march toward my master's in special education . . . But then she smoothed the silk across my shoulders and whispered, "We're so proud of you, Jessica. I've never had a student work harder than you have."

That's when I lost it.

I turned back toward the audience, tears running down my face. Most of them would never know what I'd had to overcome to get this far—what I still had to overcome every day of my life. The checks and balances I'd put into place to keep myself from making impulsive decisions. The surgeries to maintain my shunt. The fact that every time I looked down at my hand and missing finger, I was reminded that evil is a real thing that exists in our world, all around us.

I'd use all of it to help my students, I vowed. Every bit of suffering, every stupid decision I'd ever made, every hour of physical pain I'd endured. Every time someone made fun of me for being "slow." I knew better now. I wasn't slow—I was *different*, and that difference was what made me one of the best fucking special education teachers in the state.

They weren't making fun of me anymore.

The dean shook my hand as London and Reese and all the others started whooping and hollering for me. That got them some looks, but I didn't give a shit. They were my people, and they'd been there for me when I needed them.

Now it was my turn to make them all proud.

We'd blown off the formal reception at the University of Idaho in favor of a party out at Spring Valley Reservoir. Not all the club had been able to make it down, but enough were there that the Moscow chapter had come out to welcome us. One of the local brothers had a barrel smoker, which was already full of ribs. London was in her element, bossing all the old ladies around and making sure the food would be perfect. Not a single paper napkin was out of place.

Mellie took off right after the hooding ceremony, which sucked. She had to work later in the afternoon, but the fact that she'd driven down at all meant everything to me. Her path hadn't been the easiest over the years, but we'd both made it through, friendship intact.

"Auntie Jess, will you braid my hair?" asked Kylie, Em's youngest. She was two weeks shy of her fourth birthday, but in her mind she was already a full-on adult. "Mama said she needed to help Daddy with something in the tent. I'm not s'posed to bother her."

I snickered. Yeah, I'll bet he needed "help" with something, all right.

"Sure, c'mon over to the table."

We sat down and I finger-combed her hair, looking out across the beach. Marie, Sophie, and Jina were watching over a gaggle of kids and working on their tans. With the exception of Horse, most of the brothers were up drinking beer and supervising the smoker. He'd let the little ones—led by his oldest boy, who I swear was cockier than he was—bury him in the sand. Probably just waiting to explode up and chase them all into the water.

I finished Kylie's hair and she took off running to the beach, braid flapping behind her. Kit—Reese's other daughter—sat down next to me with a thump, passing over a beer.

"You know, I never thought I'd get sucked back into this shit," she muttered. I glanced at her, a question in my eyes. "The MC shit. Thought I'd made it out."

"Does anyone ever really make it out?" I asked. "Doesn't matter what life you choose—your family will always be part of you. Just be glad yours is a good one."

Kit nodded.

"Yeah, for the most part. Congrats on the degree."

"Thanks," I said, feeling warm and happy.

"Here you are," London said. She dropped into the spot on my other side, nudging me over with her hip. I shifted, pushing at Kit until she moved her butt, too. London's arm came around me and she gave me a tight hug. "So, you ready to settle down now, Ms. Hot Shit Graduate? Maybe give me some more grandbabies?"

"Not every woman lives to have children, Loni," I said, my voice dry. "I seem to remember you focusing on building your business for a long time."

"I was focused on raising your ass," she replied, grinning at me. "You gave me hell. Only fair that someone should make you suffer, too."

I rolled my eyes.

"I think I'll wait a little longer. I have it on good authority that raising a kid on your own is a lot of work . . . Who mentioned that to me? Oh, yeah. That was *you*, Loni. Remember?"

"Speaking of you turning into a lifeless old maid with a vag full of cobwebs, I have someone I want you to meet," Kit said, a wicked smile crossing her face. "He should be out here soon. I think you'll like him a lot."

"God, just one day . . ." I muttered, shaking my head. "Just one day without one of you trying to fix me up? Is that too much to ask?"

"This one is different," Kit said, her voice indignant. "He's—"

I heard the roar of a motorcycle and looked up to see who was pulling up to the campsite.

Holy shit. Was that . . . ?

"There he is! I can't wait for you to meet him," Kit grabbed my elbow, dragging me to my feet. I followed her, stumbling. *No. Fucking. Way.*

"Told you he's different," Kit said, grinning. *Yeah, he was different all right.* We came to a stop and he pulled off his helmet, giving me that slow, sexy smile I loved and hated so much at the same time. I just stood there, staring at him like a dumbass until Kit pushed me from behind. The move caught me off guard, and I literally stumbled into his arms.

Seriously?

"Hey, Jess," he said, the words a slow, sexy drawl. "Never thought I'd see you again. Happy graduation."

Fuckballs.

"So you know each other already?" Kit demanded. "Why didn't you tell me, Jess?"

"I was trying to forget," I muttered.

"Some things you just can't forget," he said, which sucked because he was right.

"I gotta get out of here," I said, trying to pull away. He didn't let me go, though. Nope. His hands tightened on my arms as he leaned down to whisper into my ear.

"Really? Running away again? Can't leave your own party, Jess. That's just rude."

I closed my eyes, inhaling his scent. Oh, God. I'd forgotten how good he smelled, how tall he was. What he felt like when he . . .

"Looks like someone has unfinished business," Kit said, her voice full of predatory glee. "I want details. Now."

Oh hell no.

My brain started to work again, and I jerked away from him in full retreat. He was laughing behind me, but I didn't care because I was well and truly over his shit.

Our story was *done*.

Finished.

The. End.

Wasn't it?